HIGH RISK

A Point of No Return Novel

Brenna Aubrey

SILVER GRIFFON ASSOCIATES
ORANGE, CA, USA

Book Layout ©2018 BookDesignTemplates.com
Cover Art ©2018 Sarah Hansen, Okay Creations
Cover Image: ©2018 Eric David Battershell
Model: Joshua Scott Brown

High Risk / Brenna Aubrey. – 1st ed.
ISBN 978-1-940951-61-4

For Dad. I miss you. *Dooset Daram.*

ACKNOWLEDGEMENTS

With huge mega-thanks to my earliest readers, Kate McKinley and Sabrina Darby. Also, to my in-office romance expert, Tessa Dare. Much gratitude to beta readers, Leigh Lavalle, Natasha Boyd, Tessa Layne, and content editor Gretchen Stull. Many thanks to Zoe York and Viv Arend, also, for expert advice.

Thank you to my "tribe" of amazing kickass next-level lady authors—you know who you are and you are da bomb. And HUGE SHOUT OUT to my super-readers in the Brenna Aubrey Book Group and the lovely Kelly Allenby.

My design team, Sarah Hansen (cover design), Joshua Brown (model) and Eric Battershell (photographer) without whom I would not have that amazing cover! Also huge thanks to Julianne Burke for the gorgeous promotional graphics.

Most of all thank you to my family...for your encouragement, your unconditional love, understanding and for all you do to keep me safe, fed, loved and sane while I'm getting the book out—especially during the home stretch of insanity. I love you to the Moon and back again.

CHAPTER ONE
COMMANDER RYAN TYLER

HOUSTON WOULDN'T HAVE CUT COMMUNICATIONS between Xander and me unless something had gone terribly wrong. But as I'm clinging on to the Canadarm robotic arm of the International Space Station, I'm getting zero answers while it carries me to the airlock.

Without having to be told to do so, I again check the reading on my suit—less than 2.5 psi now. I'm still losing pressure and will begin suffering hypoxia symptoms anytime now.

But none of that matters because I'm not the one in the most danger here.

"CAPCOM," I bark into the mic. I need an update on Xander, dammit, and there's nothing but a long stretch of silence. "Houston. Do *not* leave me in the dark. Where is he? Why did you cut me off?"

"Ty," Noah's voice fills my ears. Am I imagining the shaky nervousness? Typically, he's such a cool customer that it startles me to hear his emotion. "We are working both problems. You have to concentrate on getting yourself to safety. Leave Xander's situation to us."

I grit my teeth in frustration at the brush-off. Pointing my head to look up above the plane of the station, I search for him against an inky blackness studded with stars. He was thrown in

1

that general direction when his suit collided with the live current of the solar array.

But Houston can follow my line of sight, due to the camera attached to my helmet. They know where my mind is. I can't see a damn thing.

"Ty, follow orders," Noah says, reading my hesitation.

"I can do this. My SAFER is working perfectly. Let me go get him."

"Negative, Ty. Get to *Quest, now.*" He refers to the airlock by name. "We'll fill you in the minute you're out of danger."

Fucking fantastic.

I let loose a string of filthy epithets, aware that the channel is open and he can hear me. I have zero fucks to give at this point.

Though it isn't logical, I visualize Xander getting control of his suit, activating his SAFER, jetting back to the station, and using a tether to secure himself. I grit my teeth, willing it to be so. As if somehow, I can make it real.

Silence on the comms makes the time stretch out interminably until I reach my destination.

At the *Quest* airlock, I make ingress without incident. No one speaks during the seven-minute repressurization process. I can barely hear anything over the low-pressure alarm ringing in my ears anyway, and the light-headedness is starting to kick in, spots floating in front of my eyes.

When the inner hatch opens, my last hopes for Xander are dashed when our commander and the station's two cosmonauts enter the airlock.

One look at their faces and I know we've lost him.

Sergei takes hold of the handle on the front of my suit while the other cosmonaut unlatches the helmet. My ears immediately pop, sharp pain stabbing through my eardrums from the change in pressure. I'm almost certain one of them has ruptured—all sound coming as if from a great, great distance. That burned metallic smell of space on my suit and the perpetually new plastic smell of the station assail my senses.

"Someone tell me what the *fuck* is going on!" I bellow.

Sergei tenses, his grip on me tightening. It's only then that I realize my colleagues are anticipating me trying to go back out there and get Xander. Sergei has already pushed my helmet in the direction of the inner hatch so that it floats far beyond my reach.

He's right. It would be suicide, but he knows me too well. I swallow a lump in my dry throat. Penny, our commander, looks up at me, tears beading around her eyes. Everything in me drops, pulled only by the gravity of my own sudden grief.

On the comms, Noah's voice is tight with emotion. "Ty, I'm sorry. He's too far away, and we have no way of getting him back to the station."

"Take a deep breath, Ty," Sergei says to me in Russian. And I have no purchase to pull back from him. We are all weightless here, but he's anchored to the wall by a strap over his feet.

My mind races, and I know they are out of options. The Soyuz capsule has not been prepped and cannot be used in such an operation even if it were. But in my mind, I'm grasping at anything. Any hope when clearly there is none, or they would have found it by now.

"No, *goddammit!*" I shout, slapping a frustrated hand against the canvas wall of the airlock. The two Russians look away from my face, allowing me some privacy in my grief.

I can't don another suit. And even if I could, it would be useless for the same reasons the Russians couldn't egress in theirs. An EVA required at least four hours of proper breathing preparation to avoid getting the bends from the change in pressure.

Noah very loudly clears his throat into the mic. "We, uh, we have him on comms, Ty. He's asking to talk to you."

I rub my eyes hard and bite down on the inside of my cheek to control my emotions. Penny nods at the Russians, who slowly leave *Quest* with concerned glances in my direction.

"How long does he have on his life support?" I ask her.

"Little over an hour...maybe two. He used up a lot of it when he was trying to deal with the situation. The secondary oxygen tank isn't working either."

That punch to my gut again. I swallow, take a long breath and struggle to compose myself. Memories flood me—from our first day at the Naval Academy together, Xander's shit-eating grin that gave him away whenever he was about to pull a joke on me, the night we got locked out of our dorms during a particularly harsh Maryland winter, my throwing a bash for him as best man for his wedding. The hours and hours in the hospital waiting room with a giant teddy bear next to me during the birth of his son.

Fucking fuck. He has everything to live for.

Penny pats my arm. "Do it, Ty. He's been asking for you for the last twenty minutes. We wanted you inside and safe before..." Her voice fades.

Before they told me there was no hope.

She's my commander. It was absolutely her call. But I'm so fucking pissed that I can't look at her. Helpless rage scorches through me, but I don't have time to be angry.

She's talking again. "They're getting Karen and AJ on the comm to talk to him, but I'll give you the time alone until then."

My eyes close. Karen and AJ—oh God—his wife and his little son. The thought only reminds me that he has everything to live for. And I have nothing.

Why am I the one safe inside this airlock while he's the one drifting off into a black void?

"Put me on with him, then," I say in a low voice to Noah. Penny backs away toward the hatch where the Russians vanished.

More static blasts my injured ear as the frequency is rerouted.

Deep in my gut, that sick feeling roils, making me feel dirty, helpless. Part of me wishes he wouldn't want to talk to me. But I know Xander.

I know Xander.

A loud click and I hear his voice cut across to me from wherever he is.

"Hey, bud. I got myself into a predicament here. I'm locked outside the dorm and we've been drinking too much. Might start snowing soon."

I suck in a quick breath as his words stab my heart. Tears prickle the back of my eyes. There's no telling how many people are privy to this conversation. But all that matters right now is the knowledge that I'll never see Xander again. And this is the last chance I'll get to speak to him before I lose him forever.

And I don't give a fuck who hears me lose it.

"I'm so sorry, man. This should be me and not you." I shake my head though he can't see me. Emotion clogs my throat.

"No way, bro. No way. There's no talk of blame, okay? We don't have the time for that, anyway. Karen will be in anytime now. But I don't want to hear anything more like that, Ty. Besides...it's absolutely gorgeous out here. I can't think of a more beautiful sight to be the last thing I see. I'm not afraid."

But I am. I'm so afraid I can hardly breathe, and even that thought strangles me with fresh guilt. "Xander."

"I have some things—some private things I want to say. Can they do that? CAPCOM, can you do that, please?"

I open my mouth, hesitating, but Noah's voice cuts in. "We can do that, Xander. We'll interrupt the moment your wife is available. It shouldn't be long now."

My heart hurts to think of Karen getting this news, of AJ being told that Daddy is never coming back. That he has to say goodbye forever.

How will I ever look them in the eyes?

There's another click, and the sound quality changes in the speakers pressed against my head through the Snoopy cap. I chew on my lip and say, "I'm here, Xander. I think we're alone."

"I mean what I said, Ty. No recriminations, okay? I'm the one to blame. I'm the one who—" He cuts himself off, and I take the cue from him.

"Xander, please. I would never ever blame you. I'm sorry. I'm so sorry."

"I know you, and I know you'll blame yourself. Don't you dare claim this clusterfuck. If you do, then I'm coming back to haunt your ass, you read me?"

"Yes, sir," I choke out. Tears pool around my eyes, clinging to them and beading around my eyeballs as they do in zero-g. *Fuck.* I'm curled up in here weeping like a baby, barely able to catch my breath. And there's this agony piercing my chest with every breath, and it has nothing to do with the pressure changes I've just endured.

Jesus, this hurts so bad.

"Make me one more promise, Ryan."

Minutes pass as he calmly outlines it to me. His voice is full of strength and clarity. It has none of the caste of a dying man, and I have to cut through my own panic and grief to hear him.

There are things I promise—all kinds of things. I'd promise him the sun if I could.

I promise him I'll watch over his wife and child—they are like family to me anyway.

I promise him my future. Readily. Easily. Without even thinking about what I'm doing.

"Promise me, bro." His voice is hoarse, barely edged with emotion.

"I promise."

Chapter Two
Ryan

*A*PPROXIMATELY *One Year Later...*

I pressed the icy bottle of beer to my lips and knocked it back, ignoring the eyes that were glued to me. Only I was drinking beer at this hour.

Maybe I was the only one of us so acutely aware of the empty seat next to me. The one Xander should be filling with his laughter, his teasing grin as part of this group. For the thousandth time over the previous year, I wished he were here.

For the thousandth time, I missed him.

My friend, Kirill Stonov—a cosmonaut from the Russian space program—eyed me, subtle in that way only Russians can be. No doubt he figured I wouldn't notice the concern in his ice-blue eyes.

Why the concern? It was lunchtime, and I was drinking a beer, for fuck's sake. In his home country, beer had been classified as a soft drink until very recently.

Still, we were on the clock and anticipated being called into the investor meeting they were holding across the street to show off the new XVenture Private Astronaut Corps—XPAC. To go in reeking of beer wouldn't be the smartest idea.

"I'll brush my teeth after lunch. *Ne vyprygivay iz shtanov.*" In his mother tongue, I warned him not to get overexcited. Everyone at this table had at least a little passing fluency in the language. He laughed and looked away with his typical nonchalance. Nothing much fazed Kirill.

"How do you think it's going over there?" Mika Katoa, dubbed "Hammer" as a call sign, asked. He shifted in his seat, visibly nervous, as he had been for days. As a veteran at NASA, a couple years ahead of me, he was one of that institution's favored sons. And, unlike me, he *still* was. If the XPAC didn't get the necessary funding, then he'd be years from flying again with NASA, since he was out of the flight assignment rotation there.

Right now, XPAC was looking like *my* only hope to fly again, so this funding had *better* go through. Every anxious twitch in Hammer's face was mirrored with an anxiety of my own, buried deep inside and visible to no one. Just a sharp pang somewhere near my heart.

I had a promise to keep, and I was going to keep it. I would fly again, one way or another.

"Anything involving our golden poster boy is bound to succeed." Kirill grinned at me. His rich Russian accent lent a beauty to the English language in that simple sentence. "All they must do is show his pretty pictures from that big photo shoot. America's greatest new hero. Isn't that right, brother?"

The whole table snickered, and I threw them all a glare. "Oh, so it's shit on Tyler day, is it? I forgot to mark my calendar."

Typical deflection on my part. I hated it when they started goading me with that Great American Hero shit. It did nothing but stir that emptiness inside, and I had no desire—especially not now—to be reminded of it. Any more of that hero crap and I'd find myself diving for another beer.

"*Every* day is shit on Tyler day," muttered Noah Sutton from the far side of the table, and our eyes met. Had I not detected the tension, the element of truth in his words, I would have laughed along with him. But he wasn't laughing. And that tension wasn't my imagination. Ever since the accident. After one long, gut-wrenching year for the both of us, it had not gone away.

His eyes flicked away even as he kept talking. "It's how we keep you humble. Kirya and I have a designated rotation on who torments you on what day."

"Good to know. So I should jettison the lot of you out the airlock, then," I said, capping my sentence with a pull from the bottle.

As always, when I was with my former—and hopefully future—colleagues, it was easy to forget that our professional fate was being decided across the street in the conference room of XVenture. The successful aerospace corporation was about to launch the very first private astronaut corps, pending funding from certain very rich men who were equally excited about space exploration.

I was not a superstitious man but I'd cross my fingers, toes and eyes if it would help.

"We've got some space fanboys in today's group," Hammer was saying. "Adam Drake is over there in the meeting. He's pumped."

"One of many rich guys." Noah nodded. "Except he designed my favorite video game, so he's already on my good side."

Kirill swallowed his bite of sandwich. "Seems legit coming from *you, Dragon*," he said with a smirk. The cosmonauts didn't typically give each other call sign nicknames like the NASA astronauts did, but Kirill liked chiding Noah about his. At one time, I'd had one too. Now I was that controversial yet laudable figurehead regularly splashed across the headlines. A caricature instead of simply a human being trying to make it from day to day without losing it.

"I was on Station with Adam a few years back during my first mission when he traveled as a private citizen," I said. "He's a good guy. Smart, hardworking. Humble, for a rich dude. Obviously a big fan of the space program. More importantly, he's beyond wealthy, so he's probably in unless Tolan *really* fucks up."

Tolan Reeves, the CEO of XVenture, was handling the investors presentation himself and though he was a one-of-a-kind visionary with a warm personality, he was shit at public speaking. He'd asked us astronauts for tips since we'd had to do public speaking often as part of our job at NASA. Tolan had been so nervous about these venture capitalist meetings that he'd worked with a coach for weeks on the presentation.

"Tolan won't fuck up," Kirill said with an emphatic head shake. "I did vodka toast with him beforehand to help loosen him up." I shot Kirill a dirty look. He'd already been shooting vodka with Tolan. And he was judging me on my beer?

"Because everything's better with alcohol when it comes to Russian protocol, right?" Noah glanced over at Kirill out of the corner of his eye. "I heard a rumor Conrad Barrett is over there."

My brows shot up even as Hammer nodded vigorously. "I also heard that and texted Victoria to confirm. No reply yet."

I sipped my beer thoughtfully, sad that my bottle was almost empty. Yet I'd have to debate with myself whether it was worth the shit I'd get from the guys to order another one. Conrad

Barrett was one of the top five richest men in the country. For him to sign on to our project and help fund it would be *huge*. Huge. So huge it could make all the difference.

XVenture, an already successful private space exploration company, contracted with companies and governments all over the world on unmanned missions to send their satellites into space and even resupply the International Space Station. But now, for the first time ever, they were adding a manned program. The very beginnings of privatized human exploration: the XVenture Private Astronaut Corps. And for such a monumental addition, they needed new funding. And a *lot* of it.

But if we got it, I'd be able to fly the test flight this fall as planned. God, I wished the rumor about Conrad Barrett was true. And while I was at it—I also wished I had another full bottle of beer sitting in front of me.

And almost as if I'd hit a call button, our cute waitress, Cheryl—a new girl—was at my side again, leaning in so that I could get a good view of her lovely rack. My eyes fastened onto her cleavage like glue before I willed myself to pull my gaze away. Her grin widened, and she licked her lips, having noticed.

Don't shit where you eat, the saying went, and I ate here often enough not to follow up on her obvious interest. Besides I already had a very lovely—and enthusiastic—bed partner lined up for tonight.

"Another beer, Commander Ty?"

I blinked, my mind running through the possible outcomes of another order. The struggle was real. "No, thank you, Cheryl. Maybe some ice water."

Without even looking at the other guys at the table, she hurried to fill my order. There were scowls and rolled eyes, but she was back in minutes with the glass of water.

But again, she ignored the guys to lean in. "Can I please ask you a favor? My nephew is a huge fan. Can I get you to autograph a cocktail napkin for him?"

I patted my jeans pocket, checking for a pen, but came up empty. Noah had already whipped one out with an emphatic eye roll and presented it to me with a flourish. My face heated a little. God, I hated doing this shit in front of the guys. They always made sure I heard about it afterward. For far too long.

Jealous bastards.

"If your nephew's an astronaut fan, you know, all these guys have been to space, too. Some of them for longer than me. And they also give autographs."

She looked at the others, laughed and shrugged, but she didn't ask them to sign anything. Apparently, only "space heroes" got that honor. I clenched my teeth against the ever-present resentment that NASA had relentlessly branded me that way.

She laid a fresh cocktail napkin before me, and I poised my pen above it. "What's your nephew's name?"

"Uh." She blushed again. "Well, actually, it's for me. My girlfriends can't believe you're one of my customers."

I signed the napkin with my usual cheesy tagline.

For Cheryl,
Keep reaching for the stars!
Commander Ryan Tyler

"Don't forget your phone number. It's what she's *really* after," said Kirill in Russian, and the other guys snickered.

"*Zatknis,*"I snapped without missing a beat. With his smartass mouth, it wasn't an unusual command to order him to shut it on a regular basis—in either language.

"What did he say?" Cheryl asked as I handed her the napkin.

"He wants your number," I replied, and Kirill belted out a laugh, leaning back in his chair.

She grinned big and smiled, glancing quickly from me to him, probably sizing us both up to decide which one she liked better. The only thing I had on Kirill was darker hair, several TV appearances, and questionable notoriety that often served as tabloid fodder.

Two seconds later, Cheryl was leaning close to me, angling her phone in front of our faces. "Selfie time!" she chimed in a singsong voice, positioning the device and snapping three photos in quick succession.

"Please don't tag that with the location if you're posting it online," I begged. That was all I needed. *More* astronaut groupies.

"No way! I want to make sure you stay all mine." She reached down and patted my cheek before I pulled away. When she frowned, I smiled to cover for the awkward moment. She then quickly asked the others if they needed anything, took their orders and then walked away.

"Check out her ass, Ty," Hammer said. "You screwed the pooch turning *that* down."

I shrugged. "I'll save it for later. Suzanne's coming over tonight. We're training together."

"Ah...training *together*," Kirill mocked, making air quotes, as usual, on the wrong word. It never ceased being hilarious how he always got it wrong.

"No, Kirya, it's *training* together," Hammer corrected him with his own air quotes.

"Bah! Who cares? He's fucking her. That's what it means."

It sure as hell *better* mean that or I was in for some disappointment, and I'd had more than my share lately.

That letter from the director of NASA had arrived only the week before, but it felt like a year or more. *We feel this is in the best interest of all parties involved and wish you well in your future endeavors.*

Fuck him. Fuck NASA. I clenched my jaw, and the guys all exchanged looks as if having easily detected the change in my mood. We'd spent hours, months and years training together— sometimes in the direst of circumstances. We'd crisscrossed mountain tops in Alaska during high-altitude training. We'd locked ourselves into a twenty-foot square isolated habitat for weeks during space travel analog training. We'd spent countless hours submerged together in one of the largest indoor pools in the world, the Neutral Buoyancy Lab in Houston. And we'd run simulation after simulation. We knew each other's body language and the slightest change in voice tone—in more than one language. We read each other.

If any small group of men was more attuned to each other than we were, I had no idea who they'd be. I'd only known this close of a camaraderie when I'd served in the teams as a Navy SEAL during my pre-astronaut days.

Noah seemed to perceive it first, his head tilting in my direction as if directly receiving my melancholy. I darted guilty eyes at him and then away. Noah was the hardest to be around. He'd been there the day of the accident—not on the station with us, but down in Houston, guiding the astronauts through our spacewalk as the voice of the mission, our CAPCOM.

He cleared his throat. "What's up, Ty? Is that flat-earth fucker still harassing you? I heard something about him filing a lawsuit against you for punching him. I never know when to trust the tabloid headlines." He shook his head. "The idiot had it coming."

Kirill laughed and slapped the table with his large hand. "He'll keep his distance now. His nose did not look pretty after it met Ty's fist."

I pinched the skin on the bridge of my nose.

And that image brought up the fact that there was now a lawsuit pending, and the story had gone viral. Being known as Ryan Tyler, American Hero was at least better than being known as the drunk astronaut who'd punched out a flat-earther and gotten fired from NASA. Curiously, the tabloids hadn't mentioned that the asshole had literally shoved a Bible in my face and called me a fucking liar for refusing to swear to the truth on it for him. He'd told me that my best friend was alive and well in the witness protection program somewhere and had not suffocated in his own suit during a spacewalk hundreds of miles above the surface of the earth.

The worst part? How much I wished *his* "truth" was the correct one. How much I ached to have Xander alive again—even if hidden away under a fake name and identity. At least he'd still be walking this earth instead of having his corpse burn up in the atmosphere months after his death.

All I had to show for that dumb-ass confrontation was a bruised hand, a probable lawsuit, and tabloid headlines. And the "fuck off" letter from NASA, of course.

"There's Victoria," Kirill said, running a large hand over his dark-blond hair to smooth it down.

"How cute. Someone's got a little crush," said Noah with a loud chuckle.

"Russians don't have crushes," he growled back.

Hammer spoke up with a hilariously exaggerated Russian accent. "In Soviet Russia, we do not crush on women. The women crush *us!*"

"Very funny. I make rude gestures at every one of you," he replied. But in spite of his words, he didn't, because Victoria Breckenridge, a very attractive African-American woman, approached us, looking almost like a buttoned-up business version of a femme fatale in her dark red business suit, perfect updo and designer stilettos. Someone I didn't know lingered at her side and a step behind her. A thinly built woman wearing jeans and a sweatshirt with a picture of a planetoid and the slogan: *Pluto: Never forget. 1930 – 2006.* Her dark-blond hair was tucked up into a NASA baseball cap. I couldn't help but laugh at the shirt and wonder about the young woman wearing it.

My eyes drifted back to Victoria, Public Relations Director for XVenture in charge of publicity for the XPAC. I almost winced at the possibility that she might ask me to hit the talk show and radio circuit again. During the past year since the accident, NASA had not hesitated to parade me around like their trained pet bear. And like the trained bear, I'd gone along with it, hoping it would help me make good on my promise. I should have known they'd disappoint me—yank that away and leave me with no future with them.

In truth, I'd kill to avoid that whole publicity circus again, but if it was my only way back to space, I'd already resigned myself to the possibility I might have to endure it for the sake of the new XPAC. If it meant I'd fly again, I'd jump through flaming hoops like a tamed lion.

Hopefully, it wouldn't come to that.

In any case, I had a very important promise to keep.

The two women approached our table and, with his old school eastern European manners, Kirill immediately shot out of his seat. He never sat when a woman nearby was standing.

Victoria came to a stop and smiled wide, her dark lipstick glistening on perfect lips. "Hey boys, we're here to double-check on the catering order for our investors. They're on the tail end of the big tour and almost ready to eat. Tolan pulled out all the stops with simulated launches and everything."

"They'll think they've died and gone to Disneyland," I said with a grin, and she tilted her chin up and laughed.

"How is Tolan doing? He hasn't vomited from nervousness, has he?" Kirill asked.

Her grin widened. "Not yet. But he hasn't had to do much. He's mostly following along with the tour and making small talk as they walk along. Crossing fingers for now." She held up a perfectly manicured hand with scarlet-tipped fingers twisted around each other to demonstrate. "They'll go into the conference room and talk business over lunch. That's about an hour from now, so I want to make sure everything goes off without a hitch."

Her eyes fastened onto the now-empty beer bottle sitting on the table, and, after everything, I started to feel a little sheepish though her expression didn't change. Always the smooth operator. "You boys all know Gray, right?"

"Who's that?" I blurted before noticing that Victoria was gesturing to the nonentity in the planetary sweatshirt and baseball cap beside her.

"She's recently joined the behavioral health team," Victoria added, ignoring my interruption.

The girl—she looked *young*—peeked out from behind the thick frames of her glasses underneath the bill of her cap. Now that she was closer, I could get a better gauge on her. She was of medium height, with a slender—almost boyish—build. When she turned her head to look at Victoria, I spied a short dark-blond ponytail peeking out from her baseball cap.

"Hey, guys." She smiled nervously. "Good to see you all again."

To our credit, none of us groaned, though I was sure we all wanted to. Flight psychologists were the bane of every astronaut's existence at NASA. We had to answer their questions, suffer their evaluations and, ultimately, live or fly by their decree.

I doubted it would be anything more than the same here, too. Kirill, who was still standing and would remain standing for as long as the women were on their feet, reached for her hand. She shook it with an enthusiastic nod, a becoming smile on her lips. I rose from my seat beside Kirill, reaching out my own hand.

"I don't believe we've met. I'm Ryan Tyler."

The smile melted off her face immediately, and she stuffed both her hands into her pockets. An awkward silence hung in the air. Apparently, Kirill's hand was good enough to shake, but not mine. *What the hell?*

"We've met. You don't remember," she replied curtly, staring at the floor. Hammer snickered across from me as I stood there with my hand still extended like a fool. Like I had some kind of disease or something—maybe even the type of disease that wasn't spread from a handshake. I got checked regularly—no danger of *that.*

Noah and Kirill both joined in the laughter now, making the situation that much worse. And she refused to meet my gaze, hands shoved so far down in her pockets she could practically touch her knees. So that's how she wanted it to be? Fine. I didn't need a fucking counselor sniffing around me in any case.

Pulling back my extended hand, I held my palms out. "No worries, sweetheart. You can't handle this? Not every girl can." I punctuated my smartass remark with a big ol' shit-eating grin. Okay, it was a complete douchebag thing to say, and I realized it after the fact. I may even have apologized had her reaction not completely distracted me.

She immediately flushed a deep pink, her thick brows knitting above the rims of her glasses. Infuriatingly, it made her look adorable and even more innocent. I pulled my gaze away from her troubling green eyes and fell into my chair, effectively turning my back on her.

Gray. Who named their kid that anyway? Especially a girl. It was the blandest color ever. Why not pick Mauve or Chartreuse instead? Not that I even knew what colors those were, but they sounded much more interesting. Gray was the color of miserable weather, mammals at the bottom of the food chain, and dirty socks that had been worn way too long without being washed.

Hammer *finally* stopped laughing—the ass—and leaned forward. "Hey, Victoria, you never answered my text."

"Haven't even had time to look at my phone. What did you need, Hammer?"

"I heard a rumor that Conrad Barrett is over there. Is that true? Please say it is, and that he's a big space fan."

Victoria and Fifty Shades of Bland Gray exchanged a long look before Victoria responded. "Half is true. He is over there. Not sure how much of a space fan he is, but I'm hoping he's a much bigger one than when he entered the factory today."

"And hoping he lays down some of his fat money to go along with it," Noah whistled, holding up crossed fingers. "Let's pray anyway."

Kirill knocked three times on the table and jerked his head toward his left shoulder, a Russian gesture for luck.

I sipped at my ice water before interjecting. "Eh. Conrad Barrett is well known for being a self-righteous tightwad. Wanna bet he throws in with the flat-earthers instead?" In spite of my flippant attitude, I hoped it was true, too. That bastard could mean the difference between this program getting off the ground or not. I hated—so much—that it was all coming down to us being at the mercy of investors. But in corporate America, what else could you do?

Victoria shook her head and checked her fancy smartwatch. "We need to go check on that order. You guys are on call for a few more hours in case the investor group wants to meet you. We'll call you over. In the meantime, no cocktails or beer. You're on imminent flight status." She arched her eyebrows up as if she were a scolding mother trying her best to speak "astronaut" to her wayward boys.

"We've been officially schooled, guys," Hammer muttered as we watched both women retreat. I couldn't help but notice that the newcomer had a nice little butt inside those jeans despite her boyish silhouette from the front. Her fists were still thrust deeply inside her pockets, and her shoulders were rigid. Was she upset about something? Or maybe she had a permanent stick up her ass. Who knew? Fifty Shades of Uptight.

I checked my watch and sat back with a sigh. We were in for a long wait and all needed something to take our minds off it. Either this meeting went well and we got our money, or it would be months yet, more months of limbo while we waited.

I clenched my teeth, then forced them to relax. When Cheryl came to the table again, we asked her to turn the channel on the TV to the game, hoping to ease the tension of anticipation. We settled in uneasily and waited for our time on the stage.

CHAPTER THREE
GRAY BARRETT

I T WAS DEFINITELY ONE OF THE UNIVERSE'S CRUELEST JOKES that the more toxic and junky the food, the better comfort it gave. Half-gallon cartons of ice cream and a spoon for breakups. Gallons of coffee and/or caffeinated soda for frenzied all-nighters. I was now adding greasy potato chips for nervous anticipation to that list.

I anxiously paced outside the conference room, a nondescript reception area with tables, desks and futuristic-looking chrome office chairs. The brilliant lime-green-and-cyan color scheme splashed across a white marble floor.

Halting in my tracks, I trained my eyes on the extra-large bag of salt and vinegar chips that my friend and coworker, Parvati "Pari" Sharma, now dangled in front of my face. It had all the promise of calming the rambling mind of the nervous wreck I'd become over the past week.

I knew I should resist, use all the willpower in my brain. My jeans were already a little too tight in the butt—*too much junk in the trunk, Gray.* Wasn't that exactly what I'd told myself this morning when I'd wiggled into them?

But damn it, I'd been on edge all day, and it was noon, with no time to stop and indulge in a healthy lunch.

25

My stomach roared. Carbs were beneficial for brain function, allowing for quicker thought processing. After all, more than eighty billion neurons send and receive electrical signals during any given twenty-four-hour period. And the brain consumed almost half of the body's glucose. And carbs converted straight to glucose during digestion, and chips were full of carbs so...

Those chips were good for my brain. Yeah. I snatched that gigantic bag of chips out of Pari's hand faster than you can say *metabolic cognitive psychology*. And tore it open.

"Wow, you *are* a nervous wreck." Pari's black brows crawled up her forehead, dark eyes widening. "I knew it the second you started sending me texts full of autocorrected gobbledygook."

I shrugged, digging in for some chips and shoving them into my mouth. "My hands might have been a little too shaky to make much sense."

"A *little*? You told me to *Get oven to the confession room innocently*. I took my best guess." She bit her lip. Her thick black hair fanned around her face. "Fair warning, though. I don't do *anything* innocently."

I didn't reply. I was too busy cramming chips in my face.

"For the love of Asgard, Gray. Slow down. Breathe. Swallow. You're going to choke to death on your own gluttony."

I crunched some more. "I can't. Mmm. So good."

She shook her head. "No, don't do that. Don't make sex noises over chips. It's just sad."

Last year, Pari and I had met through our mutual friendship with Tolan Reeves, CEO of XVenture Space Co. and had become fast friends and, recently, coworkers.

We were complete opposites in so many ways. She was a rocket scientist, and I was an aspiring psychotherapist. I was fair-haired and she, due to her Indian heritage, was brunette. She made friends instantly, while I freaked out when confronted with hunky famous astronauts who wanted to shake my sweaty hand.

Yeah, Pari and I were different, but we both loved space, binged all kinds of science fiction and fantasy shows, and were both fresh and full of ambition in our respective careers.

Pari walked over to a nearby table, picked up a roll of paper towels, ripped off a section, and handed it to me. "Wipe your mouth and your hands. This isn't a pretty sight."

"*You* brought the chips," I said, complying by dabbing at my mouth.

Her dark brows furrowed. "Are things going that bad? Did Tolan screw up the capsule tour for the investors?"

I shook my head, then held a finger to my lips, quieting her, and pointed at the door to the conference room. Inside, Tolan, Victoria, and the venture capitalists who would hopefully become the future investors of XVenture's Private Astronaut Corps, the XPAC, were having lunch. With any luck, they were discussing their plans for bankrolling it—and, therefore, my dream job as an experimental flight psychologist—over a catered meal.

"What did your dad think?" she asked in only a slightly quieter voice.

I shot her a baleful look. The reminder that my dad was in there among said investors only made me want to start double-fisting the chips into my mouth.

"Come on, Gray. Everyone in the world wants to know where Conrad Barrett is going to throw his money next. *My* dad follows his stock tips like it's a religion. Like he's Ganesh himself come down from on high. But he's *your* dad, and I can't imagine him not peeling off a few hundred million to help your future career."

I blew out a sigh. Yeah, that would make sense to everyone else in the world, but not to anyone who knew my father. "Dad is unconvinced that this is what I should be doing with my future."

Pari rolled her eyes, laughing. "White people problems. At least you had a choice when you opted for psychology over investment banking."

I licked my salty lips, wishing for a sugary drink to suck down my throat. The salt and vinegar had parched me like it always did. But it was oh, so good.

Pari snatched up the bag of chips from where I'd left them on the reception desk. Carefully spreading out a napkin, she poured a pile for herself and flicked one up, pressing it delicately to her small mouth. Pari was petite, with long and straight shiny black hair tied back in a ponytail, and ebony eyes to match.

The silence stretched between us as we both listened, heads tilted toward the door. But we could only discern voices rumbling from inside, punctuated by occasional laughter or a cough. Yes, Pari helped make the rockets, and XVenture had definitely proven they were *very* good at making rockets and making lots of money at it. But sending their own astronauts to space? That had never been done by a private company. This was all virgin territory—very exciting territory for people like me who wanted a hand in the future of humans working in space.

But everything, as was often the case, was hanging by the delicate thread of the purse strings. Without it, we'd never get off the ground—literally or figuratively.

"I spied on the tour a little, to see who all was there. Pretty impressive group." She crunched a few more chips, her be-ringed hands glittering under the industrial lights. Temporary Mehndi henna tattoos on the backs of her hands and wrists, remnants of the festivities for her sister's wedding, were fading but still visible. For the twentieth time, I studied them, fascinated by the delicate artistry.

"I had no idea Adam Drake was that hot in real life," she said out of the blue, shaking her head in memory. "He's an eleven on a scale of Thor to Loki."

I raised my eyebrows at her. "Were you ogling him? His *wife* was with him." I cleared my throat of chip crumbs. "Besides, dudes aren't your thing, remember?"

She grabbed another chip and nipped it between her lips. "I go both ways. Dudes haven't been my thing *lately*," she corrected. "Besides, a girl can always appreciate a good-looking man and his bank account. He makes my inner gamer nerd squee."

"Not so inner." The girl played Dragon Epoch for hours on end. I leaned forward, grabbing more chips from the pile despite having vowed not to eat any more.

"Your dad seemed to be very interested in the details of the tour. He asked a lot of questions, anyway."

I shook my head. Questions—one of Dad's preferred stalling tactics. He regularly used it during negotiations as a way to bring up his objections.

"So...how are you reading your dad?" she asked, pressing her greasy fingertips to her napkin.

"I dunno, he's hard to read. Even for me. Ugh, I think I'm getting a migraine, this is stressing me out so much." I rubbed my temples helplessly. Normally, I had a bit of a gift when it came to reading nonverbal cues and body language. But Dad always played things close to the vest. He was famous for it. You didn't get to be one of the richest people in the country, yet known for frugality and driving a hard bargain without discretion.

I brushed my fingers together, fortifying my resolve not to touch another single chip and get them greasy again. "Tolan can be inspiring when you listen to him. The other day, when he was talking about our goal to go to the Moon, then Mars and beyond. Our goals as an institution... *I* was getting chills from it."

"But you're already sold on it all as a bona fide space nerd. Would your dad care about all that?"

I shrugged. "I knew he'd be a hard sell when they chose Commander Tyler as the poster boy for the program." The thought of Ryan Tyler gave me the urge to cram a fistful of chips into my mouth. Damn it. I had been *this-close* to convincing Dad on my own before they'd made that announcement.

"But Ty will bring in other investors," Pari countered. "The PR angle alone..."

"PR," I scoffed, throwing up my hands. "If you count tabloids as PR."

She tilted her head as if she couldn't believe what I was saying. "He's the ideal all-American hero with a story that immediately engenders sympathy. Commander Ryan Tyler, an astronaut who survived a tragedy in which he saved the entire International Space Station and showed uncommon bravery while doing it. *And* his best friend died in that same accident."

I avoided her eyes, staring off into space while considering her words. She was right, of course, and I understood all that, but it didn't change how uneasy the man made me every time I was in his vicinity.

"Besides it's not only tabloids, Gray. He's been featured in *Time* magazine, *Newsweek,* and others. He's got that big book coming out and a feature film in progress. Documentaries, speaking tours, TV appearances. He's in the public eye for his heroism." She crunched a few more chips while I pursed my lips in protest.

She let go a long sigh. "And on top of all that, he's hot as fuck." She fanned herself. "Personally, I think they should make Ty pose for posters in front of the Rubicon III rocket without his shirt. Now *that* would get people's attention!"

I rolled my eyes and looked away to cover a blush as I remembered rejecting his handshake a short hour ago and then his douchey comeback to my supposed slight. Like, every woman in the world wanted him, and because I hadn't shaken his hand, I was making some kind of sexual preference statement. I'd shaken Kirill Stonov's hand, sure. But he'd also remembered who I was as a person.

But when the mighty Ryan Tyler stood up and held out his hand, I'd immediately started to sweat. And that, combined with the embarrassment of his obviously not remembering me, had caused me to panic and stuff my hands into my pockets. Odds were if I hadn't made an impression on him the first time we'd met, he'd likely already forgotten about my perceived snub. He had a different hot woman on his arm every week. No way he'd remember me, and likely the whole scenario would play out again the *next* time I was stuck in the room with him.

Pari hadn't been exaggerating. The man was a living legend. I'd been around famous people often, being my father's daughter. But a famous astronaut? A hero who had saved the ISS? And yeah, it didn't help that he had better-than-average looks. Quite a bit better than average.

I blew out a long breath, feeling like it had been knocked out of me.

"Dad's more focused on the negatives of Ty's involvement in our program. You have to admit that his life's fallen apart in the year since the accident. All the partying, womanizing. Trashing a hotel room. Punching out a guy on video. Wrecking a motorcycle in an accident where it was questionable whether or not he was intoxicated. Getting fired from NASA—"

Pari smiled, folding her arms over her chest. "Oh, Gray, you're a psychologist. You've gotta understand why XVenture made Ty the spokesman for the XPAC."

"I'm an *aspiring* psychotherapist, to be precise, and I don't get that title until my dissertation defense and clinical hours are completed."

Pari twitched her head. "Well, I think his heroism will rub off on the XPAC—the *Right Stuff* and all that."

"Nobody hopes so more than me." I put an emphatic hand on my chest. "But if Dad doesn't buy in, then there's no program this year at all. *Nobody* flies. Not even Ty." Dad's money would make the difference between being able to do the test flight in September—which would be huge for publicity—or having to push it back a year, maybe longer.

And then where would my research be? I had training protocols to write and simulation analogs to develop. The mere thought of it got me giddy, but unless the program was fully funded, there'd be no manned mission, and the astronauts would have to find some other line of work or go back to their former employer.

As I was trying to change the subject, the four astronauts who'd been sitting at the table in the restaurant across the street sauntered into the room with Tyler at the forefront.

As I'd noted the previous two times I'd seen him, Ty was a stunning specimen of maleness in his prime. Just under six feet tall, dark hair, striking blue eyes, in his mid-thirties. He carried himself with confidence and not a little swagger. He had the self-assurance of a man comfortable in his own body and in commanding the space around him.

It didn't help that he had the face and body of a Greek god, either. That jawline could cut diamonds, topped with generous lips, a straight nose, and heavily lash-fringed eyes. *Damn.*

A gorgeous human—who seemed to draw my eyes to him like the gravitational pull of Jupiter. And as with everything locked in orbit around the biggest planet in the solar system, there was a real danger of being crushed or changed in ways I couldn't even contemplate.

So, though he made my insides tingle, I knew he was someone from whom I needed to stay far, far away. *Avoid, avoid, avoid.*

Now, if only I could give my eyes and my thumping heart that same message. They seemed to want to act of their own accord. I swallowed, working moisture into my dry throat, and ripped my eyes away, hoping there were no grease stains or chip crumbs around my mouth.

"Parvati!" said the big Russian cosmonaut.

"Kirill Andreivich!" Pari replied, beaming.

"Why are you not working on the rockets? We need you working on the rockets."

"A girl's gotta get a break sometime." She stood up and wiped her greasy hands on her jeans. "But now that you mention it, time for me to get back to work before Vic comes out."

And it was only then that I realized Pari seemed to have been studiously avoiding Victoria for the past few weeks. I made a note to ask about that later. But definitely not now.

Right now, I had four pairs of eyes staring at me expectantly. I shrugged. "What?"

"Victoria called us over here," said Hammer, as everyone called him. "Any idea if we should go in or not?"

I opened my mouth to tell them I was absolutely clueless about Victoria's plans when the double doors to the conference room opened and Victoria poked her head out. "Guys! Awesome. Uh, I only need Ty for right now." Her eyes scanned the room and landed on me. "And Gray, get in here too," she said with a meaningful expression on her face that most likely meant my dad was being a pain in the ass. I'd seen that exasperated look on many a person's face who had worked with him before.

I ignored Ty's curious stare. No doubt he was wondering why a nobody—whom he hadn't even bothered to remember meeting—was being dragged into this important discussion. And clearly, I wasn't dressed for it. But oh well. Flexibility was one of my strengths.

At least Ty had the good sense not to make any more of his stupid, sexist jabs.

I followed him into the room. Despite his irritating personality, he had an admittedly gorgeous posterior. I fought hard not to notice the muscular, veiny forearms exposed in the short-sleeved black golf shirt he wore. For an instant, an impossible picture solidified of me—jeans, sweatshirt, messy hair, and all—hanging off his perfectly rounded biceps, leaning in to smell him. What *did* he smell like, anyway? I meant his pheromones, the smell of his sweat underneath the soap and the aftershave that he might wear?

Damn, Gray. Get a hold of yourself. He's an alpha dog jerk. I shook myself out of the temporary psychosis. *That's it. Shake it off.* It wasn't like I'd never been around a good-looking man before. *Jeez.*

The main conference room at XVenture was a large space. The sectional white table had been moved aside, and the outside windows shaded to allow a projected presentation to show on the screen behind us—now on the last slide. Fortunately—or *unfortunately*, in my case—the lights were brought up enough for us to be able to see the two dozen or so people in the room, all with neatly assembled portfolio-style folders in front of them on glass and chrome tables. Vivid color banner-style posters of rockets in various stages of flight hung along the walls, and a fifteen-foot scale model of a miniature Rubicon III rocket was suspended horizontally from the ceiling across the length of the room.

All eyes were on Ty who stood beside me, stiffly, confidently. Clearly, he was comfortable being the center of attention and had been for a while. My eyes shot to Dad's face. He was sizing up Ty too.

One thing I'd assumed might work in our favor was the Navy connection. Dad had served as an officer in the Navy aboard an aircraft carrier after his college years, and Ty was a former Navy SEAL, before his selection by NASA to be an astronaut. Naval officers tended to revere those elite warriors. So maybe that would make Dad able to see the potential good in having Ty attached to the program. I crossed my fingers again, behind my back, aware that my hands were cold and shaking.

If this program didn't fund, it would mean the end of one of my biggest dreams. I'd have to resort to corporate counseling— or worse, working for my dad. And I was half aware that he was counting on that.

After introducing the people in the room, Victoria explained that we were there to clarify a few points for the investors.

"Commander Tyler, we wanted to hear from you about recent events." Victoria began, but her voice died out when Dad sat up straight and Tyler folded his arms defensively over his chest. *Uh oh.*

"Certainly. I made a statement about this to the press, but I'm glad to repeat it. I was approached by a flat-earth fanatic who shoved his Bible in my face and demanded I swear on it to God that there was an International Space Station and that I'd spent months there working on orbit."

Dad cocked his head to the side, disbelief written on every feature as well as in his body language. "You punched out a man for poking a Bible at you?"

"He was insistent and incredibly insulting."

"You punched a man out for *insulting* you?" Dad fired back, increasingly skeptical. Oh...oh crap. My heart rate sped up, and the walls felt feet closer to me than they had only moments before. I swallowed a spiky ball of fear. This conversation did not bode well for the remainder of the meeting.

A dark-haired man sitting near Dad leaned forward to interject. I pushed my glasses up my nose to get a closer look. It was Adam Drake, the video game designer whom Pari had been fawning over. He was the only one in the room who'd actually visited the station before as a private citizen a few years ago. My panicked mind reached out to him as a tiny ray of hope that perhaps he could turn this around. He'd been a passionate advocate for this program for months, and he was the type of businessman my dad respected—a self-made man.

"I've read that some of those flat-earth nutjobs can get mean as hell and, in some cases, violent. And besides, Ty's in good company. Buzz Aldrin also got into an altercation with a flat-earther after being called a filthy liar and a fake. They hounded Neil Armstrong about the Moon landing for years before he died, too. They can be awful when they're pushing their agenda. I can't think of better company for Commander Tyler to be in."

Dad tilted his head, acknowledging Mr. Drake's contribution before turning to give Ty the once-over. "But don't astronauts learn in training not to lose their cool? And what about your Navy training before that? An officer. A graduate of the Naval Academy?"

During this diatribe, Ty had straightened, dropping his arms to his sides as if coming to attention under the rebuke of his commanding officer.

"Mr. Barrett—"

"We both know where this is going, *Commander*," Dad said. "I'm going to question you. You're going to stumble over real news items reported about you in respected media outlets—"

"Not to be confused with all the lies spread or exaggerated in the tabloids." One fist closed at Tyler's side to punctuate his reply.

Dad nodded, his mouth crinkled, considering. "In addition to that video of you punching that guy, there are reports of partying and trashing hotel suites. Different women every week—every public appearance. A real playboy cashing in on his heroic image to score. Are they truly lies, or is the train wreck of the truth more interesting?"

Oh crappity crap. This was not good. Not good at all. I scanned the room. A few heads were nodding, hanging on Dad's every word. He had that effect on people.

Any more of this and he'd have even the most diehard space nerds in here pulling out of this. I caught Victoria's eye and glanced meaningfully at Ty's back. She clenched her jaw and shook her head tightly.

I stepped forward, wobbling a little like I was about to walk into a war zone. It was no-man's-land with Dad in one trench and Ty in the other, each wrapped up inside barbed wire and staring across at the enemy.

"I'm going to intervene and suggest we steer this discussion in a more…productive direction," I said at almost the same time that Ty opened his mouth to—doubtless hotly—contend with Dad. He jerked his head in my direction, animosity shooting like bullets out of his eyes.

I turned to Dad. "Obviously, you have some objections. I'm sure the PR issues will be addressed. Victoria is *very* good at her job."

Victoria spoke up. "Yes, we have an entire campaign prepared—"

But Dad hadn't even turned to look at her. He was still focused on me. "What do you think, then? Honest opinion. If it were up to you, would you make Commander Tyler the face of XPAC?"

I froze. Oh shit—and other swear words I was too panicked to think of. Every eye in the room focused on me—Dad, Tolan, Victoria, Adam Drake, all the others. And Ty himself. I shot him a sidelong glance. "Uh, I'm more than willing to answer that question...in private."

Tyler's jaw dropped. Apparently, even the slightest hint of doubt in him was not acceptable. He stiffened, folding his arms over his chest. "Anything you've got to say about me, feel free to say it right here and now. I can take it. But your *professional* opinion is hardly worthwhile since we just met."

I blinked, irked by that reminder that he still thought of me as a nobody unworthy of remembering. "We didn't just meet, Commander Tyler, but okay. Duly noted."

I cleared my throat, noting out the corner of my eye how Tolan was biting his bottom lip, staring at me stone-faced. I turned back to the people facing us. Dad leaned forward, putting his chin in his hand and focusing on me. The best way to deal with him was with direct honesty. Dad did not suffer fools and bullshit gladly. That was actually his motto.

After a prolonged pause, I continued, "I don't think that placing Commander Tyler as the face of our program was the wisest choice. I would have preferred we go with Noah Sutton. He is much less controversial. But it wasn't my call. It was Tolan's and the team leaders. But I'm sure they have very good reasons for choosing as they have."

The rest of the room was absolutely silent, and I could feel the hostility oozing off of Tyler a meter away. But everyone seemed to be holding their breath, waiting for what Dad would say next.

"Noah would be excellent," Tolan said before Dad could reply. He seemed to be choosing his words carefully. "But he doesn't have the same public draw that Commander Tyler has."

I nodded. "True. Like I said, you had good reasons, and I was giving my honest opinion. That doesn't mean we shouldn't proceed with Commander Tyler. He'd be much less risk under certain conditions."

"What sort of conditions, kiddo?" Dad interjected, and I tried hard not to show my irritation at him by clenching my teeth. I did *not* need the added heat of him revealing our relationship to the room. "He seems like a man out of control to me."

I flicked a glance at Tyler, who now appeared even more pissed off at me than he had at my dad. Oh well. No danger of him forgetting who I was now. "He's not out of control. He *does* have issues. But he's been through a lot in the last year. He's not superhuman. Anyone would be affected by the things he's been through."

"Wait a minute—" Tyler started, but he cut himself off when Victoria reached out and touched his arm.

"Are you diagnosing a temporary psychosis?" Dad asked, a smile teasing his lips.

"You know I can't diagnose yet. If Tolan thinks Commander Tyler is a good face for the program, then I trust him. While the commander might not be ideal—not with everything being said about him in the press—there are things that can be capitalized upon. I do think he needs a tighter leash. For his own sake and for that of this program."

"The narrative about him in the press can be changed too. That all plays into the plans I have," Victoria said in a slightly fainter voice as people focused on us, rapt, as if watching a Greek drama unfold onstage before them.

Dad leaned back, eyebrows climbing his forehead. He turned to Tyler, who was now steaming mad, staring daggers at me. I avoided his gaze as much as possible, trying to ignore my own racing heart and the definite onset of that migraine I'd felt coming on earlier.

"So how do you control what's being said?" Dad asked with another vicious once-over of Ty. "Even if he does get his act together, hasn't the damage already been done?"

Tolan leaned forward, putting his hands on his knees to address Dad in that sincere voice he used for nearly every human interaction. "Mr. Barrett, we are doing all we can to repair Commander Tyler's image over the summer before the test flight. I'll let Victoria explain."

"We change the narrative." Victoria picked up smoothly from where Tolan served her the pitch. "Give Commander Tyler's life the appearance of stability by crafting a perfect relationship for the cameras. They do it in Hollywood all the time. Like Kara Jean and Jimmy Kane, for example."

"What? I thought they were for real," said one of the potential investors, a prominent real estate magnate and friend of Tolan's. He was sitting behind my dad. After a cough and a couple of smiles and snickers, he heaved a big sigh. "Karimmy forever."

Victoria smiled as if suppressing laughter. "That brief relationship skyrocketed them both. They ended up coming out of that 'breakup' with a new recording contract for her and a three-movie deal for him. People adore love stories. The public fell in love and was rooting for them. We could do the same for Ty. Nothing changes the narrative more effectively than an irresistible and glamorous love story. Especially one involving a reformed bad boy."

Tyler blinked, staring at Victoria as if wondering if he'd heard her right. I almost laughed at the obvious shock written on his face. Could the thought of being tied down to one woman for a few months be unfathomable? Could it be worse than all the unpleasant things he had to do while training to become a Navy SEAL and then an astronaut?

He certainly seemed to be reacting as if capture and torture behind enemy lines would be a preferable fate.

And who knew, maybe for Tyler it was preferable.

"So, the question is...assuming Commander Tyler is on board—" Victoria turned to speak to the room. "Who would we cast to be Commander Tyler's girlfriend and love of his life?"

1-2-3-Not it, was my first thought before chomping down on my tongue and wincing. The next moment was swallowed up in a startled laugh when I saw the expression on Tyler's face in reaction to Victoria.

He looked like he simultaneously couldn't believe what had come out of her mouth and he wanted to wrap his hands around her throat and throttle her.

The room practically rang with the unanswered question— did Tyler want this bad enough to go through with it?

CHAPTER FOUR
RYAN

WELL, WELL. LOOKED LIKE I'D JUST BEEN THROWN under the bus.

I fought my instinct to interrupt as Victoria droned on. All I could hear was a distant incoherent mumbling—like all the adults did on the *Peanuts* cartoons. "Wah wah, wah waaah wah waaaaaah."

Instead, I watched Conrad Barrett listen intently to Victoria's crazy plan. "Photo opportunities at charity events. Concert attendance. Accompanying her on the red carpet. Back in March, I arranged for Commander Tyler to take Keely Dawson to the Academy Awards right after the announcement about the opening of the XPAC to give us visibility. She's becoming very popular in the media, and I think she'd be perfect for this. Since they appeared together two months ago, it wouldn't seem so sudden. And I'm friends with her publicist."

The others were nodding. There were some smiles. Even Adam Drake seemed to be listening intently and muttering that it was a "viable solution" to the "PR dilemma."

I clenched my jaw so hard it might have shattered, a thread of a heartbeat throbbing at my temple. How on earth could I have lost control of the meeting so quickly?

It felt like they were talking about someone else's life.

43

As if they were planning to showcase someone else—serve them up as chum to the sharks of today's media, both professional and amateur. I might even have had the wherewithal to laugh at the poor schmuck they were discussing.

But *I* was the schmuck. And I was not amused.

Miss Gray the Uptight was asking questions of Victoria. "Would a summer romance suffice? It's already May."

I stiffened, interrupting Victoria's answer. "I have training, obligations—"

"We can work around your schedule, Commander," Victoria said.

My face flushed hot. "And how—"

"Commander do you want to fly again or do you not?" Conrad Barrett's nasal Midwestern twang cut through the crap conversation. "Because I will invest—if there's a sound plan. And it sounds like one is forming, provided you go along with it. Perhaps all this would help you get your life straightened out."

What the—was he fucking serious?

My life wasn't so fucked up—okay, there were issues. But damn it, I wasn't giving up control of my life to some damn committee for the sake of money and a PR stunt.

Except his question kept ringing in my ears. *Do you want to fly again or do you not?* That was the million-dollar—in this case, multimillion-dollar—question.

And the answer was yes. Hell yes, I did. And apparently, a lifetime of study, honed skills, and expert training wouldn't be a high enough price to pay.

"Listen, Barrett—" I stepped forward, pointing a stiff index finger in his direction.

"Thanks for your honesty, Mr. Barrett." Adam Drake rode over me, leaning forward to catch Barrett's eye, and they nodded to each other. "I think it sounds like a good plan too. I know when I was getting my company off the ground, funding was everything. It's a huge step for XVenture to go from being a solid rocket supplier and contractor to becoming a competitive force in manned space exploration."

Adam turned his head to catch my gaze as he continued talking, seemed to be communicating something unspoken—to me, most likely. I didn't need the reminder, but apparently, he thought I did.

Et tu, Drake? Damn it. They were all falling into line behind Conrad Barrett like soldiers—or drones. Figured. My uncle used to follow his stock tips and financial advice like it was Biblical scripture carved into the stone of Mount Sinai. No one represented the salt-of-the-earth capitalistic American dream like Conrad Barrett.

"A history-making step," Adam added.

I took a breath and expelled it, stopping the outburst I'd been about to make. I was only strengthening Barrett's objection by refusing to contain my emotions, anyway.

I am a leaf on the wind. That shit was going to have to be my new mantra. Not that I'd had an old one.

What even was a mantra? *This is bullshit*—now *that* was a mantra.

I cleared my throat, willed my voice to speak in an even tone. "I've sacrificed a lot in service to the government and my fellow Americans. I've sacrificed a lot to fly in space, but—"

Fifty Shades of—Annoying—Gray spoke up. "Looks like you're going to have to sacrifice a little of your time this summer to have a beautiful actress on your arm and pose for kissing pictures, Commander. It's a hard life." The room dissolved into soft laughter. I turned back to study her, back rigid, arms folded over her chest. Without her baseball cap on, her hair was in disarray.

It wasn't unattractive, but still, she was the mirror opposite of the impeccably put-together Victoria, who stood at her shoulder nodding. If I weren't so annoyed at the words she was speaking, I'd be impressed she had the backbone to stand up and interrupt me in the first place. Who *was* this girl anyway?

She'd appeared out of nowhere and was now giving professional-sounding opinions on whether or not I should head the new private astronaut corps. And to make it worse, providing ideas bound to change my life in the most uncomfortable of ways.

More resentment burned, but I swallowed it. Keeping my cool at the moment was paramount. *I am a leaf on the wind. Watch how I soar.*

"So assuming you can get her, you'd choreograph this cute little romance with Keely Dawson." Barrett shifted in his chair and focused on the young woman to whom he was giving entirely too much credence. "But Gray, you did say that certain conditions should be laid down. I assume you meant restrictions? So would this actress be able to get him to toe the line?" Barrett's eyes traveled from my head to my feet as if inspecting a defective used car someone was trying to dump on him. I'd never wanted to punch a guy as hard as him, except maybe that flat-earth fucker from last month.

But Barrett was a close second.

Nevertheless, he had an epic ton of money we desperately needed. And I desperately needed to fly again. And with NASA having stabbed me in the back, this was my only hope. My promise to Xander was never far from my thoughts. *Ever.*

I'd be a fool not to jump through Barrett's stupid-ass hoops. But on top of the hoops, I now needed a police officer?

"No, I don't think any actress we could employ would agree to enforce any type of restrictions." Victoria shook her head and laid a scarlet fingernail against her matching lip. Attagirl, Victoria. That was the answer I needed. "Usually in a staged relationship such as this, the couple is brought together for high-profile events and photo ops. Or we arrange quiet little getaways and tip off the press to show up for a more candid experience."

Barrett looked less than impressed. "But what happens if we get all this in place, I plunk down money, and he screws the pooch by going out on a drinking binge and causes more problems?"

"So you're proposing what, a damn babysitter?" I laughed and then stopped when I realized I was the only one laughing.

"That's exactly what I'm proposing," Barrett said, pointing a finger at me. "I think Gray would do a good job at it, actually." He turned to Miss Perfectly Uptight, who looked as shocked as I had been at the beginning of this conversation.

"That's not—" she choked out.

"It's not a bad idea," Victoria chimed in, and I mentally yanked back that attagirl I'd given her. "If I choreograph everything, use my connections to put the plans in place, you could be my boots on the ground, help manage the details," Victoria said. "Since I've also got the PR campaign to launch, you could travel with him, assist him with his obligations and publicity opportunities with the actress. Things like that."

Gray's eyes widened, and she shook her head, cramming her hands into her pockets, her shoulders hunched. I almost laughed, and were I not so annoyed, I would have said something to her. Talk about throwing out a boomerang and then being shocked when it spun around to dig into your own back. Fifty Shades of Cornered—by her own doing.

Her face flushed. "I've got work to do here."

"This is more important. If you can make this work, we all benefit," Tolan Reeves spoke up. Shit. If he was on board with this, then I was well and truly fucked.

It was either parade around and smile with this actress, playing the part of the smitten man in love, or never fly again. Because NASA had made it clear—even before they'd let me go—that I'd never fly with them again.

And I had to go up again. I'd promised Xander. My last words to him, in fact, when he'd begged me to promise him. I wouldn't let the accident end our dreams. I'd fly again, in his honor. I didn't go back on my promises—and most especially not that one. That promise to a man whom I'd never again see in this life.

And NASA had let me go. Well, fuck 'em. They weren't the only way to get to space. And if this was the way I could show XVenture—and the world—that Commander Ryan Tyler, American Space Hero and whatever other dipshit title they had attributed to me, was *just fine,* then I'd do it.

Goddamn it all.

"I don't need her to babysit me. I'll do it," I said finally.

Conrad Barrett smiled, leaning back. "Good. Because if you're in, then so am I. And I insist that Gray manage the situation. I'll feel a lot better about where my precious dollars are going."

Gray shook her head vehemently.

"Now come on, Gracie," he purred to her in a weird tone of voice that was almost creepy. Almost parental.

She stiffened at the reference, and I opened my mouth to speak up for her when he added, "If anyone can make this work, it's my little girl."

The room was silent.

You could have heard a pin drop. Well, I did hear a *pen* drop. The one I'd been clenching inside my fist dropped to the floor.

His little girl.

Gray was rolling her eyes and turning away, but not before I heard her mutter, barely audibly, "*Dad.*"

Well, didn't that put a new spin on things?

Time passed, and the discussion continued for a few more minutes. The group asked me questions about the test flight. It was a quick shot into low earth orbit and a brief parabolic arc back down again, mirroring Alan Shepherd's historic first trip into space in 1961. It would be the first such voyage beyond Earth's atmosphere for a private astronaut.

The meeting wound down shortly thereafter, and I was still reeling, piecing together what it meant that my new babysitter was the daughter of the biggest investor. It explained a lot, and yet, left me more confused.

What exactly was her relationship with Tolan?

My question was partially answered when, as I was fielding questions from the clump of people who had surrounded me, I saw Tolan wind his way around the group and approach her.

With one eye on what I was doing and the other on the two of them, I tilted my head to see if I could pick up what they were talking about.

Tolan took her upper arm in his grasp and bent his head toward hers as if to speak in confidence. But his voice carried enough for me to hear it.

"Checking in. Are you up for this? I'll make sure we clear your schedule of everything else and make this a priority."

The young lady flicked a glance in my direction, and I tried to focus on the conversation I was having. A few investors were asking about the nature of the test flight planned for this fall.

I missed Gray's answer but noted again how Tolan's hand slid to her shoulder before he removed it, nodding. There was a smile on his face. "He's right, you know. You can pull this off, and I'd be—"

"You must be so excited to fly again." My questioner pulled my attention back to him.

I nodded, taking a deep breath. "It's an honor and a privilege." And yes, probably worth the ridiculous hoops I was now being asked to jump through.

The babysitter, however, was more than I'd bargained for. My eyes drifted to the spot where little Miss Priss had been standing, only to note that she had faded away and headed toward the door.

"Excuse me a moment. I need to use the restroom."

I pounded through that door, hot on her heels.

She was walking fast and had a few paces on me. We zigzagged through the empty halls of XVenture's headquarters—all high ceilings, white walls, glass, and chrome accents. Huge high windows and skylights provided as much natural lighting as possible during the day. There were posters and brightly accented frames around every doorway.

And that girl had the nerve to speed up once she heard the footsteps coming up behind her.

Ah, no, Miss Daughter-Of-Barrett, you weren't getting off the hook that easily.

She made to turn down another hallway that dead-ended into a side door leading to the parking lot. I reached out and caught her arm above the elbow. "Miss Barrett—a word, please."

She jumped, turning toward me, her mouth falling open. When she stiffened, whipping her hair around, I caught the distinct aroma of fresh strawberries. Strawberries and...vinegar? And something else I couldn't quite put my finger on. A pleasant smell. A warm feeling washed over me.

I tightened my hand slightly on her arm in astonishment. Where had *that* feeling come from? I blinked and forced myself to ignore it, focusing on the physical. Gray Barrett had a surprising amount of muscle mass under the sleeve of her thin sweatshirt. My thumb slid up her inside arm for a better gauge.

She blushed furiously. "Hands off," she said firmly, yanking her arm out of my grip and stepping back, rounding on me, her tiny fists clenched alongside her thighs.

I raised a brow and held up an open palm in surrender. "Sorry to be grabby. Didn't want you making a break for it like you seemed determined to do."

Her pink mouth thinned, and I could hardly see her eyes from the glare of light on the lenses of her glasses. "What do you want, Commander Tyler?" Her tone was clipped, irritated.

What goddamn right did *she* have to be irritated? Honestly.

"I want to know what the fuck you were thinking when you engineered that little maneuver."

She stiffened. "I didn't engineer anything. I'm as shocked by my father's request as you are. What could I possibly have to gain by spending my precious time managing an unwilling person—"

"—Who's got issues. Don't forget about my *issues*," I mocked.

She cocked her head and folded her arms. "Ah, I see. I bruised your ego, and you want an apology." She shrugged. "My dad expects total honesty, and when he asked my opinion, I had no choice but to give it to him *honestly*. He can tell when I'm lying."

"And you think I'm unfit to fly."

She frowned. "It's got nothing to do with flying. I think you're unfit to be the face of this program. I think your penchant lately for the dramatic will hurt us. And yes, you've got issues."

I took a step forward, and she backed up against the wall across the hallway. Her eyes widened as she looked at me. She looked intimidated. No, I wouldn't be grabby or touch her again, but I was fine with intimidating her. I braced my hand on the wall above her head and leaned in close. *Mmm.* More of that delicious strawberry smell. It was almost overpowering.

"And you're perfect and willing to fix me, right? Admit it. You have some shrink wet dream in your little head about *fixing* me."

She shook her head, the array of dark-blond hair settling around her shoulders fetchingly. My eyes traveled up her long neck to her mouth, her upturned nose, her dark brows hovering over her frames. She wasn't plain. She was actually kind of cute…when she wasn't being downright infuriating, or *honest*, as she was selling it.

She seemed to be finding it hard to breathe. Inhaling deeply, she coughed once, cleared her throat, looked away as her face flushed pink. "Sorry to burst your bubble, but it's not all about you. You can have all the issues you want. It's not my job to fix you."

"Whose job is it, then?" I smirked.

"Yours, Commander." She licked her lips and raised those thick, dark brows at me, and the smug smile melted right off my face. Oh, when this girl pushed back, she knew where and how to do it, didn't she?

I swallowed, a tiny pinprick of emotion piercing me to the core. Was it fear? Anger at her challenge? Who *was* this woman?

Drawing back, I looked at her...really looked at her, getting a good glimpse of deep green eyes under all that shielding.

She jerked her wrist up stiffly to glance pointedly at her watch. "I gotta get going. I'm sure we'll see plenty more of each other soon. More than either of us cares to."

Footsteps approached from behind us. Miss Not-So-Bland glanced at whoever was approaching, eyes widening. "Mr. Drake." She nodded, her voice softer. I straightened and pulled away from the wall, turning toward him.

"So this is where Ty disappeared to," Adam Drake said. "I wanted to introduce you to a few people from the meeting. Mind if I steal him from you, Gray?"

Her thin mouth dissolved into a wide grin. "Be my guest. I'm sure I'll survive it somehow."

The acid sarcasm of her mild tone was not lost on me but was subtle enough that Drake answered with his own smile. "Thanks. C'mon, man. You don't want to miss this."

I threw one last glance in her direction to see that she was covering her mouth with her hand, shoulders shaking gently in laughter. *Laughter.*

So, she thought this shit was funny? *I'll show you funny. I'll give you plenty to laugh about.* I began to fantasize about the myriad of ways in which I could make her squirm.

Following Drake back to the conference room, I pasted on a smile, shook hands with cronies, and indirectly begged for money.

It was actually only times like these that I really hated my job.

CHAPTER FIVE
GRAY

FIFTEEN MINUTES AFTER MY CONFRONTATION IN THE hallway with Commander Egotistical, I was still waiting in the parking lot, leaning against the familiar bronze-colored, fifteen-year-old Cadillac Seville. I stuffed my phone into my pocket after sending its owner another text, only to see him coming through the glass front doors followed by three other men from the investors meeting.

They all seemed to be pelting him with questions. I shook my head and watched him. His suit was ill-fitting in some places. He'd recently lost a little weight and hadn't wanted to order new suits. Hadn't seen the point when the ones he had were perfectly fine and still fit him "good enough."

And he'd never ever order a bespoke suit when something off the rack modified by a skilled tailor was good enough. *Dad.* One of the richest men in the country—in the world, in fact—was also thrifty as a miser. And yet he had the smartest head for money and investments of just about anyone. People hung on his every word, looking for the magical keys to the kingdom he must have been handed.

The problem was that even in his early sixties, hardly anyone I knew—or had ever heard of—worked as hard as my dad. He was the son of a salesman and a school teacher. Born in Illinois, a product of middle-class, middle America. He'd fought and clawed his way to immense success using his ingenuity and smarts.

And everyone admired him. He was known for being fair and honest—sometimes too honest. He had a strong drive to take care of his own.

No one would ever suspect it wasn't all that easy being his daughter. His only child.

"Gray!" he said once he was within earshot. With a wave of his hand, he dismissed his admirers. "Sorry, fellas. I have a date with the most beautiful girl in the world."

I rolled my eyes, and the men laughed. He approached.

"Took you long enough," I said with a smile. "I've been texting you for half an hour."

"Oh, honey. You know I don't check my phone that often. Plus, I think it's probably out of battery." He reached into his suit pocket and pulled out an old-style flip phone. Typical Dad.

"You need to plug that in when you get in the car. What if someone's trying to get a hold of you?"

He puckered his lip as if having tasted something bitter. "Then they can damn well wait until I get to the office like they used to twenty years ago. Back in the good old days, people didn't all carry these nuisances around. Now, they suck up more time and steal everyone's attention. *Smart*phones. Pfft!" He waved his flip phone before tucking it back into his suit pocket. "People don't get distracted while driving with this kind of phone. It is a *very* smart phone."

I tempered my grin at his theatrics. I was still irritated with him, after all.

He bent and planted a kiss on my cheek. "So am I having dinner with my best girl tonight?"

I bit my lip. "No, Dad. Apparently, I have a new job to prepare for. One you gave me. Babysitting a full-grown astronaut for the next three months."

"Oh, that," he laughed.

He *laughed*. And that confirmed my suspicions. Even though my dad was sweet and kind and loving and took care of his own, he could also be a full-on pain in the ass. "I knew it."

He clicked his Cadillac unlocked and opened the door, putting his briefcase on the driver's seat. "What do you know?"

"That you did this on purpose. That this is another one of your tests." I should have known. An old dog like my dad seldom came up with new tricks when the tried and true ones worked fine.

He shrugged. "You seem to know very clearly what you want. If this is what you want, then you shouldn't have any qualms doing the necessary work for it."

"I'd think by now you'd realize that I am a hard worker." Try as I might, I could hear the slight tinge of hurt in my own voice. As usual, my dad did not.

He quirked his mouth. "You know me better than that. I don't just plunk my money anywhere. And having my daughter involved makes no difference."

"I thought you were doing this for Tolan as much as you were doing this for me. You were his mentor, after all." In some ways, for Dad, that relationship meant as much—or more—than blood. And Tolan idolized him in an almost ridiculous way.

I swallowed, reminding myself not to get defensive. "XVenture is already a proven profitable business—"

He held up a hand. "I don't advise you about psychology and the science of the mind, do I? I didn't even object when you chose the soft sciences to focus on. Please don't you advise me on my business practices."

I sighed. It came out more explosively than I'd intended, perhaps as a vent to my inner frustration. I probably sounded more like a rebellious teen than a woman trying to argue her very valid point.

He lifted a hand to my cheek. "You're looking a little pale today, Gracie. Have you been taking your medication every day like you're supposed to?"

I bristled, stiffening, both at the childhood nickname and at the ill-timed reminder that, in spite of craving independence, I was reliant on medication for the rest of my life.

"Don't try to change the subject. I'm twenty-five years old and can take care of myself." I gently turned my face away from his touch, and he let his hand fall, still watching me closely. "I'm frustrated, Dad. You don't trust my judgment. And for some reason, you find it necessary to throw obstacles in my way."

"It's business. Family or no. And I *do* trust you. I trust that you will make this happen. In fact, I trust you so much that I'm willing to double down on my initial investment if you manage to make Commander Tyler presentable by the time the test flight happens. If everything's good, then your flight is a go and my investment doubles."

My jaw dropped, and I watched him suspiciously. My stance swayed from one foot to the other, hands shoved into my jeans pockets. There had to be some kind of catch. I knew him too well. He was sweetening the deal before throwing in the clincher.

There was a "but..." in here somewhere.

"And if I can't make things work?"

His eyes drifted off to the side as if he were considering the answer to that question. An answer I already knew damn well he had in mind before he'd even made the offer. *Double or nothing.* It was one of his trademark moves.

"Well, I reckon if you can't make it work, then there won't be much for you here at XVenture. No manned astronaut program, no need for flight psychologists—or a behavioral health program. And there's still that job at that human resources management corporation my holding company just acquired. I sure could use you there."

I blinked, my features frozen. Learning to hide my emotions from my parents—particularly anxiety, fear, pain—had come at an early age. But even I wasn't perfect at it. My dad had originally made me this offer when I'd finished my doctorate program months ago.

Dad took care of his own, and he wanted more than anything to continue taking care of me. It didn't matter that he'd be crushing my own dreams in the process. He didn't see it that way because his need to have his loved ones safe and secure was stronger than that.

And that generosity came at a price. It always did.

I didn't even twitch a nostril.

"You're setting me up to get your way," I said.

"I'm not setting you up to fail, but to succeed." I stared him down for another minute before he cracked a smile and shook his head gently. "I'm surprised you have so little faith in your ability to heal. You're a natural born healer, Gracie."

I locked my arms over my chest. "I can't cure someone who doesn't want to be cured. I won't even try."

He shrugged. "You've got your work cut out for you, but I have every scrap of faith that you can do this. You *will* do this. You can do whatever you set your mind to. I've seen you do it. You spent half your adolescence in a hospital bed. But look at you now. All healthy and grown-up and beautiful."

My mouth creased sardonically. "Nice sweet talk. Apparently, I'm pale and looking like I haven't been taking my medication."

He laughed. "Of course, I'm gonna worry about you. I always will. Now, come have dinner with me, and you can figure out what to do with that belligerent jackass hotshot later."

With another deep sigh, I relaxed my shoulders and followed his gesture, going to the passenger side of his car. "Gee, when you put it like that, why am I not jumping up and down and going *Yippee!* at the thought?"

He chuckled but, wisely, didn't reply. Instead, he settled himself behind the wheel of the car and turned the ignition once I was belted in. Hours later, he dropped me back at my car, and I made it home early enough to start my research and notes on the new task at hand.

**

I adjusted the legal pad on my knee and stared at the frozen image on the screen—the *Special Edition* interview with Ryan Tyler shortly after the accident. I'd long since changed into my yoga pants and fuzzy socks, resting my feet on the coffee table. Pari was coming over later for weekly movie night, but I had some homework to do before she got here.

I set down the highlighted printout of Commander Ryan Tyler's Wikipedia bio and picked up the remote, cueing the video of the interview that had originally aired last winter. Diana Hunter, esteemed journalist and primetime anchorwoman, appeared on my screen with her perfect updo and in her smart skirt suit, standing before a life-sized image of Ryan Tyler and Xander Freed in their dark blue NASA flight suits, arms slung around each other's shoulders as they posed in front of a T38 Talon fighter jet at Cape Canaveral. Tyler was tall, dark-haired and blue-eyed while his close friend had tawny eyes and hair the color of wheat.

Their grins. Their rugged handsomeness behind their ubercool aviator sunglasses. They looked ecstatic, sporting mission patches from ISS Expedition 53, their doomed mission. Damn. I knew the overall story, but this was going to be difficult to watch nevertheless. I pressed play, and Diana began her narrative, her beautiful features placid.

"This is the story of two all-American boys from two dramatically different backgrounds who found the deepest of friendships through service to their country. They forged a brotherhood that would take them literally across the world and to the stars, only to be ruptured by tragedy and the ultimate sacrifice of death. An accident that would destroy them both in very different ways."

The image of Diana was replaced by a pan across the campus of the United States Naval Academy in Annapolis, Maryland. A formation of sailors in their white uniforms marched in front of a myriad of historical buildings.

"That unlikely friendship started here when, as plebes, Ryan Tyler and Alexander Freed were assigned to be roommates. A relationship which quickly grew into an unbreakable bond."

"We were complete opposites in almost every way." Commander Tyler's voice came on as a montage of snapshots and videos from their time at the Academy played out—their first military buzz cuts at the barber, an image of them running during physical fitness training, pictures of them studying. "Xander was the outgoing one. He could make friends with anyone—and he did. He was so popular. I was the more reserved one."

The montage continued, this time of childhood pictures, first of Xander, as she described his background.

"Xander Freed was an All-American athlete, the eldest of four children from an upper-middle-class family in Ohio. The star of the baseball and track team. Ryan Tyler was the driven valedictorian and swim team champion. The only child of fallen Navy SEAL Joshua Tyler and his wife, Anya, who had emigrated at a young age from Ukraine, Ryan grew up in Las Vegas, Nevada. When he was still a child, his parents divorced, and at the tender age of fifteen, young Ryan was told his father would not be coming home from deployment in the Middle East."

The montage of childhood photos faded, the last image a young Ryan with his father who bore the golden Eagle and Trident pin of the US Navy SEALs prominently on his lapel. The image resolved with Diana seated against a dark background, an image of the International Space Station orbiting the earth below, her seat facing Tyler.

He was dressed in dark slacks and matching blazer. A white dress shirt unbuttoned at the neck revealed the strong column of his throat. The NASA astronaut badge—a star with three rays extended beneath it encircled by a ring—was pinned to his lapel. It was gold, rather than silver, indicating he had flown in space. His ankle rested on his opposite knee, and he sat, despite the casual pose, looking tense. And he was as devastatingly handsome as ever, with no trace of the arrogance he'd shown toward me today.

He was speaking again. "Even our goals were wildly different. We were both in the Navy, but Xander was headed to pilot school from day one. I wanted to be a Navy SEAL, like my dad."

"But those different goals didn't seem to get in the way of you maintaining your friendship, even after you both graduated from the Academy," Diana prompted.

He shook his head. "No, we kept in close contact. I was best man at his wedding." An image appeared onscreen of Xander, smiling, standing beside a beautiful, petite brunette bride. As the image faded, Tyler continued talking. "He stayed in Maryland for flight training school. I went off to California for BUD/S. We talked all the time. Hung out whenever we could."

"Like brothers," Diana said.

He nodded. "Yes. Like brothers." He huffed a sad, ironic laugh that speared me right through the heart, despite my resolve to watch the interview with an objective eye. "The brother I never had."

The interviewer leaned back and allowed a moment of dramatic silence while she told the audience they'd be right back after the commercial break.

I was streaming the episode so there was no commercial break, but I fast-forwarded regardless, aware of my time limitations.

"You and Xander applied to NASA the same year." Diana prompted.

"Yes. That was Xander's goal from the start," Tyler replied.

"And not yours?"

He shrugged and gave a lopsided grin. "I had to be talked into it."

Diana's eyebrows rose. "But you were the one accepted right away. Xander didn't make it that first round."

"Xander was injured in an accident around that time. So his application was put on hold."

"So you got to start your training. You flew first... Did he ever resent that?"

Tyler's expression did not change. "No. Not once. That's not the type of person Xander was." I scribbled more observations, frowning, noting how he spoke of his friend and glorified him. Whether or not that was for the sake of the broadcast or how he really felt would be another matter, but it led me to wonder what amount of guilt he might have been suffering since the accident.

Did Tyler feel responsible since he was the lead astronaut on that EVA and Xander was the rookie? I added that to my list of questions and briefly glanced at the variety of headlines he'd racked up since the accident.

Drunken and disorderly conduct. Assault. Tabloid rumors almost every week pairing him with various women—single, married, it made no difference. The motorcycle accident. The media certainly weren't leaving him alone, but he wasn't helping the matter. I scribbled another question down on my bullet list.

• *Alcohol consumption?*

By the point in the interview where Diana started asking questions about the accident, Pari had arrived with snacks and sat down to join me, thankfully having left the potato chips at home. I hit play after finishing up my latest batch of notes.

"It's standard protocol that astronauts are constantly tethered to the Space Station by either one or two cables. So how did Xander become untethered from the station?" Diana Hunter asked.

Tyler hesitated, tightening his strong jaw, which only served to make him more handsome than he already was. There was an intensity in his blue eyes, and his right fist tightened where it sat atop his knee.

"It's unclear. We were in the middle of a situation. A stream of pressurized ammonia had blown me back against the truss. My suit was punctured and began losing pressure. But we had to get the valve shut off to stop the leak. We were losing coolant at an alarming rate, and beyond that, the venting of gas was causing the station to veer off course. And even a minor leak can cause major problems for orbital stabilization."

Diana nodded. "And as you fought to get the valve closed, Xander was knocked against the live current on the solar array."

"Yes. His EMU—his extravehicular mobility unit, which is what we call the spacewalking suit"—he clarified for viewers—"was shorted out. He lost control of his mobility, many of the joints in his suit were frozen and unmovable. He couldn't even use his SAFER."

"Can you explain what the SAFER is?"

The less threatening question seemed to cause him to relax. His shoulders dropped a little, the fist on his knee loosened. His foot, resting atop his other knee, bobbed a little.

"Sure. NASA loves its acronyms. The SAFER stands for Simplified Aid For EVA Rescue. Essentially, it's a little jetpack at the base of the life support backpack that allows, in the event of an astronaut becoming untethered and knocked away from the vehicle, to fly his or her way back to the airlock."

"The accident had frozen half of Xander's suit so he couldn't use the SAFER jetpack to get back to the station? And he'd been thrown out and was continuing to move away very quickly. Could you not have activated your SAFER to go after him?"

That jaw tightened again, and though he fought hard to hide it, I could see the pain in his eyes before he cleared his expression and returned the interviewer's gaze. "I had to follow orders and get the valve shut. Moreover, my own suit was quickly losing pressure from the initial blast—"

"The pressurized ammonia breach?"

"Yes."

Diana leaned forward as if to emphasize the dire story being told. But it was riveting enough on its own.

"So your suit is losing pressure, and if you don't get the valve shut, what are the consequences for the station?"

Tyler's features were absolutely blank, as if talking about launch sequences instead of the life-and-death event he'd lived through only months before. "The array overheats and fries. The entire station loses power. Life support. Orbital correction ability. Possibly even a way to launch the Soyuz capsules for the astronauts and cosmonauts to return to Earth."

Diana tilted her head empathetically. "So you had to make the choice then and there to sacrifice the chance to save your friend in order to save the station and everyone on board."

Pari grabbed the remote and hit pause as I added to my notes. I listed some of the "tells" of his facial expressions and body language that I'd noticed from this and a few older interviews. Anything that might denote hiding deeper emotions. These things would be useful for when I dealt with him one-on-one...*hopefully.*

Pari shook her head. "Horrible situation," she said breathlessly. "I've read articles about what happened, but to hear him tell it like that." She mimed putting a fist to her gut. "Gets me right here."

My eyes flicked up to the paused image, his face frozen in a half grimace, half frown. He'd eulogized Lieutenant Commander Freed a week before that interview, during the memorial at Arlington National Cemetery. Of course, there had been no body to bury.

I hit play and listened to the last bits of the interview. Tyler's recount of his last moments with his friend. Xander had not been recovered, and Tyler could only speak with him over the intercom. And then Xander Freed had said goodbye to his family while he waited for his life support to run down. It had taken hours. Hours where Xander drifted farther and farther from the station and had eventually died.

The scene of the interview faded to black, and the credits rolled.

"I wonder if he blames himself," Pari asked, scraping a fingernail along her bottom lip thoughtfully. "I mean, these military guys—especially the SEALs—they get it drummed into their heads constantly. Leave no man behind. But he had to do exactly that. Exactly the thing he'd been trained for years never to do. He was *ordered* to leave Xander there while he fixed what he had to fix and got his leaking suit back to the airlock. And then he had to hear his best friend die—suffocate—over the intercom. How fucked up is that?"

I shrugged, thinking of his words to me today. *You have some shrink wet dream in your little head about fixing me.*

He'd been such a jerk, but even now, I couldn't help but feel sorry for him. Emotion welled up in my own throat as I imagined the situation. But he'd been insulted and angered when I'd implied that no one could go through what he had and come out unscathed. A dragon should never show its underbelly, the chink in its armor.

And Ryan Tyler was heavily armored, indeed. But I swallowed that emotion, the sting of empathetic tears that threatened my own impartiality. I couldn't allow myself to feel for him. That would be my downfall.

Ryan Tyler was a means to an end for me. That was it.

"His issues are his problem. He made that clear to me today. I'm going to focus on managing him."

Pari turned shining eyes on me, a knowing smile. "Ah, c'mon, doesn't the whole challenge of healing that marvelously wounded hero light your fire, even a little bit?"

An ache throbbed deep inside me. I'd like nothing more, but he didn't want that. And I couldn't help a person who didn't want my help.

"A lot of people are depending on him to rehabilitate his image back to the All-American hero everyone wants to love and root for. If he does that, we get funding for XPAC." I turned back to her. "XVenture is already doing a great job making and launching their rockets—and thus, you have your dream job. Working as a flight psychologist is my dream job. If XPAC doesn't get funded, there will be no astronauts for me to work with—and thus, no job for me."

Her smile deepened. "So, you're his babysitter."

I raised my eyebrows at her. "I'll be his freakin' jailer if it means we don't see a repeat of this crap." I waved to the printed-out headlines on the coffee table. "He has a chance to clean up his image. Still, I'm not leaving it all up to him and mere providence to get him to that launchpad in Florida on September 14th in one piece."

"But if he's being so belligerent with you, how are you going to make sure he cooperates?"

I adjusted my glasses on my nose and fought rolling my eyes. "That is the money question. Astronauts are notoriously suspicious of psychotherapy and flight psychologists."

Pari smiled. "Then don't be his shrink. Be a friend."

"Hmm. A friend?" I wrinkled my nose.

She laughed. "Yeah, you remember how to do that, right? Don't ask so many questions, and don't do that—that look you do."

I frowned. "What look?"

"The one that makes it feel like you are peering into the depths of my soul. It's unnerving."

I shook my head and laughed. "I do not have a look."

"Yes, you do. Don't do it with him, or he'll close off. Better yet, find something to bond with him over. You're a space nerd, he's an astronaut. You know... Be his *friend*."

I scoffed. "While maintaining a professional distance?"

Pari shrugged. "You're gonna have to figure that one out." She tapped the image of Tyler in his dark blue flight suit that had printed out with his Wikipedia page. "Look at this man. He's the perfect package. Navy SEAL. Master's degree in mechanical engineering. Physically fit and gorgeous. Too bad he's broken as hell."

I pursed my lips but didn't reply with what I wanted to say. *And too bad he acts like an asshole at will.*

"So, what's the plan?"

My eyes glided down over the legal pad of notes I had been taking—items circled, other things starred or underlined. I'd been meticulous in my observations. "I'm going over to his house tomorrow to get the lay of the land."

"Hmm…would be way more interesting if you got the lay of the *man*. Wink. Wink."

I rolled my eyes. "You're hopeless."

"So my mom tells me all the time," she said with a light laugh.

"All innuendos aside, Commander Tyler has no idea that I'm going over there yet, but I'll get Tolan to set it up for me. Any suggestions on getting him to meet me halfway?"

Her thick dark brows went up. "Wear body armor?"

I laughed. "I'll do this. I'm determined."

Determination had got me through a lot. It got me through school years earlier than I normally would have been. I was a doctoral candidate at twenty-five with a dissertation already defended. All I lacked were the necessary clinical hours to have my PhD.

Pari understood me. We'd bonded over being among the youngest—and among the best-educated—at XVenture. Our friendship had started from there, and we had each other's backs. I'd been trying to inch my way into this job for nearly a year. And it was close. *So close.*

My boss had pretty much told me that if XPAC was a go, a permanent spot on the behavioral health team was assured. So now, all I needed to do, thanks to my dear ol' dad, was deliver one shiny, squeaky-clean astronaut to the launchpad in the early fall.

Easy, right? I blew out a breath, my stomach knotting with the stress of the thought.

***

My laptop rang way too early, and I remembered groggily that Mom said she was going to call today. Moving it to my lap, I fought to sit up in bed. As usual, my darling mother had forgotten the exact time difference between California and Wales.

I was still rubbing the sleep from my eyes and blinking at the clock at the upper right-hand corner of the screen. Barely after six a.m. *Ugh, Mom.*

"Hello, *cariad,*" my mother chirped too loudly—and far too cheerfully—at this time of morning. Which obviously, wasn't this time of morning in Cardiff. The afternoon sunshine beamed across her garden behind her.

I rubbed the sleep from my eyes. "Did you forget what the time difference is again?"

"Oh—" She glanced off the screen as if to look at the clock. "I forgot to check the time. Well, you need to get up for work soon anyway, right?"

I struggled to sit up. "It's Saturday, Mom, ya ditz."

She laughed that musical laugh of hers. Her blond hair was disheveled around her head and partially pulled into a messy bun—though not quite long enough to stay there. Her eyes crinkled at the corners when she laughed, the only times lines showed on her face despite her being over fifty.

"Well, you *used* to be such a morning person. College certainly changed you."

Lots of things had changed me, but Mom hadn't been around for much of the last seven years, so she wouldn't know.

"How did your big investors meeting go? I was thinking about you yesterday—or was that this morning? I can't keep track of the eight-hour shift. Whenever it was, if I wasn't sleeping, I was thinking about you."

I scratched my nose. "Thanks. It was late afternoon yesterday, so you were probably sleeping, but I appreciate the gesture."

Mom's mouth creased. "Did your dad show up like he said he would?"

I nodded, my mouth pursing. I hadn't quite decided how much I'd tell her. Mom and Dad were amicable with each other when in the same room or in contact over things that pertained to me. But they didn't go out of their way to stay in touch with each other otherwise.

They weren't enemies at all, but they certainly weren't good friends either. And I often wished they could be. Sometimes I grew tired of being their go-between.

"What's that face? Did it not go well? You know how picky he is with where his money goes."

"Um, he's going to invest."

My mom could be an airhead sometimes, but she was as perceptive as I was. She read through my bullshit immediately.

"Under what conditions?"

With a heavy sigh, I told her about my babysitting job for the next three months. Her brows hitched up higher with every sentence, until finally, she doubled over laughing.

"It's not that funny."

She straightened, wiping her eyes with her index finger. "It's hilarious, Gray. And so typically your dad. I could have told you he would do this."

I gritted my teeth, wanting desperately to change the subject. Mom sobered, and before I could ask her about the weather in her homeland, she followed up. "He offered you that human resources job at HRQ again, didn't he?"

I bit my lip. No one—*no one*—on this planet knew Dad better than my mother. It made sense. They'd been married for almost twenty years before divorcing. Mom, originally born in the UK, had grown up in the US and met Dad while they'd worked on a joint project together—and shortly before he'd purchased the company she worked for. Their romance had been a whirlwind—so out of character for my dad.

But they'd been too different, and for too damn long, they'd tried to make it work for my sake. Their world ended up revolving around me even more so than normally happened when a couple had children. When your kid is undergoing health crisis after health crisis, it tends to shape your entire world. I blinked, returning my focus to what my mom was saying.

"Let me tell you. And I tell you this all the time, but I'm going to keep repeating myself in case you don't listen. You have to get out from under your dad's thumb. I know he makes you feel safe and secure, but..."

"...'It comes at a price.' Yeah, I know, Mom."

"Don't settle because it's what he wants. You have the right to strike out and find out what you love to do."

I smiled. Sometimes these talks with Mom were all I needed to firm my own resolve.

"Dad likes to take care of people."

She nodded. "Your father is an excellent man. *But...*" I blinked, realizing maybe that was why Mom had fled back to Wales after the divorce. She begged me regularly to go visit her, but because I'd been in school continuously since I was barely seventeen—including during the summers—I had seldom taken her up on it.

"Just remember your cousin, John," Mom said. She brought him up often. "He lives and dies by your dad's approval—his house, his whole lifestyle, even who he married. He seems happy, but it's a gilded cage he inhabits."

"Not to worry, Mom. I told you that I want to prove I can succeed on my own despite being Conrad Barrett's daughter."

Her smile faded a little. "Did the company need the money so badly that you had to go ask him for it? It would have been better if you'd kept him out of it."

I sighed. "Tolan asked him."

Mom's brows drew together in a slight frown. "Tolan's a good kid. How's he doing?"

I almost laughed. That "good kid" was nearing forty. But Mom obviously remembered him as one of Dad's most loyal fresh-out-of-college mentees.

"Good. Better if Dad had agreed to hand over the money."

"Which you and Tolan both know Conrad Barrett would never do."

I fell back against my pillow and stared at the screen with a wistful smile. "I guess you got me there."

Mom's smile grew, and she waved her hand as if to clear the air in front of her. "Enough of that...how are you doing? Have you been up to our spot lately?"

I stifled a yawn and replied. "Whenever I go over to Dad's, I try to squeeze in a walk around Griffith Park."

"I bet all the white jasmine is blooming there right now. It smells *so good*. I miss how Southern California smells in May."

I laughed, and we chatted for another half hour before Mom declared she needed some tea and had to go. Of course, I never got back to sleep, so I texted Tolan with my plan for the day and asked him for help.

I had a full-grown astronaut to wrangle. It was about time I got to wrangling.

CHAPTER SIX
GRAY

TOLAN TEXTED ME HOURS LATER TO TELL ME THAT Commander Tyler had been notified of my visit. And thus, I prepared as best I could for "friend mode." I dressed nonthreateningly in a T-shirt and jeans. Okay, so maybe they were my preferred clothing choice, but they said "girl next door" and "nonthreatening friendly person" easily enough.

Tyler was smart, though, and I couldn't be obvious about this approach. Likely the minute he detected me trying to manipulate him, he'd dig in his heels, and it would make an awkward situation worse.

When I pulled into his hilltop driveway in the exclusive, hilly Cowan Heights neighborhood in North Tustin, it was a little after four p.m. Tolan had made the arrangements, and as it happened, I caught Tyler's assistant, and biographer, Lee, on his way out the door. He grinned and extended a hand.

"Hey there, Gray. Good to meet you. Ty's in the middle of his workout, but I let him know at lunch when you'd be here. You can wait for him in the front room. He should be down shortly."

The house itself was huge, hanging off one side of Peter's Canyon, overlooking the dry scrub habitat of California coastal chaparral and sandy reddish cliffs. It was a lovely setting and a remarkably huge house that was probably grander and more impressive than any place he'd ever lived before.

Ryan Tyler had major endorsements and appearances—motivational speeches at six figures a pop—in the wake of his notoriety. In addition, he had recently inked an eight-figure book deal—with movie rights to the as-yet-unpublished memoir optioned for an undisclosed amount. So he could easily afford a place like this now. I couldn't help but marvel over the cost that wealth and fame had come at, though. And I wondered how he truly felt about it, deep down.

I checked my smartwatch to make sure I wasn't late—nope, right on time. The front room was empty, but I assumed it would be as Lee had said. Ty would be down shortly after finishing up his workout. Maybe he'd opt for a quick shower.

I burned a few minutes walking around the room to take in the furnishings and décor—none of which were personal enough to reveal anything about him at all. The place had been professionally decorated in black, cream, and a muted aqua color. And it was beautiful, but definitely not him. I wasn't quite sure what I'd expected—bachelor pad-style decorations. Leather couches, big overstuffed recliners, massive TV and game console with super expensive sound system, maybe. None of that was present here.

Maybe he'd saved it all for the master bedroom.

I immediately blushed when thinking about his bedroom, then reminded myself what an idiot I was. Jeez. I was a grown woman thinking about a very hot man watching TV or playing console games in his bedroom, and even that got me flushed.

I'd spent all day yesterday studying up on him, reading articles about his life pre-accident and the event itself, taking notes and making cross-references. Now, I wandered around his front rooms, checking my watch far more often than I needed to, and looking for clues about who he was.

Thirty minutes in, I decided one thing he definitely wasn't was *punctual*. Strange, for an astronaut. But maybe he was purposely blowing me off? I wouldn't put it past him. He'd been pretty annoyed yesterday, accusing me of setting the whole situation up.

I wandered down a hallway toward the kitchen, having caught sight of a row of large framed and glass-covered expertly mounted photographs.

They were gorgeous—professional quality, to be sure—and each one of them displayed a location on the planet's surface as shot from low earth orbit. I paused next to one, a string of islands, straits, and isthmuses—interlaced with about twenty different shades of blue and green. *Stunning.* I was moving in for a closer look when a bang thumped the wall.

Like someone or something had fallen in a nearby room. Oh, jeez. Had Ty dropped the weights he'd been lifting? Was he in trouble? Had he fallen?

I took a step toward the sound when another bang followed the first one—and then another. And *another* hit against the wall.

There was a certain...rhythm to those bangs, as a matter of fact. And as I approached the sound, someone cried out with a loud moan.

Are you freaking serious right now?

I shrank back in the direction I'd come.

Either people were having sex a few rooms away, or that was one over-the-top realistic sound system accompanying a porn video. I stepped backward again—and bumped into the wall *loudly*.

Shit. I froze, holding my breath. I never thought I'd catch myself thinking this, but I hoped they were too wrapped up in messing around to be bothered by my intrusion.

Fortunately, they were. Either that or she was deeply wrapped up in calling upon a higher power during some very intense-sounding prayer.

The picture behind me tilted on its hook, and I turned to catch it before it fell off the wall. Crap. I'd come this-close to knocking it to the ground and breaking it.

Thump. Thump. Thump.

The rhythm was speeding up now, and I fled down the hall, leaving the picture horribly askew on its hook.

By now, even back in the front room, I could hear the woman's shrieks of ecstasy.

I checked my watch. Almost an hour past our appointment time.

My blood boiled. This was intentional. He was deliberately blowing off an important meeting so he could bang someone. Okay, so it was probably what most men would do, but this felt like definite pushback in my direction as revenge for yesterday.

Jackass.

American hero, my ass. More like American manwhore.

How obnoxious! I almost wished I had bumped that wall louder so that they'd know I was here. That they'd know they were so loud it was obvious what they were doing.

Maybe I should knock this very expensive-looking vase off the coffee table to create an extra-loud crash. Fury and embarrassment burned in my face and stiffened the muscles in my jaw, my shoulders, even my arms as I paced circles around that couch and coffee table, arms folded tightly against my chest.

I was so wrapped up in my private daydream of a vendetta that I hadn't even noticed when it stopped—or finished or whatever. I didn't want to know. Too. Much. Information.

Way too much.

I fanned my heated face and ordered myself to calm down. They were talking now, but I couldn't pick out the words. Grabbing my phone, I battled over the next question. Should I text him? Call him? I didn't even have his number. Should I turn around and storm out of here while I mentally flipped him the bird?

No. I couldn't do that last one. Jackass or no, I needed him. XVenture needed him. Commander Ryan Tyler, All-American Hero, was vital to getting the XPAC launched.

And Dad had tasked me with this as his version of a test. And I wasn't about to prove that I needed to come running back to him for a job. Maybe he secretly hoped XPAC was a losing bet. Well...

Challenge accepted, Dad.

I reached into my messenger bag and began pulling out things. A legal pad, a bundle of sharpened pencils. My tablet, which had been fully charged. An assortment of gel ink pens that glided when you used them and didn't smear all over my hand when I wrote because I was a lefty.

He wanted to get rid of me? Well, screw that. I was establishing myself, whether he liked it or not. I wouldn't leave until *I* was ready.

I lined everything up on the glass coffee table, careful to keep my legal pad of notes tucked away where he wouldn't accidentally see them. Then I plunked myself down on the gigantic couch and tapped my foot, waiting.

Would he come out? Or would he roll over and go to sleep? It was the middle of the afternoon, after all. But who knew? Maybe he was a napper?

God, I hoped I wasn't going to have to sit through another round. Nope, just *nope*. If that started, then I'd have to come crashing through the bedroom door to interrupt—with my hands over my eyes, of course.

Before that thought resolved or led to another string of thoughts that would chase each other down the rabbit hole that was my brain, I realized the voices were louder than before—and accompanied by footsteps. Approaching.

I stiffened—crossed and then uncrossed my legs on the couch before resolving to lace my fingers together and hold them primly in my lap.

Regardless, I shot out of my seat the moment the two people rounded the corner. When they caught sight of me, they froze. The woman, a pretty, petite but very fit, platinum blonde in a designer velour tracksuit with an expensive gym bag over her shoulder, raised her brows and glanced at Ty.

The American Hero himself was wearing sweat pants slung low on his torso and not a stitch of clothing above his waist. Well, at least they were maintaining the ruse of a workout semiconvincingly.

I might have believed it, even. But sex did not sound even remotely like working out.

I couldn't help but notice his perfect body. He was sculpted in all the right places. His arms bulging with veins, defined biceps, powerful shoulders. His thin, solid torso, every rock-hard muscle delineated under his skin. Abs, abs, and more abs. *So many abs.*

Like, more than a six-pack. I caught myself counting them. I stopped at ten when he cleared his throat and spoke.

"Oh, you're here."

I blinked, tearing my eyes away from the ridge along his hip that dipped into those sweat pants. Ugh. He was a rude pig, so clearly, the pretty packaging shouldn't matter.

Damn it, Gray! I set my jaw and narrowed my eyes at him and reminded myself he was just a man. A jerkwad douchebag of a man. Who happened to be incredibly hot, but I could and would ignore that part.

"I arrived on time. At the exact time I believe Tolan told you." I said, with particular emphasis on the name.

He rolled his eyes.

Yes. He did that. *He rolled his eyes.* Right where I could see him. He didn't even bother to turn his back or look away or anything.

Without another word—and no introduction to his lady love—he turned and escorted her to the door. As he reached to open it, she gave me another long glance before smiling and falling against him, throwing her arms dramatically around his neck and kissing him like they were long-lost lovers who were bidding each other farewell forever. And there were a dozen movie cameras focused on them. And the sound score had reached a massive, dramatic crescendo as the tormented pair realized their fate was never to be together again. She even moved her head against his, bending backward so that her long hair swung toward the ground.

For his part, he stiffened and put his hands on her shoulders and quickly separated himself from her. "See ya next week, Suz," he said quietly.

"Call me before that, 'kay? We can hang out even when you're not training."

"Sure—yeah." His hand was already on the door, ready to shut it on her as she stood in the doorway. It was like he couldn't get rid of her fast enough, and I wondered if that's how he treated all of his lovers or if this was a show for my benefit.

My innards sank, and I could almost see Dad's victory smile already. How the hell was I supposed to wrangle this without constant surveillance?

As soon as the door clicked in the frame, he turned toward me, while glancing pointedly at his watch. "So, when exactly was our meeting?"

"Over an hour ago. Four o'clock." I folded my arms and tapped a finger. "But you were busy or *getting* busy, I should say. Good thing it didn't take long." I mirrored his action with my own cheeky glance at my smartwatch.

He didn't even bother to disguise his annoyance as he walked toward me. Then he stopped, grabbing a T-shirt that I hadn't noticed was lying in a pile on the floor—likely hastily discarded in passionate frenzied foreplay. He scooped it up and pulled it on all in one fluid motion. The NASA logo was emblazoned across his broad chest. All that stunning male beauty was now covered. Of course, the shirt fit him like a glove, clinging to his prominent pecs and solid torso. If only that T-shirt could cover his stupid, cocky grin.

"Haven't had any complaints yet. Feel free to let me know if you'd like to go for a test ride."

My face flamed hot. *Hot.* So hot, I was positive he could see the color. My complexion was fair, and when I blushed, it was very noticeable. I fumbled, covering by coughing into a fist and telling him, "We're supposed to discuss the plan to change the narrative, not how deftly you can flip through the pages of the *Kama Sutra.* And if you want to convince people you're perfectly fine, blowing off an important meeting for compulsive sex is not a good start."

"*Convince people.* What people am I convincing?"

I raised my brows at him as if to say, *Take a wild guess.*

He put a hand over his heart. "Well, Ms. Barrett, if—"

"It's Gray. Don't be late again," I interrupted, lest he fire another sexual invitation at me.

His brow twitched up, and that smile widened. "So is that a thing? Dropping your last name on purpose so people don't immediately figure out who Daddy is?"

So that was how it was going to be? Huh. This showing up late—and loudly screwing his trainer—was grandstanding rather than absent-mindedness. I wouldn't have expected a proactive military man, an *astronaut,* to be passive-aggressive.

"This isn't about me. But so you know, I'm not the type of person to take advantage of a famous name." *Unlike other people in this room,* I added mentally. Though it was a weak comeback anyway. After having gotten a good look at him, I was sure he didn't have to rely on his famous name—or face—to get women into his bed. Even as a nobody, he was hot AF—as Pari had attested the day before.

His features froze. "Still. It would have been nice if you'd clued me in when I met you yesterday."

I fought rolling my eyes—*someone* had to take the high road here. "We didn't meet yesterday, and you were given my full name the day we did meet. It's not my fault you didn't deem me important enough to remember."

He blinked, clearly irritated again, a fist clenching beside his solid thigh. "Let's cut the bullshit, and you can tell me why you're here."

He made no effort to sit down. In fact, he looked like he was going to flee the room at any moment.

Straightening my spine, I was aware that I looked like a nobody. I definitely dressed like one. Silently, I cursed my decision to dress casually so that I could seem like more of a friend. Instead, I should have worn a power suit and designer heels. These macho military types responded to suits better than my own faded jeans and T-shirt.

I lifted my chin and met his gaze and…ugh. Those eyes of his were so blue, it was impossible not to notice.

Like, what color even was that, anyway? Indigo? Sapphire? Cornflower? No, cornflower was too light for that shade of deep blue. Like the deepest blue beneath the black of space. The color of the upper stratosphere, maybe, or even the thermosphere—not that I'd ever been that high.

Damn it, even his eye color was fascinating to me. WTF. They were just stupid blue eyes. *Ugh.* I tore my gaze away and forced myself to remember the douchebaggery that came along with those heavenly blue eyes. It helped.

"I'm here to discuss the plan." *And to figure out how much of a hot mess you are.*

His brows shot up. "Oh. I get to have input? I thought Daddy Dearest was running this show."

Oh God. *Here we go again.* He was invoking my dad at every turn. Either he was using his dislike of Conrad Barrett as a shield to deflect me, or the honest but not-so-kind things my dad had said to him yesterday were sticking in his craw.

Either way, it was time he realized that I was not my dad.

"I'm here to help you do your job, Commander Tyler. That's it." I raised my palms toward him. "Do you think I would agree to go through with this dog and pony show if I could easily talk my father out of his decisions?"

I hoped it wouldn't have to go further than daily check-ins. Maybe an imposed curfew if there was a need. I did not want to fight with him every step of the way.

But I would. I would if I needed to.

The ball's in your court, Mr. All-American Astronaut Hero. I braced myself for whatever quip he'd volley back at me.

He surprised me.

CHAPTER SEVEN
RYAN

WITHOUT ANOTHER WORD, I SPUN AND LEFT MS. Barrett in the living room, her arms crossed, her face flushed. The wet bar was in the next room. She could follow me there if she wanted to continue this conversation, and if she didn't—so much the better. I walked across the living room to the wet bar, ducked behind it, and pulled out the half-empty bottle of Stolichnaya Elite. I poured myself a shot.

Ms. Gray Barrett trotted after me. Her face was placid, eyes keenly observant, but no emotion showed as she watched me under the heavy rim of those glasses. She did, however, very noticeably check her watch again. It was close enough to the acceptable hour.

I grinned at her before knocking back the vodka. This moment was worth it. I poised the bottle to pour myself another shot, but she leaped forward, holding her hand over the top of the shot glass, blocking it.

Well, well, well. Spunky...and irritatingly nervy.

I looked up, my brows raised. "Never come between a drinker and his vodka," I said in Russian.

Her mouth thinned, but that was the only clue to her emotions. Her voice was steady and self-assured. "Okay, you've made your point. I get it. You're not happy about this."

A laugh burst forth from my chest before I even realized what was happening. "You have a talent for understatement, Ms. Barrett."

"Gray, please. I—"

"Fine. *Gray*," I barked. "Couldn't your parents think of a more interesting color to name you after?"

Her white teeth worked against her bottom lip. "It's a nickname."

"So, you want to be my friend? Is that what this is all about?"

Her dark brows knit. I bumped her hand with the base of the vodka bottle. She didn't budge.

With a drawn-out sigh, I recapped the bottle and set it aside. "I did a full year of the whole media circus for NASA after the accident. Paraded around like a prize pony for interviews, speeches, appearances, dinners, and press events. Been there, done that, got the fucking T-shirt." I pointed at the NASA logo on my chest to emphasize my point.

Her eyes dropped to my chest, and she rolled those pink lips into her mouth. It was only then that I realized how fascinating her mouth was. It was small, at the base of an exquisite pair of cheekbones. Her lips weren't particularly thick or pouty, but she had this deliciously deep valley where her top lip bowed, from the bottom of her upturned nose to the top of that coral-colored lip. It was prominent and...alluring.

Kissable. I bet her lips tasted very sweet.

I blinked and shook my head. *Damn.* I hadn't touched the vodka in over a week. That one shot was hitting me harder than I'd imagined it would. *Mental note: go easy on the Russian dew.*

I straightened from the wet bar and took a step back even as I fortified myself with a deep breath. She watched me with those leaf-green eyes.

"What's it a nickname for?" I blurted before I even realized that I cared to know.

She blinked and drew back. "Um, what?"

"Gray. What's it a nickname for? Why do they call you that?"

Her thick brows arched over the top rim of her glasses, and she cleared her throat. "It's short for my actual name. Angharad Grace."

"Oh. Yeah, that's...that's a mouthful."

"Says the guy who bursts out spontaneously in Russian?"

I laughed but didn't reply.

"I was named after both my grandmothers. And 'they' don't call me Gray. *I* call me Gray."

I narrowed my eyes at her. "You seemed surprised that I'm annoyed by this situation."

She shrugged. "I'm surprised you aren't bothering to hide your irritation. I'm surprised by your flat-out rudeness. I'd figured that the logical part of your brain and your years of training would have helped you come to grips with getting done what needs to be done."

I shrugged, irritated at being called out. "I see no problem with getting the shit done that needs to get done. XVenture has rockets. They have astronauts. Now, let's fly them. Let's do this."

She shook her head. "We both know it isn't that easy."

My eyes roamed her face as she talked. She had the most beautiful skin. It glowed, even in the darkened room with half the shades drawn against the late afternoon. As each moment passed, the more she stood up to me and pushed back at me, it dawned on me what an idiot I was to have forgotten meeting her that first time. She was the complete opposite of forgettable.

A spark of attraction—tiny, surprising—popped in my chest and smoldered a little lower. Lingering.

"Bottom line is this—are you ready to do your job?" she asked.

"Why are *you* here?" I shot back.

She readjusted her glasses and tilted her head to the side as if studying me. "I'm here for my future. For my dream job. And for Tolan. And for everyone else who dreams of being a part of the first-ever commercial astronaut program. People who want to make history, who no longer feel the government is doing what it should to advance humankind's goals in space exploration. Why are *you* here?"

My brows twitched up. Huh. She gave as good as she got, it seemed.

I stayed silent, not quite knowing what to make of her candor. Lately, people didn't show me much of it. They were too busy with the hero worship. No one ever spoke their mind anymore. And even though hers rubbed me the wrong way, it was refreshing to hear an honest opinion once in a while.

From this angle, her dark-blond hair caught the light, and it glowed golden. It only added to that strange aura of know-it-all innocence she seemed to project. She was like...grown-up Hermione about to school Ron Weasley for the hundredth time. *Wow.*

"I can't help but wonder what it is you really want, Commander Tyler." She gestured to the room around us. "Maybe it's to sit around all day in a mansion paid for with book deals and speeches to your adoring public. Oh, and enjoying the perks of sleeping with women who think worshiping you is their patriotic duty."

Damn. Hermione indeed. "Any woman sleeping with me, I make sure that *duty* is the furthest word from her mind."

A fair bit of color washed over that glowing skin, and I had to admit to being satisfied to see it.

And I decided right then and there that I wanted to cause more of it.

"Obviously, you're bothered by our plan to rehabilitate your image. Do you want to talk about that?"

My mouth pursed like I'd sucked a lemon, overtaken by the feeling I should be lying on a couch. "Don't play act the shrink with me."

A faint smile appeared on that pretty little mouth. "I'm not playacting."

I looked her up and down—a slender slip of a girl. She didn't look older than twenty or twenty-one at the oldest, though I knew she had to be older than that to have finished enough schooling to hold a PhD.

"Well, I don't need a shrink—*or* a babysitter. I'm thirty-five years old."

She shrugged. "Don't think of me as a babysitter, then. Think of me as your personal aide."

I scowled. "I already have an assistant."

"A chaperone? Overseer? Governess? Take your pick." She held her hands up, palms open.

"Escort?"

Her hands dropped, mouth thinning. "Not that one."

"I don't need—"

"It doesn't matter what you think you need." She gestured to herself. "Or even what I think you need. The facts are that the investors aren't going to toss in their money until they're convinced your life isn't a shitshow. We're here to change the narrative, remember?"

I stiffened. "*A shitshow?* Is that what you think my life is?"

She pressed those little pink lips together. "Uh-uh. We aren't going to do that. It doesn't matter—"

"It matters to me. What do you think?" *You have issues,* she'd said. Exactly what issues was what I wanted to know. And since she hadn't held back before...

She blinked, cleared her throat, and then adjusted the frames of her glasses on her nose. I stood, waiting, and finally, she folded her arms over her chest. Most women I'd been around did something like that to draw attention to their assets, but not this one. She was openly studying me. And besides—she didn't have many assets. Not on her chest, at least.

But I found her fascinating nonetheless. The way her collarbones peeked up from the scooped neck of her T-shirt like a stylized pair of wings. Parallel, slightly curved, graceful, ready to take flight. With my eyes, I traced the length of them. Then I raised my gaze and met hers.

That spark popped again and seared hotter than before. I had the urge to taste that slender neck, those graceful collarbones— run my tongue along the length of them and feel her shiver in reaction...

Frowning, I fought hard to hide those thoughts, though I was satisfied to note there was a similar struggle mirrored on her delicate features. Her brows drawn together. That intense stare of hers. Her mouth slightly open.

She looked downright shocked.

For something to do—to dispel the power of that moment—I repeated my question. I wasn't about to let her off the hook. "Well? What do you think?"

Her voice was shaky when she spoke. "I'm...reserving judgment." She squared her shoulders in an almost adorable gesture. "But it goes without saying, especially in my field of study, that post-traumatic stress disorder is real and—"

"I do not suffer from PTSD," I bit out, closing a fist on the bar between us. Her eyes zoomed to that gesture, and I yanked my hand back, stiffening. Damn it. How had I let her rile me like this?

It was shocking, really. She was so not my type. And lately, I had not been hurting for plenty of my type.

Maybe it was that old conqueror's instinct. It coursed through my blood like nourishment from mother's milk. If I saw an insurmountable obstacle, I set my cap for it. It was as automatic to me as breathing. And right now, Ms. Gray Barrett seemed like a challenging and formidable obstacle indeed.

A tasty little obstacle. My eyes drifted over her slender body again—only to take in her thin T-shirt embroidered with rockets and stars, her snug jeans.

A space groupie, as we liked to call them. Funny, she didn't seem as starstruck by a real-live astronaut as most of the Cape Cookies were. Maybe she preferred women. The next thought was that it would be a damn shame if she did.

I drew back, startled, and forced myself to think about something else. Flight trajectories. Launch sequence—no, no, definitely not launch sequence. *What the hell?*

I rounded the bar and quickly strode out of the room.

Maddeningly, she trailed after me as I walked down the hall to the front coat closet, opening the door to grab my cross-trainers.

"Come on, Commander. You were a Navy SEAL. If you can do three tours in the Middle East, you can—"

"That's a cheerful thought." Been reading my background info, had she? Sounded like she had it committed to memory. Probably complete with psych notes on a notepad.

"I'm just—where are you going?"

"I'm going for a run," I said, having slipped on my shoes. I threw a meaningful glance at her feet. "I'd say feel free to join me but those sneakers are never going to make it in the canyon."

"But we're—"

"See you when I get back, if you want to wait around that long. I'm sure I can be trusted not to throw myself off a cliff."

With a scowl, she followed me to the side door that led out to the backyard where I could enter the canyon via a trail and hit my usual running loop.

She threw her slight body against the door before I could get it open. "You are not walking out on me after keeping me waiting for an hour while you screwed your trainer."

I pulled back, staring at her.

"I want to go for a run. I need exercise."

"You just got plenty of horizontal exercise!" she shot back.

I blinked, confused. She'd certainly waited a while to show her inner firecracker. Who the hell was this girl? Blocking me from pouring another drink, throwing herself across my door to keep me in the room, getting me tangled up in this horseshit scheme in the first place.

My blood boiled. Yeah, I could have easily pulled her off the door. I could throw her over my shoulder and physically remove her from my house too. But she was Conrad Barrett's daughter, for God's sake. And yeah, he was a motherfucker, but his wallet was going to get me back to space. *Hopefully.*

So, was I really stuck with this little pain in the ass of a waif?

My jaw clenched, and I bent down to get in her face. "Get off the door," I growled.

She didn't flinch, not even a blink. Instead, she took a deep breath and didn't move. "I never said you had PTSD. I said I was reserving judgment."

I straightened. She was right. "But your implication—"

"Listen, everyone knows you've been through a lot in the past year."

Christ. I liked it better when she was calling me on my shit. "Don't patronize me."

"I'm not. But it is virtually impossible not to have trauma after what you've gone through. It doesn't make you weak. It makes you human."

I leaned in and met her, nose-to-nose, much as I had yesterday in the hallway at XVenture. "I do not have PTSD, got it?"

Those green eyes held my gaze unflinchingly. "I don't care."

I tilted my head, certain I'd heard her wrong. "*What?*"

She straightened, lifting her chin. "I said, I don't care."

I let out a breath I didn't even know I was holding. This girl was surprising me more with every new thing that came out of her mouth. "Really? So why bring it up?"

"You asked me what I think. I gave you my honest answer."

"Well, you're wrong." My skin burned.

"So you've said. I'm not afraid of being wrong. But you haven't done or said anything to convince me otherwise." Her eyes shot through me like darts. "Don't ask me again, and I won't have to tell you my opinion."

I shook my head. *Damn.* Why was the fact that she refused to relent on a wrong opinion bothering me so much? Maybe she didn't care, but why the hell did I care so much?

She nodded grimly. "Go ahead and go on your run. I'll definitely still be here when you get back. In fact, while you're gone, I'll be picking out one of your spare rooms to stay in—obviously not the room you banged *Suz* in. I'm assuming you didn't bang her in your own room."

I blinked. How did she know that? And—wait...what?

She stepped away from the door and waved at it as if to dare me to step through it now. With an obvious shrug, she turned, glancing one last time at me over her shoulder before heading back into the living room.

I glared after her and then, of course, followed her, aware that this was probably some reverse-psychology trick.

"You are not staying here."

In the living room, I glanced at my coffee table, noticing her line of pens, some file folders, and a notebook all neatly arranged there. But there was no overnight bag of any kind, only a flat laptop case.

"You don't even have your things with you."

She turned to me. "I'll survive until tomorrow. Then after our meeting with Victoria and Keely Dawson in the morning, I'll slip out to get some clothes and come back. From then on, I plan on sticking to you like velcro."

"You aren't staying here," I repeated.

"I keep a bag of toiletries and other emergency items in my car all the time. Tonight it comes in handy." She punctuated her words with a cheerful smile. An almost gloating smile. She was daring me to kick her out.

I stared at her in wide-eyed disbelief as she picked up a roll of cloth I hadn't noticed. "And look, I've still got my towel with me from yesterday, Official Towel Day! A towel is about the most massively useful thing in the universe."

I blinked. This interaction got more bizarre—and strangely, more intriguing—by the moment. My hands on my hips, I watched as she unrolled it and wrapped it around her. "See? I can wrap it around me for warmth or lie on it or wave it for emergencies as a distress signal or...or..." She seemed to be trying to remember the rest.

I blew out a breath and continued in a dry voice. "Or use it to avoid the gaze of the Ravenous Bugblatter Beast that assumes if you can't see it, it can't see you."

She brightened. "You've read it—*The Hitchhiker's Guide to the Galaxy*! May 25th is Official Towel Day."

I gave her a look as if to say, *Of course, I've fucking read it.* "Astronaut. And by the way, you're not staying here."

She spread her hands out. "You have tons of rooms in this house."

"Not happening," I replied.

She pulled out her phone from her back pocket and held it up. "Okay, I'll let Tolan know of the change of plans. You're kicking me out."

I held out a hand. "Wait—"

Her brows went up as her thumbs poised over her touchscreen. "I'm waiting."

"I don't need you here."

She held up a hand and began to count off items on her fingers as she listed them. "Aside from all those interesting headlines you've taken part in, let's look at your behavior in the past hour alone. Blowing off an important meeting for compulsive—and impulsive—sex. Hard liquor at a barely acceptable hour."

"It was almost five o'clock—"

"Shitty attitude."

Well, okay. She had me there.

And yeah, having sex while she was waiting for me had been rude. I'd known she was coming, but I'd wanted to avoid the meeting. When Suz had started tearing off my shirt three minutes after coming in the door, I didn't say no. What man was going to put off sex with his hot trainer because some pain in the ass young shrink had an appointment with him at the same time?

"The bottom line, since we are being dead honest here?" She raised her brows at me, and I nodded to give her the go-ahead, bracing myself for another onslaught of her special brand of honesty. "You have a body of work lately that shows you don't have your shit together, and I'm here to help you get it and keep it together until the test flight. That means no partying, no benders, and no womanizing."

I scoffed. "Why don't you just check me in to the local rehab slash monastery?"

She smiled. "It's all about public opinion and what they think. And the investors. And Tolan, for that matter. If you want to fly again, then you'll do this. We have the same goals, Commander. I want you to be able to fly. I want that test flight to happen as much as you do. We are on the same side here. Besides...this house is so big, you'll hardly notice me. I won't get underfoot."

I scowled. Having a shrink under my nose was going to cramp my style. I didn't care how huge this house was. There was no way I was going to allow her to pry into my life.

I glanced at the phone in her hands again. But could I afford for her to rat me out to Tolan, along with the rest of the astronauts on the XPAC?

They'd all have questions too, and no doubt, they'd berate me for not doing the simplest of things to cooperate. Tolan could remove me from the flight as easily as he'd put me there. Sure, he wouldn't get the PR benefits...

And again, I wasn't so far gone I could forget that this girl was connected. Her father. Tolan. My back was up against a wall.

Jesus. *Fuck.* How did I get myself into these situations?

She held out a hand as if I'd walked into her shrink office and she was pointing out the couch to me. "Please, sit down."

"I prefer to stand. Unless you put out your little cup and stool? *Psychiatric help, 5 cents?*"

She smirked. "That's the Snoopy discount. It's going to cost you a bit more than that."

Too bad it wasn't going to cost me a few kisses, maybe a grope or two of that sweet ass of hers. I put my hands on my hips and refused to sit.

She blew out a breath. "Fine, we'll stand."

I cocked my head to study her. At least my jailer for the next three months was cute—in her own little way.

She waited patiently, scratching the side of her nose, and for a fleeting instant, I caught the flash of gold on her left hand—on her ring finger. My breath caught. Was she married?

Then I spotted a sparkly red stone in the middle. I turned my head to get a better look. A year imprinted along the side. And upon closer inspection, it was on her middle finger, not her ring finger. Clearly a class ring. I tried not to contemplate the way my heart had skipped a beat at the possibility she might be unavailable.

Why the hell did I care?

She could have a live-in boyfriend for all I knew, or steadily dating someone. She didn't have to be married to be unavailable, and again, why the fuck did I care so much? Her right hand held nothing except for a plain silver chain around her wrist with a medallion hanging from it.

"Well, you don't leave me with much of a choice, do you?"

She frowned. "I don't want you to feel like that. I don't want you to feel cornered. We're on the same—"

"Team, yeah. I was listening during your pep talk. But you've got rules for me while you're my jailer and I'm on house arrest. Do I have to wear an ankle bracelet? Report my whereabouts at all times?"

She shook her head. "I'm here to keep you on the straight and narrow."

My jaw clenched and then relaxed. I looked away. "Sounds boring."

"Boring is good. Boring is stable. Boring is—"

"*Safe.* Just like bringing in Daddy for the investment money. You like playing it safe, don't you?"

"I like playing by the rules." A genuine smile rose on her delectable lips. "Rules are essential, and I'm very good at following them."

My eyes fixated on that mouth, that delicious bow in her top lip, that crease below her nose. I wanted to taste it. And God, how much did I want to make her break rules the moment she'd said she liked them?

So much.

Just wait, Ms. Gray Barrett.

Just you wait, that wicked voice in my head warned. Not only would I have her breaking those rules, I'd have her enjoying every moment of it too.

CHAPTER EIGHT
GRAY

FOR A LONG MOMENT, WE STARED EACH OTHER DOWN. I couldn't read a thing in those deep blue eyes. The tension in the air between us was real and thick. Like taffy, peanut butter, maybe creamy soup. With bread. Damn, I knew I shouldn't have skipped lunch. It was after five o'clock, and I was starving.

My stomach growled. *Loudly.* I mean…not simply growled. It roared like Smaug awakening and emerging from the Lonely Mountain after sleeping for two centuries, smoke flaring from his nostrils and fire in his eyes. Ready to rain down death and flame on the nearby Lake Town.

Yeah, my stomach sounded like an angry dragon greedy for treasure—preferably in edible form.

The look on Ty's face asked the question he never put voice to—*WTF was that?* Without responding, I busted up laughing. It was either that or die of embarrassment, and I had too many close encounters with embarrassment on any given day to be self-conscious about the fact that I was such a hard worker that I'd skipped lunch.

The dragon roared again even louder. And now I was laughing even harder.

And so was he. It was a sexy sound, a low sort of rumble that rose up from the base of his chest—his big, wide chest. And, thanks to his shirtless situation earlier, I knew it to be solid and muscle-bound too.

"You're hungry, apparently," he said as I wiped moisture from the corner of my eyes. "Either that or someone should release the Krakken."

"It's a dragon, actually. Smaug."

"Huh. Where's Bilbo Baggins when you need him?"

I raised my brows, impressed by his knowledge of fiction. First *Hitchhiker's Guide* and now *Lord of the Rings*. I wasn't aware astronauts had much time to read for pleasure. Nevertheless, he'd gotten the story details wrong. "Bard," I corrected. "Bard killed Smaug."

"But Bilbo told him how."

I nodded. "Fair enough."

The dragon roared once more, and his brow went up, face still looking pretty grumpy. "Got the number for a local pizza delivery?" I asked with a hopeful smile.

He heaved a sigh and had an *I'll regret this* look on his face. "I'll make you a sandwich. I've worked up an appetite too."

My mouth curved up and, stupidly, I didn't bite my tongue when I should have. "I'm sure you have."

He shot me a look and turned around, leaving me where I stood. Oh, jeez. Sometimes I couldn't keep my mouth shut, and we were not in a place where I could tease him for his offenses— no matter how tease-worthy his offenses were.

I trotted after him toward the big, shiny kitchen with gleaming, brushed-copper appliances and fancy, cream-and-black granite countertops.

He turned and pointed to one of the stools at the counter across from the refrigerator, and I obediently sank down onto it. Meanwhile, he pulled things from a gigantic fridge—whole grain wheat bread, mayo, greens, tomatoes, fresh deli-sliced meats wrapped in brown wax paper.

"Are you a vegan or gluten-free? Because I can't help you out if you're any of that. Well, if you're vegan, I suppose I can toss a spinach leaf at you."

I frowned, confused by his sudden switch to problem-solving mode. I watched him for a moment, noting his quick, jerky movements that seemed to express lingering irritation. He was most likely going to try to smooth this situation over—try to negotiate his way out of it—and get me out of his house for the duration. I narrowed my eyes and prepared for his next angle.

These alpha-warrior types all used the same playbook. Commands. Grandstanding. Other theatrics. And, depending on their personalities, sprinkled in sweet talk and charm. I'd steel myself and not think one bit about how he was impossibly gorgeous even while making a sandwich—those dreamy forearms, those strong, capable hands. I tore my eyes away and tried to focus on what he had asked me.

"I can't eat spinach or kale." I pointed to the bag of fresh baby spinach leaves. He frowned but shoved it back in the fridge. "But other than that, I'm okay."

My stomach growled again as if participating directly in the conversation and lodging its own—very loud—protest.

"I'm working as fast as I can," he said when his back was turned, but the laughter was easily detectable in his voice and in the way his shoulders shook as he assembled the sandwiches.

"It's super nice of you to make me food. But I want you to know that you won't have to feed me for every meal. I'll hit the supermarket on the way back tomorrow. I'm not a very good cook, but I do make killer breakfasts."

He threw a sly look my way but seemed to be biting his tongue. Most likely another sexual innuendo—this time suppressed, thank God. He grunted noncommittally as he sliced a tomato and placed the slices on two pieces of bread.

"How about we compromise," he began in that same mild tone of voice. "I don't think you want to stay here any more than I want you here. We could meet every day. I'd report to you—"

I sat up straight and put a huge grin on my face like an excited puppy dog. "You mean I could give you therapy?"

His face darkened. So predictable.

He unwrapped the meats from their deli papers and listed out the choices—thinly sliced roast beef, honey ham, spicy chicken. I chose the chicken, which he laid out on the bread for me, choosing the roast beef for himself.

"What makes you think I need therapy?"

I arched a brow at him as he bent over his creations, then wiped his hands and got two plain white plates from a cupboard. *Poor wounded soul doesn't think anyone else can see it.*

I swallowed but, wisely, held my tongue this time.

He glanced up at me as if expecting an answer, and I blinked. "So you refuse to call it therapy, but you'd promise to attend regular daily sessions with me in which we—what?—play chess?"

His cheek bulged where he clenched his jaw. We held that long, weighted stare until long after it started feeling uncomfortable. It felt like an accusation—no, like a challenge. But I wasn't sure who was the challenger and who the challenged.

Finally, I conceded, dropping my gaze. A split second later, he moved back to the sandwiches, pressing the slices together and finishing them off with one clean cut through the middle of each.

He placed my spicy chicken sandwich in front of me. "What do you like to drink?"

"Ice water is fine."

He pulled out a cold bottle of water for me. And some sort of green liquid for him—something probably handmade from his trainer-with-benefits. Juiced kale, he clarified with a rueful smile and poured it into his own bright orange Anaheim Ducks souvenir glass.

It looked awful. I suppressed a shudder and looked away. Amused, he brought his sandwich and drink to the counter and sat on a stool opposite me. He seemed to wait until I looked up before gripping his glass and downing half of the smoothie. This time, I did shudder.

Laughing, he used a paper napkin to wipe his mouth. "It tastes like ass, in case you were wondering. Suz made it for me."

I grinned. "Then I'm sure it's packed with high-potency vitamins and minerals for extra long-lasting virility."

This time, he actually fought rolling his eyes. "Are you ever going to let it go?"

I pursed my lips. "Probably not. It was pretty epically rude of you."

"It won't happen again—"

"Good!"

"—if you're not staying here."

I narrowed my eyes and bit into my sandwich. He watched me for a long moment—probably expecting me to capitulate—

which I wouldn't. Then he bit into his own sandwich. Soon we were both wordlessly demolishing them.

"If you're trying to assure me that things like this aren't going to happen again, you aren't doing a very good job," I finally said after I'd swallowed my last bite. I could get painfully honest now that there was no chance he'd spit in my sandwich.

"So, what? I'm supposed to convince you that I'm toeing the line before you'll let me off the hook?"

"If letting you off the hook is your euphemism for no longer living at your house, then, no. I won't be doing that until the test flight."

He blinked. "Three months? Are you out of your mind?"

I grinned again, reaching my hand out for his empty plate and glass. "Some people have that theory about psych majors."

He frowned and handed over his plate and glass. I promptly took them to the sink where I—unwisely—sniffed at the brownish green residue in his souvenir glass. Shaking my head, I filled the basin partway with warm, soapy water.

"Jeez, this stuff smells vile. Hopefully, she's better at training than she is at making smoothies."

He laughed. "Oh, she's *very* good."

He'd lobbed that one to me on purpose. I narrowed my eyes at him, and he stared as if daring me to say anything. Instead, I very visibly bit my tongue, then said, "That one is going to leave teeth marks."

When I set the dishes in the soapy water, he said. "I have a dishwasher, you know."

I shook my head. "It's two plates and a glass. Easy peasy."

Except it wasn't. I saved his green goo glass for last, and taking it up, pushed my hand in to get the sponge to hit the bottom of the glass. Inexplicably, the thing shattered in my hand after having put the slightest pressure on it.

Pain stabbed me in the fleshy part of my palm, right at the base of my thumb. I dropped the glass, and it shattered further against the ceramic sink.

"Shit!" Ty exclaimed as he moved up quickly beside me. I put my hand down to fish out the broken pieces.

"I'm sorry—"

"No! Don't do that." He grabbed my wrist and yanked it out of the water, holding it up. Blood streamed down my forearm from where the cut was oozing above my wrist.

"I'm making a mess," I said as drops of blood stained the rug where we stood. Red streaks quickly formed, dripping down my arm past my elbow. Ty cursed.

Oh crap. Not a good time...not a good time at all for this to happen. A pang of icy fear slid through me, but I willed myself to stay calm.

"Don't worry about that. Keep this up above the level of your heart, and especially keep it out of that dirty dishwater."

He grabbed some paper towels and doubled them, pressing the wad firmly against my cut. "Cheap-ass souvenir cup. I dropped another one like it last week, and it shattered everywhere. I knew I should have thrown this one out. It's a hazard."

"It's..."

He was standing near, and I could smell his hair as he bent over me, pulling off the paper towel to inspect the wound. For some strange reason, I found his nearness, his warmth comforting. Like I wasn't in this alone. Now, if I could only gather my wits about me enough to tell him what he needed to do to help me.

"Christ, it's deep, and you're still gushing blood. Must have cut the radial artery. You'll need stitches." He pulled off the soaked paper towel and pressed another one to it. Pins and needles prickled the flesh of my arm from holding it above my head.

He frowned, looking into my eyes. "You okay? You look pale, like you're going to pass out."

I inhaled sharply. "I'm fine, but I need you to go grab my toiletry bag in my car. It's in the glove box."

He looked at me like I was an idiot. "You're cut and bleeding profusely, and you want me to run an errand?"

"It's important, believe me. In the bag, I have some powder wound sealant. It's in a round container—"

He grabbed my unwounded hand and pressed it to the cut and stepped away, springing into action. Then he scooted his stool up to me. "Sit. I don't want you passing out. Your car keys?"

"In the front pocket of my bag. On the sofa."

He disappeared and was back in minutes holding the round container, instructions-side up, walking and reading at the same time. He set my key chain—complete with a dangling space shuttle replica—on the counter, continuing to read the directions on how to use the powder sealant. When I reached for the medicine, having used it before, he pulled out of my reach, continuing to read before taking my hand and following the directions to the letter. He'd be accustomed to that sort of thing, wouldn't he? Quickly scanning checklists and protocols while on board the ISS, speeding across low earth orbit at 17,000 miles per hour.

"No spinach or kale. Both have Vitamin K, which aids blood clotting. And you carry wound sealant with you, which means you're on blood thinners." He spoke in a clipped voice as he worked on me.

"Yes."

His tone was like ice. "You should be wearing a medical alert bracelet."

I held up my unwounded hand to show him the medical alert medallion dangling from my right wrist. He flicked a glance at it and then went back to inspecting my wound. His large hand enveloped mine, which had never—ever—felt so small before this. His palm was callused—a working hand. The roughness felt good against the back of my own. In fact, I could hardly notice the slight throbbing pain because of his nearness. His smell.

He smelled like seashells—wind, sand, ocean—salty and earthy with a hint of lime. He bent his head again to inspect the progress of the clot. My lower arm was sticky, coated with a thin layer of my own blood. "Deep enough cuts can be life threatening on blood thinners. Even bruises are dangerous."

He'd taken on a lecturing tone to deliver to me facts I already knew—rather well.

For once, I bit my tongue instead of speaking out against mansplaining.

I swallowed, trying hard to ignore the way my heart knocked irregularly against my ribs with his nearness. The clicking sound from within my chest was loud enough that he surely heard it too.

I tried not to think about how he was beyond gorgeous and smelled oh, so good. The thump in my chest reverberated through every part of my body. Why was it always the *heart* that was associated with these feelings? Why not the liver or the kidneys or—

Oh. Now he was blowing on the wound, and despite the slight sting, I shivered—and *not* from pain either.

This man was making me tremble and flush from his attention and touch. Those fingers idly cradling my hand? I felt them clear up my arm, in the center of my chest. Tingles, warm and sparkly.

"We need to clean you up and get you to a clinic."

"A clinic? Why?"

"For stitches. It's deep, Gray."

"Can't you do it?" I asked.

He hesitated. "Yes, but I'm not a doctor."

No more doctors. No more hospitals. Not now. I'd had so much of that my whole life and would probably have more too. I didn't want to sit in a clinic for this. Not if he could help me.

"But you're trained to perform minor medical procedures. Do you have the supplies?"

He took a breath and let it out, straightening. "I can easily do this. I assumed you'd prefer a doctor."

I shook my head vigorously. "I have no desire to go to an ER or clinic for something this minor."

Images rushed through my head unbidden—mind-wrecking pain through the middle of my chest for weeks. The smell of astringent and cleaning fluid. The sandpapery feel of hospital sheets. *Ugh.* No.

He sighed, turning my hand over and inspecting it again, to ensure the bleeding had completely stopped. Then he straightened. "Wait here. I'll get my med kit," he muttered.

He came back with an impressively sized plastic container that had been latched closed. Placing it on the counter, he asked again. "You feeling okay? No headache or light-headedness from the blood loss? You still look pale."

I fought against bristling at the accusation—the one I heard all too often from my father. I glanced up at him. Instead of biting sarcasm or mild mockery, there was genuine concern in his deep-blue eyes. I swallowed and nodded. "I feel fine. Thanks."

"Then let me get this cleaned out and closed up. I want to check and make sure there aren't any micro pieces of glass in the wound, so I'll numb you up a little and poke around in there."

He pulled out a pair of glasses from a case and slipped them on. Then he put on some rubber gloves and pulled out a syringe of lidocaine to numb the area of the cut. I bit my lip when he shot me up. He tenderly held the hand while we waited for it to numb. Through this, I was grateful he didn't pepper me with probing questions.

I couldn't look when he used a swab to poke around inside the cut. I couldn't feel anything, but the sight of it was grossing me out. Satisfied, he pulled out antiseptic to clean the wound.

"I can't use the surgical glue because of the way the cut went through the heel of your hand. But I'll use plenty of stitches to minimize scarring."

"I'm not that concerned about having a scar on the heel of my hand." I had plenty far more prominent scars to worry about.

He glanced up at me, over the top edge of his magnifying glasses, his features all too serious. "I only do my best work. *Always.*"

I bit my lip and nodded. "Okay."

Well, well, well. I'd found at least one situation in which the American Douchebag was likable. When he was taking care of someone else. It was almost a marvel to see how well he fell into the role so naturally. So capably.

The protective instinct ran very deep in him. That much was obvious. It was almost endearing to see. *Almost.*

"I'll clean up your arm after we get you closed up. I don't want to chance you starting to bleed again."

"The wound sealant usually works extremely well."

His brow shot up. "You use it often? Maybe you should be more careful, especially while on a blood thinner."

"The blood thinner is a permanent thing. So I just have to deal."

"Then you need to be more careful about the activities you choose to participate in," he growled in that voice that sounded like he'd become my self-appointed guardian.

I raised a brow. "You mean make the *safe* choice?" I mocked his earlier words to me.

With a huff, he didn't reply. Then he bent his head to begin his work. And instead of looking at what he was doing, I bent my head too. Because at this angle, I got a whiff of his amazing-smelling hair. It was soft as it brushed against my cheek, and my heart started bumping loudly in my chest again. And...

There it was, the telltale *click-click-click* in the silence. I straightened and he muttered, "Hold still. Just a few more to go."

But I wanted to pull away before he heard. Oh, who was I kidding? He'd already heard. Everyone could hear it sooner or later, unless they had hearing impairments.

He straightened and looked at me, our faces inches from each other.

"Did you feel anything?"

I blinked. "Oh, uh, no." *At least not physically.*

He reached up and whipped off his glasses. "Okay. So when I say stand still, I mean it. Don't get all wiggly on me."

He glanced down at my chest. That same cold fear sliced through me again. Had he heard me ticking like an antique watch? What was he thinking?

He frowned. "You have blood all over your shirt and your arm. Let me lend you a fresh one to wear."

Inexplicable relief washed over me. I glanced at his broad chest—right in front of me. *Too* close. So close it was making it difficult to breathe.

Upon examining that broad chest more closely—purely for professional reasons, of course—I said, "Your shirt would fit like a dress on me."

He shrugged. "Better than looking like a victim of attempted murder."

I looked down at my ruined shirt, embroidered stars and rockets all over it, the pale blue blotched with blood. "You have a point."

"Also, peroxide for the stains will get it out good as new."

My brow crept up. "You seem more knowledgeable than you should be about things like laundering clothing. Or maybe it's specifically about blood. Hidden a few bodies, have you?"

The words, they slipped out without my checking them, and his slight smile froze on his features. The awkward moment hung there between us, and I felt like complete crap, blinking like an idiot and feeling a little light-headed with embarrassment. "Oh, I'm sorry. I'm such a—"

He shook his head. "It's all good. Besides, I only hid the bodies of the behavioral health professionals we had to work with." He punctuated with a good-natured wink and a laugh. And, the moment dissipated, I laughed along with him.

He sobered a little after a minute. "When I was on the SEAL teams, we had to deal with blood quite often."

After delivering that disconcerting bit of news as if he were describing another day at the office, he turned on his heel and left the room, returning minutes later. In his hand was a folded black T-shirt much like the one he was wearing, with the giant NASA logo in the middle of the chest. He pointed out a small bathroom off the kitchen and handed me a washcloth to clean off my arm.

I sighed when I realized that the T-shirt had a V-neck, but put it on anyway. As I'd suspected, upon inspecting myself in the mirror, the shirt was huge on me, practically hitting my knees. The collar drooped down low, almost to my bra. The red scar that stretched from my navel up past the top of my sternum, almost to the notch where my chest met my throat, was plainly visible.

I pulled the collar up, scooting it back on my shoulders so that the V of the collar rested against the base of my neck. It looked weird, but maybe he'd just take me for being overly modest or something. To keep it in place, I pulled the base of the shirt tight around my waist and knotted it there. Who knew if it would hold? It was worth a shot anyway. It was either that or wear it backward.

It was stupid to feel self-conscious about the scar. I usually wasn't. But for some reason... Well, if the blood thinners and the loud, clicky heartbeat hadn't clued him in, I didn't feel like discussing my all too in-your-face weaknesses with a man who projected such outward physical perfection and chose not to admit to any weakness at all.

I came out, and he glanced briefly at my getup, before his eyes flew to my face, scanning my features with narrowed eyes. "You still look pale to me."

"I didn't lose that much blood. It's not like I need a transfusion." I'd had several of those before, too.

He drew a deep breath and released it, considering. "Well, I'd feel better if you didn't drive home like this."

Good, because I was staying anyway. I bit the inside of my lip to keep from giving a snarky reply. He was trying, in his own way, to be nice, after all. But I was also half certain he was going to suggest calling me a cab.

"And since Victoria is coming over for a meeting in the morning, you might as well stay. *Tonight.* That way I can keep an eye on you since it's my fault you were injured."

My brow twitched. *Fine.* At least we could start here. Once Victoria was here in the morning, we could both put pressure on him to let me stay.

"You're taking responsibility for a crappy souvenir cup randomly breaking in my hand." *What else have you taken responsibility for, Commander?*

"I feel badly that you were hurt." He waved toward my hand. "Especially considering your health issues."

I straightened my spine. "I am fine. The health issues aren't dire." But I wasn't going to assert my independence so much that I'd leave. He'd finally capitulated. Partly, anyway.

He leaned against the doorjamb and continued to stare down at me. "So since you were so quick to impose rules on me. *No benders. No partying. No womanizing—*"

"Yes?" I arched my brows at him.

"Well, I have some rules of my own." His features were serious—somber, even.

I pressed my lips together, half expecting him to forbid me from going into the west wing of the house where he kept his enchanted rose under a glass.

"Well, like I said—"

"You're good at rules. Yes, I remember," he finished. "Then that means you will observe these... First of all, no shrink talk. No psychoanalysis. No talk of PTSD or trauma or however you choose to label it."

I blinked. "Is that—is that all one rule?"

His gaze narrowed at me in clear irritation, and I held up my uninjured palm as if to give up the point. No need to agitate him.

And was he even serious with me right now? How could he possibly convince anyone that his downward spiral wasn't because of trauma from the accident? That horrific accident I'd watched him narrate on video as if he'd been discussing the latest NFL score.

As they said, denial wasn't just a river in Egypt.

Instead of arguing, I cleared my throat. "Anything else?"

"My privacy. Respect it. This is my house. You leave everything as I have it. For example, if a light is on. It stays on."

Lights? What an odd example. "I'm happy to grant you as much privacy as you need. But please, no having sex while I'm under the same roof."

He scowled. "You already gave me your rules."

"Consider it an axiom under the no-womanizing rule. And I get to add it because of your behavior this afternoon."

"So...what, should I hang a tie on my front door?"

"How about you endeavor to control your urges?"

He didn't respond beyond folding his arms over his chest and looking at me like I was insane.

And before I forgot, I added. "Also...Wheaton's law."

"I'm sorry. What?"

"Don't be a dick."

He laughed. "Sorry, not going to apologize for breaking that one."

"Are you planning to?"

"I thought I already had?"

I straightened. "You have. But I'm willing to grant amnesty for the recent past if you can get it together."

"Does that mean I get probation from you living here?"

"How about I consider giving you time off for good behavior—after you've proven to me that you're doing better?"

He pushed off from the doorjamb, still not looking happy about my proposal.

I pressed. "I promise to be as unobtrusive a roomie as possible. You won't have to pick up after me, either. I—" I glanced at the sink, and it was pristine. He'd cleaned up everything during the few short minutes I'd been in the bathroom. "Astronauts are good housekeepers, too."

"Habit. There's no cleaning service on station. One day out of the week, we are on cleanup duty. And since all the mess floats everywhere, it's extra motivation to keep things clean."

"Do you care which of your spare rooms I use?"

A brow went up. "Apparently not the one I used earlier."

"Definitely not that one. But I'm sure you have others. I'll go gather my things." I said, grabbing my toiletry bag off the counter and heading to the living room for my laptop bag and other items.

He followed me until we rounded a corner into the hallway, past his row of gorgeous, professionally framed photographs.

He paused at the one I'd knocked into earlier, straightening it with a frown before sending me a sidelong glance. I could feel my face flush hot with embarrassment, remembering the circumstances in which I'd backed into the picture, nearly knocking it off the wall. He'd been playing headboard percussion against the wall with his moaning trainer.

I gestured to the photos. "Did you take these from LEO?"

His brow spiked at my use of the jargon. "Yes, from the cupola windows on station."

I glanced at them again. One of them was a network of lights over a black landscape—a major city captured at nighttime. Another was an azure river's complex delta gleaming from brown landscape. "The mouth of the Nile," he said, pointing to it. "And this one, that you're already quite familiar with, is the Bahamas." He indicated the picture I'd admired before, the islands and water of different shades of blue and green, streaming in between them. "That's everyone's favorite landmark from low earth orbit."

"Not yours?"

He shrugged. "I didn't have a favorite. Everything was amazing and gorgeous from that vantage point, even the stuff that's not so beautiful on the surface." His eyes flicked from the picture to me. "Guess it takes another angle to prove you can see beauty in anything."

I stared for another long minute, admiring his skill with the camera, and the silence stretched out between us. I tried hard not to look at him even when I could tell he was staring at me. Soon, it got awkward, and my face felt like it would melt off, so I backed away and continued to the living room to grab my things.

Gingerly, so as to favor my injury, I stuffed my things back in my bag. He smiled, seemingly amused that I'd come so overly prepared. It was pretty safe to say that anyone with any reasonable amount of intelligence by now would have figured out I was a huge nerd. I didn't lie to myself about fooling anyone.

He nodded to the front door. "You need to lock up your car— unless there's something else out there you need?" He laughed. "Like another towel or something?"

"Is this a ploy to get me outside so you can lock me out?" When he shook his head good-naturedly, I continued, "I do have to put the windows up in my car."

He followed me out to the driveway. The sun had just set, and the outside lighting came on. Everything was lit up bright— planters, the steps, all along the driveway. Big spotlights on the house. It seemed strange. You'd think an astronaut would be more concerned about light pollution—and energy conservation, for that matter.

Hell, under this lighting, he could probably perform surgery out here.

Ty pointed out the battery-operated fan in my front seat. "These new BMWs sure have interesting climate systems."

I laughed. "The AC is broken, and I blew off my appointment to take it in today to come here instead."

Once we returned inside, he gave me a very brief tour of the parts of the house I hadn't seen. There was the deck out back that looked eastward over the reddish clay of Peter's Canyon, where the sky was now purpling with a chipped, silver-white moon above the horizon. Off the lower floor of the house was his home gym with sliding glass doors leading to a beautiful saltwater pool. It was surrounded by a drought-resistant garden that was all the rage in Southern California these days.

When we went back upstairs, I noted at once that inside the house was also well lit-up by timed lighting. I thought back to that strange comment he'd made. *For example, if a light is on. It stays on.*

I flicked a glance at his back as I followed him down the hallway toward a spare room. It was the farthest room possible from his master bedroom on the other side of the house.

Did he have a thing about lights? Or, rather, the dark? And if so, was there any way I could address it without violating his "no shrink talk" rule? I'd have to consider that. I'd made one breakthrough tonight. Best not to push it any further. For now.

He entered the bedroom first and walked to the bed to make sure his housekeeper had put on fresh sheets. Flipping back the comforter and blanket to check, he glanced around the room. It was Spartan in design—a dark blue bedspread and a few more of his amazing photographs on the walls by the closet. "Bathroom is down the hallway." He pointed. "You need a toothbrush?"

I shook my head, pointing to my trusty toiletry bag. He nodded and walked toward the doorway, turning around.

"You're okay for the night?"

I nodded. "I have lots of work to do. I brought stuff with me."

He didn't react to that. After all, he had no idea that I was going to type up my notes about him. Yeah, he wasn't my patient, but I could make observations about him nevertheless.

When he turned to leave, I stopped him, asking for his phone number so we could keep in contact. Without comment, he typed his number into my phone, calling it so he'd have my number too.

When I looked up from putting the contact name into my phone, he was scrutinizing my chest with narrowed eyes. Either he was fascinated by my nonexistent cleavage or, despite my attempts, the V-neck collar of the T-shirt had slipped down and he could see the scar.

But I didn't want to have this conversation now. That was all I needed in my life—more male overprotectiveness. He'd let me stay under the pretense of keeping an eye on me, and I hadn't protested because it aligned with my own goals of keeping an eye on him. But I wasn't going to let the protectiveness get out of hand.

"Good night," I chirped, grabbing the door.

"Sleep well, Gray," he said gently. I shut the door and moved to the bed. Plopping down, I stared up at the white ceiling, thinking.

As disastrous as the day had started, at least things had ended on a semipositive note.

I could only hope that things would take an upward turn from here.

But who knew? The trainer would surely be back next week or maybe even tomorrow.

And I'd had to shed my own blood all over the kitchen to get him to agree to let me stay here for a night.

So, in some ways, it did not bode well for the near future. But I preferred to see myself as a glass-is-half-full sort of girl.

CHAPTER NINE
RYAN

ARLY THE NEXT MORNING, I OPTED TO MAKE UP FOR MY missed run in the canyon, taking advantage of the cool morning breeze. It was late May and the weather would be heating up soon, but after a winter of profuse rain, the landscape was still green and fresh on my usual running loop. An excellent way to clear my head. To think.

Upon my return, I realized I'd apparently taken longer than I'd planned. The intended meeting with Victoria and my new—and very temporary—housemate was already underway. For the second time in as many days, I was late to a meeting involving the mysteriously intriguing young daughter of Conrad Barrett.

But I didn't expect they wanted me to show up sweaty, fresh from a run. So I excused myself to take a quick shower, appearing back downstairs in sweats and a T-shirt minutes later. Gray and Victoria were sitting on the couch quietly talking. It sounded like they were synching their calendars for the next few months.

My eyes flew first to Gray, who was dressed, of course, in the same clothes she'd worn the day before—jeans with holes in the knees and a T-shirt. She'd turned the huge shirt I'd loaned her backward and knotted it to hug her waist. I hadn't said anything the night before when I'd seen the scar on her chest, but it, along with the other things—the blood thinner medication and the clicking heartbeat—had clued me into her medical issue. Gray had a prosthetic heart valve.

It made me consider all the things I'd said to her about playing it safe. No wonder.

Instead of pulling it back in a ponytail, Gray wore her dark-blond hair brushed out and around her shoulders. It was still in that usual messy style—not quite curly, not quite straight—fluffy and disorganized around her face. Like she'd woke up and run a brush through it once or twice and hadn't bothered with it much beyond that. Her face had very little if any makeup on it—probably because she hadn't packed any in her emergency toiletries. Or maybe this casual tomboy look was her usual style.

It wasn't unattractive. It was rather fresh. Different. A lot different from the women I usually spent time with, and it was strangely enticing.

I stopped my close inspection when I glanced at her chest again, noting the way her knotted T-shirt tightly hugged her slender figure. There was something...strangely arousing about seeing her in my shirt. I couldn't help but enjoy an image of her in something I'd worn the night before—that she'd picked up and slipped over her naked body after sliding out of my bed in the morning.

And before I could stop myself, I immediately wondered if she was wearing a bra. I forced myself to look away before my mind went too far down that path. *Too dangerous*—especially considering who she was and the fact that she was my unwelcome houseguest for a very short while longer.

Victoria, in her usual tailored suit, stood up, almost to my height in her expensive heels. "Ty, good to see you," Victoria said, reaching to shake my hand.

"Hey, Victoria. Sorry to keep you waiting." I nodded to Gray as I slid onto the couch opposite them.

"That's not a hobby of yours?" Gray said affably, softening the sarcasm with a light smile.

I narrowed my eyes at her as if to say *cute*. Because that's exactly what she was. At least it was better than a sexual innuendo. She could have said something about riveting waiting or pounding desire to meet with me or whatever.

Victoria shot a quizzical look at Gray before turning back to me. "I've had a chance to finish up on my notes and work out a tentative plan over the summer for this campaign. We're doing things with very little notice and on the fly, but I'm confident it will go the way we like with some effort."

I scratched the stubble on my jaw, my eyes again flicking to Gray, who was now looking down at her phone screen. I turned back to Victoria. "I hate to beat a dead horse, but I have some real concerns about how this whole plan is going to go down."

Victoria smiled. "Then let me resolve your concerns. I do this all the time."

"For actors," I protested.

That smile widened on her perfectly painted ruby lips. Gray was now keying a message into her phone, not appearing to pay any attention to our conversation. And strangely, a spark of irritation ignited in my chest.

I frowned at myself, wondering where that came from. I wasn't entitled to her devoted attention at all times. Didn't mean I still didn't want it.

Something about this meeting was clearly making Gray uncomfortable. Maybe it was Victoria herself.

"Ms. Dawson is a very accomplished actress," Victoria spoke slowly as if addressing a grade schooler. "She was up for a Golden Globe award last year. And she's a pure professional too. She'll treat this with all the dedication of any of the roles she's played. She also stands to benefit from this publicity opportunity."

I laughed. "Well, Keely Dawson might be the best actress in the world, but that still doesn't mean that I'm any kind of actor. That wasn't included in astronaut training."

Victoria ran a scarlet-tipped finger through her gleaming raven hair as if to tuck it away from her face. The gesture was completely unnecessary as her hair was done up in a neat, high bun. There wasn't a single hair out of place.

"But public appearances have been and *are* a part of your job. You're used to that part of it. And we'll guide you through the rest, every step of the way."

"We?" Again, my gaze darted to Gray, whose eyes flicked up to meet mine before skittering away again almost as quickly. So, she was paying attention to this. Perhaps she was annoyed by my continuing protest. She probably thought she'd had me nailed down yesterday.

I shook my head, leaning forward to rest my elbows on my knees. "Seriously, though—"

Victoria grinned. "You lie to all those flat-earthers about there being a space program, right?" She laughed when I scowled. Her joke might have been funnier in other circumstances. But the media had widely reported that my fight with that jackoff had been the reason I'd been fired from NASA.

"Too soon," was my only reply.

She sobered, detecting my mood change. "Don't sweat it, Ty. Keely is the pro. Just follow her lead. She can even lead you in some improv work to loosen you up. Give you a few acting lessons. She is very excited about this project."

"Glad one of us is," I muttered out of the side of my mouth.

She laughed—a laugh that was as measured and as carefully manicured as the rest of her. My eyes fell on the threadbare hole and the side of knee peeking out from Gray's jeans. Even there, her skin appeared soft—as soft as that hand and wrist I'd held yesterday when I'd patched up her cut.

I blinked, pulling myself away from the distracting thoughts. "I'm not a romantic type of guy, and I've never had a public relationship."

Victoria straightened. "I'll have everything choreographed. Like a perfect dance."

Laughing, I shrugged. "I don't dance either."

Gray's head popped up from her screen. "Then think of it in terms of your job, Commander. Checklists for protocols. That's what you understand. Victoria can even give you homework to study."

I grimaced at her. "I can't create an illusion of something that isn't there."

Victoria stood. "You won't have to. Our prompts to the press and the cameras will take care of all of that. Let me show you." She motioned for me to stand, and I complied. "Now, go stand over there at the far end of the room, in front of the fireplace."

I did as she asked, and she grabbed her phone, fiddling with an app. Without looking up from what she was doing, she said. "Gray, go stand next to him."

Gray jerked her head up again from her own phone. "What?"

"I'm proving a point to him, and you're going to help me. Just do as I say and go stand next to him."

Gray blinked and slowly set her own phone down as Victoria started snapping pictures of me. "You've done a ton of press conferences, interviews and public appearances. You've been to the White House and met the president. And you've been on the red carpet with Keely before. Part of the reason we selected her was for the aesthetics. You two looked amazing together back in March. All we need are picture-perfect poses and a projection of intimacy between you. For example, put your arm around Gray's waist."

Gray stiffened, clearly shocked, but before she could protest, I moved fast, sliding my arm around her slim waist. Hmm, this felt easier than I'd anticipated. I settled my hand on her hip.

"Loosen up a little," I muttered so that Victoria wouldn't hear. She was busy snapping photos anyway and giving her own orders.

"Okay, Gray, turn toward Ty and put your hand on his chest."

Gray's eyes widened. "Uh..."

"Do as the lady asked." I struggled to hide the grin that so wanted to escape. The more uncomfortable Gray felt, the more I wanted to crow that I was right. What made either of them think I could pull this off any better than Gray could?

"See?" I muttered to her. "Even you have a problem with it, and no one is asking you to do it in full view of the public."

Gray's teeth clenched, but her dark brows arched haughtily. "I can do it just fine. I was taken by surprise."

"Okay, so let's see you convince Victoria, then."

She turned to me, steel and frost in her green eyes. "Fine. I can do this. And so can you."

"Gray, tilt your head back and look into his eyes. Ty, move in a little closer to her, would you? Lean in."

Oh, I was so enjoying Gray's discomfort. Suppressing the *I told you so* on the tip of my tongue, I leaned in as close as I could get, invading her space. The more I leaned, the more Gray tilted her head back as if to keep looking into my eyes. Her cheeks were flushed that too-becoming shade of pink again and her smell.

That delicious strawberries and mint smell. I breathed in deeply through my nose, feeling a surge of awareness of her. My heartbeat sped up. Hell yes, this was turning me on a little bit, but I wasn't quite sure *what* about it was turning me on.

"Stop blinking and breathing so fast, Gray. You look like you're about to pass out," Victoria instructed. "Turn your head a little away from me and the camera, but put your mouth near Ty's. If you lean in close enough from this angle, it will look like the two of you are in the middle of a passionate kiss—Yes! Like that."

Her photo app kept clicking, and I decided to ham it up by wrapping my other arm around Gray and pulling her slight body even closer to me. She placed a hand flat on my chest, and it gave enough resistance to let me know it was there. And I enjoyed how her hand felt there, like I wanted more of it.

Then she licked her lips, and that surge of awareness skyrocketed into arousal. I lifted my hand to her hair and whispered in her ear. "Let me take you to the Moon, baby girl."

Instead of the intended result, which was laughter to ease the tension, her eyes widened with shock. Suddenly I felt her weight in my arms as if she had lost her balance.

At that exact moment, Victoria's phone rang. She looked at her screen and let out a breath. "Oh, shoot! I have to take this. It's about that *LA Times* reporter covering this week's launch at Vandenberg. Be right back and don't move." And in seconds,

Victoria had trotted off through the front door and onto my porch to take her call.

I gazed after her—immediately confused as to what was happening, but also all too aware that the girl in my arms was trying to pull away. And I wasn't going to let her.

"You can let go now," Gray said quietly.

I shook my head, tightening that arm around her waist to hold her fast to me—up against me now. Shooting her a wicked grin, I said, "Victoria explicitly told us not to move."

The hand against my chest trembled a little bit, and she turned her face away from mine as if to gaze after Victoria for help.

"Victoria is probably going to tell me to kiss you when she gets back in here," I teased. "So I can practice like I'm kissing Keely."

Her posture changed again, tensing like she was stiffening in my arms. "The whole point of this exercise is that you don't actually have to kiss. You can't really fake kissing anyway. You probably shouldn't bother with the kissing part when you're with Keely." She flicked a glance up into my eyes as if to gauge my reaction to that. Just as quickly, her gaze fled.

Hmm. What was that brief flicker of something I saw in those moss-green eyes of hers? A green-eyed monster maybe? Or maybe it was a figment of my imagination. *Projecting*, she would say, in her psychobabble language. Maybe it was my own attraction to her.

When she very visibly swallowed, I had to think again.

"But I like kissing," I goaded. "I'll kiss her if I want to kiss her."

Her brow twitched in a frown, and she cleared her throat. "Yeah, but if you can't make it convincing, then—"

And that was all I let her say before I swept in and took advantage. With my hand on the back of her head, I pulled her face to mine, and I stole that kiss from her. My lips swooped down like a bird of prey to capture hers.

I hitched her body up against me, and that pop of energy between us from the day before was nothing compared to the heat and crackle between us now. Like a flare of solar energy.

Such a blast could kill an unprotected man in minutes. Even on station, we were advised to seek cover in the event of a solar storm.

And this scorching heat between Gray and me, generated in seconds, felt much like a burst of that powerful energy from a star. A jolt hitched in my chest, rumbling through my internal organs like the thrust of acceleration achieving escape velocity.

When her mouth opened to mine and she sucked in a breath, my arms tightened around her. Our tongues danced with each other, and she trembled against me.

And distantly, I wondered how hard it would be to pull myself away.

Her mouth moved on mine and her tongue teased. With a surge of arousal, I responded, tracing the edge of those delicate lips with my tongue, wanting to plunge and probe inside of her, to explore what she was hiding under that quiet, sweet surface. I suspected an ocean of depth within, and that realization more than intrigued me.

Her hand curled over my pec, fisting in my shirt, pulling it taut. Reality shivered—just a bit. My hand cradled the back of her neck where her skin was soft and fragrant with that minty, fruity fresh smell of hers.

Her hand relaxed, and with the bar of her forearm, she pushed against me. Not enough to propel her away but enough to communicate her wish to end it.

Me? I'd all but lost awareness of my own surroundings. Maybe I'd originally dived in to prove a point, but the speed with which I'd forgotten myself was not a little shocking. Only now was I realizing it, like coming out of a dream.

I didn't pull back from her until I heard the doorknob rattle when Victoria reentered the room. My arms went slack, and Gray was breathing hard, looking at me wide-eyed. But she didn't step away.

The moment stretched between us, and when Victoria finally looked up from her phone, she frowned at us. "You okay in here? Anything wrong?"

I drew back slightly, aware of the buzzing static of some other energy present in the room—gamma rays and dangerous radiation from my imaginary solar flare, no doubt. Through a fog, I blinked, stunned that no one could see it or sense it but me.

Gray blinked heavily as if trying to pull herself together. She turned partly away from me, her thin shoulders hunching slightly with self-consciousness.

I cleared my throat, aware that my own heartbeat was galloping and my body had begun reacting to that anything-but-ordinary kiss. "Oh, we were—ah—settling a disagreement, that's all." Victoria's elegant eyebrows arched to ask the question she didn't bother to voice. I flicked a look at Gray, who was staring at the ground, her face sunburn-red. "She was saying that there was no way I could pull off kissing for the cameras—"

"I said it wasn't necessary," Gray protested.

"You said it would be unconvincing," I fired back. "So I was proving you wrong. I think I succeeded."

Victoria frowned and shook her head, likely choosing not to pursue the subject. She'd already begun fiddling with her phone again immediately.

But for a slight flush of pink, Gray appeared unaffected, her features placid. When she took a step back, I instinctively grabbed her hand before realizing exactly what I was doing.

She froze as I thought quickly. Almost as an afterthought, I brought her palm up and inspected it.

She'd covered her cut with a large square bandage that I'd given her the night before.

"I'd like to have a look at this," I said. "So I can see how it's healing."

She pulled back the bandage, and I bent over her hand, getting a good look at the pink-red wound that, fortunately, did not appear to be infective. Before replacing the bandage, I made sure to lean close, running my thumb over her palm. I must have hit a tender spot because she flinched, yanking her hand back.

"Did that hurt? I'm sorry," I muttered.

She looked away with those same stained cheeks. So innocent and so damn sexy in her own way. Her eyes dropped to the floor, but she didn't reply.

Before I had a chance to follow up, Victoria poked her phone in my face, to show me how convincing our pseudokissing pictures were. But all I could think of was how good it had felt to do the real thing. There was something about that pink staining Gray's cheeks. The way, in the photos, that she had her hands on my chest.

And I remembered how she'd grasped onto my shirt while we were kissing, the cloth bunched up in her fists. Like she was holding on for dear life right up until the second before she'd pushed me away.

It caused an unfamiliar tightness in the back of my throat and an all too familiar ache in my cock. Still, it was different from that typical surge of empty lust.

There was something else I dare not question. An undiscovered territory fraught with peril.

"See?" Victoria beamed. "If you can make a fake almost-kiss look this convincing on the fly with Gray, think about what you can do in front of the press with a real professional actress." Victoria was grinning from ear to ear with glee, downright convinced that her scheme was going to work—and take the media by storm.

But I knew that no kiss I'd share with a beautiful Hollywood starlet would compare to the one I'd shared with Gray right here in my living room. I'd kissed more than enough women before to know what the real deal was.

What the...what the hell was that all about?

And *her*...

Gray had crossed the room, keeping her back to me, flipping idly through pages on a notepad. She hadn't said a word, but the back of her neck was still flushed that becoming pink. My eyes drifted down her body again, wondering why, just why, this woman was ensnaring my thoughts and attention so thoroughly. She was the complete opposite of my usual. I wanted to pull that ill-fitting T-shirt off of her and touch her everywhere underneath, sure. I definitely wanted to know if her skin felt as soft as it looked.

But there was something else. I wanted to know more about her. I wanted to know why she was so interested in space yet had decided to study psychology instead. I wanted to know about her struggles—health struggles, among them—but also her triumphs.

I'd been collecting facts about her for the past two days, and they'd only served to intrigue me enough to want more. She loved nerdy sci-fi and fantasy books. She knew a lot about space flight and the history of the space program. And those endearing things—carrying a towel for Towel Day, lining up pens and paper pads like soldiers in an army, or naming the growling in her stomach after a famous dragon.

I pushed those confused thoughts of her away for the moment, frustrated. Turning to gaze out the window, I waited while Victoria emailed some of the photos to her assistant for "reference"—whatever that meant.

Gray seemed to be avoiding me. Maybe this awkwardness would encourage her to run along after the meeting and not come back. I still hadn't figured out how I'd get rid of her as my houseguest.

And strangely, part of me felt like keeping her around.

I hadn't been staring out that window long before a sporty convertible Mini Cooper with the top down pulled in. It was painted bright pink, and two girls wearing gigantic designer shades sat in the front seat.

I recognized the driver as she stepped out, miles of bare leg from her heels to the edge of her Daisy Dukes, as Keely, a fetchingly attractive redhead. Exactly my type.

Victoria let out a little shriek and laid down her phone to go meet them outside. I turned to Gray, who continued to read her notes.

"So," I said, clearing my throat to get her attention. "Is everything okay?"

She spun, almost startled. "What?" she croaked.

I gestured to where we'd been standing when we'd kissed. "You've sufficiently recovered?"

She shrugged—a very exaggerated gesture—and very obviously unnatural. As if she really wanted to make sure I knew she didn't care about the whole thing. It wasn't one-tenth as convincing as that kiss had been.

She looked so fresh, young, innocent. I wondered how the hell she knew how to kiss like a siren.

She sent me a glance out of the corner of her eye—probably to check and see if I was teasing her. Her back stiffened. "Why wouldn't I be?"

Our gazes met, and that warm feeling from the day before washed over me. I was going to hell already anyway, so why not take a few swipes at the pure little Saint Angharad Grace of the Holy Barretts?

"I might need to go over the finer points of all that later."

Her dark brows furrowed. "The finer points of what?"

"That kiss. I may need a few..." I gestured with my hand in a rolling motion. "Repeat performances. To practice nuance. Purely for research, of course."

A moment later, the three women walked through the front door, and Gray had no chance to reply.

It was hard, really hard, not to laugh at the perplexed look on her face, her mouth slightly agape. But as much fun as it was to tease her, I wanted to kiss her again more.

No contest whatsoever.

Victoria was making introductions. Keely gave a high-pitched squeal as she turned to me. She trotted up, throwing her arms around my neck and kicking up a leg behind her as she kissed me on the cheek.

"Commander Tyler! My favorite astronaut."

Did she know any others?

"Hello, Ms. Dawson."

She blew out a breath and rolled her eyes. "Call me Keely, please. We're going to be kissing each other in front of cameras, after all."

I smiled but hid what I was thinking with my usual expertise. If only there were a way to get that cute psychologist to play the part instead. This bizarre little project could take on whole new levels of interesting.

"Then you should call me Ty like everyone else does."

"Deal," Keely said with a grin.

"Let's get started, shall we?" Victoria said, plastering on her widest smile. "Commander Tyler, have you met Sharon, Keely's best friend and assistant?"

I turned to Keely's plain and rather dour friend who ran her agenda like a drill sergeant. "We've met. Good to see you again." The woman, unshockingly, did not respond.

Victoria concluded by introducing the two women to Gray, who quietly but graciously shook their hands. Then at Victoria's instruction, we all took seats and proceeded to go over her asinine outline.

I tried hard to bite my tongue like a good little astronaut. I'd been through enough Monday morning Astronaut Office meetings at NASA to be an expert at it.

"What's this event?" Keely's assistant asked, pointing at the calendar. "Next week—

Make-A-Wish Foundation? Keely has an engagement then. Could we reschedule?"

Victoria's penciled brows pinched together. "There is press involved in that one, but I can see—"

"No," Gray interrupted, and everyone's heads turned in her direction. She straightened her spine and raised her chin. "That one is high priority. He can't reschedule, nor can the sick little boy who is involved. It's not some random event. It's very important. He's been waiting months to meet Commander Tyler."

"Okay," said Keely, turning to Sharon. "Contact my publicist and get my event changed."

That perma-pink on Gray's cheeks was now deepening to a more intense shade of red. At first, I was puzzled by why this event had stirred such passion. Then I remembered her own health challenges—very likely springing from a childhood illness. If I were a betting man, I'd say that scar had come from open heart surgery—a surgery that had come at the end of a sickly childhood.

All the more reason she identified with a sick child on the Make-A-Wish Foundation list.

"I agree," I chimed in. "I've done a few Make-A-Wish events already, and the top priority is the child. This one has been scheduled for months. I make it work with my schedule where I can." Even though—goddammit all—this one was in Houston, the last city I wanted to be in these days.

Keely smiled. "I can go to the Make-A-Wish thingy with you and meet the little boy. It's a good cause."

Victoria tore her sharp gaze from Gray to look at me. "Well, to be fair, he's there to meet Commander Tyler, tour the Johnson Space Center with him, and then ride in the Zero Grav Experience."

Keely drew back. "What the heck is that? A simulator?"

I nodded. "Yeah, it simulates zero gravity, like in space."

"Fun! I bet he'll love that." Keely laughed and threw me a flirty look, batting her eyes.

Uh oh. As gorgeous as Keely was, I did not want this girl to get the wrong idea that this might be anything more than exactly what we'd signed up for—fake playacting, photo ops and public drama. Nothing more. Certainly not anything real.

I didn't do real. *Ever.*

My eyes drifted inexplicably to Gray, who was scribbling more notes on her legal pad with a pencil.

I'd have to keep a handle on the Keely situation. Though it was strange how I didn't even question why it was not okay to get with the hot and flirty actress, but it was more than okay to fantasize about the quiet but fetching girl next door.

I studied her as Gray watched Keely over her notepad, chewing on her lip. The ridges above her top lip were prominent, her introspection half-hidden by the thick frames of her glasses.

Gray was perky and a little tomboyish. With a heavy dash of college nerd. But damned if I didn't find that combo sexy as hell. And surprising enough to me to cause me to marvel at it every time.

It was a quiet, understated...unawakened sort of way. The way that made it crystal clear that I wanted to be the one to awaken her. *All of her.*

Awaken her in ways she didn't even realize had been sleeping. That thought made my blood burn, and I had to force myself to stop thinking about it and focus on this goddamn snooze of a meeting. But if I could deal with twelve-hour days filled with tedious sims or even isolation testing, then I could survive this. Hollywood farce and all.

Chapter Ten
GRAY

THE MEETING BROKE UP, AND VICTORIA, KEELY AND HER assistant eventually gathered their things. We aligned our calendars for the first photo op and public date when we would leak the "exciting new love story" in a few days.

"Gray, Tolan said you're staying here for the next little while?" Victoria asked, flicking a long look at Ty. I tried to act like I hadn't been expecting her question. Victoria and I had already discussed the entire thing in texts the night before, so this conversation was for his benefit.

For his part, he didn't even react. No protest, no eye roll. Nada. Well, that was a good sign. I turned back to Victoria. "Yeah, I'm going to be Commander Tyler's assistant and, you know, keep things running smoothly from here. I'll be your point person too." There was no reason to go into the details about the mess I'd found here yesterday—sex in the other room, vodka in the afternoon, and a belligerent jackass astronaut. I was willing to start off on a new foot today if he was.

Victoria nodded and smiled. "Gotcha. Thank you. I have so much going on with this launch at Vandenberg and then the XPAC announcement event that I can barely squeeze this in. So, I might be the mastermind, but you're the one getting it all done."

I smiled and tried hard not to look at Ty, whose stare I could feel irradiating my skin at 1,000 degrees Celsius. I was steel. I was frost.

However, when Victoria and Keely left, I immediately fled to the bathroom down the hall from the room I'd slept in the night before.

And no, not because I had to go.

I closed my eyes, splashing cold water on my face and patting it dry with my trusty towel. Then I stared at myself in the mirror, noting that my cheeks were still flushed from that encounter in the living room with Ty an hour before.

I hadn't *stopped* thinking about it.

My mind spun, caught in a whirlpool—no, a maelstrom—a swirling current of overpowering force centering around one locus.

That *kiss*. That goddamn kiss.

If thunder had a taste and a texture, they would be that kiss.

He'd pulled me against him, and I'd felt that hard body—so unyielding and yet, ultimately responsive to mine. Or maybe I'd imagined that tremor—like he was holding back from unleashing its full power. Like a rocket pinned against the launchpad before blowing its bolts and pounding its thrust against the ground in order to propel it skyward at a speed faster than that of a bullet leaving a gun.

Ty's body had felt like that as he kissed me. Like he was holding himself back. And the only thing I could think of right now was—if that was holding back, what would the real thing have felt like? The thought of it left my throat dry.

A rocket burns at 3,000 degrees Celsius, and I was certain his kiss could have equaled that temperature. *Easily.*

My eyes drifted half closed, and I was scorched by the memory of each detail. With every movement of his lips and the tip of his tongue, which had extended just enough as if he was tasting me before being pulled back under that intense hold of control. But that flicker, that taste had permanently changed something inside of me. As if it had caused a chemical reaction— much like that of rocket fuel when it propelled a rocket upward.

And chemical reactions could not be reversed. The change they wrought was permanent.

And the way my stomach had bottomed out the moment his tongue had slipped through his lips to touch mine on a clandestine spy mission of its own. As if I might not detect what he was doing. *Let me take you to the Moon, baby girl,* he'd whispered in that deep, sexy voice of his. The line had been cheesy and he'd clearly been joking, but with that kiss, he'd practically done just that.

And then that look in his eyes when he'd pulled away. It had flashed in an instant and vanished—*raw hunger.*

It had kept me from speaking—or even breathing—for the minutes afterward. I'd had to turn away to hide the shock that was all over my face.

And minutes later, I'd been rankling in the corner while Keely flirted with him. Ugh. Him and his stupid gorgeous looks. He was a magnet for the male-loving gaze. And not only *mine.*

But I reminded myself of the importance of this situation. I needed to keep this professional for so many reasons. For the most important reasons. Wrangle him. Keep him on the straight and narrow and get him to make the XPAC look good, exciting, squeaky clean, and yeah—maybe a little sexy.

In recent years, NASA had made going to space look anything but sexy. But we needed a little of that appeal. I hadn't been as willing to admit it in the meeting yesterday in front of my dad, but we needed Tyler badly for this. And damn, but we needed him to cooperate.

Which probably meant I'd have to start fighting off the women who'd gravitate toward him. But alas, not Keely. If something flared up there, then I'd have to stand back and let it happen, and hope it didn't end badly.

Did every one of them want to jump his bones—even if they didn't particularly like him? I certainly wasn't that type, but he was having a seriously profound effect on me. My head felt light, and there was a buzzing near my ears, bowled over as I was by this realization. *I am steel. I am stone.*

After talking myself down, I resolved to make a quick trip home to get my things. I lived about forty-five minutes away in Long Beach, in my own little one-bedroom condo not far from the university there. It would take me several hours to get there, get my stuff packed up and loaded in my car, and return. Hopefully, I'd be able to trust him alone for those few hours.

I'd taken some measures last night when he'd gone to his room, so I'd have to check later to see how much I could trust that he'd behaved while I was gone. If he let me back in, that was.

Opening the door, I was startled out of my skin by the hulking shadow hovering nearby. I turned and gasped in fright before realizing Ty was waiting for me outside the bathroom door. I put a hand over my heart and coughed—hoping to cover for the loud clicking as my heartbeat raced.

He grimaced and muttered his apology, holding out a folded bit of cloth. It was my T-shirt from the night before, laundered and without a stain. "I figured you'd probably prefer to wear something more your size."

I took it from him slowly. "Thank you. I would...not that I don't love wearing a NASA shirt. But..." I waved to point out the baggy fit. But I'd forgotten about cinching it tight around me so it wouldn't slip like last night. It fit me so tightly now that it hugged me like a second skin.

His eyes followed my action, gravitating to my chest. There was something in that look, an obvious pop of tension where he noticed me. Noticed me in a way that men didn't usually notice me—or at least not as far as I knew. For myself, I couldn't tear my eyes away from his mouth. I heated again, remembering that kiss. And—damn it—my nipples tightened just reliving it. The shirt wasn't thin, but I didn't have a bra on. I gulped. Did he notice?

My hand squeezed tight around my own T-shirt, and we stood in silence before he finally looked up. "I thought that—as an apology for yesterday—I'd come along and help you gather your things."

I blinked. *Say what?*

In response to my obvious befuddlement, he cracked a smile. "I'm not an asshole all of the time, Gray, only some of the time. Okay, maybe *most* of the time."

I frowned. "Commander—"

"Ty. Everyone calls me Ty." He laughed. "Or better yet, call me Ryan."

I hadn't heard *anyone* call him Ryan. I blinked again. "O-okay."

"Besides, who knows how long I'll hold that rank? Technically, I'm still in the Navy, but I have no idea for how much longer."

His voice trailed off, his blue eyes drifting out the window. Astronauts who had entered NASA from the military were still on active duty, still held their rank—and were promoted—while they served as astronauts. But since Tyler had broken with NASA, it was as yet undetermined what his status in the Navy was. He might have to retire before his test flight in September. But I suspected he might be having trouble letting go of his rank.

I almost—*almost*—asked him about it. But he'd immediately target that question as "shrink talk." Far be it from me to threaten this newfound détente between us with a violation of the rules he'd set yesterday.

He nodded toward my guest room. "Why don't you get changed, and I'll take you in my car? I have air conditioning, after all."

I pressed my lips together and nodded, retiring to my room to make quick work of changing my shirt and grabbing my phone and keys. I met him near the front door.

He'd changed into jeans, grabbed his own keys and had put on a pair of mirrored aviator sunglasses. His butt looked fantastic in those jeans. And those glasses. Oh God. He had hotshot pilot written all over him. I took a breath and blew it out. *I am a rock. I am ice.*

We got into his hybrid SUV—a far cry from the flashy sports cars the astronauts of the Space Race era drove. It still had that new car smell and appeared as clean as if he'd driven it off the lot yesterday. I was relieved he'd chosen to use his car instead of my sweatbox full of empty coffee cups that rolled around on the floor in the back seat whenever I made a sharp turn.

Our small talk turned interesting when we hit the freeway. "This is a time-consuming way to apologize, you know," I began. "*I'm sorry* takes probably three nanoseconds to say. And then you have hours of your weekend day to do whatever you want."

He made a face at me. "I doubt it. A nanosecond is a billionth of a second."

I rolled my eyes. "It's a figure of speech. I'm just saying, two words are easier than...all this."

He shrugged with one shoulder. "I prefer action to words." Hmm. *Unsurprising.* It was probably easier to do it this way than to admit he'd been wrong to go loudly sex up the trainer while I was waiting to meet with him. But I let it stand.

I shot him another glance while he kept his eyes on the road. "Are you feeling okay with all of this?"

"This fake romance BS?" he clarified for me. "It doesn't matter how I'm feeling about all of it. If it's my only way back up there, then I'm doing it."

I frowned. "Of course, it matters. It's important to understand your feelings going forward, because—"

He held up his hand abruptly in a chopping motion to stop me as he stared out the windshield. "Is that shrink talk? I thought we had a rule about that."

"*You* have a rule about that." I folded my arms and gazed out the window, trying to think my way around the roadblock he'd thrown up so quickly. Damn. It was not going to be easy to get this man to open up about himself.

"I'm trying to say..." I started again. "That first and foremost, I'm here for your support, okay? I've got your back."

"We say *I've got your six*. And in my line of work, trust is earned." His words were stern, but his tone was mild.

I turned to him. "Well, then I hope to at least be given a chance to earn it."

"We'll see." He cryptically ended the subject by turning up the volume on the talk radio station that had been playing in the background.

It being Sunday, the freeway was clear, and we made good time to my place. I invited him in, and he followed me up the steps to my one-bedroom condo on the second floor. "I can show you around if you like. It will only take a fraction of the time it took you to show me your place."

My place was modest, and he voiced almost immediately what I knew he was thinking—what I'd heard before. "Not where I expected the daughter of Conrad Barrett to live."

I shrugged. "I like it. Dad is known for sensible investment, so I followed his advice and bought a place I knew would have good resale value."

His eyes immediately flew to my hodgepodge décor—a beautiful framed poster of the iconic shot of the earth rising over the Moon taken during the Apollo 8 mission. Space memorabilia I had collected during my teenage years. Mission patches from the Space Shuttle era. Some model Redstone and Saturn V rockets propped along the top of a black bookcase. Colorful and exotic paintings of imagined planetscapes on the walls.

I left him to study one of them while I packed a suitcase in my bedroom and scurried around the apartment to grab toiletries and personal items.

By the time I was ready to hit the road, it was well past lunchtime, and this time, his stomach growled loudly. With a laugh, I suggested a nearby, quiet English-style pub. Since it was a student haunt, usually, when school was out for the summer—and on long weekends, of which today was both—the place was mostly dead.

Nevertheless, before we got out of the car, he donned a red Angels baseball cap and kept his mirrored sunglasses on. I threw him some major side-eye, knowing he feared being recognized. "All you need is your hoodie to complete the starter pack."

He frowned. "I'm sorry?"

"Your Marvel Civilian Starter Pack. They all wear them in the movies—Tony Stark, Steve Rogers. You fit right in. Cap, hoodie, sunglasses. It's a foolproof way they are never recognized when they don't want to be."

"Too bad we're not in the movies."

He chose a back table along the wall behind the empty stage that usually hosted live musicians on the weekends. We quickly placed our orders—his double-bacon heart-attack-on-a-plate avocado cheeseburger and my fish and chips.

While we were waiting, he struck up the conversation again. "Did you go to school here, at Cal State Long Beach?"

I shook my head. "No, I attended a tiny women's college, Scripps, up in LA. And UCLA for my doctorate."

"All-girls' tiny school." There was an enigmatic smile on his lips. "I should have known."

My brows twitched. "What's that supposed to mean?"

Declining to answer, he merely smiled and shrugged while fiddling with the salt and pepper shaker. He instead asked another question, apparently the self-appointed King of Curiosity today.

"So tell me how a woman who is obviously crazy about space and space travel came to study psychology instead of going into a STEM field."

"You really don't like psychologists, do you?" I laughed, now feeling nervous.

His face was unreadable. "I had to speak to my fair share after the accident...and it wasn't by my choice."

I thought about that for a moment. *Hmm, no wonder he had that brick wall up and determined to keep me out.*

"So, are you going to answer my question or just stall with another question to me?"

My brow twitched. *Touché.* Usually, I was the one who asked the questions and controlled the conversation. It was weird to be on the receiving end. But I reminded myself that it was a good sign. If he was asking questions, it meant he was interested in looking for common ground and hopefully finding a way to work with me. I took out a few of the sweetener packets from the plastic box and idly rearranged them on the dark wooden table in front of me, thinking through my answer before looking up again.

"When I was a kid, I insisted on wearing shiny space suits instead of princess dresses. And I decorated my bed like a rocket ship. When I was afraid to go to sleep, I'd imagine myself taking flight in my ship and that I'd wake on a new planet in the morning. I grew up in LA, right on the edge of Griffith Park, and my mom liked to take walks all up through the hills. We'd often end up at the observatory planetarium. I spent so much time there looking at the exhibits, the displays. The moon rocks. It fascinated me." I shrugged and rocked from side to side on the wooden bench where I sat. "I've wanted to be an astronaut since

I was tiny—and I'm sure you've heard a bazillion little kids tell you that."

He listened intently, considering my words with his head tilted to the side. "I have, but that doesn't make it any less valid. I had no desire to be an astronaut when I was little."

Interesting. I opened my mouth to follow up that tidbit with another question of my own when he headed me off. "So why psychology? Why not physics or aerospace or engineering?"

I began to stack the packets on top of each other like miniature beanbags. "You mean why not a valid field of study instead of a 'soft' science?" Typical STEM snobbery. Only the smartest people went into STEM fields. I'd heard it before.

"Well—" he began, but I didn't let him finish.

"Because I wanted to work with astronauts." My eyes flicked up to meet his, which widened in surprise by my interruption. "I'm fascinated by the human element in space flight. We won't be able to go and explore out there until we figure out how to keep people sane and healthy during long-duration space flight and planet-side missions. And while it will always be possible to build a bigger, faster, better spacecraft, the one element that won't change—until we evolve—is the human element."

He pushed the salt and pepper back into their cubby and sat back. "Valid points," he said noncommittally.

My fingers fiddled with the stack of packets. "Besides, it became clear to me very early on that becoming an astronaut was out of my reach, due to my health issues. I never gave up that dream, though. I just decided to tweak it a little so it would work with my personal circumstances. I did the next best thing. I would have tried for a job at NASA if Tolan hadn't been ready to start up the XPAC. You can agree with me that this is way more exciting. And I got lucky. *Very* lucky."

Our gazes locked and held when I looked up, and there was this moment—much like the one the day before—where something changed between us. A noticeable thickening in the air. He didn't blink, his Adam's apple bobbed when he swallowed, and the glimmer in those blue eyes—was it my imagination, or did it look a bit like grudging admiration?

I drew back when our server—a good-looking college kid around my age—showed up with our plates of food. "Fish and chips for the lady. And...one out-of-this-world burger for Commander Ty." Ty grimaced at being recognized but recovered quickly, looking up at the guy. "I also brought you a beer, on the house. The bartender insisted."

He plopped the beer down in front of Ty with several coasters and a pen. "Commander, can we get your autograph?"

Ty was very polite, but not chatty. So, once he'd signed the coasters, the server scooped them up, slipped them into his apron, and walked off.

"Jeez," Ty said before picking up his burger. "You'd think people wouldn't be so starstruck in LA."

I laughed. "You aren't a star, Commander. You're a hero."

His gaze sharpened as he poised his burger in front of his mouth. "You're not calling me that anymore, remember?"

"Right...sorry, er, Ryan." I pursed my lips awkwardly. "That's going to take some getting used to."

"Well, get used to it. And no using the h-word either." I nodded affably, pondering that. He seemed more annoyed at me for using the word *hero* rather than messing up and using his rank.

"Aren't you going to eat?" he asked after swallowing his first bite.

I picked up the bottle of malt vinegar and began drenching my fish and chips. "I'm waiting for my fries to cool off. I always wait at least five minutes. I don't like burning the roof of my mouth."

His brows twitched up for a moment. "Ah, you're playing it safe. I should have known."

I fought rolling my eyes, but just to annoy him, I picked up a fry, blew on it, and then popped it into my mouth. It was hotter than I would have liked, so I proceeded to suck down a bunch of ice-cold lemonade while he laughed at me.

I wrinkled my nose. "Needs more vinegar," I said, raining down more on the fries so that they grew soggy—which seemed to baffle him.

"How long has it been since your valve replacement?" he asked after having devoured most of his burger.

For someone who'd forbidden me from talking like a "shrink," he certainly was asking a lot of questions today.

I popped a couple more fries into my mouth to stall my answer. When I'd swallowed, I shot a question right back at him. "How'd you know it was a valve replacement?" *Stupid question, Gray.*

He shrugged. "I'm no Sherlock Holmes. Just observant. The clicking heartbeat was my first clue. The blood thinners were another."

He'd seen the hideous scar too. But mercifully, he didn't mention that. Open heart surgery survivors all had some variation of the zipper scar—enough to call themselves members of the zipper club or even incorporate the scar into some cute little tattoo that implied the same. Some wore their scars proudly, like battle wounds.

I wasn't usually so self-conscious about mine, but I didn't go out of my way to show it off either. And something about Ryan knowing my situation made me more insecure than normal.

"I was sixteen for that surgery. So, nine years ago."

He brought his hands up to lace his fingers together and rest his chin on them. His focused gaze grew unnerving. "What was your diagnosis?"

"It's a congenital heart defect," I said, moving the remains of my lunch around on my plate to keep from fidgeting. "I was born with a hole between the chambers of my heart, some thickened walls, and valve deformities."

When he would have followed up with another question, we were interrupted again—this time by the bartender. He brought Ty another beer though he'd only drunk half the previous one.

"Commander Ty—I'm Jay, your bartender." He held out his hand, and Ty shook it. "I had to come meet you after you signed the coasters for me and my buddy. Thank you."

Ty nodded and smiled and immediately scanned the bar, probably hoping people wouldn't notice the fuss. It was still pretty empty in here as it was well past the lunch hour and a few hours before dinnertime.

Jay pulled out his phone and showed something to Ty. "Can you settle a bet with me and my buddy? I say these NASA photos are evidence of structures on Mars, but he says no way."

He plopped down a blurry black-and-white photo—presumably from a satellite in Mars orbit—in front of Ty. Pointing at some blurred angular edge among darker mountains, he said, "I mean, that right there. That looks like architecture, don't you think? Man-made structures. It's an anomaly."

Ty blinked. "I dunno, man," he said evenly. "I haven't been to Mars yet."

Jay's eyes widened. "But you've been to space—and lived there. You work for NASA. You guys are all in on this, right?"

Ty's face immediately darkened into a scowl, and I could only think that he was associating this guy with the flat-earth creep who'd pestered him the previous month. Anything that implied he or the other astronauts or NASA as a whole was lying was bad news.

I leaned forward to catch Jay's attention. "We're in a hurry to get going. Can we get our check?"

Jay barely glanced at me before turning back to Ty, who bolted out of his seat and pulled out his wallet. "Yes, I gotta get going. Thanks again for the beers, Jay. I guess I wasn't so thirsty."

Our server appeared beside Jay, and we took care of the check on the spot. I insisted on splitting it, and Ty was in such a hurry to get out of there, he didn't argue.

On our way home, we laughed about it. "You should make up some random crap," I said. "Something really out there. Like green Sasquatch on Mars. Or like you saw some guy in a bad gorilla suit floating around in space outside the station trying to monkey with the equipment. *Nightmare at 250 Miles*."

We laughed together about it, and I wiped my eyes. "Does that happen to you a lot?"

He rolled his eyes. "Way too much." He shook his head. "And while you think it might be funny to mess with people. It's not so great when you see your own words—either said jokingly or willfully taken out of context—printed all over the tabloids. And then people treat you a certain way based on it. When everyone writes down your words or wants to sell a photo of you to the press, you're accountable for everything that comes out of your mouth."

On that sobering thought, we ended up driving the rest of the way back to North Tustin, each lost in our own thoughts.

***

Over the next few days, we settled into a pattern which consisted, mostly, of staying out of each other's way. We happened to work at the same place and live in the same house. But evenings—particularly when night fell—he studiously avoided me.

On weekdays, he left far earlier in the morning than I did and came home later than I did. He kept long hours, something I was sure was no different from his days at NASA, especially while preparing for a flight.

Sometimes we'd eat together, but more often, we didn't because of his late hours.

Thankfully, he was cordial—most of the time.

Except for the night he noticed what I'd done to his booze bottles.

"What the hell is this?" he snapped from behind me. He'd entered the little den beside his office. I usually did my work in here, at his behest, probably because he didn't want me sprawled across his living room couch otherwise.

I pushed back from the desk where I'd been staring at my open laptop and turned to him, pushing my glasses back up my nose.

He held up his bottle of vodka, and I almost lost it, realizing the source of his annoyance. I bit my cheek to keep from showing my reaction.

And I played dumb. "It looks like a bottle of vodka."

He blew out a breath. "Yes, of course, it's a bottle of vodka. I went to pour myself a drink, and I saw *this* on the side." He held the bottle in front of my face at eye level, so I could see the marks I'd made along the side with a Sharpie. In tiny writing, I'd marked the level of the liquid inside the bottle along with the date.

The good news was this was days after I'd originally marked those bottles and he was only noticing now, which meant he wasn't hitting the liquor every single night.

When I was silent, he locked his arm. "Did you do this?"

I bit my bottom lip before looking up at him. "Yes. But only as a tool for assessment and...introspection."

His brows knit. "What?"

"Just so we can figure out if you're overusing alcohol."

He retracted his arm, spine stiffening. "This is over the top. I don't need this sort of policing."

I rose out of my chair so we could be on a more even level—futile because he was still four inches taller than me. "Good. Then there's nothing to argue about. It's to keep you accountable."

His cheeks bulged where he clenched his jaw several times before he spoke. "I do *not* have a problem with alcohol."

I blinked. "But alcohol has caused you some problems, right? The night you punched out the flat-earther, you were drunk. That party that trashed the hotel room in Chicago—"

"That was not my fault. I was—" He cut himself off and shook his head. "I'm not going to bother explaining myself to you."

"You definitely don't have to do that. And you know what? I'm not even going to look at those liquor bottles except to mark new levels once a week. Those marks are for your reference. Not mine and not anyone else's. They are there to help you."

He blew out a breath, face darkening to an even deeper shade of red. My desire to laugh was gone now as my heart sped up and the loud clicking was now noticeable. His eyes flicked to my chest and then back to my eyes again. Maybe he thought I was afraid of him. Maybe that would make him feel better.

Instead, he turned and walked out, muttering something about not feeling thirsty anymore. I all but collapsed back into the chair, then gathered my things and decided to call it an early night.

Criminy. I would be happy when I could go back to the peace and quiet of working at my own place.

A little while later, I crawled under the covers, exhausted. My phone chimed right as I was closing my eyes.

Pari: How's your watchdog job with Astro-Hottie going?
Me: Ugh.
Pari: That good, huh? LOL
Me: Don't want to talk about it rn.
Pari: Did you leave that package of Oreos on my desk today, btw? That wasn't the cookie fairy?
Me: It was my return favor for the bag of chips last week.
Pari: Me and my extra five pounds thank you. :p
Me: Gotta hit the hay. Tomorrow is the big beach photo op with "Astro-Hottie" and the movie star. Lots to prep.
Pari: Exciting. Send me some shots!

***

In the tiny hotel room at the Malibu Country Inn right off Zuma Beach, Victoria masterfully went through the prep for Ryan and Keely's first photo op session. This would be their "coming out" as a couple on the sandy Malibu beach that had started so many famous romances—both real and orchestrated—before them.

I glanced out the window, squinting at the gleaming surf of a late Friday afternoon. People were out—but not in droves. Which was why we'd chosen this time and day, rather than a crowded Sunday or Saturday or a holiday.

Victoria briefed the couple thoroughly on what was expected of them. She explained where they should pause and for how long. She told them where they should kiss and how—right down to where their hands should be. They'd asked questions, and I half expected Ryan to pull a tiny notepad out of his shirt pocket and take notes.

While they chatted, I snapped a quick picture of the three of them and sent it off to Tolan, to keep him apprised.

He responded half a minute later with a thumbs-up emoji. We were a "go" for launch of this new "it" couple.

Victoria had doubled-checked to make sure her media contacts were in place, poised and ready to snap the seemingly candid photos. Then she dismissed Ryan and pulled Keely aside for a final once-over of her hair and makeup.

I took the opportunity to excuse myself to use the bathroom.

Upon exiting, I was stopped short by Ryan, who hovered right outside the door. I moved aside to let him by, assuming he'd been waiting to use the bathroom after me. But he squeezed into the doorway beside me and didn't budge, wedging his arm across the doorjamb to block my way out.

"Yes?" I said quietly, my eyes flying to Victoria and Keely, who were engrossed in their final touches.

"I want you to know before you freak out that I had two shots down at the bar just now."

Well, it didn't take a rocket scientist to detect that. The moment he'd opened his mouth, I smelled booze on his breath. His tone was tense, clipped, and I brought my gaze up to meet his burning eyes.

"You're still pissed about the marked bottles, aren't you?"

His brow twitched. "Should I not be?"

My breathing felt tight and my heart raced, though I couldn't tell if that was because I was dreading a possible confrontation or because I found his proximity so incredibly distracting.

His smell—seashells, lime, and salty seaside spray. *Eau de Ocean God.* A vision of his perfect abs popped into my brain, dappled with drops of ocean water. I'd seen that amazing torso of his a few more times since that first incident in his living room—coming in from an early morning swim and grabbing ice water in the kitchen after a workout. He was so damn gorgeous I had to stop short of physically pinching myself to remember this was a job and he was a jerk—some of the time anyway.

"Are you nervous about this?" I asked in a quiet voice.

He smiled lazily. "I know how to kiss a woman. I think I proved that to you last weekend."

I swallowed thickly, shocked he'd bring that up. I'd been so positive he'd never given that kiss another thought. But I sure had given it many thoughts. I couldn't not think about how amazing that kiss had felt. During the past week, that kiss had never been far from my mind.

But in that same week, he had kept himself distant. Remote. Almost as if he were actively avoiding me. It was as if, after we'd kissed, he'd turned everything off and I was a nobody again.

But for that half a minute, I'd felt like his everything.

He might have snapped back easily. But my mind had not. Not yet anyway.

Now, however, he was staring at my lips. "Maybe I could use a little...warming up, though. You know, like a lip-fluffer."

I frowned. "A lip-fluffer?"

He smiled, tilting his head a little closer, his voice quiet. "You know, like in porn? You know what a fluffer is."

I drew back and did a double take. "Uh, how much vodka did you say you had?"

He laughed. "Enough to ease the stage fright, but not enough to blow it."

I reached up and fixed the collar on his blue button-down shirt. Our faces were *very* close now, and mine was getting warmer by the minute. "You'll do fine."

He lifted a thumb to brush my bottom lip. "How about one for good luck, then?"

I looked down, stunned by the zing and rush, and incredibly shy all at the same time. He was teasing me, and it wasn't all that funny. But I was trembling all over now, because damn it, I wanted to kiss him again.

"You shouldn't be such a tease," was the only lame thing I could come back with.

Without a word, he let his hand drop, and he slowly pulled away from me. I looked up then, and our gazes caught and held.

"Good luck...Ryan. You'll do great." I cleared my throat and then straightened my spine. "And you're right. You do know how to kiss a woman."

Keely now stood at Ryan's shoulder and looked from one of us to the other. "What's going on here?" Her big baby blue eyes flitted from his face to mine and back again. My face burned with what I assumed was an obvious blush.

Ryan gestured to my chest. "I was reading her T-shirt."

It was yet another piece in my nerdy wardrobe. Keely's gaze flickered to it. "That color green makes your eyes ding, Gray, but I don't get the shirt."

I pointed to the complex formula depicted—the orbital velocity formula. Below it, in pale yellow script it read, *The first step is admitting you have a problem.*

"Just a little psycho nerd humor. This is a physics problem."

Ryan seemed amused, his eyes glued to my chest, which made me blush even more, and Keely smiled and nodded, but I wasn't quite sure my explanation had helped her.

Minutes later, Victoria was leading us out of the hotel room, pointing out the path they were supposed to take on their leisurely stroll across the sand before pausing near the pier for their public smoochfest. Victoria and I watched them go, and I couldn't pull my eyes away when Ryan reached out and took Keely's hand.

Keely turned to him and laughed, her red hair dancing on the breeze, and a bolt of lightning cracked through me so swiftly it took my breath away. I was crazy jealous of Keely at this very moment.

Biting the inside of my cheek, I turned and went back into the room, vowing not to look anymore. And willing the jealousy away.

I failed on both counts.

CHAPTER ELEVEN
RYAN

"WELL, IF THIS ISN'T THE MOST GORGEOUS DAY TO start a public romance, I don't know what is." Keely turned and beamed up at me and squeezed my hand simultaneously. She had a thousand-megawatt smile, with star power and charm to go along with it. She was in her element, and I couldn't help but be affected.

"It's been a long time since I just walked at the beach. It's nice." I turned to look at the water. The surf pounded relentlessly to our left. A light, cool breeze danced over my skin, bringing the earthy, briney scent of the ocean, wet sand and seaweed along with it.

Keely made a face. "I want to walk on the surf side! I used to love playing that game, you know the one, where you walk on the wet sand and try to see how close you can get without the water coming up and getting your feet wet. But Vic said I had to walk on this side because of the pictures."

I smiled, pulling her closer to the water. Her light skirt caught the breeze. "We can still do that if you want."

"Damn, Ty. You're so nice. And here I thought you were such a bad boy."

I grinned. "Don't spill my secret."

169

She giggled and flicked her designer-perfumed hair, turning up the flirtation. She was every man's fantasy of the Manic Pixie Dream Girl.

Except *mine*, apparently.

No, I couldn't get my mind off that sweet young thing I'd left back in the hotel room. The one who wore the faded jeans that hugged her tight little ass and nerdy T-shirts with esoteric logos that made me laugh.

The one who slurped her breakfast smoothies through a straw so loud it echoed through the house. Who always had her nose buried in a big, fat nonfiction book or her e-reader when she wasn't watching me with those eyes that missed absolutely nothing.

The one who smelled like strawberries and mint and had skin that looked so soft that I itched to touch it. Every single time.

I also wanted to make her moan.

And gasp my name.

And—

Keely elbowed me. "Houston, we have a problem."

"What?" I turned to her.

She widened her eyes and grabbed my arm, hanging off it and staring up into my eyes as she smiled dreamily. "Wake up, Ty, bae. The show must go on. And I just spotted our first pap off the...what would you call that in pilot speak? Two o'clock?"

Without turning my head, I flicked my eyes in the general direction and was rewarded with the glint of a camera lens reflecting the sunlight as it pointed toward us. We hadn't quite hit the spot where we were supposed to stop and stare dreamily into each other's eyes before kissing, watching the surf for a few minutes and continuing on to the pier, so we kept walking while

I leaned my head toward hers as if every word she spoke fascinated me.

Oh God, I'd get through this somehow. Keely was a pro who took it all in stride, so I followed her lead and walked the predetermined two miles. And hopefully, we'd managed to convince a few that we were giddy new lovers aching to publicly display our affection to the world.

It was enough to make any red-blooded man's man puke.

But NASA had trained a good little astronaut to jump through their hoops. And I'd jump through these too. Because XPAC was going to get me back where I needed to be.

And there was no time to be distracted by a too-perceptive young shrink who seemed to stare right through my barriers and zoom in on the problematic pieces of my soul, like an X-ray machine, poised and ready to diagnose my weaknesses.

Before long, we were edging our way across the sand toward the beach access road, having left the photographers behind. We hopped into the back seat of the Mercedes Victoria's assistant drove. And our obligation for the day was done. We'd be sharing an intimate dinner date on Sunday night. One that included the eyes—and the camera lenses—of the awaiting public as well.

**

That night, as the sun went down and the timed lighting came on, making everything as bright as if it were still noon, I sat at the counter in my kitchen staring down at my phone, vaguely aware I should do my usual disappearing act for the day to avoid the tasty Ms. Barrett.

I'd been doing a good job of evading both the drink and the prying shrink, much as she intrigued me. Far too much, in fact.

So I'd devised a plan to keep her out of my way for as long as I could. This house was big enough to lose two people in it. I momentarily thanked my foresight for not buying that tiny but luxurious condo on the beach in Newport I'd been eyeing. That would have made my evasion tactics damn near impossible.

Right now, Gray was somewhere else, probably on the deck watching the sky at sunset. I'd noticed that was one of her favorite things to do. Then I'd scolded myself for paying enough attention to notice her favorite things to do.

I fingered the home button on my phone again, resting my forehead in my palm. I'd been reluctant to unlock it—four texts and two missed calls. All from the same person.

I swallowed thickly, feeling that same pang of guilt and self-recrimination. I'd been avoiding responding for weeks—even months. Sometimes I'd send short answers, but most often, I ghosted. It was easier that way. Then I'd send something—a check or some flowers, candy or a bunch of toys for the little guy.

My eyes froze on that first text.

Keep wondering how you are doing out there in Sunny California. The boy keeps asking about you.

I blinked. That was unfair, bringing AJ into this. A stab of pain almost stole my breath as I pictured the little guy, round cheeks wet with tears as he saluted the monument erected in honor of the father he would never see again. That day a five-year-old child became a member of the same club I'd been inducted into at fifteen.

My jaw clenched, and my finger hovered over the reply button.

Just then, the sliding glass door to the back deck scraped in its frame. And I jerked my head up. Gray opened the door barely wide enough to allow her slim form access, then shut it almost as quickly. She turned and looked at me, stopping in surprise. "Hey."

"Hi." I clicked my phone off and stuffed it into my back pocket.

She tilted her head. "You okay?"

Christ. Five seconds in the room and she was doing that uncanny perceptive thing again. It irritated the fuck out of me. Time to throw up a smoke screen. "If by 'okay,' you mean mildly annoyed by the paparazzi circus game I've had to play, then I'm just dandy."

Her dark brows came down, and she took a step toward me. My cue to hop off my stool and leave. "I'm gonna turn in."

It was eight o'clock. In reality, I was going to go watch a movie or three in my room before nodding off in exhaustion. But for her benefit, I faked a big ol' yawn. After this stint with Keely, I'd be ready to make a run for an Oscar.

She nodded, then went to the cabinet, grabbed a glass, and filled it full of ice water from the fridge. "I've got some reading to do myself."

I clenched my jaw and refrained from replying. Any reply would be an attempt to strike up a conversation, and doing that was not compatible with my goal of avoiding her. So I kept my mouth shut.

She turned and left the kitchen ahead of me, but I was on her heels. Her hand swept down to flick off the light switch. The room was cast into darkness.

And without a thought, the breath caught and froze in my lungs, and my head spun. Without fully realizing what I was doing, I clamped my hand around her wrist. She gasped, turning to me and spilling water from her glass, sloshing it onto the floor.

"What the fuck are you doing?" I ground out between clenched teeth before flinging her hand away and turning the light back on before the darkness could take hold.

She froze in place, staring at me wide-eyed and visibly swallowing. That heartbeat—

click, click, click—came fast.

I'd scared her.

Well. *Good.*

She blinked, staring at me. "I, ah, turned off the light."

"And what was the rule?"

She frowned, something changing in the quality of her gaze. Moving around me, she grabbed a wad of paper towels and stooped to mop up the mess on the floor. She didn't look up when she finally talked. "You told me to leave everything as I found it—"

"That means the lights too."

"Yeah, you gave me that example at the time. I…forgot." She straightened, dumping the wet paper into the trash and taking up her now half-empty glass. She filled it again, and I waited by the light switch while she walked around me and out into the hall toward her room. Before I could turn the opposite way to head toward the stairs, she stopped me.

"Uh, do you mind if I ask what's up with the lights?"

I turned my back on her. "Yes, I mind. Keep them how you found them."

They'd turn off automatically according to the timer—long after I was holed up in my room and wouldn't be coming down again until the morning. But her flicking them off meant they wouldn't come on tomorrow night, and I couldn't have that. Everything had been set up perfectly according to my routine. And I wasn't about to have her mess it up.

She was already messing up enough shit as it was.

CHAPTER TWELVE
GRAY

A FTER A ROLLER COASTER WEEKEND OF PHOTO OPS, A fake dinner date, and one astronaut hissy fit, we were ready to hit the runway on our way to Houston for the Make-A-Wish Foundation event.

Getting out of the town car at the private airfield near LAX, I scratched at the scab on my palm where my stitches had been. Ryan had dutifully removed them on Sunday during one of the rare instances I'd seen him all weekend. He'd said maybe ten words during that entire conversation.

Since his blowup over the kitchen light switch on Friday night, he avoided me the entire day Saturday by working out for hours in his gym, swimming in the pool and walking in the canyon. A very active day. On Sunday afternoon, he'd hung out with his astro-buddies until it was time to get ready for his dinner date with Keely, which he—thankfully—showed up to completely sober.

I'd made sure not to touch a single light switch, to the extreme of leaving my bathroom light on all night as well. I'd puzzled over the intensity of his reaction, and of course, I'd documented it in my notes. Obviously, my flipping the light switch was a trigger—but for what, exactly, I didn't quite know. Neither did I know what exactly the trigger was.

Did he not like the darkness? Or did he dislike not having control over the lighting in his home? Was it a PTSD issue?

Well, that was a dumb question. Obviously, it was. But I didn't know enough yet to make an assessment about how serious it was or what exactly it was. I'd noted it, reserved my judgment and tried not to do anything else that would push him any further away than he'd kept himself for the rest of the weekend.

I boarded XVenture's private jet behind Ryan, Keely, her assistant Sharon, and the Russian cosmonaut, Kirill Stonov. Our flight time to Houston would be just under three hours.

Watching Ryan's back as we climbed the steps into the plane, I wondered about how this trip might be affecting him. There was a good chance that going back to NASA's most important center within a month of being sent packing was awkward for him. He showed no inkling of it. Then again, he was an expert at veiling his inner thoughts and emotions.

Not unusual in astronauts. They played everything so close to the vest due to the highly competitive nature of getting flight assignments. One of the most famous stories involved celebrated test pilot, Colonel Chuck Yeager. He broke the sound barrier in his experimental plane within hours of cracking his ribs during a horseback ride. He'd neglected to divulge that little detail to his flight surgeon before the life-risking flight.

I was familiar with this mentality, having had the opportunity to study many hopeful astronauts during my graduate program. Fully experienced astronauts with their gold wings were exponentially guiltier of this same mind-set. Never show a weakness. *Ever.*

Ty was greeted enthusiastically by the private jet's flight crew, pumping his hand with wide smiles and fawning over him. They asked for autographs, selfies, and offered him a tour of the cockpit.

None of them could have any inkling their hero was hiding some seriously dark, deep suffering.

But I did. And he was so damn afraid of me right now, that I'd figure it out, he could barely look at me.

I could feel the animosity sloughing off him in waves.

***

Hours later, our cars rolled to a stop at the VIP drop-off at Johnson Space Center in Houston. NASA had allowed us entrance away from the prying eyes of the hundreds of tourists who regularly visited.

Exiting the car, we were hit by a wall of summer humidity that was so unlike the dry heat of Southern California. My clothes stuck to me during the short walk from the driveway to the door.

Despite Ryan's recent dismissal from NASA, they had allowed this event to take place for the sake of a sick boy's wish. Our group was met by a tall and thin NASA outreach representative and vice director of public relations. He pumped Ryan's hand, a grin on his lips. "Ty, welcome back! We miss you around here."

"Thanks, Ron," Ryan intoned flatly and then proceeded to introduce the rest of us before disappearing into a nearby locker room. When he emerged, he was magnificent in the dark blue flight suit of a NASA astronaut, complete with his name stitched in over the left breast pocket and flight patches on the front and sleeves.

Blank-faced, he led us to a predetermined meeting place. The photographer had Ryan and Keely pose in front of a few displays for shots to release to the Associated Press and news blogs.

Keely snuggled to his side, and he slung an arm around her hips. For the hundredth time, I admired how amazing they looked together. And how weird it made me feel inside to notice it. Though I tried not to examine that feeling too closely, even as she leaned up and whispered something in his ear, kissed his cheek, laughed at something he said. Ryan seemed affected, smiling back at her as he made her laugh, adjusting his hand on her back.

Something gripped me then, with barbed claws and razor-sharp fangs sinking into my chest. An ugly, heated feeling that made me feel like I might combust.

Jealousy. But not simply a pang. Oh no. This was a full-on flaming-eyed monster that wanted to rip itself out of my chest, Alien-style, and spit acid everywhere. I took a deep breath and made myself look away until the pictures were done.

Ryan wasn't mine, and I had no right to be jealous. This weird reaction was purely irrational and emotion-based. I blew out a breath. *There.* Nothing like psychobabble to cool my jets. *Emotional intelligence for the win.*

The Make-A-Wish Foundation Ambassador appeared with the young family of the sick boy. Ryan asked Keely and the rest of us to stand back and allow the family to be photographed with him.

Francisco Martinez, about six or seven years old, had recently finished chemotherapy. He was adorable—and far from frail. His black hair was thin, but growing back, and he had the most heart-melting, bucktoothed smile.

Looking at him, I couldn't help but think about my own hopes with Make-A-Wish when I was a child. I'd been desperate to be chosen, having decided, like Francisco, to meet an astronaut—though in my case, it was to meet Dr. Sally Ride.

But that chance had never come for me. Dad had convinced me to turn it down. He'd given me two reasons—one, we were too privileged to take the chance away from another child who didn't have the resources our family had, and, two, I wasn't sick enough to think about something like final wishes.

I was sick—*very* sick—but Dad had refused to acknowledge that. He'd told me that accepting a wish would be like giving up. Like putting a knife through his heart. And after he'd said that, how could I go through with it?

So I hadn't, even though I'd cried about it when he wasn't around. And he never knew.

I clenched my jaw and reminded myself to be present in the now and not lost in the past. Besides, watching Francisco and Ryan together was magical and made it easy to forget old hurts.

The boy gazed up at his hero with wide eyes. Then he snapped to attention, offering him a salute. In response, Ty sank to one knee in front of the child, holding up a hand. "Give me a high five, Francisco. I heard you made it through your last round of chemotherapy with flying colors."

Francisco's parents shared a look. His mom smiled and said something encouraging to her son in Spanish. The boy enthusiastically slapped Ryan's hand. "My dad said if I can do that, I can do anything, like go to Mars someday. Do you think I can do that, Commander Ty? Can I be an astronaut and go to Mars even though I've been sick?"

Ryan grinned wide "You should never give up on your dream, Francisco." His gaze flicked toward our group, meeting mine before he turned back to the boy.

"I have a friend who was sick when she was little, and she told me she never gave up on her dream. And you shouldn't give up on yours. In fact, going through everything you have proves that you're strong—and a fighter."

I blinked, listening to his words, remembering our conversation in the little pub in Long Beach when I'd told him I'd refused to give up and decided to work with astronauts when it became apparent I'd never be able to become one.

He'd had a look in his eyes then—an admiration.

I swallowed a lump in my throat and fought prickling tears as Francisco's smile widened at this new hope given to him. He hopped up on his toes and gave Ryan another high five, and I tried my hardest not to blubber like an idiot.

Ryan stood and took Francisco's hand, and they moved toward the full-scale model of the Harmony node of the ISS, where the crew living quarters were located.

"We're going to need a lot of new astronauts in about twenty years. By then, you will have concentrated on getting better and staying healthy. And spending a lot of time getting good grades. That's super important if you want to be an astronaut. You have to study a lot."

He led us all through the module, and we got to explore. I had been here once before—years ago—but I was thrilled to be back nonetheless. Some were fascinated by the tools velcroed to the workbench, others were trying to figure out the exercise equipment.

Me? I'd shut myself inside the tiny phone-booth-sized crew sleeping quarters where the astronauts slept standing up and strapped to the wall because of weightlessness.

Francisco was continuing his conversation with Ryan. I could hear it right outside the door. He seemed determined to reject Ryan's plea to study and do well in school.

The boy's tone was downright skeptical. "Do *you* study every day?"

"I have to take care of myself, both my mind and my body. If I don't, then I don't get to fly. And flying is the most important thing in the world to me."

"Hmm. That doesn't sound as interesting as having fun. Don't you drive cars real fast and fly your fighter plane?"

I tried hard not to giggle at Francisco's questions. *Don't forget to mention guzzling vodka and punching out flat-earthers,* I felt like prompting. I put a hand over my mouth to muffle the giggles.

Ryan's voice came from right on the other side of the canvas wall from me. "I have fun too. But not too much fun."

"I think you should have more fun. Being an astronaut is hard work."

Oh, believe me, kid, he has plenty of fun. Too much fun. My other hand went over the first when my laughter couldn't be held in.

Abruptly the cloth "door" to my little cubby was ripped aside. Ryan and Francisco both peered inside at me.

Ryan's mouth quirked. "I can't have too much fun, or else I get in trouble with Ms. Barrett here."

I rolled my eyes at Ryan and was rewarded with a cheeky smile from him.

"Are you his boss?" Francisco asked, squeezing by me to look inside the crew quarters as I made my way out. I looked shyly up at Ryan before glancing away.

When I would have returned the cheek and said *yes*, Ryan answered for me. "No, definitely not my boss. More like...my babysitter."

Now I scowled at Ryan, and his grin grew exponentially.

"Your *babysitter?*" Francisco said, turning back to look at me while Ryan velcroed him inside the sleeping bag that held him to the wall. "You're too old to need a babysitter. Only kids like me do."

Ryan straightened and turned back to me, still amused. "See? Even Francisco thinks I'm too old to have a babysitter."

With my hands on my hips, I muttered quietly so the boy couldn't hear me. "That's because Francisco doesn't play Slam the Headboard with his 'trainer.'"

Oh, how satisfying it was to see the cheeky smirk melt off his face. I turned and exited the module with the rest of the group.

Next, I made straight toward my favorite display—the one that let visitors touch a moon rock. I shoved my hand in and ran my fingers over the smooth surface of a polished cross-section, lost in thought until I saw the boots standing beside me.

"Your babysitter likes the moon rock," Francisco said.

I straightened, blushing, and pulled my hand out.

"Your turn, Francisco," I said with a smile and made a wide berth around the astronaut, proud I hadn't looked up into his face, and thus, his mocking smile was wasted. That time, at least.

By this time, our group attracted the attention of other visitors to the Space Center. A crowd formed near the astronaut as people held up their phones and took pictures of Ryan, calling out to him. But both the NASA rep and the Make-A-Wish ambassador were keeping the crowd at bay.

As it was, Ryan ended up staying almost a full hour after the tour ended to sign autographs, not refusing anyone when he very well could have.

I blinked back an unexpected sting in my eyes when, upon saying goodbye, Francisco broke ranks from his parents on the way to the car to run back and give Ryan a big hug.

"I will never forget this day. This is the happiest day of my life, Commander Ty." Ryan wrapped his arms around the boy's thin shoulders.

"You'll have many more happy days, Francisco. And after you go to Mars, I will ask for *your* autograph, okay?"

"Anything for you!" He snapped off a salute and ran back to his parents' sides, talking eight-hundred miles a minute while Ryan watched them go, his face unreadable.

He'd never shown any indication that he disliked or was uncomfortable with all the hero worship. I'd seen firsthand how he was constantly subjected to it.

But what was all of it doing to him, deep inside?

Maybe someday I'd have the courage to ask him. Provided that didn't qualify as "shrink talk."

We'd be returning home early the next day. But Ryan had requested the evening to attend a small get-together with a few friends here in Houston. And surprisingly, we were all invited. He mentioned the advantages of being seen with Keely enjoying some Houston nightlife, but I suspected a deeper reason.

Maybe we were there to act as a cushion. There could be no other reason for Ryan to want us along with him. We were there to protect him against anything emotionally untoward. I doubted anyone else had perceived that as the reason, but I sure had. I'd probably have to ask Ryan about it at some point. If I ever got the chance to talk to him alone, that was.

At our hotel, I took a long nap, then showered off the Texan summer humidity and dressed for the evening.

On my way to the elevator, I ran into Keely in the hallway, her hair still in curlers, holding a diet soda from the vending machine. "I'm not sure why I'm bothering with all this." She waved at the curlers. "The humidity here is insane."

I laughed. My hair had a special kind of unique curl here, too. And it was big. If it were any longer, it would look like eighties hair.

Her eyes slid over me. I was wearing dressy black jeans, a nice button-up blouse, and my Doc Martens. "You're going to the thingy tonight, right? You have to go. I need you there."

I nodded. "I'll be there. Was headed down to the lobby a little early."

She frowned at me. "Don't you have a dress?"

I shrugged. "Not with me, no." I didn't add that I maybe owned two dresses, if that, hanging, almost never-worn in the back of my closet at home.

Her brows arched. "A skirt?"

I shook my head again.

"Girl! I know everyone's got their personal style, but get your butt in here. We can dress this up." She hooked her hand around my upper arm, and I let her pull me into the two-bedroom suite she was sharing with her assistant.

"Sharon where is that maxi dress you kept insisting I bring? Gray, how tall are you?"

"Five eight. Look, I—"

"Perfect! We are the same height." She turned and gazed at me again. "A maxi dress with those Doc Martens might look kinda cute. Grunge retro."

Sharon was expressing her doubts, but Keely interrupted her. "Just tell me where the dress is."

When she pulled it out of the closet, I knew it was a hard pass—strappy with a scooped neckline. I mentally grasped for excuses. "I don't have a bra that will go with that."

Keely glanced at me for a moment, but she held the hanger up to me, letting the dress drape down my front. She pointed to a nearby mirror. "Look at that color on you. Dusty rose. Perfect with your complexion. No matter how much of a tomboy, a girl's gotta try a dress every once in a while, you know?"

I frowned at myself in the mirror. I'd loved wearing these casual sorts of dresses once. But nowadays, they made me feel too...exposed. I didn't like to stand out.

Flying under the radar—*that* was my style.

"Options. Go without a bra. You could totally manage that." When I gazed at her sharply, she shrugged. "Sorry."

I nodded. She was right, after all. It wasn't unknown for me to opt out of wearing a bra when the occasion called for it. "Or you could wear this pretty blouse you already have on over the dress so it's more like a maxi skirt."

I frowned.

"Come on, Gray." She wiggled the hanger in front of me. "Go change in the bathroom. You know you want to." I bit my lip and tried to keep myself from smiling when she got into my face with a wide grin on hers. "You'll look gorgeous."

I sighed and did as she asked. Not sure if I was more frustrated by her makeover instinct or the fact that she was so cute and charming I couldn't even hate her for how she'd inevitably capture Ryan's eye.

I slipped on the dress. The length was perfect, but the dress hung loosely on me. It was still flattering, tucking in around my hips before flaring out in attractive folds around my legs. Of course, my scar was in full view.

But I did as she suggested and put the blouse on top. Buttoning it up part of the way, I was thankful to see the scar remained hidden underneath.

I studied myself in the mirror from several angles, liking the effect. I felt...pretty, feminine. And I'd applied some makeup, so my complexion looked great next to the color. Well, I'd be damned.

No doubt Pari would faint dead away if I walked into XVenture like this. I made a mental note to send her a selfie for shock value.

Sharon was putting the finishing touches on Keely's blowout at the vanity when I exited the bathroom. The two of them looked me over when she shut off the hair dryer. Keely nodded, smiling. "Sharon, did you end up packing those rhinestone flip-flops of mine? Those would look great with that dress."

"You were going to wear them tonight, I thought."

Keely shook her head. "No way, Ty is tall. I need to wear my heels. Besides, they will look way cuter on Gray with that dress." She beamed up at Sharon, who rolled her eyes.

Keely slipped into the bathroom and came out minutes later asking me to zip her up. She wore a gorgeous formfitting pale-blue silk minidress that came down above mid-thigh. Unsurprisingly, she was glamorous and stunning. Sharon handed her a box of jewelry, and she poked her earrings into her ears.

Though wearing her maxi dress had made me feel feminine and romantic, I now felt shabby beside her. My shoulders slumped, and she immediately tsked me, bringing her hands up to cup them, now several inches taller than me in her heels. "Shoulders up and back. Stand up straight. Oop, let's do up one more button!" Her gaze met mine, her smile only faltering a little. I assumed she'd seen the scar. Then she turned that grin on full blast. "Gotta show off that pretty dress to the best angle. Make sure our Starman notices you."

"You're the one he needs to notice."

She shook her head. "Only for the cameras. You're the one he looks at when he thinks no one is watching him."

My face burned bright red. Wow. She had a vivid imagination, didn't she? I frowned, shaking my head. "Um, no way."

Her eyes crinkled as she laughed. "Gray, stop making me laugh so much. I'm going to ruin my mascara! Now...admit it. You've got yourself a little crush."

I glanced at her assistant, who was paying no attention to us as she tidied up the vanity.

I bit my lip. Had it been so obvious? Had I been mooning over Ryan without even realizing it? But what about my emotional intelligence? Why hadn't that allowed me to hide what I was thinking?

And crap, did *everyone* know? Did *Ryan* know?

Keely was now searching around for her clutch, which Sharon dug out of the rumpled bedspread. Then, after looking at the time, Keely ushered me out of the suite, and we walked to the elevator.

She smiled at me when she bent to press the button, picking up our conversation right where it had left off. "I like you a lot." She beamed amiably. "I think you should be in my squad."

I laughed. "Not sure I'm the squad type."

She shrugged. "We can talk about it later. Right now, back to the subject. It is completely understandable that you would have a thing for the astro-bae. So don't feel self-conscious about that. Ty is smoking hot. Who doesn't have a crush on him? I'd do him in a second if I had the chance."

I blinked, nauseated at the thought of having to listen to her and Ryan bang the headboard against the wall in his house.

"I suppose that would be good for your public romance if you did," I said in the tiniest of voices.

She grinned. "He's not interested. I've tried a couple times. He's...preoccupied."

I looked away. "I can't imagine it's been easy for him to come back to Houston."

She shrugged, checking the clasp on her bracelet. "I have no idea about any of that. I was mostly referring to the fact that he's preoccupied with you. And I think you should go for it."

I stared at her, wide-eyed.

"Stop blushing, Gray. You look like a teen virgin."

I sputtered in response, and she laughed, bending to press the elevator button again. "I'm so going to make this happen. But be warned, I've got my eye on that hot-as-hell Russian friend of his, and I may be hanging a sock over the doorknob tonight if you know what I mean."

My eyes widened. "Jesus."

"I have a feeling he's going to have me saying that a few dozen times too." She winked as we stepped in and the doors closed.

Down in the lobby, we met up with the others. Naturally, my eyes gravitated to Ryan—like they always did, despite my brain chastising me for the action. It didn't matter. It was like they had a mind of their own. And damn, he was gorgeous in dark brown chinos and a button-up blue shirt. It matched the deep azure color of his eyes and managed to emphasize his powerful physique underneath the clothing. His short dark hair was combed back as if having come straight from the shower.

Stealing my breath. He was a virtual thief when it came to my breathing. In truth, constantly guilty of making me forget to draw the next one. Like he himself was the vacuum of space.

Maybe I needed to don a spacesuit to protect myself from him.

His gaze met mine, then slid slowly down my body, apparently taking the surprising wardrobe choice in stride. When his eyes returned to my face, my skin warmed thinking about Keely's revelation about how much he looked at me, *when he thinks no one else is looking.*

The air felt thick, riddled with tension. I yanked my eyes away and tried to think of something else—as if mentally donning that suit of protection.

I was feeling vulnerable and shaky tonight, twisting and turning in reaction to Keely's revelation.

A hired driver opened doors for the four of us, and we filed into the SUV. Keely shoved me toward the back door, and in my haze and without realizing it, I ended up sandwiched in between Ryan and Keely. I guess that was what she meant by *making this happen.*

Subtle, she was not.

And though it was a wide car and there was plenty of room for the three of us to sit back there, Keely inexplicably "needed space." She scooted as far over as she could get away with, pushing me up against Ryan and his amazing smell.

I turned and scowled at her, but she jerked her head away, keying something into her phone intently before holding it up to her face and angling it to include us.

"Smile for a selfie!" she sang.

"Sorry," I murmured to Ryan for invading his personal space.

"You're okay," he muttered back, his posture seeming to relax against me.

I swallowed, my heart racing with its ubiquitous clicking. My cotton-clad thigh pressed against his muscular, iron-hard one, and through the material of his trousers, I could feel the warmth of his body.

He bounced his knee up and down, and then the pressure increased as if he was doubling down on the close quarters. He turned his head to me and breathed in deeply.

Which reminded me. I could smell those sexy alpha-man pheromones. Man of Action scent. We rode in tense silence, the scenery of Houston melting away on both sides of the car. I stared straight ahead, my fingernails digging into my palms.

I forced myself not to think about how amazing it felt to be pressed up against a stunningly attractive man who kissed like freaking Casanova. *Don't go there, Gray. Don't even think of that kiss right now.*

Holy cripes. I had a feeling this fifteen-minute car ride was going to last a whole lot longer. Or maybe I was merely hoping that.

CHAPTER THIRTEEN
RYAN

I HAD TO ADMIT, I MORE THAN ENJOYED THE CAR RIDE TO the restaurant with Gray's slight body pressed against mine. There definitely should have been enough room for the three of us in the back seat of that car. We didn't have to push up so close to each other, but I didn't care. Kirill had peered back at us from his front seat—the bastard. He'd grinned and muttered quietly to me in Russian when he noticed the same thing. "Cozy."

Gray looked more fetching than ever tonight, much younger than even her twenty-five years. She wore a white sleeveless blouse and a long dusty-pink skirt that floated around her ankles when she walked, giving a peek of glittery sandals underneath.

And in the back of that car, I'd taken advantage of the situation and got my share of that strawberry scent of hers. The only thing it made me want was more—more feeling her body against mine, more heavenly smell. Even more of the rushed clicking of her unique heartbeat.

That teasing I'd dished out to her today at the Center with the kid? That was nothing to what she was in for tonight. Getting out of the car, I held the door for her and Keely, trying to suppress a wicked grin of anticipation.

But as we entered the restaurant, it didn't take long to see that things were not going to go as I had anticipated. My first clue was the sign at the entrance indicating that the bar and accompanying section of the restaurant were closed down for a "Private Party."

And I'd hoped, though I knew better, that my group of half-dozen close friends had not morphed into a horde of folks from NASA. That happened all too often, and I should have known better. Once word got out, gatherings like this grew like strings of particles in a chemical chain reaction. Houston was a big town, but the smaller NASA community in Clear Lake and the surrounds was close-knit.

I stopped and stared at the sign, overwhelmed by the urge to turn around and blow Dodge. Kirill's shoulder nudged mine, and I looked up. His expression was somber as he nodded to me then moved into the restaurant. "Let me go see what that's all about."

The women stood on each side of me, Keely's eyes scanning the room. Gray took Kirill's place beside me, her eyes on my tense shoulders before flicking up to meet my gaze. "How can I help?"

Not, how's it going. Not, is there anything wrong. No.

She'd perceived those things immediately in the half minute I'd had to react to this new development. Putting her hand on my upper arm, she narrowed her eyes and I tensed. *I've got your back*, she'd said, and I'd been so quick to blow her off.

I'd been skeptical, of course. Like she didn't even understand, fully, what it meant to have my back. The most astonishing thing about her statement was the way I'd responded. With hope that she meant it. That she'd be around long enough to. But I still didn't know yet.

I clenched my jaw.

"Should we step outside?" she asked.

I shook my head, my gaze flying back to where Kirill had disappeared. I'd stand here until he returned to fill me in.

An impromptu get-together of the local NASA community—astronauts, control directors, and other support personnel to the astronaut office—wasn't unexpected. And shouldn't be dreaded. It was just…

Facing my past. Facing the reality that I hadn't fully admitted I'd run from.

In California, at that safe distance, it was easy to forget. It was easy to imagine Xander still alive back in Texas living with his family. It was easy not to notice his gaping absence from all our lives.

Here. Not so much.

The subject of Xander would come up in our conversations tonight. We'd laugh and reminisce. We'd toast him, for sure. It was unavoidable—and deservedly so. I would never ask anyone to forget Xander. But he would be here, like a ghost, haunting the back of every sympathetic look, weighing down every sad smile, every hushed memory—even the happy ones which people would repeat to try to make each other laugh.

And God, I wasn't ready for this.

Kirill came back and filled me in—yes, the restaurant was sectioned off for us, and there were a lot of familiar faces. "Come, Ty." He nodded toward the bar and lifted his hand to flick his throat with his middle finger—a Russian gesture indicating alcohol was in our near future.

Great minds thought alike. I followed him toward the bar. I had to properly numb myself with alcohol to get through the night. Or maybe indulge in some raucous sex with a willing and lovely participant. Depending on how shitty this evening went down, I'd have to avail myself of comfort by any means possible.

The lights were low, but every surface glowed with the reflections of the silver and red neon lights in the brushed nickel that covered the bar, the tables, the chairs. This was the futuristic—and somewhat cheesy—décor of one of Houston's several space-themed hangouts—The Gantry.

Loud music with a pounding dance beat came from a live band in the other room. The smells of beer, barbecued beef and tangy bacon assailed my senses.

Once the four of us hit the bar area, every eye in the place gravitated to us. Kirill filed off to the side to slap hands with a couple of our compatriots. And he called upon his well-known talent for procuring a shot of vodka whenever he wanted one. Russians and their unique skills.

I picked up oohs and aahs over Keely, who gravitated to my side and flirtatiously hung on my arm. People were talking about her latest movie, how beautiful she was in person, how much of a lucky bastard I was. Without a doubt, Keely would get pestered for her autograph. Better her than me for a change.

"Ty!" a familiar voice called behind me. I spun to face my former commander, Thor Mickelson, from my first mission on station.

I shook his hand heartily as his grin grew, and he offered me a bottle of beer. I introduced him to Keely, and he did his usual awkward sort of nerd flirting we'd often teased him about. Thor tended to get tongue-tied around pretty girls, which was amusing since he had no trouble attracting them with his tall and fair Norse looks.

Kirill appeared at my other side, and I nudged him. "Did you know this thing would get so big?" I asked in Russian. The other astronauts would probably understand us to one degree or another, but aside from Kirill, I spoke the best Russian of the crew, hands down.

"No idea," Kirill answered. "I didn't even think you had this many friends in NASA."

"Fuck you," I answered. We laughed. He pushed a shot glass in front of me and asked the bartender to fill it with vodka.

I took a shivering breath, my body aching with tension. When the shot appeared, I snatched it up, gripping that little glass like my lifeline. I'd only have to tighten my grip a little to turn my knuckles white.

"Commander Ty, it's an honor," the young bartender said when he recognized me. "First one's on the house, sir."

I gave him a tight smile. "Thank you."

Turning to Kirill, I clinked my glass to his. "*Poyekhali!*" Russians had thousands of different ways to toast, depending on the occasion. But for this night, I chose the famous words of the first man in space, Yuri Gagarin, right before being launched into orbit. *Let's go!*

Kirill and I drank in unison and slammed our glasses down. Before I could get a refill, however, there was a nudge at my elbow. I expected it to be Keely, so I turned to ask her what she wanted to drink.

Instead, the woman standing there was much shorter. With long dark hair gleaming over her shoulder like a shining curtain. My entrails froze. *Karen.*

Oh fuck.

"Ty," she said with a tremulous smile on her lips, her doe eyes wide. She was a lovely woman. And as always, I knew exactly what Xander had seen in her.

She'd cut her hair and looked a lot thinner than the last time I'd seen her—at the memorial six months before. That usual mischievous gleam in her eyes—the hint of one of the sharpest tongues I'd ever come in contact with—was gone. Now, they only reflected sadness. Seeing it was like a punch to my gut.

I swallowed hard, and to cover my utter shock, I took her in a gentle hug and kissed her cheek, like old times. As if I hadn't been blowing off her emails and texts for the past six months.

"Heya, KareBear." The nickname was my joke from our college days. She'd always hated it, and I had no idea why it jumped out of my mouth at this particular moment.

Maybe deep down, I did want to offend her so we wouldn't have to have the confrontation I knew was sure to come. My chest tightened so much it was hard to draw the next breath. She stepped back and gazed up at me again, the hurt in her dark eyes stabbing at me like twin daggers.

"We missed you," she said simply. "They have Internet and phones in California still, right?"

It felt as if things around us were moving in slow motion— colors blurring, sounds fading into silence. Eyes were on us from all directions. I swear I felt so much like I was in a fishbowl that I was about to grow gills and start breathing water. I'd certainly welcome the fins so I could swim away. And God knew it was getting harder and harder to breathe by the minute.

I cleared my throat. "I got real busy. Kirill will tell you—we've been working like *sobaki*." I raised my hand to the bartender. "What are you drinking, Kare?"

She flicked a baleful glance at my shot, which had now been refilled, then looked up at me in that way that always made me feel like a chastened schoolboy. "I'm not thirsty."

"Hey!" Another hand landed on my shoulder, a blur of blond hair appearing. Whoever it was, I was about to embrace him or her as my savior from this awkward situation. I jerked my head toward the newcomer.

Gray. The babysitter. Well, she had said she'd have my back. And in this case, she was proving that very thing. The relief almost washed over me like a powerful ocean wave. She'd break the tension of this moment. She had a talent for that.

Her hand squeezed my shoulder in an unusual gesture. "Everything going good here?"

I blinked, and she threw a pointed look at Karen. So I did what was expected and introduced them. "Gray Barrett, this is my good friend Karen Freed. Karen, Gray is my, uh..."

"Personal supervisor," Gray interjected quickly—too quickly. She'd already spent some time thinking that one up. If I weren't feeling so crappy and anxious to scramble away from this meeting, I'd laugh at the irony of it.

Karen's eyes flicked to Gray, but she didn't smile. "Nice to meet you, Gray." Then she turned back to me. "Ty—"

"You know," Gray interrupted again. "I bet you two would love to get caught up in private. There's a little room at the back with only a few tables in it. It's a section they've closed up for the night. You'd have privacy there."

I blinked at Gray. Throwing Karen and me together in a room alone when I was trying to avoid the hell out of her? That's not what having my back meant.

I opened my mouth to protest when Karen chimed in with her enthusiastic acceptance of Gray's invitation. "Yes. Can we do that please, Ty?"

I clenched my jaw, then relaxed it. "Sure. Let's go."

I pushed the second shot toward Kirill. "Call me in fifteen minutes," I told him in Russian. "If I don't answer, call again." He barely nodded, didn't even look at me. "And would you buy Keely a drink for me?"

This time, he did look at me. "That would be my pleasure."

I turned back to Gray. "Lead the way, *personal supervisor.*" We locked gazes, and I added a heated glare to leave her in no doubt of my feelings about her intervention. *I'll deal with you later, little Miss Buttinsky.*

She tore her eyes away and walked in front of us toward the back of the restaurant. Karen didn't appear to see the people who were trying to wave at her and catch her attention, her eyes fixed on Gray's back. Damn, she was upset with me. I rubbed my jaw, wishing I'd downed that second shot before we'd left the bar.

I so did not want to do this. Not here. Not now. There wasn't even an optimal time or place I could think of, to be honest. But what choice did I have? My *personal supervisor* had intruded, sure, but could I have possibly blown off Xander's widow in person, although I really wanted to?

I exhaled a long breath. Didn't matter what I wanted.

One thing I'd learned from my years within the disciplined military structure—take what was coming to you. Accept it and don't avoid it. *Adapt. Improvise. Overcome.* One of the many mottos used in the teams.

This meeting was long overdue.

I'd had to kill people at point-blank range—sometimes with my bare hands. I'd had to face the cold vacuum of space with only the thin layers of a vehicle or suit for protection. But now, a slightly built woman of barely five feet tall was causing me to shake in my boots. It was ridiculous, really.

I pulled out the metal chair for her, and she sank gingerly into it. I took a seat across from her at a now empty table. Gray waited for a moment. "Can I get either of you anything?" When we shook our heads, she vanished.

Karen produced her phone and began swiping through photos. She stopped and showed me a set. "AJ's birthday party. We were hoping you'd call."

She held up the picture for me to see, and I glanced at it, unable to stare at it for very long. AJ in all of his adorable, toothless glory, grinning at the camera in front of a cake with six candles alit. I was nauseated, and my eyeballs felt like they were starting to sweat.

I missed him...so much.

I coughed into my fist.

"Did he get my present? I hope he liked it. I bet he's rocking that new big-boy bike."

She didn't answer, instead yanking the phone back from me, searching for another picture. "His first day of school this year." This one, I could barely look at. Instead of a grin, he looked very serious, his hazel eyes—*Xander's* eyes—staring out at me from a child's innocent face. His hair was slicked down, and he wore a perfectly pressed school uniform, carrying an *Avengers* lunchbox. That lump in my throat grew exponentially. I fidgeted in my seat.

Karen laid the phone on the table, and it clicked off, mercifully. "Last year, for kindergarten, he was so sad because his dad couldn't be there. Remember? And you always filled in when Xander was away for work. When I told him you were both going to be in space at the same time, I think it broke his heart. Because then 'Uncle Ty' couldn't fill in for his dad."

I rubbed the bridge of my nose with my thumb and forefinger, awash with shame. Guilt. You name it, I was feeling them all. Spin the Wheel of Torture and whatever it landed on, that's what I was feeling.

God forgive me.

"Karen..." I began in a shaky voice, not even sure where I was headed.

She leaned forward, laying her arms across the table, palms up in supplication. "We *need* you, Ty. AJ. Me. You haven't been there for us."

I promised I'd watch over his wife and child.

I blinked. "I-I've tried my hardest. I've sent—"

She shook her head and made a sharp cutting gesture with the blade of her hand. "Can you honestly say that? You've tried your *hardest?* And I don't care about your money. Guilt money."

I sucked in a breath, sat back, and stared at her. So the gloves had come off and so quickly too. Well, Karen never was one for holding back on her honest opinions so I shouldn't be surprised, but goddamn, this was hurting more than I had even suspected it would.

"What the hell is going on in your head? You're out there trashing your life and forgetting about the people who care about you—whom you love. Unless you never cared for us at all. You lost your best friend, I get it. But you didn't have to lose his entire family—who was like *your* family—unless you actively choose to do so. And yet, that's how you keep choosing."

My jaw was clenched so tightly my head began to ache. *Fuck.*
Just hold it together, Tyler. I couldn't lose it. I couldn't unleash on
Xander's widow, no matter how low the blows, no matter how
much she was pissing me off. I fought for a breath, marveling at
how much tighter things felt in my chest.

"I do care about you and AJ. I love you both. And I promised
Xander—I promised him that I'd take care of you."

Her eyes snapped to mine. "For God's sake, stop burdening
yourself with that obligation. Whatever Xander asked of you
when he was minutes from dying wasn't fair of him to ask."

I swallowed a huge lump in my throat. How could we talk
about fair? If life were fair, Xander would be here right now,
sitting at this table instead of me.

My fist clenched. "I'm very serious about that promise, Karen.
You can't give me 'permission' to let it go."

Her face flushed and her features hardened. "We don't need
the money or gifts sent from over a thousand miles away. We
need your presence in our lives. You can't take care of us. You
can barely take care of yourself. Drinking. Womanizing. Getting
violent and hitting people. The motorcycle accident and the
trashed hotel room—"

I rubbed my forehead, more ashamed than I had ever been in
the past year for my irresponsible behavior. The hero who
couldn't even be heroic for his dead best friend's son.

Pain blossomed deep inside my head. "I-I'm not in a good
place right now."

She let out a tight breath of exasperation. "Well, no fucking
duh. You were fired from NASA. There's a lawsuit from some
flat-earth nutjob who keeps talking to every news outlet in town

that will have him. It doesn't have to be like this. Come back here and stay. We can all heal together."

I buried my face in my hands, resting my elbows on the table to support my head.

"Ty." She reached out and wrapped her hand around my forearm.

I pulled back and dropped my arms. "I can't. I have no future here, Karen. You know that as well as I do."

She frowned. "Burned bridges can always be repaired and rebuilt. One incident with one jerk harassing you—or even your lapses in judgment over the past year—are all your grief. The world has watched us all grieve—very publicly. It's time for us to take our lives back and not live for the public anymore. And NASA will forgive."

Obviously, she believed like everyone else, like NASA wanted everyone to believe—that I'd been let go because I'd drunkenly punched an asshole.

If she only knew…

But she had no idea about the real reason NASA had sent me packing. No one did. It was my burden to bear alone.

I shook my head, unable to reject her ideas in words. It hurt too much to talk to her, to speak about her loss. To know that I was to blame, ultimately, for it all.

"Kare—"

She slammed her hand down. "Don't shake your head. It *is* possible. For God's sake, stop it with this guilty burden you insist on carrying around. Xander died doing what he loved. It wasn't your fault. Stop acting like it is." Her face flushed scarlet, her breath quickening. Much as I wanted to, I didn't look away. I owed her that much, to acknowledge her words.

She spoke in ignorance of the truth, and she was a grieving widow.

And I had to find a way to overcome this and be there for her. My feelings weren't important in the face of hers. But how could I fake it when inside, it honestly felt like I was falling apart?

She shook her head, now fighting tears. "I want you back in our lives, Ty. Come back to us."

I hesitated, trying to choose my words wisely. No more promises I couldn't keep. I was already breaking the ones I'd made to her dying husband. "I'll try my best. I'll see what I can do."

She stared at me as if I'd spoken Russian to her. "That's all you have to say after I poured my heart out to you and begged?" She scowled and stood up, shocking me. I sat back and held her accusing gaze, swallowing more lumps in my throat. She threw down a 3x5 card on the table between us. "Get help, Ty. You need it."

She turned and walked into the hallway toward the front of the restaurant, wiping her cheeks with the back of her hand. I buried my own face in my hands the moment she disappeared. *Fuck. Fuck. Fuck.*

That had gone about as well as I thought it would—or *remarkably well*, considering the circumstances. I wondered what Xander would say if he were here right now, sitting where his widow had been, watching me with an accusation in his eyes.

Why are you alive when I am not? When I had so much more to live for than you did?

I flipped over the card Karen had tossed down on the table before storming off. It was AJ's school picture. He was smiling but with sad eyes. His father's eyes.

My stomach bottomed out, and I could not tolerate the emptiness a second longer. I needed alcohol to numb this pain. *Immediately.*

I kissed that photo before tucking it into my wallet, then I wandered back inside. Without seeking out either fake girlfriend or former friends with sympathetic ears, I made straight for the bar, knowing the crowd would soon form around me.

It always did.

CHAPTER FOURTEEN
GRAY

T HIS SIDE OF THE RESTAURANT MAY HAVE BEEN crowded with NASA personnel, but the ladies' room was deserted, and I took full advantage of this quiet place to gather my thoughts and slowly wash my hands after using the toilet. It had been ten minutes since I'd led Ryan and Karen Freed to that quiet corner in the back to have their chat.

Having recognized her the instant she'd entered the space, I'd witnessed her immediate approach to Ryan. I'd taken it upon myself to facilitate something between them that wouldn't be so publicly awkward, as I suspected it might. And one glance at Ryan's face the minute he'd turned and seen her there had been enough to tell me my hunch was right.

And yes, the man had made it more than clear with his heated glares and the rest of his body language that he was furious with me. I'd deal with that when I had to. But I liked to think I'd helped him avoid an uncomfortable incident, and maybe—just maybe—he'd come around and appreciate that.

Well, I could always dream, right?

I'd been watching him closely as he drank at the bar with Kirill, and when Karen had approached him, I recognized her instantly from the plethora of interviews and the one documentary I'd watched about the accident. She'd been a frequent interview subject.

Ryan's usually stoic demeanor had immediately radiated intense stress. So I'd jumped into action.

After drying my hands, I pulled out my phone to check and see if he'd replied to my text yet. My green bubble was the last thing on our conversation stream. *Are you ok?*

I couldn't even tell if he'd seen it yet. He was probably still deep in conversation. I was tucking the phone back into my pocket when someone else burst through the door and headed straight for the farthest toilet stall in the row.

Karen Freed. Well, that hadn't taken long. In fact, less than fifteen minutes. There were obvious tears on her face, and her cheeks were streaked with mascara. She promptly shut herself into a stall and let out some muffled sobs, as if weeping into her hands.

For a moment, I stood frozen, watching myself in the mirror as I figured out what to do. I could leave her alone and go look for Ryan.

Or I could do what I'd been trained to do and at least offer some help. Some small comfort, maybe, where I could. And though I was concerned that their encounter had obviously ended unpleasantly, I knew I couldn't just walk out of here to find Ryan.

My eyes gravitated to the tissue box on the marble counter of the bathroom. I snatched it up and walked over to her stall. "Um. Hey. I have tissues...so you don't have to use that crappy TP."

I slid the box under the stall door, and there was a long hesitation before she picked it up. After a moment—and a nose blow—she thanked me quietly.

"Are you... Is there anything I can do to help you? Anything you need?"

Another long pause. "No."

"Okay." I cleared my throat before slowly stepping back, unsure how to proceed. "Did, uh, did Ryan go back to the bar after you two...talked?"

There was a definite pause. "Thank you for that, by the way. He probably wouldn't have left the bar to talk to me if you hadn't suggested it." Her voice seemed stronger, as if she was no longer crying.

"Please, don't mention it." And because it was getting weird talking to her through the stall door, I stepped away. "I'm going to go see if I can find where he wandered off to."

I turned to go but stopped when I heard the latch being undone. She opened the door to the stall and stared at me.

I frowned, wishing I had pockets to stuff my hands into. "Are you sure there's nothing I can do to help you out?"

She stepped toward the trash can and discarded a wad of used tissue, putting the box back on the counter. "Actually, there is something."

I waited.

"Can you keep an eye on him?"

I almost—*almost*—laughed at the irony of her asking me to do that. Had I not introduced myself to her as his personal supervisor? From the expression on his face, he'd loved that one.

I nodded. "Absolutely."

"He's..." She shook her head. "We used to be good friends. Close friends. I have no idea what's going on with him these days. I watch the TV and read the horrible stuff in the tabloids like everyone else." Her voice choked up, and she grabbed a fresh batch of tissues.

Instead of interjecting or protesting, I nodded. This was far from a counseling session, but I'd learned long ago that if a person wanted to talk, the best thing you could do was *listen.*

"He's taken on a lot of the blame for what happened, you know? I'm just—I'm worried about him."

I approached her slowly. "I am working with Commander Tyler now. He's pulling it together. I know it doesn't seem like it now, but we're still at the very beginning. He's very motivated to fly again. He'll do whatever it takes." I smiled. "But if you want, we could stay in touch. I'll give you my phone number. You can text or call me whenever you want to know how he is. I'll have to respect his privacy, of course, but I'm glad to put your mind at ease if you need it."

I held up my phone, and she took it, dialing her own number so that we'd have each other's info. Then she handed it back to me and went to the mirror to tidy up her face.

"Thank you. I don't know what we would do if we lost him too." She dabbed at her eyes with a tissue. "I mean, he doesn't come to see us anymore, but I worry. We were like family." She turned on the faucet to splash some water on her face, then dabbed at it again with a paper towel.

"He was never like this before—the partying, the women, the fighting. And all that drinking." She frowned. "All the stuff I see in the tabloids."

"A lot of that is exaggerated." I thought about saying more, but it was a tricky area, to respect his privacy—and I didn't want to lie to her. Hadn't I told him to his face that his life was a shitshow?

I put a hand on Karen's shoulder. "And you? Are you getting the help you need?"

She looked at me with guarded eyes. "I get lots of support. Lots of attention. And I'm right here in my support network. I never left. My family's here. Xander's family is here. NASA has been amazing to us. And all our friends, I—" She swallowed hard, and her eyes filled with tears.

"I'm sure Ty will come around, and you'll see him as much as you always did. Time."

She dabbed at her eyes. "I'm selfish. I want him now. I want him for my son. It's like I lost both my husband *and* Ty."

I nodded. "Give him time."

When I went to step back, she reached out and grabbed my hand. "Thank you, Gray. Thank you."

Back in the restaurant and against my own better taste and judgment, I positioned myself at the corner of the bar, where it bent in an L-shape. It was the perfect vantage point from which to observe the astronaut hero who was already well on his way to getting hammered.

He still hadn't answered my text, but in addition to that one, I sent another. *Please watch what you are doing before I sic Keely on you and have you dragged away from the bar.*

A minute later, he pulled his phone out of his shirt pocket, glanced at it then looked up, scanning the room as if looking for me. When we made eye contact, part of his mouth quirked up before he very deliberately shoved the phone back into his pocket without dignifying my message with a reply. Not even with the middle-finger emoji, which I was half expecting.

I scanned the room to find out where Keely had vanished to. Both she and Kirill were conspicuously missing from the goings-on at the bar, and I began to suspect she'd already swooped in for the kill as she'd promised to do.

Ryan continued to drink with a dozen of his best friends all around him, egging him on. As he pounded vodka shots, I was attempting to devise a plan. It would probably have to involve some Russian muscle if I could track Kirill down. Someone would have to drag him out of here soon, and I'd have to get strategic about his removal.

Someone plopped into the seat next to me and leaned over.

"Hi," he shouted so I could hear above the general barroom din.

"Hey there." He looked like an average guy in his early forties, fit, with a face I vaguely recognized, as if I'd seen it before on the NASA website. Another astronaut, most likely.

"I'm Strom Bogart." He held out his hand for a shake. I hesitated then shook his hand. I definitely recognized the name, one of NASA's thirty-nine active astronauts.

He smiled and I leaned back. Was he hitting on me? I didn't have a lot of experience in this area because I was seldom in situations where random unknown people—or anyone, really— hit on me. But if he was trying to pick me up, it seemed kind of a stiff and awkward approach.

Although, who was I to judge awkward?

"My name is Gray." I left off my family name, blushing as I remembered Ryan's accusation. *Is that a thing? So people don't figure out who Daddy is?* I flicked a glance at the man of the hour. He was now sipping at a beer bottle—probably taking a breather in between more vodka shots—watching me talk to his former coworker. A cluster of women had now gathered around him.

"I haven't seen you around here," he said. "But I recently got back from Russia myself. Star City. Been training on the backup crew for the ISS."

"Ah, you're an astronaut," I said, stating what I already knew. What the heck else was I going to say? It's not like he asked any deep, probing questions or even tried to charm me. His sole approach, it seemed, was based on the fact that he was an astronaut. Admittedly, that did carry with it a certain wow factor.

I imagined he rarely had to do much else in your average bar. Since the dawn of the program with the Mercury 7, astronauts were notorious for womanizing—even the ones with families.

I picked up my phone and sent Kirill a quick text. *You around? Ty is getting a little rambunctious.* Hopefully, he understood what rambunctious meant. His English was good, but that was not a common word. I bit my lip. Maybe I should have used an easier word?

Strom Bogart captured my phone hand in one of his. "What are you drinking, Gray? Let me pick it up for you."

"Uh..." I pointedly pulled my hand away from his startling grasp. Then I glanced at my phone. No answer.

"They've got all kinds of fun cocktails here. Pink—like your pretty dress. How about a cosmo?"

I blinked. If I let this guy buy me a drink, I'd be stuck here for far longer than I cared to be. I scooted off the barstool. "I think I'm going to—"

"She's not thirsty," Ryan slurred from the other side of me. I jerked my head around. He'd appeared there like a stealthy ninja. Ninja astronaut hero. Wow, there was no end to this man's talents.

"Good to see you, Ty!" Strom stood and held his hand out for a shake.

"Keep your hand to yourself, Bogart."

Strom dropped his hand, and the two exchanged a look that was chock-full of heated animosity. I had to wonder, if these two had a history, why was Strom even here tonight at a function obviously honoring Ryan?

Ryan stood at my side, his shoulders stiff, a hand clenched. And he was quite obviously *not* sober. Ryan towered over the shorter man who did not seem to want to back down.

Instead, Strom turned back to me. "So, I was saying. Something pink?" He turned to the bartender. "A cosmo for the lady, please. And whatever's on tap for me."

"Does your wife know you're here buying drinks for other women?" Ryan asked. How the hell had he gotten so far gone in the half hour since I'd been in the bathroom talking to Karen Freed?

Strom threw Ryan a disgusted look. "Don't be a prick. You know I got divorced. Or maybe you don't since you were too busy living in your own little world."

"Nobody cares," Ryan answered. The bartender placed the martini in front of me, and Ryan pushed it over toward Bogart. "She's not drinking your fucking pink drink."

When his hand drew back, it clenched into a fist, the veins in his forearms bulging. *Uh oh.* I clamped my hand around his wrist. "Ryan."

"Jesus, Tyler. Calm the fuck down. Didn't you come in here with that actress? Who is this? Your sister? Or maybe the third in your ménage?"

I scooted away from my barstool at the same time Ryan leaped forward and grabbed Strom's shirt.

But I was there, pushing between them. I looked up into Ryan's irate face. This was all we needed, another violent incident for the tabloids. "Ryan. Back off."

He ignored me, tightening his hand in the other man's shirt. Strom reached up and shoved Ryan's shoulder. "Back the fuck off. Let the woman decide if she'd rather hang out with a real astronaut or a has-been who will never fly again."

I put my hands on Ryan's solid pecs as his face clouded. Everyone at the other end of the bar froze, watching. But no one stepped in to offer help. They might as well have been eating popcorn.

I shoved Ryan as hard as I could. It didn't get me very far. "Ryan! I'm not going to step away, and you'll have to go through me if you want to hurt him."

He looked at me *finally.* "Move, Gray."

I shook my head fiercely. "Nope. If you go after him, you have to take me too." He opened his mouth to reply hotly when I added. "Or...I can take you back to the hotel."

He hesitated but didn't move. Finally, Strom succeeded in freeing his shirt from Ryan's grasp while Ryan stared him down. The other man backed off. "You've lost your mind, Tyler," he muttered as he disappeared with a dismissive gesture.

Did I imagine it or did a few of the spectators at the other end of the bar exchange money? Shit, they were betting on the outcome? When the phones started coming out to take pictures and video, I gently turned him away from them.

He was still stiff and solid as a brick wall. I had to think fast. Maybe playing the damsel in distress would help.

"Ryan? That, um, that was stressful for me. Can we... Can you take me back to the hotel?"

He turned back to look at me, frowning as if confused. He was clearly tanked. I scanned the bar again for Kirill and found nothing. Putting my hand on Ryan's thick biceps, I nudged to guide him away from the bar. "Can you please get me back to the hotel? I need your help."

He blinked. "Yeah."

"Let's go. Come on. Help me to the car?"

As soon as we were out of sight of the bar, I steered us toward the front doors. "Gray..." he breathed.

I glanced up through the glass doors that led to the parking lot. Some people loitered there—one of them with a ginormous camera around his neck. "Reporters," he slurred. "That's Jack." He nodded to the man standing next to the photographer. "He stalks me everywhere in Houston. Someone must have told him I was in town."

"Crap, we can't go out that way. Stand here." I patted the wall, coaxing him to stay put. Then I texted the driver to meet us around the back.

Despite the recent almost-altercation with Strom Bogart, he watched me with a doting smile. "You're really cute when you're bossy."

I waved over the hostess at the stand, asking her for a discreet way to get us out the back while avoiding the bar.

After a long, appreciative look at Ryan, she nodded and led us through the kitchen. I looped my arm around his to keep him from bolting or straying in case he decided to get mischievous. He still had a goofy smile on his face.

Of course, members of the kitchen staff, under the bright lights, called out to Ryan, "Commander Ty! Hey Ty, how's it going?" We dodged shiny metal bowls and large wire racks on wheels, making it through the small storage area and into the alley where the SUV was waiting for us.

Thank God.

"Come on. Let's go," I muttered, reaching out to open the door, but he pushed my hand away.

"Let me." He fumbled with it a few times, but I waited patiently. As long as he thought he was helping me out, he'd be much more malleable and much less resistant to the idea of going home.

I jumped into the back seat of the car and held out my hand for him. "Come on."

He shook his head. "No. I need to stay and drink some more."

Oh *no*. "Ryan, I need your help. I'm upset." It leaped out of my mouth out of sheer desperation. "Don't make me go back to the hotel by myself."

He blinked, wavered, but, miraculously, entered the car and sat down beside me. I told the driver to take us to the hotel. As I was going to sit back, Ryan put an arm around my shoulders and looked into my face. "Are you okay? I will kill that fucker with my bare hands if he touched you."

"I'm okay, thank you. He didn't touch me."

"Only because he didn't have time to. That bastard is a pushy creep with women."

"Thanks for looking out for me, then. And for making sure I get to the hotel okay." And to punctuate my diatribe lest he be onto me, I rested my head on his shoulder.

He was tense—as stiff and as hard as that brick wall I'd compared him to earlier. He turned his head and very obviously inhaled the scent of my hair. His body relaxed against mine, and he fell back into his seat while muttering under his breath, "*Mmm. Strawberries.*"

With everything in me, I tried not to think of the tingles that ran down my spine, my arm, everywhere that his body pressed against mine.

And God, I *really* didn't want him to puke on me.

Thankfully, there were no reporters waiting in the hotel parking lot a few short miles away. We made our way to his room, which was down the hallway from mine, a fair distance from the elevator. I'd make sure he got in okay before leaving him to sleep it off.

That was the plan, at least.

"I need something else to drink. Does this hotel have a bar?" he muttered as we stepped out of the elevator.

"You've had enough to drink, Ryan. You're going to be sick as a dog tomorrow."

He shrugged. "I don't get hungover. It's my superpower. Strong Ukrainian genes."

"I don't think it works like that." My mouth thinned. "*And* that's not the greatest superpower a person could have."

"It's great if you want to drink."

He fumbled with his keycard, waving it the wrong side against the keypad. I held out my hand. "Want me to do it?"

He pulled away from me. "I think I'm going to go down to the bar."

"It's closed," I lied, snatching the card from his hand and opening the door with it. "Come on. Let's sit in your room and talk."

That seemed to appease him. We entered the room, which looked like a smaller version of Keely's suite. But unlike her rooms, these were completely spotless. Housekeeping had been in for the evening turn-down service, complete with a foil-wrapped chocolate on the white counterpane. But otherwise, there were no personal effects anywhere to be seen. The room was pristine and untouched.

Before I even realized what he was doing, Ryan was unbuttoning his shirt and pulling it off. *Holy cripes!*

Oh—undershirt. White undershirt. Thank God he was still covered. And I tore my eyes away once they caught glimpse of how the sleeves of his shirt hugged his biceps, how the torso molded to his very well-developed physique.

Look away, Gray. He's not for you. Not for you.

But damn did I ever hate that voice of reason inside my head right now, because I wanted to look. He was beautiful beyond words.

"You like chocolate?" he asked, plucking the candy off the bed and seeming more sober than he had been.

"Who doesn't?"

He shrugged, plunking it down on the nightstand. "I don't."

I snorted. "You going to tell me you prefer freeze-dried astronaut ice cream?"

He laughed, sinking down to sit on the bed. "That's not a thing. We don't eat that shit. And no, we don't drink Tang either."

I smiled. I knew all that, but hey, it was something light-hearted to break the tension.

"There's a minibar in here somewhere, right? They've at least got those little tiny bottles of cheap vodka." His blue eyes scanned the room, but he didn't move.

"Hmm. I think coffee would be better for you right now. How about something to eat?" I went over to the dresser and picked up the menu. "I can order something from room service. Did you even eat before you pounded all those shots down?"

He rubbed his forehead with thumb and forefinger in tiny circles directly above his eyes. "You never eat after the first toast. It's custom."

"Hmm, sounds like a quick way to get hammered."

"That's the idea."

I put down the menu, noticing the slight slump in his shoulders. Carefully, I came around the edge of the bed and sat beside him.

"You were particularly motivated to get wasted tonight."

He shrugged and didn't look at me.

"More so after your talk with Karen Freed."

That got his attention. He turned and peered at me through narrowed eyes. "I have you to thank for that."

My hands fidgeted, smoothing a slight wrinkle in the bedspread. "You mean to tell me you would have blown her off and turned your back on her? The only thing I did was offer you two some privacy from all the prying eyes."

He glared at me but didn't argue. That was it. No word, no change of expression in his face, nothing. That narrow-eyed gaze made my internal organs twerk.

"You're obviously in a lot of pain after your chat with her. Probably why you were seeking alcohol."

His eyes fluttered closed briefly, then open again.

Then, without warning, he was in my face, the smell of vodka imbuing my perception of everything around me. "You are violating my rules," he said with only the slightest slur to his words. "I specifically said no shrink talk."

His face was inches from mine, and he didn't back off after saying what he had to say. I pulled my head back but stopped, coming up against an unexpected barrier—his hand. He'd raised it to cup around the back of my neck, preventing me from pulling away. His gorgeous face was as close as ever. Those blue, blue eyes starting to cast a spell.

My innards went from twerk mode to melt mode in ten seconds flat, my throat so tight I couldn't even swallow. Underneath that vodka smell, I could catch hints of the seashells and salt, a faint breath of sage from his aftershave. The room around us jerked and then jolted to a stop.

My eyes fluttered closed. "I-I was making conversation," I said faintly, though any idiot could hear the lie on my lips, the tremble in my voice.

There was a shift in weight on the bed. Why had I sat here instead of on a nearby chair? Why had I gravitated to his side like this? And now, why was I letting him move closer, so that our faces were an inch apart? His hot breath caressed my mouth and my breathing seized—as if willing him to breathe for the both of us. So close now, I could feel his body warmth on my skin.

So close I couldn't even think of a reply. He'd caught me red-handed.

"I'm willing to forgive that violation of the rules, provided…"

My eyes cracked open. Oh God, his blue eyes stared down into mine. "Provided?"

"I'll answer those questions, Gray. But I get something in return for each and every one of them."

Clouds and fog and...I could barely hear him over the thready beating of my heart. Click, click, clickety, click.

He heard it too, the corner of that sexy mouth tugging up into a knowing smile. Confirmation of what he was doing to me with hardly any touch besides the one holding my head in place. Just his proximity. Just his words.

He knew. And *what* he knew pleased him so much that there was a very satisfied smile on his mouth when he proclaimed, "For every answer I give you, I get a kiss."

Oh God. *Oh God.* I knew I shouldn't be this weak. *But I was.*

My eyelids fell to half-mast, burdened under their own weight, too exhausted to fight the tension between us, too thrilled to acknowledge all the improprieties involved. For the thousandth time, I reminded myself that he was not my patient. And I was not his therapist.

Good thing, because he kissed like a god. And the twinge in my lips told me I wanted more of what he'd given me last week.

Against the voices screaming in my head to say *no.* To put a stop to this. Instead, very slightly, I nodded.

"Say yes, Gray."

My eyes flew open and locked on his. He didn't blink, didn't look away. Those eyes were laser-focused on mine.

One beat, two. *Click, click.* And then a breathy, "Yes." But when his face pressed closer, I turned to the side, narrowly escaping him. "But answers first."

More hot breath against my face. A sigh. Then his hand dropped from around my neck. "Fine. Yes, I deliberately got drunk as a result of talking to Karen."

"Why?"

His eyes narrowed. "That's another question. And I want that kiss *now*."

Damn it. I was so close to getting him to open up. So close to—

His hand was at the back of my head again, pressing me toward him, and his mouth sank to mine, firmly but tentatively. He let his warm lips linger there, but he did not open his mouth or attempt to open mine. My lips tingled under the pressure from his, though, and my spine felt like it was losing all structure, slowly liquifying as hot desire zinged from my lips down through my inner core.

It was embarrassing how quickly I was breathing when he pulled back from that simple kiss—nothing nearly as passionate as what we'd shared the week before. But that was because I suspected he *knew*—he knew there were more to come.

He knew that my intellectual curiosity saw this as a rare opportunity learning what made him tick. And my indisputable attraction to him—that didn't hurt, either.

He was scrutinizing my face again. From the way my skin burned, I was sure he noticed the deep flush in my cheeks.

"Your next question? And fair warning, I'm not going to make these come cheap. The more it costs me to answer your questions, the more it will cost you...in kisses."

I swallowed, attempting futilely to work moisture into my dry throat. Then I gave a slight nod. "Okay, then tell me..." My voice faltered and I took a deep breath, tried to calm the dizzying turn in my head. "Tell me why talking to Karen upset you so much that you had to go drink in order to numb yourself."

"Because I'm a hero and he is dead," he said in a voice as lifeless and as dry as moon dust.

"Because you *survived*—"

His eyes flicked away. "Yeah. I survived the only spacewalk to result in an astronaut or cosmonaut dying. *Ever*." He was wrapped up in his own world for a long moment. He shook his head. "Xander is the hero. I'm a failure. The man who failed to save his best friend's life. And yet, they all want to call me a hero. Ask me for interviews, autographs."

"And talking to Karen reminded you of that."

He grimaced. "I need no reminder of that. I know it. Every single goddamn day."

My heart twisted to think about the irony of his conundrum and how such a thing could play with his mind. *Failure is not an option*, the famous saying went. *Work the problem*. And yet, he hadn't been given the chance to do either of those.

He'd been ordered to return to the airlock so NASA wouldn't lose two astronauts instead of just the one.

I blinked back a sudden pang of sympathetic pain for him, but I tried very hard to keep the pity out of my face. Instead, I clasped his very solid arm. "I'm so sorry."

The arm beneath my hand tensed, and he pushed off the bed. "I'll be right back."

He went into the bathroom and shut the door. When he emerged a minute later, he washed his hands at the sink in the vanity area, splashing some water on his face before patting both his hands and his face dry with a white hotel towel.

My eyes ran down his tall form. He was looking more and more sober with each passing minute, but he still had a restless energy about him. When he emerged, his eyes gravitated toward the fridge across the room where the minibar was located. I should leave. I *knew* I should leave.

But if I left now, I was certain he'd start drinking again and make things worse. And how could I possibly leave this conversation when he was finally opening up to me?

I pushed my glasses up my nose. "How about room service?"

His eyes jerked back to me. "I'm not hungry." Then he approached the bed again, sinking to his previous spot beside me. "But I do believe we have some unfinished business."

He turned to me and reached up to gently remove my glasses, setting them on the nightstand next to the piece of chocolate. I blinked. Since my prescription was not a strong one, I was able to see fairly well without them. Nevertheless, it was always an adjustment when I took them off.

Then slowly, so slowly, he brought his hand to my chin, tilting my face up so he could get a closer look at me. He glanced from one of my eyes to the other, and I swallowed, holding my breath so that it was tight, almost painful in my chest. "You have beautiful green eyes."

I bet he said that to all the girls.

And that thought made me close them with a disheartened flutter. His thumb came up to run along my chin until I opened them again to see that his mouth was inches from mine—again.

"Gray."

"What?"

His mouth sank to meet mine, and just before, he whispered, "Don't panic."

This time was as sweet and thrilling as the first time we'd kissed in his front room the previous week. He tasted of vodka, of course, but also fresh and soapy—presumably from his aftershave. Cold and heat swirled together in my insides, jumbling every feeling and sensation.

But unlike last time, this one had something more—an added hint of...desperation? A hook of white-hot desire impaled me, searing me down to my core.

His free hand wrapped around my waist, pulling me against him. And when his tongue entered my mouth, it claimed me. That was the only word I could use to describe it. He unleashed that tongue like an intrepid explorer who wasn't looking back, plunging forward into new territory. Planting boots on the ground and staking an unequivocal claim.

I swallowed, stiffening at that realization, and he must have perceived it as hesitation because his hold on me tightened. He added the hand that had been holding my face into the mix, wrapping it around my shoulders, pressing our chests together.

It felt like nothing I could compare it to, like being pressed up against a warm, solid wall. A wall that also happened to smell very sexy.

His bottom lip aligned on mine, sealing my mouth to his. Our breath was coming quickly now. And things were escalating faster than I ever could have suspected. I gasped for air against his mouth, my heart rushing as I was lost and losing myself. Wandering a strange planet alone with no guidance, no knowledge of where I was going.

Just trusting Ryan to lead us there, and yet...

If I continued this, I'd be taking advantage of his drunkenness.

Because he probably would not have initiated his little game if he were sober. Not with me anyway. Who knew. When he woke up in the morning, perhaps he'd be cursing his beer goggles.

At that thought, I pulled away from him. Our heads separated, slowly, so slowly. I watched first his nose, then the fringe of his dark lashes. Pulling away gradually, both he and I, his handsome face took focus. Those blue, blue, wickedly blue eyes.

This man was pure sin and danger. And he knew it. And he'd known it the moment he had proposed the kiss. He was mocking me.

Unless…unless Keely was right about his interest in me. But the odds of that were much lower than the odds that he saw me as an easy bed partner to distract himself from his pain. That could be the only explanation as to why he was actively trying to seduce me.

But how to explain my becoming easy prey to his seduction?

Easy prey, indeed. I turned to him, inevitable given the way his eyes weighted me down. Our gazes clashed, and though I saw no mockery, no calculation, I knew it had to be there.

He shifted his head as if studying me from a different angle. "You know what is the sexiest thing about you?"

I tried to disguise my shock. It was like he'd been reading my mind. I snort-laughed. "That is the last word that should ever be used to describe me. There's absolutely nothing sexy about me—"

He cut me off with a fierce shake of his head. "You're wrong. So very wrong and that is the sexiest thing about you. That you don't know how sexy you are. You stand around and hope people won't notice you." He reached out and twirled a strand of my hair around his finger. "But I notice you, Gray. You're the first person I look for in the room."

I laughed as if I was finally on to him. But in reality, I didn't want to question why his words were making my heart soar. "Proof you really are drunk."

He moved in as if approaching me for another kiss, invading my space. "You don't get to do that. You don't get to tell me what I find irresistibly attractive and what I don't. You of all people should know that, Ms. Shrink."

I drew back and licked my lips but didn't reply, my eyes drifting away. His finger flicked forward, coming under my chin to redirect my gaze. "That scares you, doesn't it? To be noticed. It's *safer* when you're invisible." He said the word like it left a weird taste in his mouth.

I swallowed. "Maybe."

"And the questions…you like asking these questions because then nobody's asking you questions about yourself. When you're the one asking, it keeps you safe. Protected."

My eyes fluttered as I considered that. I'd never thought about it that way before, but he might have had a point there. I frowned—there was definitely some self-evaluation in my near future.

His face inched closer. "Does it scare you?" He repeated the question. "When I tell you that I see you—that I think you're sexy and worth noticing?"

Our eyes locked and my mouth opened, but the tightness in my throat prevented speech—seemed to prevent *breathing* for that matter. And the clicking. The endless clicking. It was so quiet in here that the only thing to disturb it was my rushed breath and my heartbeat.

Ryan tilted his head as he moved closer, his eyelids drooping. He was going to kiss me again.

I pulled back at the very last minute—though it took a ridiculous amount of willpower. "Don't I get a question and an answer first?"

His jaw tightened—almost in irritation—as if he'd hoped I'd forget about that little game. But I could not. Yes, I was enjoying his kisses, and it was a good thing to keep him distracted from the liquor cabinet. But getting him to open up was too valuable to me. And I wasn't going to back down while that rarely opened door was still ajar.

He sat back and ran a hand through his hair. "Okay." But there was caged impatience in his voice. He was humoring me. Until—until the next time.

That next kiss would be a costly one. I could see the tension building in his eyes. They were like mirrors—like shielding, reflecting only my own perceptions back at me. I looked deeply into them, trapped as if in a gravity well.

"Does the hero-worship make you hate yourself?"

He blinked, eyes listing to the side as if considering my words. That took all of two seconds. Then. "No."

His hands—both of them—were in my hair, my head being steered toward his. "Wait—"

But he didn't wait. Now he was more insistent about getting what he wanted. And apparently what he wanted was deep in the back of my mouth because he went there with insistence, persistence. Unmitigated confidence.

His mouth fastened onto mine, and he drew a deep inhalation through his nose, one hand knotting in my hair and the other on my back. But I couldn't tell whether he was holding me to him or holding on to me for support.

It didn't matter. The tone of this kiss changed into something rawer. More desperate. More *hungry.*

I pushed back, and his mouth left mine. I couldn't stop staring at the rise and fall of his chest, for he was clearly as turned on as I was.

"All that and all I get is a *no?*" I finally said after waiting for my own breath to calm down enough to keep me from embarrassing myself.

His blue eyes were cold and aflame at once. Ignited ice. As if the only thing he'd let me see was how much he wanted me, how much he wanted another kiss. "What more is there to say? I have scars. You don't live as long as I do—or how I do—without them."

I nodded. "Physical scars, yes, that's true. But also, emotional ones. The ones you won't acknowledge."

He tilted his head toward me slowly and curled his mouth seductively. He raised a finger and pointed to the middle of my chest. "I'm not the only one here who hides scars."

I shivered when his hand moved to the first button of my shirt. He eased it through the buttonhole, then watched me carefully as if waiting for me to stop him.

Instead, shivering inside, I nodded, giving him permission to proceed. He wanted to prove his point using my scar? Fine. Let him.

He had no idea that I was planning to flip that back on him in a way he wouldn't see coming.

With my shirt unbuttoned, my scar was now in full view under the revealing, low-cut neckline of Keely's maxi dress. An angry dark red slice into the pale skin of my chest.

"Do you-do you know about the parable of *Kintsugi*?" I asked.

He flicked a cautious gaze into my face and then stretched out onto the bed, leaning his head on his hand to prop it up. He looked up at me where I hadn't moved. "No. It sounds like a Japanese word, though."

I nodded. "It is. It's—" He patted the bed in front of him as if inviting me to lie down beside him and talk. With only a second's hesitation, I concluded this might be a less threatening way for us to have this discussion. There was a reason most psychologists' offices were decorated with the ubiquitous couch.

I faced him a little less than two feet away, mirroring his body language by propping my head on my arm. "Anyway, the parable talks about the *maki-e* technique in Japanese art. Broken ceramics or porcelain pieces are repaired by filling the cracks with pure gold dust mixed with lacquer. Instead of trying to hide the cracks, the art glorifies them as part of the item's history and richness."

A brow quirked. "Hmm. Interesting. You think I'm hiding my brokenness?"

I knew he was, but in spite of my previous bold honesty, I refrained from saying it outright. I chose a more indirect path instead. "I think your profession has encouraged that sort of behavior."

His face was curiously blank when he replied. "Why don't you live by that philosophy, then?" he asked, reaching out a long, thick finger to gently stroke my scar from where it appeared at my neckline up to the notch at my collarbone where it ended. Hot desire streaked through me even from that simple, light touch. My nipples tightened into painful, erect buds. "Why don't you think this makes you more beautiful?"

I tilted my head toward him, acknowledging his point. "I never said I was perfect, Ryan. We do, after all, live in a world that judges women by their physical perfections—or imperfections." I shrugged a shoulder. "We all have our issues."

His gaze narrowed as if to a sharpened point. "Some of us have more issues than others."

I never let my eyes leave his—even when it would have felt more comfortable to do so. "Some of us have been through a whole lot more than others."

"But this right here says you are a fighter. A survivor. That your heart is in the right place." His fingers lingered there again, this time not as accurate in his slow tracing. His knuckles grazed the side of my breast, and I caught my breath. That twinkle in his eyes told me it had been deliberate. His cocky smile said it all.

And those words...*you are a fighter, a survivor.* That same brief glint of admiration in his eyes from before. And when he'd told Francisco about his friend, he'd meant me. He'd said that going through everything proved I was strong—and a fighter. And now, as he said this, I realized he was serious. And he was so much more than all that pretty packaging I'd tried to warn myself off of. *So much more.*

I bit my bottom lip, thinking, and he smoothed it with his thumb again, smiling. "That lip is way too delicious for you to bite like that."

I swallowed, and he tilted his head as if to look at me from another angle. "Any more questions for me? I'm surprised you've given up so easily."

I laughed. "I haven't given up. I have a ton more questions for you."

And I wouldn't say it to his face, but I was damn near craving his next kiss. Like a dieter trying to justify that luscious dessert on a plate that was currently tempting them, I began to tell myself similar thoughts.

Instead of, *If I eat this, I'll work out a little longer or harder today.* In my case, it was, *Just a little kiss. But it's doing so much good. He's opening up to you.* And on it went, justifying caloric intake, the "just one hit" theory, and every other addict's nightmare.

But I was in no danger of growing addicted to his kisses, was I?

No. Definitely not.

I was strong, like steel. I was ice. *Solid ice.* I was compacted water molecules with virtually no vibration. I was solid and cold and...and... I looked away from that penetrating gaze. *Oh yes, Commander Tyler, you are a dangerous substance indeed and you could grow addictive.*

"I never ever thought I'd say this, but *please*, ask away, Dr. Gray."

I blinked, suddenly shy. This was getting real, and I had better make the questions worth it. *Worth it.* I almost laughed at myself. Like I was making some huge sacrifice here, to be kissed by a gorgeous, intense, hero of a man who was wanted by thousands.

But again, the door was open, and his offer had a very clear expiration date on it.

"Why did you get so angry when that guy at the bar said you'd never fly again? Especially when we both know he's wrong?"

He broke gazes with me and rolled onto his back, staring up at the ceiling for a moment. Then he slowly drew his lips into his mouth, as if wetting them. "Because he knows about the promise. It was spoken over the comm system—supposedly privately, but I have reason to believe it has since leaked out, at least internally at NASA."

I almost asked, *What promise?* But that was another question, and he'd call me on it. And I'd lose this opportunity to continue the conversation. So I did like any good therapist and I nodded and made a conciliatory noise, to indicate I was listening with great interest—which I *was*. And a nice big juicy prompt. "So he was taunting you."

Ryan continued to stare at the ceiling. "Bogart knew the importance of that threat to me. Xander made me promise I'd fly again. That I wouldn't let the accident stop me, no matter what the outcome."

I mulled that over for a moment. Wow, talk about laying a heavy charge at Ryan's feet during a horrendous time for both of them. But perhaps Xander's concern had been about giving Ryan something to live for instead of blaming himself.

"Are you flying for the right reasons, then? Because you want to and not because it's what Xander wanted?"

He rose up again, his face approaching mine. "Another question. And I never got my payment for the previous one."

My breath stuck in my throat. Ryan put a deliberate hand on my shoulder and nudged, pushing me flat on my back. The entire world did a loop-de-loop as he hovered over me, unmistaken desire in his eyes. Slowly, his head sank toward me and my mouth opened, ready to accept him when...

When he changed direction, and his mouth landed on my chest, slowly, hotly outlining the shape of my scar with his kisses. Erotic traces of his mouth across my sternum, my collarbone before bringing his face up to hover above mine. "You smell so good."

Click. Click. Clicky. Click. Click. My prosthetic valve was a traitor, exposing me, letting him know so clearly his effect on me. Of course, the fact that I could barely catch my breath had something to do with it too.

No one had touched me like this. *Ever.* And he seemed to be capitalizing on that fact—without even knowing it.

I had no illusions that I came across as experienced. To someone like Ryan, who had been with lots of women, I was certain my lack of skill was beyond obvious. But it hadn't seemed to deter him one bit. Quite the opposite—that flame behind his eyes appeared to burn hotter than before. Maybe even enough to melt the glacial blue ice there.

"Do you want to fly for yourself, or is it just because of what you promised Xander?" I asked, rephrasing my earlier question.

His dark brows trembled, but his mouth twitched up. "Ohh...that one. That's a very deep, probing question, Dr. Gray. I think I'm going to demand that I charge you up front for that answer. Are you willing to pay the price?"

I couldn't help it. I couldn't breathe. All I could do was lock gazes with him and nod wordlessly, unable to even fathom where he'd go next but all too willing to follow him there. *Far* too willing to follow him there.

Reason shouted at me from the back of my mind, told me this shouldn't go any further. But he did not tear his gaze away from my face when his hand went to the strap of my dress and gently scooted it off my shoulder, exposing my right breast.

I only barely suppressed a whimper as his dark head sank to envelop my nipple with his lips. My mouth dropped and my back arched up to him as he made hot contact, his tongue circling, his mouth closing in, sucking. Fire and bliss and tension all rolled into one.

My mind—even that voice at the back of it—blanked out, and all I could feel was Ryan's mouth on me, his hand closing over the other, still-covered breast. The deep, guttural growl in the base of his throat as I let out an involuntary moan. I was consumed, body and mind, by his touch.

White-hot fire bloomed in my chest, in my core, between my legs. I shivered under him, delirious and drunk for more.

I *needed* more. I needed him. *Everywhere.* He shifted his weight onto me, and our mouths were together again, my body writhing underneath him, as little under my control as my own thoughts and desire were in that moment.

Now he was whispering, his mouth pressed to my ear as he pushed against me. "Gray, I want to fuck you so bad right now. I need you."

I closed my eyes, thoughts swirling. Knowing I couldn't. I shouldn't.

But dear God, how I wanted to.

CHAPTER FIFTEEN
RYAN

S HE WAS EXQUISITE, THE TASTE AND THE FEEL OF HER slender body against mine intoxicated me quicker than alcohol entering my bloodstream. I nudged a knee between hers, opening them. My hand immediately gravitated to the dress hem—which was ankle-length, but with a couple tugs, I had the skirt bunched up above her knees. I brushed my hand against her soft thigh, and she sucked in a hiss between her teeth.

It was obvious she didn't get enough of this—or at least, hadn't got enough of it lately. Must have been a long time since the last man in her life had touched her. But she sure was enjoying it now. Enthusiastically so. And that was making it even hotter for me. My hard-on was painful, tight in my pants.

So I wouldn't be following the original plan to binge vodka and make an utter ass of myself at the bar. This was going to be a whole lot more fun. And if I was honest with myself, I'd been desperately wanting inside Gray's panties since the minute I'd kissed her in my living room the week before.

Her sweet sighs, the way she moved against me. She was making it goddamn hard to hold myself back. My hand scooted up her thigh under the skirt. I made sure to do it slowly, so she could stop if she wanted to. But I'd be fucking crushed if she stopped this now.

My mouth was on her neck, my hand and mouth moving in concert with each other as if in some complicated training maneuver, flying a T-38 Talon.

I had to be very careful. Because this was different. This wasn't like other times. *She* wasn't like the others.

Those tempting sighs as her fingers trailed through my hair, tightening to pull at the roots. The slight pain only inflamed me more. Those tiny catches of breath. One of my hands pressed against her back, and a tremor wavered through her body beneath the thin cotton of her dress.

Arousal surged, my body hardening even more in response to this new rush of lust. But I resisted rushing her the way my body was rushing me.

"I need to be inside you," I murmured into her mouth as I pressed my hard cock against her leg.

And that, apparently, was where I made my mistake. I felt it the second she stiffened, her hands sliding from my hair to press against my chest. As a last-ditch effort, I moved my hand higher on her thigh, to rest on the hot mound covered by her panties. But I didn't go diving in, allowing her time to process.

She shivered again, and I felt it rip through me too. I closed my eyes to savor the feeling, but before I could move my hand or do anything else, she turned her head away from mine and pushed against me. "This needs to stop, Ryan."

Fuck.

Her breath came fast, and I couldn't help but notice how gorgeous she looked when her face was flushed. I drew back, keeping my hands exactly where they were. Maybe she'd change her mind? *Yeah, keep hoping, idiot.*

With jerky movements, she reached down and locked her thin fingers around my wrist and pulled my hand away from her panties. Damn it. So close and yet so far. My cock ached. She was calm but very firm with her actions, leaving me in no doubt whatsoever. I drew back, pulling my other arm out from underneath her. She'd probably go on about how this was a mistake and should never happen between us. I was sure as fuck not going to acknowledge that.

It hadn't felt this right with a woman in a long time. Like I cared less about getting myself off and more about making her feel good. Of course, I always made sure a woman enjoyed herself in bed with me, but this was different.

Because it wasn't only about getting her off.

Maybe I was hoping that some of her goodness, some of that tenderness, would rub off on me for a short amount of time, like Tinker Bell's fairy dust. Like sprinkles of hope.

Hope. That was something I hadn't felt for a long time.

Gray slowly sat up and fixed the bodice of her dress to cover herself, then recommitted to that plan completely when she rebuttoned her blouse. I watched, blinking, trying to clear my head of the lustful thoughts running through them right now.

Her hair, more disheveled than ever, her face, flushed and pink. Her eyes, bright with arousal. She wasn't simply cute. She was fucking gorgeous—breathtaking.

And I wanted her without question.

I was supposed to respond, I guess, but I had no idea what the question was, so I sat up. Running a hand over my hair to smooth it down, I tried to forget how it felt to have her thread her fingers through it, scraping over my scalp, running tingles down my entire body with each one.

Stupidly, I held out hope that maybe she wasn't actually slamming on the brakes. She could want to talk about birth control or express her consent or some possible medical complication given her various health issues or who knew what. *Yeah, keep dreaming, chump.*

"Why are we doing this?" she finally asked with a shake of her head, that fine, unruly hair of hers puffing out at the sides, making me itch to run my fingers through the mass of waves and curls. I swallowed, my throat tight, every pulse point throbbing with need.

Yep, it looked like the brakes were officially being slammed. "Well, I thought that was obvious. I also thought it's what you wanted."

She looked away from me and reached over to the nightstand to grab her glasses and replace them on her nose. I might have liked to, but I was completely unable to rip my eyes away from her every movement. I watched her like a hungry tiger in the bush, stalking prey.

And she was watching me too. With equal intensity.

Then she shook her head, those innocent green eyes widening, her dark brows rising above the rims of her glasses. She looked sad or disappointed. Disappointed? In me?

Join the club, Gray, I wanted to say in response, but I kept my mouth shut. Forcing my gaze away, I let out a long sigh and willed my stupid body to calm the fuck down. A dark thought at the back of my head said I should have put the moves on one of those random women at the bar instead.

Maybe I'd enjoy that. But it wasn't what I wanted. What I *needed.*

What I needed was right in front of me, folding her arms over her less than ample chest, studying me and looking somewhat like a comic book character drawn with a lightbulb over her head.

"Why are you doing this?" she repeated.

I turned back to her, giving her my own unwavering scrutiny. "I want you."

She raised a brow. "Do you? Do you *really?*"

Enough with the fucking games. "Isn't it obvious? Now you're being ridiculous with the, *You couldn't possibly find me sexy.* I thought you were smarter than that."

Her mouth thinned and she stiffened. "That's not why I asked, but thank you."

"Why did you ask, then?"

"Because it's clear that you're using sex to numb yourself."

I drew back, blinking, ready to deny her assertion. But in the back of my mind, a voice yelled at me, calling me a hypocrite. She was right. I'd just been chastising myself for not finding someone who'd be more willing to go along with it for the ride. I clenched my jaw, scowling.

Her gaze dropped to the bed, and almost involuntarily, she blushed, biting her bottom lip. My breath stuttered, watching that mouth, the way she chewed her lip, the way it was clear her nipples were erect under the thin cotton of her dress. The way that dark, rosy pink nipple had tasted in my mouth, the gasp in the back of her throat, the arch in her back.

Christ. I closed my eyes and rubbed the knot in the top of my spine.

"I'm not going to be the scratch for your itch, Ryan."

I rolled my eyes to the ceiling. "Gee, when you put it that way, it sounds so appealing." My shoulders slumped, and I was now exhausted. The adrenaline of anticipated sex was quickly evaporating from my body, and all I wanted now was to feel the hot spray of a shower on my sore muscles. To lie down on a soft bed and sleep for hours in a quiet room.

But I didn't want to be alone—more particularly, I didn't want her to leave.

If she stayed here with me, I might have the courage to sleep through the night for once.

"I'm, uh, going to hit the shower." I stood from the bed, taking a step toward the bathroom. In response, she stood and took a step toward me.

"Ryan."

I stopped but didn't turn to her. "What?"

"I didn't mean to—are you mad? I didn't want to make you angry."

"Angry? No. Frustrated? Sure."

"But do you get why you want this? It's your instinct in response to what you're feeling from all that today. First, the push to get drunk, then the rush toward sex. You're trying to numb your pain."

I closed my eyes again. "I feel nothing. I *am* numb."

"That's not true. You're not letting yourself access those feelings. It's like a child when she burns herself on the stove. The next time she feels the heat, she pulls back—sometimes very far back. You were just in a room with your closest friends from the last decade—all but one. And his widow—"

"I'm fully aware. And yeah, it wasn't my favorite thing to do, but hell, if I can climb a fucking mountain on zero sleep and minimal food and water then—"

"No!" she rasped, quickly approaching me. "No, you can't compare those. Facing physical hardships has no bearing on how you'll handle something like this. Especially when you insist on carrying the heavy burden for it."

My shoulders slumped before I even realized what specifically she was saying. That tight feeling in my throat. I turned to her, and I could see them—tears pooling in the bottom of those big eyes, a tremble in that bottom lip.

Tears for me.

I watched, stupefied, as one tiny tear escaped the corner of her eye and traced a silent path down her cheek. Without even a thought, I reached a finger up and traced its path across her luminous skin.

She sniffed loudly and mirrored my action, placing a hand on my cheek. I squeezed my eyes shut, concentrating on every square centimeter of that skin in contact with mine, her warm palm molding to my jaw, my cheek.

"We both have a problem, then. I should admit I'm using sex to numb my pain, sure. You should admit that you are an attractive woman whom men desire."

I studied her face, her reaction. Her eyes were wide, and she swallowed before her gaze fell away from mine.

"Deal?" I asked, pushing the issue.

A faint laugh escaped her lips—an expulsion of a quick breath, not unlike that catch of breath that had so inflamed me when I'd kissed her. The memory of it struck a new spark in me, straight down to my gut.

"Deal," she agreed quietly.

I didn't get rejected, ever. But I had to admit this was incredibly arousing. I should get rejected more often. By her.

"Are you-are you going to be all right now if I go back to my room?"

I reached out and captured her wrist to prevent her from pulling away as she took a step back. "Please don't."

Her face clouded. "Nothing's happening between us, I thought—"

I shook my head. "Yeah, I know. You made that perfectly clear, but…" *Jesus.* It was hard to even ask the question, to even get it out without each word belting out more proof that I was a weak fool. Answering her questions earlier had been hard enough.

It was damn near fucking impossible to admit that I needed help from *anyone*, that I needed help from her. That I wanted more than anything to lie down on that bed and sleep undisturbed until morning.

"You want me to stay so we can talk?"

God, no. I sighed. "No. I…I want to go to sleep. I'm feeling exhausted."

Her dark brows creased together. "But you want me to stay while you sleep?"

My hand tightened around her wrist. "Please."

God, this was stupid. Why did I even want her here, and why was I begging her for it? If she stayed, there'd be all that much more danger of her discovering my pathetic secret.

"You want me to stay in here until you fall asleep?" she asked, her eyes widening like a child's.

I shook my head, almost wearily.

"You want me to leave?" I shook my head again. She frowned and then looked at the bed and back at me. "You want me to sleep here?"

I closed my eyes again, that pain growing in my chest. It almost felt as if I could burst into tears if I could ever manage to let the emotion out. Instead, it was a knot of sharp agony twisting inside me. But still, I knew I'd rather sever my own arm and abandon it by a roadside than ask for help.

"Nothing will happen," I said. "I'd rather not be alone." My voice died out.

Her brows came together, and she stepped forward with that precious gesture once again, touching my face with her delicate hand. "I'll stay. But no one should see."

Of course not. I was supposed to be having a very public affair with the amiable Keely, who was most likely getting her rocks off with her Russian one-night stand. I'd seen them leave the bar out the back right after my talk with Karen. If I knew my man Kirill, I was sure Keely would be a happy woman tomorrow.

I envied him his lack of damage.

Releasing a long breath, staring into those pristine green eyes, I felt broken. *Could you fix me, Gray Barrett? You said that wasn't your job. That it was mine. But why do I wish so much that you could?*

Her troubled expression cleared, and she appeared to go into problem-solving mode. "I'm gonna slip out to my room so I can brush my teeth and put on some yoga pants. But I'll be back. Why don't you take that shower?"

I walked over to the nightstand, grabbed the keycard, and handed it to her. She thanked me and went to the door then turned before she left. "You, uh, you don't sleep naked or anything, do you?"

I grinned—couldn't resist. "You have a problem with that?" Her brows shot up and she glared at me. I laughed. "Don't worry. I'll be decent."

She pressed her lips together as if suppressing a smile, and turned to leave. I chuckled to myself as I grabbed a pair of gym shorts and a fresh T-shirt from my luggage and went into the bathroom.

By the time I was finished, she was back in my room, sitting on the bed—clothed in gray yoga pants and a NASA T-shirt, one with the classic round logo—affectionately referred to as "the meatball" by insiders—and fuzzy pink socks. She'd also removed her glasses.

My body had not forgotten the promises of those earlier kisses and tastes of her, and even now, I was reminded of how delicious those breasts were under the thin T-shirt that was stretched over them. *Mouthwatering, as a matter of fact.* My eyes dropped, noting the way her pants clung to those long, shapely thighs.

That familiar pressure below the belt promised to embarrass me again very soon if I didn't get under the covers.

"What side do you like?" she asked, glancing at the bed, then pointed to the book and travel clock sitting there. "I assume this one since your stuff is on this nightstand."

"It doesn't matter to me." I shrugged. And it was true, I usually let my sex partners decide all that.

She pulled her feet off the floor, stretching out before rolling over to the far side, and I watched her, that reserved smile on her pretty face, the way she blushed in the dim light.

"I don't suppose you do this often, just sleep with a guy."

She frowned, hesitating, then patted my side of the bed. I lifted and slid in under the covers. It was a king-size bed, and thus, there were miles between us.

The thought of closing my eyes and opening them again to pitch-black made my blood run cold. Usually, even with a woman present, I kept the room illuminated, even if dimly. None of the women usually said anything. By the time we got to sleeping, she was too worn out to complain about the light being on.

But this was different. Not only had I *not* had a chance to wear her out in the most pleasant way possible, she was also smart as a whip and missed nothing. For the tenth time, I questioned my own sanity for asking her to stay here with me.

Once I was settled, she turned to me, and we stared at each other awkwardly. Then she smiled. I turned my head and stared up at the ceiling, before finally closing my eyes. "Good night."

"Night." she answered in a small, hesitant voice. "Are you—were you going to turn off the light?"

I didn't say anything, trying to ignore how my heart pounded at the pulse point in my throat, and I could feel it there, stealing my breath, my resolve. A trickle of fear entered into my awareness, and my thoughts drifted to that pure blackness on the far side, the dark planet stretched out miles below me as I gasped for breath in my breached suit.

Gray slowly sat up as if she sensed my unease, though I made every attempt to hide it. I was a fucking expert at hiding it. But she was no doubt remembering the incident a few days before when I'd nearly lost my shit at her for habitually flipping off the kitchen light.

My eyes fastened to the ceiling. I focused intently on bringing down my heart rate, taking long, deep breaths and expelling them in a measured way. I turned my head to her when she sat up, then scooted closer to me, looking down into my face.

"You okay? You're sweating."

"I'm fine."

She hesitated and then nodded. "So the light stays on?" Her voice was gentle, inquiring. Of course, she'd figure this out.

"Yes. And I don't want to answer any questions about it. I only want to sleep."

She blinked and nodded. "Okay." Though I could read a thousand questions in her eyes, she still hesitated. Gray had not ever been shy about asking the questions she wanted answered, but I'd already headed her off at the pass.

Instead of moving back to her side of the bed, however, she lay down right beside me. In the silence, I could hear the clicking of her heart valve—much slower and more measured than it had been before when I'd been riling her up.

I squeezed my eyes closed. God, I wanted to rile her up again. I wanted to bury myself in her heat and forget that every time I closed my eyes to try to sleep, all I could see was the blackest black, the emptiest of vacuums.

I realized that I was holding my breath when my chest felt tight. My fists clenched. My entrails cold as ice.

Cold as space. I was a lone, solitary figure fighting for my own life and for that of my best friend in the dark of space.

Her head came up again. "Breathe, Ryan. Stop holding your breath. You're going to make it worse."

I looked at her, head pressed to the pillow next to me. We locked gazes. She *knew.* Somehow, she did. She stared at me with unblinking eyes, then reached a hand out to smooth my face again, her soft hand rubbing loudly against my growth of whiskers.

"Don't let your mind wander. Just think about your breathing." I swallowed, noting that the sound of her voice wasn't unwelcome. It calmed me.

I let go of the pent-up breath, and it exploded from my chest like a pop. "I'm fine," I repeated after a desperate gulp of air. Even I could hear the lie in my own voice.

She turned toward me, pressing closer to my side, laying a hand lightly on my chest as if trying to check that I was still breathing. "Close your eyes, Ryan."

But every time I closed my eyes, I had to fight hard not to see what I always saw in the dark—the black panels of the ISS solar array against the stretch of faint stars. The panicked sound in my ear coming from Xander's frantic questions, the CAPCOM's equally frenzied responses. The warning alarms from the breach in my own suit.

"Use your SAFER, Xander," Noah was saying on the comms.

"I can't maneuver— Everything's frozen—"

I gasped again, wondering how I was going to make it back to the airlock before my own breach caused the suit to lose all pressure.

The clock was ticking. Would either of us survive?

"Ryan, you're here in Houston in a hotel room with me. You are safe."

Maybe I'd said something she could overhear or if she'd just inferred my terror. She placed additional pressure on my chest, resting her head against me. "Concentrate on the sound of my voice and on the pressure of my head on your chest... It could help."

Her head shifted, and I got a good whiff of her hair. She smelled feminine and strong. Mint, strawberries, the salt of sweat from the arousal my hands and mouth had stirred in her lithe body. She smelled of a country road in spring, and she felt like rain clouds and anticipation.

I turned my head, burying my nose in her hair, feeling a rush of something else—*comfort, longing*. I breathed her in deeply, feeling that tingle of awareness scatter through my chest, across my shoulders, down my legs to my toes.

Every molecule in my body was aware of her. Ready for her. Aching for her. I didn't move my arms, but I imagined touching her soft skin again. Fuck, I'd give anything to rest my hips between her open thighs, feel her underneath me.

Her hand reached out toward mine, and her fingers threaded through mine, tightening their hold. "I'm here with you. You are safe," she was repeating over and over again.

Home.

I pulled her close, that hollow ache inside intensifying. And then she did something that surprised me—she molded herself to my side, lifting a leg to interlock with one of mine.

I wanted to kiss her again.

Want was a weak word for what I was experiencing.

Crave. Desire. *Need.*

Damn. Was I starting to need? That was an alien experience for me. I'd never needed anyone.

But as my heart rate slowed and my nerves calmed, I concentrated on the gentle sound of her regular breath and that clocklike ticking of her heartbeat until it was clear that she was sleeping. I closed my eyes and let the darkness take me peacefully.

Chapter Sixteen
Gray

I AWOKE TO A TANGLE OF SHEETS AND LIMBS, WITH RYAN'S very solid arms wrapped around me. And I had to admit it was very hard to remove myself from that warm, secure place. This feeling of safety, calm wrapped tightly in his embrace made it near impossible to contemplate leaving that bed.

But the thought of being seen while I snuck from his room was enough to induce me to leave those very muscular arms. Without making a sound, I returned to my room as the sky was lightening with a predawn glow. With relief, I saw that the hall was empty, and thus, there was no one to misinterpret my two-hundred-meter journey as a walk of shame.

But it might as well have been. I couldn't stop thinking about the night before and how I'd let Ryan kiss me and touch me and make me feel so... How I'd allowed it all in the name of getting questions answered. Important questions, yes. But at what cost? My integrity?

The hotel offered breakfast in the lounge. I was the first one there, but others filed in quickly. And though I tried to prevent myself from doing it, I scanned the room constantly for Ryan's presence. But he hadn't shown up yet. Next to the coffee machine, Keely grabbed my arm. "How are you, Gray? Did you have a good time last night?"

I smiled, pondering a way to dodge her question while filling up my mug. The rich aroma of freshly brewed joe hit my nostrils. The smell of coffee alone could wake me up and get me going when I was still half asleep. This morning, with my jumbled thoughts and feelings, I particularly welcomed the magic of the bean.

"The dress was adorable. Thank you for the loan."

She smiled but thankfully did not push for details about last night. I couldn't help but notice how put-together she looked, even this early in the morning—full makeup, perfect hair blowout, complete with fresh curls. Not only that, she'd already signed a few autographs for the staff. Her lipstick was a pale, creamy taupe and perfectly applied to her beautiful full lips. I felt like a wilty daisy beside her.

"I think our Starman liked it too. He couldn't stop looking at you all night."

I shushed her, looking around to make sure no one would hear—especially Ryan himself. But he'd still not entered the room, and I wondered if I should text him to wake him up. Judging from the difficulty he'd had falling asleep, he probably needed the extra winks.

I cleared my throat and scrambled to change the subject. "Did you, uh, did you get home okay last night? I sent the driver back for you."

She smiled again. "I slipped out early with the Russian, and we caught an Uber. We had our own fun." Her eyes widened. "Oh my God, is that man talented. He's got some mad skills."

I blinked. "But no one saw you together, right?"

She laughed. "Girlfriend, I'm an expert at dodging paps when I need to."

"Thank goodness." I stirred my coffee. "I'm glad you had fun."

She glanced across the room over my shoulder then back to my face. "I think you and Ty need to have that kind of fun too." She waggled her finely shaped brows at me. She was like a dog with a bone over this.

I glared at her. "Please don't tell me he's right behind me. *Please.*"

She glanced over my shoulder again and waved. "Not *right* behind you. He can't tell we're talking about getting him laid. But I'm sure it would make him happy if he did hear."

My eyes bulged, and I shushed her, which only seemed to amuse her more.

Still, all her talk of getting laid and having "that kind of fun" was not lost on me. I was already getting radiation burns from the blushing and also from the remembered touches and kisses from that exquisite man in his hotel room last night.

"Oop!" she said after taking a sip of coffee. "Here he comes."

"Don't—" I reached out to grab her hand, but she slipped away. "—leave me."

Keely turned and waved at me over her shoulder, and the next thing I knew, I felt a presence at my side.

"Morning," he intoned, his morning voice gruff and two octaves deeper than normal. He cleared his throat noisily, throwing me a sidelong glance. "How's the coffee?"

I hadn't even taken a sip of mine yet. "It smells great." I rushed to grab a packet of sugar and pour some milk into my cup. He grabbed a mug and filled his to the brim—hot and black.

Raising the steaming mug to his lips, he sipped, and then gave a shrug. "It's okay."

I was still stirring mine. I sipped at it and watched him over the rim. Our gazes met and then seemed to bounce off each other. My breath seized. Talk about awkward.

Was it going to be like this from now on because I knew how amazing his hands felt on my body and he knew what color my nipples were?

My face burned hotter. *Stupid question, Gray.*

I was saved from further self-consciousness when my phone chimed, and I fished it out of my back pocket. It was a voice mail notification from my dad, received because the do-not-disturb setting had timed out.

"I should get this." I didn't have to, but, saved by the chime.

I stepped into the hallway outside the lounge to listen to the voice mail. It wasn't urgent. He wanted to chat, probably fishing for info on how the trip to Houston had gone. As always, Dad had lost track of time and hadn't realized we weren't even back yet. And he wanted me to meet him for lunch or dinner sometime this week. He gave me several open slots and asked me to text his assistant my answer so I'd be on his calendar. Dad always made sure we touched base regularly.

We left for the airport right after breakfast. During the short trip, I fielded some texts from Pari.

Well, you've been distracted or something because I've texted you four times with no answer, she said, pointing out that I'd missed her previous texts. I scrolled up and read her snarky remarks about Texas. She also linked me the mention and photos on TMZ about Ryan and Keely's hot dinner date in West Hollywood. And then, after I hadn't answered her, she'd texted: *Houston, we have a problem. Gray's phone is broken beyond repair. Either that or her thumbs are.*

I zapped off a quick answer to her. *Owe you a phone call and some lunch. Will touch base. We're about to take off. Home soon! We've been on a super tight schedule since we've been here.*

Her answer came back in less than two minutes, right before I hit the stairs to the plane. *If your schedule is half as tight as Ty's ass, then I completely understand. BTW, any clandestine shots of dat ass you can snag for me would be much appreciated.*

I laughed. *Not doing that for you or anyone else!* Then I stared at my answer before hitting send. I might be inclined to do it for myself, though. In a rush, I remembered what it had felt like this morning to wake up beside him. His arms, pinned across my waist, his breath hot on the back of my neck. His hard body pressed to mine and—yeah, it wasn't hard to figure out which other parts were particularly hard, given the fact that it was early morning and he was very male.

Not only had it been a good idea to hightail it out of there before anyone saw, but also before he woke up. Before I'd be tempted to let him do things he'd surely want to do. And I'd surely want him to do.

Or maybe he was cursing his beer goggles. Who knew?

Nevertheless, about an hour into our flight, most of the others were napping—Keely had stretched out across a long bench and Kirill snoozed across from her. Sharon had headphones on, her head pushed up against the bulkhead at an awkward angle, snoring with her mouth open. I was finishing off an article in *Behavioral Health Today* when he plopped down opposite me.

"Hey," he said quietly, throwing a glance at our sleeping contingent.

"Hi." I followed his gaze. "Amazing how exhausted everyone is but us."

His brow cocked knowingly at me. "Yeah, I'm thinking there was a lot of activity in other parts of the hotel last night."

I threw a look at him out of the corner of my eye before ducking my head to feign intense interest at the article in my lap. "Yeah, too bad for my no-partying rule. I'm sure you must have been bored beyond words." I gritted my teeth after I said it. But hey, might as well get the elephant in the room out into the open, right?

His brow scrunched in puzzlement. "What the hell are you talking about?" His voice was tinged with gruff amusement. "Last night was definitely not boring. And in fact..."

I looked up, raising my brows, but I didn't dare say a word. My next breath was held tight in my chest. *In fact...what? In fact, I want to spend more time with you. In fact...I find you very intriguing, Gray, and I want to know you better. In fact...*

"In fact, I got the best night's sleep I've had in ages."

My breath released with a sound much like a deflating balloon. *Wahh wahh waaaaaaah.* Sad trombones.

Not the answer I would have dreamed up. I frowned, and his sexy mouth broke out in a grin. He was messing with me, infuriating man.

"Yeah, about that," I said, adjusting my glasses to formulate a fierce stare. It was all I could do to keep from laughing. "You still owe me an answer to that last question. I, ahem, paid for it in advance, if you'll recall."

"I do recall." His eyes flicked down to my chest for only a split second, and I grew hot all over, feeling his mouth on my chest again. His warm mouth lining the length of my exposed scar, his lips encircling my nipple, sucking. Oh *Jesus.* Heat washed over me, and desire threatened to immolate me where I sat. I fidgeted in my seat, and his smile turned smug.

Smug. Damn him.

He knew what he was doing to me. There was no question about it. Was it a game? And did I have the strength to stop it, if it was?

"Obviously, here is not the place to answer that properly. Especially now that I'm sober. How about we have dinner together tonight, for once?"

I puzzled, tilting my head and trying to find his angle, wondering why I'd thought we would go back to him wandering around the house and ignoring me once we got home.

"We can't go out to eat. You're supposed to be dating Keely."

"We'll order in. Maybe watch a movie or something afterward."

Or something. He'd put a strange emphasis on that as if implying he wouldn't mind it one bit if we engaged in similar activities to the night before. What to do about that? I'd probably have to approach that subject with him too. Something I could address over dinner as well.

I bit the inside of my cheek and tested him by making two of the most ridiculous suggestions I could think of. "How about *Armageddon* or *Gravity?*"

He laughed. "Those are the worst astronaut movies. They fuck up almost every single detail."

I didn't say anything but was quite happy I'd gotten away with not answering him. I looked down, closed the magazine in my lap, and set it aside.

"Don't tell me you're going to turn away now."

"Hmm?" I glanced up at him with the question in my eyes.

"The only way you're getting the answer to your question is if you have dinner with me."

I blinked. "What makes you think I'm even free tonight?" I was free, of course, as I was most nights. And already staying at his house. "Like, uh, I might have work to do or studies to read or..."

I made the mistake of looking up and entangling my gaze with his intense stare. My throat clamped, and it was hard to breathe. Those cold blue eyes impaled me, did not allow me to look away. I blinked. "I...I'm not sure how wise this is."

His mouth twitched almost imperceptibly. "Wisdom has nothing to do with it."

I swallowed that lump of fear or anticipation or whatever it was in there that was clogging up my cognitive abilities. Then I nodded.

"Say yes, Gray." His voice had an odd tone to it—almost a desperation.

I sighed, giving in to him—and to myself. A surge of heat rose in my chest, and I smiled. "Yes, Gray."

The car took us directly to his house early that afternoon. And, though we had that predetermined "dinner date," we went our separate ways that afternoon. I to my little desk at the cubby not far from his office, and him to work on the latest biography pages with his assistant.

There was work to catch up on, particularly my follow-up study work. I had been serving as an assistant team member on a Mars Analog study where volunteers had agreed to live in a small habitat in the desert for months in simulation of a Mars mission. They were monitored closely by a psychological team and sent emotional wellness questionnaires regularly. I was working on compiling the results of the latest questionnaire for the head of our team.

But in the early afternoon, I took a break to grab a bottle of water and an apple out of the fridge. I didn't even realize Ryan had taken a break too, until I heard someone pacing around the living room nearby, ending a phone call.

When I realized I'd become an unwitting eavesdropper, I turned to go—until I heard the name of the recipient of his next phone call.

"Hey, Suz. Yeah, I just got back from Houston this morning and—yeah, I'm doing great, thanks." He cleared his throat. "I know we were supposed to get together and train later this afternoon, but I—oh yeah, you saw that? Wow on TMZ? Huh." He chuckled. "I guess I'm famous."

There was another long pause where he was listening, and I was frozen in my spot. If I moved now, he'd probably hear me. I could still hear him pacing over there. I didn't even dare bite into my apple for fear it would crunch too loud and give me away. Yeah, me of the loud clickity heartbeat was trying to be a stealth ninja while eavesdropping on Ryan and his trainer-with-benefits.

"Me and Keely? Well it's complicated. But obviously you and I—we can't see each other anymore professionally. And my schedule's tight leading up to this launch."

Another long pause and I was riveted, wishing I could somehow hear the other end of the conversation. I was simultaneously relieved that he was letting her go and revolted that he was doing it in such a callous way. I guess there could have been worse ways. Text message or sticky note. Carrier pigeon? Wall graffiti?

"I think you're talented, but for obvious reasons..." Another pause. "You're awesome, Suz. Thanks. Yeah, sure. I'll keep in touch. Text me whenever."

Text me whenever. Ugh. Gross. He was gross. Men were gross. He might as well have said, *Text me when I'm not seeing her anymore so we can start screwing again.* Blech.

Before I could so much as move, however, he rounded the corner, having finished his phone call, and caught me right in the middle of my not-so-covert spy op—an untouched green apple in one hand and a chilled bottle of water in the other. And my eyes as wide as the kid caught with her hand in the cookie jar.

To cover for myself—since it was too late to turn tail and run—I bit a huge chunk out of my apple and started to chew.

Ryan frowned, probably wondering how much of that I'd heard. He apparently decided I'd heard it all because he held up his phone before stuffing it back into his pocket. "Guess I'm on the hunt for a new trainer. You know, the *rules* and all."

My brow twitched, and once I swallowed my mouthful of apple, I replied, "Maybe you can manage to stay out of the next one's pants. Or better yet, hire a guy."

His mouth thinned and his eyes chilled, unamused. I didn't care. I probably should be overjoyed by the fact that there was no risk of having to overhear him pound some chick into next week. But for some reason, I wasn't.

Maybe it was the casual way in which he'd let her go. *I hope he gets blue balls because I sure as hell am not going to fill the trainer's shoes.*

And that's what turned my stomach most of all—the possibility that he'd been planning for me to, because of last night.

Ugh. I was so stupid. *Of course*, that's what he thought. That's what the whole "dinner tonight" thing was about. He was going to continue with whatever he started last night and try to get me in the sack.

Hell to the no.

The ease with which he'd dismissed Suzanne proved to me, above all else, what type of man he was. He would never take a romantic connection seriously. It was all just sex to him.

And that type of man was not for me.

He clenched his jaw. "I don't make a habit of that, FYI."

"That's not what I saw in the tabloids."

He rolled his eyes. "If you believe everything the media prints, then you're not as smart as you think you are."

Well, he had a point there. He moved up to the counter, resting a hand on its surface. I bit into my apple again, wondering how to end this conversation so I could crawl back to my room and be invisible.

"I'm not saying I'm a monk but, damn. That thing with Suz didn't even go that long. It was only twice. It's not like—"

I held up a hand to cut him off. "I don't need the full details about your sex life. Your love 'em and leave 'em style says it all."

He owed me nothing, in fact. We'd only shared some passionate kisses and a heart-to-heart talk. And he'd been drunk for most of it.

He straightened, folding his hands over his chest. "Are you done convincing yourself I'm the last man on earth you'd ever end up with?"

"No danger of you ending up with anyone, right?"

"Maybe the right one hasn't come along yet."

I blinked. "Isn't that what all the women hope? That they are the right one?"

He approached me and stopped when we were standing close to each other. "I don't know, Gray. Do they?"

I had no idea what to say to that. My face burned. I bit into my apple again, but before I could lower it while I chewed, Ryan reached out and caught my wrist, wrapping his large hand around it. He pulled my hand up toward his mouth and sank his teeth into that apple, never taking his eyes from mine.

When he pulled away, he was chewing his bite with a smile. I swallowed, aware of his nearness and—though I was annoyed with him—that ever-present, overwhelming attraction that never went away.

I stiffened, trying to regain some control. "I'm not eating dinner with you tonight."

He didn't miss a beat. "Yes, you are."

"I think I'll go grab an In-N-Out burger. Maybe a shake. Hole up in my room."

"No, you're having pizza with me on the deck." I frowned. Pizza did sound good. But ugh.

I drew back, but he was still holding my wrist, his grasp tightened, and I didn't struggle against his hold.

I lifted my chin and locked my eyes on his, affecting a confidence I didn't completely feel. "I'm not going to be that trainer's replacement in your bed, Ryan."

He didn't seem surprised one bit by my declaration, nor did he seem affronted by it. Instead, he shook his head. "I'm not going to ask you to, Gray."

I took another deep breath and came right out with the question that had been nagging me since the call. "Did you send her away because you thought that I...that you and I...?"

"Nope. I had several reasons to end it. Your rule being one of them. The thing with Keely being another."

I took a breath and then let it go, oddly wondering why this news didn't make me feel better. "Well...okay then."

His grip on my wrist loosened slightly. "Okay then," he repeated, searching my face.

"Then what's all this about eating dinner together?"

He smiled. "You're stuck here, remember? We might as well try to get along. Don't worry. I won't compromise your virtue or anything like that."

If you only knew. I was afraid he'd compromise my heart. But I had the power to say no, to pull away. I had the power to keep my distance while still trying to help him, didn't I?

It was a decision. And I made it then and there.

"Fine, I'll have some pizza with you under three conditions. You honestly and thoroughly answer my question like you promised. And there's no alcohol. And no kissing."

If he had an opinion on those conditions, he did not show it. Instead, he nodded, smiled again, and then left the kitchen to go back to his office and...

Did I hear whistling in the hallway?

Hours later, we sat by the poolside, the lights ablaze as the water reflected shivering light all over our faces. I had a can of Dr. Pepper in my hand, and Ryan was finishing up his third water bottle. He never drank soda, he said, when I'd offered him a can from the six-pack that had accompanied the pizza.

Between us was an open, grease-stained box of some of the best New York-style pizza I'd ever had—a chewy crust and heaps of cheese, exactly the way I liked it. Pepperoni on his half, black olives and mushrooms on mine.

My shoes were off, and I had one foot trailing in the water, kicking up a small splash every so often as we talked. The ice from our conversation this afternoon had quickly melted once we had food in front of us.

"My first time, I took up some T-shirts, coins, and other collectibles for friends and charities who had asked me as a favor. It's not that easy because the Russians only give us a kilo's worth of personal items we can bring, and the capsule is not roomy."

I nibbled on my last bit of pizza crust and watched him raptly. Whenever he talked about his job, his face became animated, his hand gestures more dramatic, engaged. It didn't take a rocket scientist—or even a psychologist—to realize how much he loved it.

"One thing my friends and instructors loved most was when I took a photo of them up with me and took a picture of myself with their photo on orbit. Then gave the picture back to them when I got home. The second time, I did that mostly. Took a shit-ton of pictures."

"You use a camera well if those photos you have on the walls inside are any indication."

He took the last bite of his third piece of pizza, chewing and swallowing before answering. "I took digital photography classes. The other astronauts teased me about it, but that's because they were jealous as fuck that I didn't have to learn Russian because I already spoke it. I mean, I had to learn how to read and write it, but I'd learned to speak it as a kid. Mom and I lived with my grandparents when Dad was gone for his job. And later, after the divorce. They all spoke Russian at home."

I frowned at him. "So the other astronauts were mad because you already spoke the language?"

He rolled his eyes. "They bellyached *constantly* about learning Russian. You can teach an astronaut any skill—we have to be jack-of-all-trades. We learn to perform minor medical procedures, major repair jobs, how to do complex science experiments. But learning the language is the one thing that stumps most of them, as brilliant as they all are."

I looked at him. "Teach me how to say something in Russian."

"*Ya ochen krasivaya.*"

I repeated it a few times, and he corrected me on my pronunciation. Once I'd gotten it down, I continued to repeat so that I'd remember it. "What does that mean?"

He smiled but didn't answer. I gave him a suspicious look. "You taught me how to say a bad word, didn't you?"

He shook his head and laughed. "Nope. I swear I didn't."

I repeated it a few more times. And he responded. "*Da, ochen verno.* Very true."

I narrowed my eyes at him. "But you're still not going to tell me what it means."

He smiled slyly. "Nope."

"Then how about you answer my question from last night?"

He put down his last crust—after having eaten a whopping four pieces—and brushed the crumbs off his fingers. "Okay. I guess I've hedged enough about that, haven't I?" He paused, taking a deep breath as if collecting his thoughts. "You asked me if I want to fly for my own reasons or because of the promise I made to Xander."

I nodded, and as it appeared we'd finished gnawing on the pizza, I flipped the box closed and leaned back on my hands to let him continue.

His gaze drifted out over the pool, and he shifted how he was sitting, unexpectedly restless. "There was a reason I put you off last night—well, several reasons." He laughed as if to himself. "But the answer is...it's complicated."

Therapist prompts. I had to remember to limit my responses to "I'm listening" cues and not come at him with more intrusive questions that would cloud the issue or derail him. So I made a noncommittal, "Mm-hmm."

"Xander, Karen, and I were friends since our first year at the Academy."

"Karen's also in the Navy?"

"She was. She left about five years ago when AJ—her and Xander's son—was born."

I nodded, wordlessly urging him to continue.

"Xander's goal from day one was NASA. Ever since he was a little kid. So he started out as a pilot in the Navy."

"What was your goal then?" I was not above noticing that he was answering this question by constantly referring to Xander instead of himself, so I did what I could to redirect him while still being a good listener.

His eyes locked on mine. "I wanted to be a SEAL. Like my dad." From his bio, I remembered that his dad had been killed in action when Ryan was fifteen. Also, that picture of them together. Perhaps he idealized his dad in much the same way he did with Xander.

Maybe there was something there.

Ryan shifted again, then reached over and pulled a few plush water-resistant cushions off a nearby lounge, handed one to me and laid the other next to him on the ground, then leaned on it. I thanked him. The ground was getting hard, but the conversation was fascinating.

"So tell me how you went from being a SEAL to an astronaut."

He laughed. "I'm not even the first frogman to do that, believe it or not." He glanced out over the shimmering pool again. I studied his face, and he seemed to realize that, keeping his features completely composed. Finally, he took a long deep breath and let it go. "Xander and I got drunk one night, and he dared me to apply when he did for the next astronaut class."

I blinked. "You became an astronaut because of a dare?"

He smirked. "Yeah, it sounds pretty ludicrous." He shrugged. "Actually, once I put in the papers and worked my way through the interview process, I got attached to the idea of working for NASA. Then I got picked and he didn't, but he was beyond thrilled for me. He was the best of me—the best of all of us." His voice faded out.

I blinked. Ryan wasn't so good at hiding his feelings this time, his jaw flexed and tightened, a haunted look passing through his eyes. Pure guilt. He tore his gaze away from mine as if he knew I'd be able to read the emotions there. He had yet to answer my question, and I wondered if he really would or if I had the heart to push him to.

Swallowing, I could barely fathom what he must be going through. How much pain he was certainly in. And yet, he'd never ask for help. And I had the sense he'd never let himself *not* feel the pain.

He'd continue to punish himself.

Ryan. I wanted to say it. I wanted him to confide everything in me so it would feel better, to let it out.

But I might as well be asking the sun to rise in the west tomorrow instead of the east.

CHAPTER SEVENTEEN
RYAN

MS. GRAY BARRETT THOUGHT SHE KNEW EXACTLY what she was doing. And that I was at the mercy of her superior psychology skills. That she was drawing me out like a snake charmer draws a snake from a basket. Coaxing, cajoling...intriguing me.

Now she sat, her arms hugging her shins so that her knees supported her chin. She looked at me from over the rim of her eyeglasses. How cute she was, how adorable even with her smallest gestures—like constantly adjusting her glasses on her nose or chewing her top lip with her bottom teeth when she was concentrating.

I couldn't help but notice those small things now and wondered how I ever thought her unremarkable before. She was the furthest thing from unremarkable. Subtle, yes. But that was because she tried to hide herself, keep herself protected and safe.

She was looking at me with her head tilted to the side. "Is now a good time to point out that you still haven't answered my question?"

I schooled my features. Would now be a good time to point out how much I'd enjoy getting her out of those clothes and doing what we started last night?

I swept the idea out of my head faster than it could take hold. Because of our conversation in the kitchen this afternoon, I'd never consider proposing that. But damn if I didn't want to.

"So, why am I flying again?"

She nodded. "Yes. Is it to fulfill your promise to Xander?"

"Yes, and..." I shrugged. "Because I love to fly, especially since I got my gold wings."

Astronauts didn't earn that badge until after their first flight—technically a height of a hundred kilometers or higher, which was considered space flight. Until then, they wore silver wings. Since Xander had died during his first mission, he hadn't had his gold wings long enough to ever wear them. Instead, they'd been presented to Karen at his memorial.

Gray was watching me in that uncanny way she had. The way that let you know she missed absolutely nothing. I hadn't been as careful as I should have been around her and, to be honest, I didn't mind. That usual barrier of caution I used to keep between myself and everyone else had relaxed, and I wasn't sure why. But for once, I wasn't uptight about it.

She thought she could help me. She thought she could fix me. She was wrong, but it wasn't unpleasant watching her try.

Besides, it got lonely in here sometimes.

"But what is it that you want for *you?*"

"What do you mean?" I leaned back, bracing my hands on the deck behind me to support myself.

"Well." She crossed her long legs and mimicked me, pushing back on her hands. "You became a SEAL to honor your dad, right?" I nodded. "And you became an astronaut pretty much as the result of a dare. You've joined XPAC so you can fly again for Xander."

I blinked.

She sat up, resting her forearms across her crossed legs. "But what do you want for you? What is your dream?"

I dropped my gaze, nudging the pizza box aside with my foot to make more room to stretch out. Coughed. I avoided her gaze while I mulled over her words. *What the hell did I really want?*

For some reason, AJ flashed into my mind, memories of holding him as a baby, putting him on my shoulders as I walked around the county fair to see the animals. The wide-eyed look of wonder on his face as he took in the world around him.

But thinking about AJ hurt. A lot. A physical stab right in my chest.

Maybe someday I'd be a father, but more than likely not. It wasn't fair that Xander couldn't be here to be a father to his own kid. And I already knew I was too broken to be anything more than a shitty husband. My jaw clenched. Yeah, maybe having my own family was a dream, but dreams were things you thought about and then forgot about as you got on with life. Dreams were mist and fairy tales.

Gray waved a hand in front of my face to get my attention. "Wow," she said when I looked up. "You just went a million miles away when I asked that."

Her stare was penetrating, observant. Sometimes she barely blinked, and it was a little freaky.

"Can I ask you another question?" She shifted how she was sitting.

I couldn't help but think about what I got in exchange for each of her questions last night. My eyes flicked to her chest, remembering the heat we'd generated the night before. The taste, the feel of her beaded nipple in my mouth. The way she'd moved and sighed when I'd touched her. Renewed desire sizzled through me. I wanted her in my arms again, her body pressed against mine.

Yet, under the circumstances, it would be a mistake to propose such a thing again. Though, I wanted to. I really wanted to.

My mouth quirked. "This one is on the house."

We shared a long, knowing look. Those green eyes held a flash of thirst like she'd crawled through the Mojave and I was an ice-cold glass of lemonade. My entire body tensed in response. Had it not been for that conversation in the kitchen earlier, I'd be all over her right now.

But she'd been seriously bothered by the thing with Suzanne, and I was now pissed at my past self that Gray had been kept waiting during my roll in the hay with Suz. Because now Gray had me pegged as a type of man that I wasn't, necessarily. At least, not until recently.

My jaw clenched and I held that stare, but I didn't move. *Baby girl, I doubt I'd tire of you as easily as the others.*

I swallowed. Goddamn, I wanted it. And so did she. But I wasn't going to make that move now. It would fuck everything up.

There was an absolute pull between us—like an inescapable orbit. *Gravity.* At one point, a body approaching another body in space risked being caught in orbit—trapped within the gravitational field of the larger body. If it wasn't traveling fast enough to get away, it would be captured forever, barring some eventual cataclysm.

I wondered if I was going fast enough to avoid this pull toward her. Because everything about her fascinated me enough to want to slow down, to notice and record everything, perceiving every single second. These collections of moments between us were tiny proofs of that magnetism, of that potential force.

It felt dangerous.

And thrilling.

She licked her lips before talking, and fuck, it was like a jolt straight down to my crotch, remembering how those lips tasted, how they'd felt underneath mine. I looked away, out over the pool, and tried to think of something else, waiting for her to voice her question. If it was something bad, I'd figure out a way to deflect it.

"I wanted to know about...about your sleeping habits."

A laugh exploded from my chest before I could even register another reaction. The question was so clinical. And probing. And personal.

And if there was a chance to bend this turn of her curiosity in my favor, you'd bet I was going to take it. "I'm all ears, Ms. Barrett."

"Last night, you seemed... Well, you were out of sorts before we fell asleep. I want to know if that happens every night."

Hmm. While the question irritated me, it also showed some promise. If I played this right, it might work to my advantage.

"What else did you want to know?"

Her brows pinched together before her forehead smoothed again. "Your coping mechanisms for it. I assume the drinking and going to bed with women are somehow tied to the sleep patterns. And...and keeping the lights on?"

Christ on a fucking cracker. How the hell did she do that? Psychologist or mind reader? Or maybe a goddamn secret Vulcan?

Disconcerted, I bought time by turning one of her techniques back on her. "Mmm."

She blinked at me. And blinked again. "That's not an answer."

I shrugged, recovering my astonishment enough to follow through with the idea that had popped into my head. "I never said I'd answer. Only that you could ask."

She rolled her eyes and looked away in disgust, and I laughed. I'd never seen her roll her eyes before. I'd even wondered if that often very appropriate—and sometimes required—gesture was in her repertoire. But she showed emotions so rarely. Maybe she was a Vulcan, after all.

"If you're curious to know about my nighttime habits, there's one surefire way for you to find out everything you want to know."

One brow rose above those dark frames. She looked adorable, like an inquisitive little owl. Like one of the post owls that brought letters in *Harry Potter.* "Dare I ask what that is? And dare you answer me?"

Here it was. Time for my new proposal. I sat up from my relaxed position and leaned forward slightly. "Direct observation. You want to know it all? Sleep with me."

Her jaw dropped, and she turned about eleven different shades of red and pink. *Oh, you want it bad, baby girl, don't you?*

A similar rush of blood in my veins surged at her reaction. *Damn.* I wanted it bad too.

But this wasn't about fucking. Though, hopefully that would happen eventually.

"Literally sleep, not figuratively," I clarified.

Her lips thinned and were almost white, though the color in her cheeks and neck had not faded. "You mean like last night? After-after the—I mean. You just want to sleep."

"Yup."

"All night?"

I nodded.

She sat up and picked at imaginary pizza crumbs on the deck around the pizza box. "Um, where?"

"In my bed."

She visibly swallowed. "And why are you proposing this? How does it help you?" Her eyes came up and pierced right through me again.

Hmm. I hadn't expected that question, and I sure as hell wasn't going to hand over the answer. "You get info by observing, while I don't have to answer questions. I've been forced, by trade, to work as a scientist—at least in the performance of tasks, if not in the formulation of hypotheses or conclusions. But I know how it works. I can give you unobstructed observation time."

"And you gain...?"

Damn. This girl was too smart. And persistent.

I shrugged. "Well, I get a good night's sleep without having to exhaust myself with hot sex first." There. Let her chew on *that*.

"And how long would this period of observation last?"

As long as possible. The thought popped into my mind automatically. But I shrugged to feign nonchalance. "I dunno. As long as you need to gather your data. We're already sleeping under the same roof anyway."

Just the thought of possibly having her next to me in bed tonight infused me with relief. I could already feel myself relaxing. To sleep like I'd slept last night, for more than one night...

Please say yes.

She didn't move. Not even to bat an eyelash. She just did that weird stare thing she always did. Sometimes it made me squirm inwardly. But tonight, I tried my best to push that back on her, to make *her* squirm. I would have loved to make her squirm in more ways than one. But tonight wouldn't be about that.

I'd woken up this morning, my arms empty, the smell of her hair on my pillow, without that ever-present gnawing exhaustion that accompanied all my mornings, afternoons, and evenings of late. At that moment, I'd made the goal to get her into my bed, via any means available to me—seduction or persuasion, if necessary.

And with her question about sleep habits, she'd handed it over to me in the easiest way possible.

"Okay," she said with a decisive nod. "I propose a week."

I think not. I think you'll need longer than that.

I know I'll need you longer than that.

I only nodded, keeping my face blank. "Fine. Observation begins tonight, then?"

She hesitated as if searching for a way to put it off. No way was I letting that happen. I was getting my way, come hell or high trauma—whichever killed me first.

I needed this in order to succeed during the test flight training. My ass was already dragging every day, and I feared making stupid mistakes. And damn it, those mistakes would lead to possibly being removed from the flight list. Which would not—*could not*—happen.

That same question again flitted through my mind. *You're flying for Xander, but what do you want to do for you?*

No time to ponder that. It didn't matter. What mattered was keeping a promise to the best friend I couldn't save. What mattered more than anything else was this flight.

I pushed up from the ground, then bent to snatch up the pizza box. She watched me wide-eyed for a moment, still thinking. *What are you going to come up with next, smart girl? I'm ready for you.*

Without a word, I held out a hand and she took it. I pulled her up to her feet, noting that she weighed hardly anything. Then we went inside where I stuffed the pizza box into the fridge.

"Movie?"

She nodded, still lost in thought.

A few hours later, we finished watching some inane rom-com—better that than an astronaut movie—starring Sandra Bullock. I was finally feeling like I could doze off under the right circumstances.

And it didn't appear as if an explosive orgasm or three was in my near future. Thus, the right circumstance was, hopefully, having Ms. Angharad Grace Barrett in my bed, just to sleep.

As had happened the night before, she changed and prepped for bed while I showered. When I came out in my shorts and T-shirt, she was sitting on the far side of my bed with an e-reader in her hands. She had on a thin T-shirt and those same tasty yoga pants. And the fuzzy socks.

I almost laughed at her, that she slept in so much clothing. It was summer in Southern California. The evenings were no cooler than a temperate seventy degrees. In addition, my house was air-conditioned to a steady low seventies temperature.

But apparently, she liked bundling up regardless. Maybe she wasn't usually a cuddler.

My bed, like the one last night, was a king-size. I hesitated before lying down, feeling that same familiar rush of anxiety whenever it got close to closing my eyes to sleep.

As usual, I'd left every light in the room blazing—from the bathroom to the overhead light, to the lamp beside my side of the bed. I didn't bother to ask her if the lights annoyed her. There was no way I was going to turn them off.

She put down the e-reader and looked at me for a moment. I raised my eyebrows. "All set? Anything you need?"

She shook her head solemnly and watched me. "I'm good to go."

My lips quirked involuntarily with a smile. "Okay then." I took a deep breath and sat down on the bed, noting the same speeding of my heartbeat as always, the same cold fear forming at the back of my throat. I was all too aware of her observation, and though it should have made me nervous to reveal myself like this, it didn't. I was relieved she was here. And it wasn't just because it was any woman in my bed. It was because it was *her*.

Because I knew she cared, and for some reason, that mattered. I still didn't fully understand it. And at this point, I wanted to be able to close my eyes for a while and be at peace instead of endlessly reliving a nightmare.

I swallowed a dry lump in my throat and lay down jerkily, pulling the covers over me. She was still sitting, though she slowly turned to lay her glasses on the night table beside her.

I hesitated, as always, not wanting to close my eyes. For some reason, lying here in the quiet of night—especially when alone—I couldn't bring myself to do it. I'd stare at the ceiling for hours under the blazing lights. And sometimes I never closed them.

And sometimes I'd have to get up and drink vodka until I passed out to quiet those horrific thoughts, the memories. Or have a woman with me to distract me from them until I was too exhausted to think.

I tried to follow Gray's advice from the previous night—to focus on my breathing and not allow my mind to wander. But it got to be too much, and I found myself frozen, holding my breath. All at the mere thought of closing my eyes.

"Ryan, let the breath go." Her soft voice sounded at my ear. I turned toward her, her face mere inches from mine. She'd stuffed her pillow under her head. "It'll do you no good to hold your breath. It'll only make you more anxious."

I blinked at her and did as she instructed. We spent long minutes like that, listening to nothing but the sound of my breathing and the clicking beat of her heart. Then, to split the silence, I spoke again. "You must think it's weird for me to sleep beside a woman without sex involved."

Her brows wavered. "I'm sure some women manage to resist you. And I hope that wasn't a proposition."

I refrained from the temptation to look down the length of her body. *And if it was?*

I turned back to watch the ceiling again. "No, just making conversation," I replied in a breathless voice.

She was silent for a few minutes before clearing her throat to speak. "It's weird for me because I've never had anyone else in bed with me before—except for last night, of course."

I studied the ceiling as I absorbed that. "You've never..." My voice died out. How the hell did I even ask something like that without it sounding awkward?

"I've never slept with anyone in a bed until last night. And I've never had sex."

That blew me away. Gray tended to hide herself. She played it safe, but how had that not happened? Surely, she'd had men interested in her before. Surely, she'd dated.

And I'd had a chance to gather that she was attracted to men— or at least, to me.

I frowned, turning to her, the disbelief obvious in my voice. "And you're twenty-five? How?"

She shrugged, but her expression didn't change. "Just not something I focused on. I was very sick during most of my adolescence. In and out of hospitals a lot. Never much time for dating or romance under those circumstances."

I blinked, watching her as she stared off into the distance, into the past. She smiled. "I did have this one special boyfriend, though, who was also a cardiac patient—he'd had a heart and lung transplant. We kissed once when I was fifteen, but that's about as far as it ever went. When I had my last valve replacement—"

I sucked in a breath, startled. "How many have you had?"

"Two surgeries for heart wall and valve repair when I was little. One tissue valve replacement when I was thirteen that didn't end up working. And then the final prosthetic one at sixteen. Like I said, lots of surgeries, tons of time in the hospital."

Jesus, she was a warrior.

"And never time to live as a typical, healthy kid," I said. No wonder she played it safe. I'd called her on it before as if it was a negative, and sometimes, it could be. Playing it safe could hold you back in so many ways. But playing it safe also protected you from danger, from the darkness.

"I was healthy almost instantly after the last replacement. And it was so weird to go from being this chronically ill child who was so limited in what she could do to, all of a sudden, a healthy young woman. To be inserted into normal life so abruptly. Be expected to go to school, college, all of that. Normal young adulthood took a lot of getting used to, and I had no time or desire to date. I was too busy catching up. I always figured there'd be time for that later."

How different our teenage years had been, but no less traumatic one from the other. My life had changed the day my dad's teammates showed up at my doorstep to tell me, tearfully, that he wouldn't be coming home. She'd had to fight for her life in a hospital bed.

Sounded like we'd both been forced to grow up well before our time. "Where's your mom?" I blurted.

She glanced up at me then began to fiddle with the edge of the sheet. "She lives in the UK. My parents are divorced too, but they didn't do it until I got better. They probably should have split up a long time before that, though."

I laughed. "I know that feeling."

"What about your mom?"

"She lives in Boston with her second husband. He and I don't get along at all. I don't think he treats her well, and she doesn't invite me over very often, to keep the peace. But I do see my grandparents on the holidays. They live in Florida."

I reached out and covered her restive hand with my own. She met my gaze but did not react in any other way, nor did she pull her hand away.

With a tiny smile, she scooted her head over so that it rested on my shoulder. My entire awareness became...*strawberries.* "There are many ways to awaken, but the only way to enter that experience is to first be asleep," she murmured.

I frowned. "Who said that?"

A long pause. "I just did."

And I pondered that, feeling my body relax even further. I shrugged her head from my shoulder onto my chest, remembering how she'd rested it there last night. She turned onto her side and fitted herself close to me so that she was resting in the crook of my arm.

I stared at the bumpy white ceiling of my bedroom, but simply feeling her here had lowered my heart rate, my breathing. The area immediately surrounding us felt different—safe. Like we inhabited our own little world. Only the two of us.

Turning my head, I buried my nose in her soft hair. Her smell made me warm all over—and not just because I wanted her. It was comfort and strength. Someone else's strength upon which I could rely for once.

We lay like that, awake and in silence, underneath every bright light in the immediate vicinity. And eventually, without any struggle, my eyes fell closed, and I slept a dreamless sleep.

CHAPTER EIGHTEEN
GRAY

THAT NEXT WEEK, I SPENT EVERY NIGHT AT RYAN'S house and every day at work. He was there too, either training in the simulator or in the astronaut office with the other guys, working on plans and paperwork. Or on conference calls with the manufacturers of the different systems that were employed by XVenture's new Phoenix capsule, which would take them to space.

While we were at work, the two of us acted distant, professional. No observer would ever be able to tell that we knew each other's preferred sleeping positions. Ryan liked to sleep on his back most of the time. Me, I was a side sleeper, occasionally flipping onto my tummy. We nodded to each other in the hallways, never ate lunch at the same table, and refrained from even speaking about our shared activities to others. It was our little secret.

Which was good because the public was getting into the blossoming romance between him and "America's sweetheart," Keely Dawson. For fake lovers, they were making quite a splash.

At work, Pari and I were walking to the cafeteria for lunch when Victoria turned the corner and approached us from the other end of the long hall.

Without warning, Pari veered, pushing me into the nearest open doorway, presumably to avoid Victoria.

"What the—"

"Shh!" She shut the door behind her.

We were in a small meeting room with physics equations scrawled messily all over the whiteboard, notepads, notebooks, and pens scattered the table, and garbage everywhere. The place smelled like a dozen college students had pulled all-nighters in there every day that week. I waved my hand in front of my nose.

"Holy crap, it reeks in here."

Pari rolled her eyes. "Wilty daisy, there you go again."

"Is this how rocket scientists live? Because...no thanks." I couldn't help myself. I started picking up fast-food wrappers and throwing them into the almost-full garbage can to keep myself from gagging.

"This team's been on a deadline, so cut them some slack."

"I hope they bathed when they went home. Ugh. Did you drag me in here to avoid Victoria? What the heck is going on with you two?"

She froze and blinked, then cleared her throat. "I, uh, had to talk to you. It's something that probably wouldn't go over well in the lunch room anyway. Gossipy gossip type of stuff."

I raised a brow. I wasn't fooled, but I figured she'd come out with whatever was up with her and Victoria eventually—no need to pry.

She leaned her back against the door and folded her arms. "What do you know about the four astronauts' relationships?"

I frowned at her. "Far as I know, they're all single and enjoying it." That gave me a pang, to think it about Ryan and the player lifestyle he'd be sure to get back to as soon as he didn't need to play nice with Keely anymore. I gritted my teeth, forcing myself not to think about it.

She blew out a breath and pushed her dark hair behind her ear. "That's not what I meant. I was asking about their relationships to each other."

I hesitated. "Well, they seem to be good friends. They all have worked together in the past—in some cases, for years. Either at NASA or in Russia." I bit my lip and stared. "Why?"

Her dark brows rose. "Hoo boy, I was here early this morning because I needed to get some shit done before our morning scrum. And I happened to duck into the break room to grab a soda..."

I nodded. "And?"

"I heard yelling outside the astronauts' office and the door was kind of ajar, so I perked an ear up to listen and maybe got a few peeks inside."

"How unsurprisingly nosy of you."

Her eyes widened. "Do you want to hear this, or do you want to make snarky comments?"

I held out a placating hand. "Okay, fine. What was the shouting about?"

"Noah and Ty were shouting at each other."

I blinked. "Really?"

She nodded. "They were never near enough to start posturing like men do—you know when it's going to come to blows. It wasn't like that. But they were *not* happy with each other. If he's in a shitty mood tonight, you'll know why."

I adjusted my glasses, absorbing this. "What were they arguing about?"

She shook her head. "Something to do with the prep for the launch? I couldn't tell, it was so out of context. But Ty was telling Noah to stop assuming he was a fuck-up. And Noah said Ty had never given him any reason to assume otherwise."

I pulled back. "Whoa. That's harsh."

Pari nodded her agreement. "Those two don't like each other very much, I've noticed."

I thought about that for a moment. Usually, I picked up on these things quickly, but it occurred to me that I'd only rarely seen them together though they worked alongside each other every day.

"So, of course, I decided to come get the dirt from you. Why don't Ty and Noah like each other?"

I frowned. "No idea. Those two have worked together extensively. In fact..." Something tickled my brain, and I paused, blinking.

"What? C'mon, I don't have all day here. I'm starving."

"I read the entire transcript of the accident. Noah was the CAPCOM on the ground during the spacewalk."

Her forehead wrinkled. "That's awkward and he's come over to work here, too?"

I shrugged. "I don't know Noah's motivation. He wasn't fired from NASA like Ty was. But he's here for some reason. Probably felt his prospects to fly were better."

"Huh, okay." Her eyes drifted to the window in the door to check the hallway, which reminded me.

"Now are you going to tell me why you are avoiding Victoria?"

Pari's eyes flicked back to me. "Yeah, I promise. Just not now." With that, she yanked the door open and was gone, leaving me inside the gross room alone. As I was getting tired of breathing through my mouth to avoid the smell, I pushed out after her and headed to the lunch room behind her.

That night, there was nothing obviously wrong or different with Ty's mood to indicate that the blowup between him and Noah had been anything unusual. And I avoided probing, as much as I wanted to.

But I was reminded of my promise to Karen Freed, and since it had been a week since coming back from Houston, I sent her off a quick text.

Hey there, it's Gray. Just wanted to drop you a line and let you know everything's going okay here with Ty. I hope all is well with you too.

Only a little while later, I received a brief reply. *Thanks. Hopefully he'll feel like telling me that himself sometime soon.*

I hesitated, then keyed in a quick reply. *No promises, but will see what I can do!*

And she answered that one too. *Bless you. Thank you.*

***

Friday of that week proved to be a very busy day. I left work early to have that promised lunch with my dad at a nearby organic restaurant.

He would have liked to go for a walk first, but the weather for the past few days had been stinking hot, so we sought refuge inside in the air conditioning instead, staring out the window at the pond full of ducks in the adjacent park.

"I don't care much for the frou-frou food here, but the view is nice," he said. "I'd never pick this place out, though. Too pricey." He scanned the menu with a curled lip, and I fought a chuckle.

"Thanks for indulging me."

"You managing to wrangle that playboy astronaut? I've been reading the news. He's coming up every so often with that cute little actress."

I nodded. "He's behaving himself, Dad, never fear. He's...he's a good person. Try not to judge him based on some past mistakes."

He darted a look at me and then back to the menu. "Hmm. This whole XPAC is risky business. I warned Tolan before he went there. He was doing great with the rocket business. The launches to resupply the Space Station, all the government and satellite work. And he's done great—followed my advice about staying private, but..." He shook his head. "This astronaut thing. I just don't know."

I tightened a fist under the table, my fingernails digging into my palm, but I didn't let him see my agitation. He couldn't yank the rug out on this now, could he? I was doing everything we'd agreed on.

"Dad, it's going great. It's Tolan's dream. It's *my* dream. There's so much of a future for the human race in space exploration. Do you want to leave it up to NASA's 'maybe we'll get there in the 2030s,' or do you want to be a part of the future now?"

Dad never had a chance to respond, because a person who'd been headed to a nearby table veered sharply toward us instead. "Conrad? I thought I heard your voice. And your beautiful daughter! How are you, Gray?"

We both looked up at Aaron Thiessen, head of Thiessen International, an investment firm. Like Tolan, Aaron had once been mentored by the legendary Conrad Barrett. Dad stood and enthusiastically pumped the hand of his former acolyte. Then Aaron smiled at me, bending to kiss my cheek.

"Please, sit down with us," I indicated the empty seat beside me.

He grinned, unbuttoned his suit jacket, and obliged.

"I'm meeting with someone shortly, but they won't be here for a bit, just texted me that they're stuck in traffic."

"It's great to see you again. How's your sister doing?" I only knew her superficially—mostly because we'd both attended the same small, elite all-girls' college, Scripps. Sheridan was older than me, and we moved in very different circles. I didn't actively associate with the plethora of socialites or future politicians. And there weren't many other unapologetic introverted nerds in the bunch.

"Finished up at Stanford, going in for her doctorate. Congrats on finishing yours, by the way. Dad must be proud." He flashed a smile at my dad, who nodded in approval. "I couldn't help but overhear what you were saying to Conrad about being a part of the future now?"

I smiled. "Yes, I was congratulating my dad about his smart investment in XVenture's new Private Astronaut Corps. They are going to change the future of space travel—of our planet, actually, when it comes right down to it."

Might as well spread the news to every billionaire I knew, right? A few extra dollars for the program couldn't hurt.

Aaron was a little over thirty, and thanks to Dad's tutelage, now a billionaire himself. He had been known to famously diverge from Dad's advice from time to time. But I wasn't above laying on some peer pressure for my dad either. I could all but feel him going skittish about the XPAC investment, so why not sell Aaron on it hard-core? That way, Dad would look like a fool for backing out.

I had no problem playing it devious when I had to.

Because no way was I going to work for a human resources firm when I could be working with astronauts and having my hands in the future of space travel. "NASA is projecting possibly going to Mars in the 2030s. But NASA hasn't transported their own astronauts into space since they retired the shuttle in 2011. They've been going up on Russian rockets instead."

I barely paused to catch my breath before soldiering on. "XVenture will beat NASA to Mars. They'll do it in the next decade. And they have plans and some of the best talent from around the world to do it. They built a rocket company from nothing. Now they are the leading provider—even to NASA—of transportation into low earth orbit and beyond."

For his part, Aaron couldn't have been acting more positively if I'd paid him. Thank goodness. He was rapt. Asking questions as fast as I could answer him. Ten minutes later, he had to be tapped on the shoulder and told that his party had arrived.

He stood up and said, "Gray, I want to talk to you more about that sometime soon, okay?"

Well done, Aaron! "Tell me when you want to come by our facility, and I'll get you a tour." I beamed.

He turned to Dad. "Conrad, great to see you again. Let's meet up soon."

Aaron was gone, and Dad was sending me a piercing stare. I raised my brows at him. "What?"

He smiled then. "Nothing. I shouldn't be surprised when I see you've picked up some of my more annoying traits, I suppose."

I grinned. "You mean like stubborn bullheadedness?"

His eyes narrowed. "I was going to call it steely determination, but that works too."

We laughed.

Later, as we walked out to the parking lot and were safely out of earshot, Dad said, "You know what might be a fun idea? What if you went out on a date with Aaron? He's a good guy, and I think he likes you. Besides, I never see you dating anyone."

I raised a brow and gave him serious side-eye. "Really, Dad? Love life advice from you? I thought you only doled out advice on stock portfolios and retirement strategies."

He shrugged sheepishly. "You're my daughter. I worry."

I threw my arm around his back and rested my head on his shoulder. "I'm fine. I'm happy."

His lips thinned. "That's all I want...for you to be happy."

"I am. It is possible to be happy without a man," I said mildly, though I tried not to question why I kept picturing Ryan and how good it had felt this past week to sleep in his arms. How safe and secure.

Minutes later, I hugged and kissed Dad in the parking lot as we went our separate ways.

The day was only getting hotter. I left the restaurant in LA and headed the thirty-five miles to North Tustin and Ryan's house. Driving along in afternoon traffic, I cursed the fact that I still hadn't taken the time to get the air conditioner in my car repaired. It was a long, sweaty slog. Seriously, only in parallel universes where time moved slower would it make sense for it to take an hour and a half to go three dozen miles.

But this was LA. A parallel universe unto itself, and this was a heat wave. Lowering the window in a car with nonexistent climate control did nothing, but I futilely hoped for relief from a stray breeze.

I finally reached Ryan's house at the height of the hottest part of the afternoon. Despite having pulled my hair back into a ponytail, it had blown into a frizzled wreck. My face was beet red from the heat and my shirt soaked with sweat. So much for the crappy little fan I'd been using. Today, it had only succeeded in making me more dehydrated by desiccating me in the nearly absent humidity.

When I let myself into Ryan's house, the look on his face said it all—I was a sweaty mess. His mouth dropped open and then... "Are you all right? What happened?"

I threw up my hands, adjusting my bag on my shoulder. "This weather happened. My AC is still broken."

Without a word, he took my bag from my shoulder and took it to my guest room. "You need water. And you need that air conditioning fixed. Keely's coming over in a little bit. We have to take some pictures or something. And she wants to go for a swim."

"Yeah, she texted me, so I grabbed my swimsuit and some other clothes. They're still in the car."

He quickly got me a glass of frosty ice water straight from the fridge. I drank it down as fast as I could then held out the glass for more. He refilled it and handed it back to me.

"I need your car keys," he said, holding out his hand.

"The shop won't take it now. I need to call and make an appointment, then get someone to follow me there or arrange a rental drop-off for the day. It's a huge pain, and I keep putting it off."

He rolled his eyes at me. "I didn't mean to take it to the shop. I'll fix it. It's a standard compressor. I can do it with my eyes closed."

I blinked. "Uh, what?"

"What do you think we have to do up there?" He pointed to the sky. "Fixing the damn air circulation and life support systems were top priority on station. Over half the stuff we do there is dedicated to vehicle maintenance. How else would the combined space agencies keep it up there and flying for over twenty years if we weren't constantly fixing it?"

"So my car has the same air circulation system as the ISS?" I asked, still in disbelief.

"Not exactly the same, but close enough. Now, keys?"

I handed them over to him, and he turned and walked out the front door. By the time he'd pulled it up in front of his garage, opened the hood, and went inside to fish out other tools, Kirill and Keely drove up in her Mini convertible—top up, of course. Only a masochist would have the top down on a day like this.

"Hey," Keely called as she got out, looking like a million bucks in her miniskirt and high heels. "What's going on here?" she asked, gesturing to the raised hood on my car.

"Auto repair," I said. "My AC is out, and he's sick of me procrastinating getting it fixed."

"Hello, Gray." Kirill nodded in that oddly formal way of his. "I'll go to see if Ty needs help."

"How's it, um, going?" Keely asked quietly. She glanced pointedly to the garage and then back to me. "With him?"

Well, I was having great success in getting him to fall asleep every night. He was waking up every morning well rested. I, meanwhile, was spending hours lying awake in his arms trying not to daydream about how amazing it would feel if he pulled me close and touched me in very inappropriate ways, but...

I said none of that. "It's going fine. He's being a good boy."

Keely's perfectly penciled brows jumped in her smooth forehead. "But we don't want him to be a good boy, Gray. That's the point. We want him to play *The Astronaut and the Lonely Martian Girl,* rated X version."

I shushed her as the two men emerged from the garage prattling away to each other in Russian. Ryan carried a big toolbox, and Kirill had rolled up the sleeves on his button-down dress shirt. Kirill, apparently, was poking fun at him for not using the right words in Russian for the tools, and Ryan said some things that I think would have been full of symbols had they been translated with subtitles.

Keely and I soon found a shady spot—some decorative boulders across the driveway from where they were working. And almost as if on cue, Ryan pulled off his shirt and wiped his sweaty face with it. "*Now,* we're talking," Keely murmured to me. "Let's hope the Russian follows suit. You would not believe the body underneath all that eastern European formality. He's *so* pretty, Gray."

Kirill was, indeed, a handsome man—tall, dark blond, very muscular, with perfect bone structure. But Ryan...Ryan. I couldn't take my eyes off the way his back muscles rippled as he worked, especially when the sweat caused his skin to glisten in the sun.

Oh Lordy.

I slept with that precise amount of perfect male under my fingertips every night.

And he didn't touch me.

And though—as I'd told him—I'd gone years without indulging in those very natural needs, it seemed as if my body had very recently awakened. My romantic side would have preferred to compare the awakening to that of Sleeping Beauty. But with the ravenous hunger I was now encountering, the analogy worked so much better to equate with Smaug, the Dragon of the Lonely Mountain. Dying to breathe fire. Dying to roar. Dying to devour scorched man flesh—

I shook myself from my daydream.

"Girlfriend, you need you some hot man injection, stat."

In spite of my own dirty thoughts, my face burned hotter than the afternoon sun, if that was possible.

"You brought a swimsuit, yes?"

I nodded. I'd brought one. *Reluctantly.*

"Did you wax in all the right places?"

I winced. "*Wax?* No. Shaved? Yes."

She blinked. "One-piece or bikini?"

"One-piece."

"Wrong. Bikini. I brought four with me. One of them will fit you, I'm certain of it."

"But—"

"No buts. You have a nice body. Flaunt it."

I looked down at my chest reflexively, and she put a hand over mine. "Stop fretting about the scar. It's not that bad."

I darted a look at her, suddenly remembering that she'd seen the scar when I'd borrowed her dress in Houston.

"We're going swimming after this. Ty and I have to do a bunch of silly selfie poses for me to post over the next couple weeks on my social media. We'll have to do a few wardrobe changes and slight scenery changes. After that, we're definitely all going swimming, having dinner and then who knows?"

I arched my brows. The way she was checking out Kirill's butt, she definitely knew.

We proceeded to watch the men work for another half an hour or so while Keely told me about the new movie she was going to be working on in the fall. I couldn't take my eyes off Ryan's perfect body—his strong shoulders, his sculpted arms, the dimples in his back above the waistband of his jeans.

I didn't know whether to cheer or boo when they declared themselves finished. Ryan had started up the car and gotten it nice and refrigerated inside. "We were lucky. You didn't need any replacement parts."

"Thank you. I *was* lucky." *In more ways than one.* My eyes tried not to slide over his bare chest and all those many, many delicious abs. And on top of it, he could sew up wounds and fix anything mechanical too. And he had those eyes.

I blinked. *Careful,* I warned myself, lest I get the idea that he was the perfect man, I forced myself to remember he was damaged goods and had a past. But since I'd started spending time with him, it seemed like he was getting better. It hadn't been very long, but things looked promising.

Hopefully, it would last.

After that, Ryan showered, cleaned up for Keely's selfie photos, and they cuddled up for cute poses around the flower planters in the front yard, in the living room. And finally, by the pool.

Keely's bikinis were not as ridiculous as I'd envisioned them to be. One, however, was only held together by strings, so I handed it quickly over to her. There was one that fit reasonably well. It was striped in several shades of blue. A little tight in the butt area and definitely loose in the cups of the top. But we made it work.

I came out and jumped into the pool as quickly as I could, against Keely's protests. The men had gone to grab drinks and, thus, had not been able to appreciate our bodies—and my distinct lack of tan.

Minutes later, the guys came out with a cooler full of beverages. Ryan gallantly offered me a Dr. Pepper without even asking. I thanked him, opened it, and took a sip. He slid into the water without getting himself a drink. But not before I'd noticed how amazing he looked in his short trunks.

The guys got wet immediately. Ryan swam a few laps and then headed straight for me. I'd been sitting on the ledge in the deep end, watching him. He flicked the water out of his hair and grinned when his gaze met mine. Keely and Kirill sat in the shallow end, talking and laughing in low voices.

Ryan treaded water, of course. He was such a natural in the water. Like he was born to it. I didn't miss how his eyes lowered to look at my swimsuit, and I fought the strong urge to want to cover up. His mouth curved into an appreciative smile before he lifted his eyes to meet my gaze again.

And I was flushed and hot all over despite being in the cool water.

"You left work early today," he said. "I saw you head to the parking lot after lunch."

"I always leave early compared to you."

He nodded, plunged himself into the water, pushed off the bottom of the pool, and then shot up again, breaking the surface with a big grin. "Wanna race?"

I laughed. "Not even if you were swimming one-armed without using your legs."

He grinned. "Smart girl. So where did you go this afternoon? Obviously, you weren't getting your AC fixed."

I bit my lip to keep from smiling, amused by his curiosity. Maybe even a little flattered by it too. "I had a date."

That seemed to throw him. He blinked and hesitated, bobbing where he treaded water. His face was unreadable when he asked, "A date? Who's the lucky guy?"

"Some old guy I've known my whole life." I grinned and splashed him.

He laughed, splashing me back. "Do you get together with your dad often?"

I nodded, remembering some of the things he'd said about Conrad Barrett when Ryan hadn't known he was my dad. It hadn't bothered me at the time. You didn't get to a place of such prominence like Dad did without having a lot of people not like you.

"We're close. I have no siblings, and my mom lives far away. My dad is always there for me."

He nodded, a somber look on his face. After that declaration, I hardly imagined he'd be repeating the same things he'd said about my dad before. Given the fact that Dad had been such a jerk to him during that meeting all those weeks ago, I had to admire his restraint.

"Is he still feeling good about his investment in the XPAC?"

I shrugged, opting not to go into detail about his hedging today at lunch. No need to cause alarm over something that was probably nothing.

"He's very cautious about his investments. It's not about the actual dollar amount for him. It's about the win. He loves the thrill of the hustle, and so it will never be about his net worth or how much he can afford to lose. He doesn't like to lose. At all."

Ryan nodded. "I know the type."

"You *are* the type," I replied with a laugh. He returned my laugh and—there it was—that haunted look at the back of those deep blue eyes. Something I'd said had reminded him of his innermost wounds.

He was the type to always win. Except when he'd lost. And when he'd lost, he'd lost *big*.

Whenever he got that look, I wanted to launch myself into his arms, hold him close, press my cheek to his chest, and tell him it would be all right. That he could heal from this. That there was hope.

But telling him that meant nothing. A man like Ryan needed proof, action, not words.

We stayed in the pool, eventually joining the others in the shallow end. There we hung out and chatted as the sky turned to gold, then lavender, and the first stars—barely noticeable out here because of light pollution—came out.

Kirill pointed out some of the summer sights in the sky, identifying Venus and Mars, which had risen beside the Moon.

"Can you see the Space Station from the ground?" Keely asked.

"Yes. It's second brightest object in night sky," answered Kirill.

She frowned. "What's the brightest?"

"The Moon," Kirill said without missing a beat.

"Oh! Duh," Keely laughed. "Sometimes I wish I was blond so I could claim to be a dumb blonde."

"You're not dumb, and I love your red hair." Kirill flashed her a smile, and she grinned slyly back at him.

"The blonde over here is mildly offended." I raised my hand jokingly.

"And most certainly not dumb," agreed Ryan.

Soon after, we all decided we were hungry. Ryan pushed himself out of the pool, and I appreciated every rivulet-covered muscle in his back as they rippled and coiled to make that action possible. Then he bent over the pool, extending a strong arm toward me.

I reached up, and with one arm, he lifted me out like I weighed nothing.

We ordered takeout from a fantastic gourmet Chinese restaurant that delivered. And then we chowed down at the table, poolside.

Ryan and Keely started to take some more pictures now that the light had changed. While they did that, Kirill and I took care of the cleanup.

In the kitchen, after having loaded the dishwasher, Kirill replaced the liner in the garbage can and chatted with me.

"How is your work going, Gray? Good?"

"Yes. Between XVenture and hanging out here, it's almost like I have two jobs."

He seemed to consider that and looked like he wanted to ask me something, but he remained silent.

"Oh, I almost forgot. *Ya ochen krasivaya.*"

His eyebrows twitched upward in surprise. "Eh...*ya soglasen.*"

I didn't understand that either. "What did I say?"

He grinned almost from ear to ear. "You told me 'I am very beautiful.' And I said that I agree."

I blinked. "Uh...oh." Then my faced flamed hot. "Wow, I sound conceited in Russian."

He smiled. "Ty taught you that?"

"I thought he was teaching me a swear word."

Kirill nodded, laughing. "He knows lots of those too. If you were listening today when he fixed your car, you heard them."

The other two came into the kitchen right at that moment, Keely shivering under her towel and jumping into Kirill's arms. "It's so cold in here!"

I turned to look at Ryan. I couldn't help but think back to the night he'd taught me that phrase when we'd sat by the pool over our pizza. The way he'd pulled that phrase out of the air the moment I'd asked him to teach me something in Russian. The way he'd smiled to himself and shook his head like a shy boy when I'd asked him what it meant. But when I'd repeated it, he'd told me, *Da, ochen verno. Very true.*

So seriously.

He'd seriously told me he thought I was very beautiful and then reaffirmed it when I'd said it.

Did that mean—did it mean he truly thought I was beautiful? And how was that even possible? I glanced at Keely, lithe and gorgeous even now, with pool-damp hair and no makeup on. He'd never shown anything close to romantic interest in her.

While Ryan put soap in the dishwasher and started it up, I stuck containers of leftovers in the fridge and threw out what was empty. By that time, Keely and Kirill had disappeared into the other room.

"So I found out what it means," I said.

"What's that?" he asked, straightening and turning to me.

"*Ya ochen krasivaya.* Kirill told me what it meant."

With no embarrassment this time, Ryan only smiled. And then me, my big mouth, and my skeptical self blew it and wiped that smile right off his face when I laughed. "You sure know how to bullshit, even in Russian."

The smile melted into an offended scowl in less than a microsecond. "It wasn't bullshit."

I blinked. "Oh."

He tensed, his eyes narrowing, and a brief scowl twisted his features before he turned away, wiping a dish towel over the damp counter with short, agitated strokes.

I reached out and put my hand on his arm. "I'm sorry."

He straightened and looked at me. "Don't ever do that again."

I blinked at the way his voice was so serious—almost angry. "Do what?"

"Tell me I'm lying because I say you're beautiful. You don't believe my opinion? Fuck that."

Then he reached out, hooked his hands around my upper arms, and pulled me to him. His kiss landed hard on my mouth without giving me a chance to so much as catch my breath. With one of his favorite maneuvers, he rested his hand against the back of my head, holding it fast to his.

His tongue was in my mouth a second later, and I was melting against him while it worked its devious chemistry, stirring things inside me—feelings, sensations, dizzying thoughts. His lips moved over mine with certainty, possession. When he pulled away, we were both breathing heavily.

"Did that kiss lie?" he asked, his mouth inches from mine.

I shook my head. The vocal answer was stuck in my throat. I couldn't speak, the breath, the feeling too overwhelming. I'd been wanting him to kiss me again for days, and yet, I'd been the one who had asked him *not* to kiss me again.

Because...because I knew exactly what it would do to me. *This.*

Good lord.

The world whirled around us for an instant and righted itself again. I felt the need to grasp the edge of the kitchen counter anyway. Very audibly, I gulped, and at that moment, Kirill and Keely walked back into the kitchen holding hands.

"We, uh, we're going to run along now. Let you two get on with your night," Keely said while making meaningful googly eyes at me. I looked away, pretending not to notice.

But Kirill was watching Ty and didn't say anything for a long time before turning to me. "Good night, Gray. Later, Ty."

They left out the back door to grab their bags on the pool deck and go. And we were left staring at each other semi-awkwardly in the kitchen. How much of the kiss had they seen, if anything?

Ty didn't say anything about Kirill's look, and it reminded me of that conversation I'd had with Pari a few days before about the astronauts and their relationships to each other. Ty and Noah had something weird going on, and I'd forgotten to ask Kirill about it.

I doubted the tight-lipped Russian would have told me anything useful anyway.

"We should get out of our damp suits," he finally said.

"Good idea. I'm exhausted."

I was dying to get the salty pool water out of my hair and off my skin. I turned to go toward my guest bathroom and the bedroom I hadn't slept in for almost two weeks.

After a hot, relaxing shower which only served to make me even sleepier, I pulled his bathrobe off the hook on the wall. I'd borrowed it because I kept forgetting my own, and it was at least two sizes too big for me. The belt wrapped around my waist twice before I'd half knotted it. I stumbled back into my room to find my pajamas and ended up curling up on the bed and dozing instead.

He found me there a while later.

"Hey." He sat on the bed. "You okay? I was waiting for you to show up, and you never came. Would you rather sleep in here tonight?"

I blinked up at him and shook my head. "I was super tired."

"Here, I got you." And he bent and scooped me off the bed, carrying me down the hall, through the house, and into his master bedroom. And I very much enjoyed the ride. He was dressed for bed, but I pressed my cheek to his soft T-shirt that covered that hard wall of muscle, his strong arms holding me to his wide chest.

It felt divine, and my heart was clickety-clicking away with excitement.

And I was no longer sleepy by the time we reached his bedroom.

He lay me down on my side of the bed, and I looked up at him. "I didn't grab my pajamas."

He shrugged. "Just sleep in that."

I thought about it for a moment. "I can't go to sleep now."

"Why not?"

"Because we were going to work on something tonight."

He sat down beside me on the bed, staring. "We were going to *what?*"

I blinked, suddenly alert, heart beating fast. Crap. Had I made it sound too much like these times sharing a bed were therapy sessions? Because they weren't. They so weren't.

"I thought maybe we could try turning off the lights."

He recoiled slightly. "No."

"I'd still be here. Right beside you."

He shook his head slightly, that strange, distant look coming into his eyes. What did they call it? The thousand-yard stare?

"How about we try it for five minutes? Then the lights go back on."

He blinked but didn't move.

I slowly sat up. "Just five, Ryan. You can do that, right?"

His eyes dropped to the coverlet on the bed. But no protest.

I scooted off the bed and proceeded to turn off the extra lights—the one in the hallway to the bathroom, the overhead light, and lastly, I sat on his normal spot on the bed before slowly reaching over to put my hand on the lamp switch. "I can count down to turning it off. So you can prepare—"

I cut myself off when he leaped forward, clamping his hand over my wrist.

"You don't want to try?" I asked in a quiet voice.

His Adam's apple bobbed as he swallowed. "If you want to do that, I need a distraction."

"Okay—you want some music on? Or a podcast? Or what would you like for a distraction?"

"*You,*" he fired back immediately, his eyes dropping to the neck of the terry robe where it had fallen open above my cleavage.

Now I was the one swallowing noisily.

"What-what do you—"

"You turn that light off, then I get to touch you. Kiss you. Wherever I want. The entire time it's off."

I recognized this characteristic bargaining maneuver. Like the night in Houston when I'd bartered questions for kisses. But tonight, the hunger in his eyes said he wanted more.

And I couldn't help it. I wanted more too.

So much more.

My body had been telling me for over a week now that *it was time.*

It wasn't like I'd had many opportunities before, but nevertheless, it felt like the right time to me. So, with my heartbeat owning the pulse at my throat, I nodded wordlessly and turned off the switch.

He caught his breath so loudly, it was the only thing I heard before he grasped me and pulled me to him, tracing the line of my neck from collarbone to chin with his lips, then he buried his face in my hair.

"Strawberries." His voice was a growl, and his body was tight, tense. Was it from arousal or the fear trigger of the darkness? He was talking, at least, so that was a good sign.

"Are you doing okay?"

"I don't need my eyes open for this, Gray." And the next sensation I felt in the dark was the firm tug on the belt of my robe. Oh, um. Yeah, I hadn't counted on him getting me naked—at least, not this fast.

He had it untied in seconds, kissing his way down my neck, to my chest. Firm, insistent hands pushed me back, flat against the mattress. It felt so good, I could barely catch my breath in time for the next one. The only sounds were the sighs coming from my mouth, the occasional answering heavy breathing from him, and that persistent clicking of my heart.

And tonight, I didn't mind that it was giving me up like a double agent. His warm hands on my cool flesh felt *so good*. And his mouth...

Oh God, his mouth. He had one nipple between his lips, his hand working the other between thumb and forefinger. I jumped at the contact, and he responded with a low groan deep in his chest.

I called out his name with ragged pleading. That seemed to fire him up because the dirty talk started.

"I want inside, Gray. I want to know what you feel like under me when I'm inside you. I want to hear you say my name when I'm fucking you. I can hardly think about anything else. All the time. What you'll sound like when you come."

My fingers threaded through his hair as his head moved down, across my belly. Had it been five minutes yet? It had felt like an hour—a year—a month. And mere seconds at the same time. I could turn on the light and stop this. But did I want to?

"Will you let me?" he asked hoarsely. "I want to make you come." Yes. *Oh yes.*

"Please," was my breathy reply. And thankfully, he required no other because what he was doing to me—every touch, every kiss, was stealing my words, stealing my thoughts until everything, my being, my *existence*, centered around him. Him. *Him.*

When he parted my legs with his wide shoulders, even that small fraction of rational thought scattered to the wind. Existence became his hot breath bathing my thighs as his head moved slowly, so slowly to close in on its target.

Being became the feel of his hands on my thighs, my knees, parting them wider. All reality was his soft lips exploring the juncture of my thighs, probing deeper, homing in on the center of sensation, pleasure.

Thoughts, breath, awareness fell into a series of beats, of pulses, each movement of his mouth on that bundle of sensitive nerves. The touch of his tongue to my clit. How his mouth moved against it, the vibrations as the deepest groans from his wide chest reverberated through his lips, tearing through me.

Was I remembering to breathe? I had no idea. All I could feel was him. His mouth on me. His lips enclosing me, sucking. My hips moved under him of their own accord, so far out of my control. My hips thrust toward him, wanting more, and yet, feeling pleasure so intense, it almost hurt.

His mouth. His *mouth*. That gifted, heavenly mouth. And that tongue.

I rolled my eyes back into my head as my spine curled, chest thrust upward. I called out and had no idea what words I was saying.

I didn't want him to stop. I think I was telling him that. Over and over again. But it felt as if the voice was coming from somewhere else, and I was all wrapped up in my own world, light-years away. *Don't stop. Oh God, Ryan. Don't stop. It. Feels. So. Good.*

Tension built, like engines firing up before a rocket launch— toward my own countdown. My breathing synced with the movements of his mouth. In the darkness, the room spun. Ryan's hands held me tightly at my hips, but his mouth didn't stop.

Of course, he knew exactly what he was doing. He sucked and licked relentlessly until—until that countdown reached zero, maximum tension. My legs, my arms, my teeth, everything clenching, constricting, and then...

With a convulsive shiver, my body let go in ecstatic, blissful release. My muscles pulsed with heat and pleasure so intense, I could only moan and sigh and gasp.

Oh *Jesus.*

How. What. Where...?

My body was still convulsing, those pleasure points still throbbing until blessed emptiness. Clouds of pleasure enveloped me. I hardly noticed when Ryan straightened from the bed and dove straight for the light switch.

My eyes squeezed shut in the sudden light, and I was aware that he was looking at me, lying splayed out on his bed with my robe wide open, my naked body in full view.

After what had just happened between us, it would be rather silly to cover up now. Nevertheless, as his eyes roamed over my body, I felt my skin warming self-consciously under his scrutiny. When I fully opened my eyes, it was to watch his back as he went into the bathroom, turned on the faucet, and began to splash water on his face over the sink.

I blinked, still getting accustomed to the light then sat up slowly. "What are you doing?"

"Taking a breather and trying to calm the fuck down for a minute. There's no way I'm keeping my hands off you tonight if I don't."

I smiled. "It's a little late for keeping your hands off me. But what if— What if *I* didn't want to keep my hands off of *you?*"

Ryan froze in the act of wiping his face dry. Then slowly, he pulled the towel away to look at me. His expression was completely impassive, but his eyes smoldered. I couldn't resist slipping my eyes down his body, from his tense shoulders to the thin T-shirt that hugged his solid torso, to his shorts—and the very noticeable bulge of his arousal in them.

I remembered his hot words from moments before. *I want inside, Gray. I want to hear you say my name when I'm fucking you...what you'll sound like when you come.*

I wanted it too. So much. Even though he'd thoroughly satisfied me, a new fire stoked in my belly. I wanted to know what *he* felt like.

I cleared my throat and opened my thighs. "I want you inside me," I said in a harsh whisper.

His lids dropped halfway over those beautiful blue eyes, and deep color spread over his skin. A fist clenched at his side, and he stepped toward me, his Adam's apple bobbing as he swallowed. I scooted aside so he could sit on the bed beside me.

After a brief hesitation, he slowly sank, facing me. But his features were still closed, still skeptical. I leaned forward and tilted my face toward his, my mouth landing for a kiss on his mouth. It was slow, careful. And yet, he was holding back, keeping himself reined in so tightly, it felt like he might break.

Unlike the other times we'd kissed, he didn't reach forward to hold my head to his. Instead, he received the kiss, opening his mouth to mine but never leaning into it. As if he wanted to be completely certain that I was initiating this. That this was what *I* wanted.

And it was. It so was.

My hand landed on his rough cheek as I pushed farther into that kiss, holding his face still so that I could deepen it. Everything was silent. Everything still.

Except that ubiquitous clicking from inside my chest.

Then, so subtly, something changed. He exhaled and, on that breath, uttered against my lips a simple plea. *"Gray..."* But I couldn't know if it was an appeal to stop or to continue.

Something in that calm whisper set my blood flowing, as if it hadn't been flowing before, as if I hadn't been awake or even *alive* before that moment. My body leaned into his, and he felt it too, that moment, because his arm locked around my waist, and he closed the distance between us until our chests were touching.

I had my hand twisted in the cloth of his T-shirt a moment after that, insistently tugging to signal that I wanted it off. I wanted it all off. I wanted to feel his skin against mine. I wanted it so badly, and I wanted it *now*.

I countered his plea with one of my own. *"Ryan."*

In less than a second, he'd pulled off his T-shirt and tossed it onto the floor. Then my hands were on his chest, and he was leaning in for more kisses, which I enthusiastically returned. On his lips, on his face, down the hard column of his neck, across his upper chest. He felt solid, like a rock. Like a wall encased in male flesh.

Under my fingertips, I perceived every crease of solid muscle, every visible vein under his skin. The hair on his arms, his chest. Every bit of it so masculine, so beautiful. I explored it all with my hands and my mouth, and he savored every moment, his eyes closed, his breath hissing through his teeth, his hands threading gently into my hair.

I shrugged off my robe then, a mere formality since it was open anyway. But Ryan mostly kept his hands from roaming. They stayed resting on my hips as I explored him, our mouths meeting every so often to reconnect in a hot kiss.

Neither one of us left each other in any doubt of our intentions or desires. But we didn't communicate with words. Touches, strokes, sighs, caresses with our lips across sweaty, salty skin.

He sucked in his breath when my hand landed on the bulge in his shorts. I stroked the length of him with my fingers, watching his face closely as he tensed. "You are driving me insane," he finally uttered the first words between us in nearly half an hour.

I smiled, laughed. "We can't have that. A psychotherapist is supposed to do the opposite, right?"

He opened his eyes and looked at me, his arms tightening. "You can drive me insane anytime. *This* way, anyway." And for the first time in all that time since he'd come back to the bed, he initiated contact by gently pushing me flat on my back. The lamplight glared down on us, but I didn't mind. And I wasn't about to insist he turn it off now.

In truth, I was way too turned on to feel self-conscious about my body under all this light. He was still sitting, looking at me, and he reached out to stroke my arm tenderly. "Are you sure about this, Gray?"

My mouth quirked. His seeking reassurance of my consent was probably the sexiest thing he had done so far—and that was a difficult list to top.

And I could see why he'd want to make sure. He'd called me on it before, my tendency to play it safe. And now I was throwing caution to the wind.

It felt thrilling. And my clicking heartbeat agreed. Smiling, I replied, "I'm really damn sure."

He stood up and shed his shorts and underwear in one fell swoop and...

For the first time, I got to appreciate his beauty in all of its male glory. *Wow.* He was...stunning. Like he'd been carved right out of marble by Michelangelo himself. Like the statue of *David* I'd seen in a picture my mom had posted on her wall after going to Italy.

One difference, though. Actually, a very big difference. Unlike *David*, Ryan was clearly aroused. And that additional hard-to-miss feature made him even more alarmingly gorgeous.

My heartbeat notched up to triple time, and every living being in the room was made aware of it. He only took his eyes off me to move to the nightstand and open the top drawer to pull out a foil-wrapped condom, placing it on top of the nightstand.

Then he came to the bed, waited for me to scoot over to make room for him, and lay down beside me, pulling me to him with a passionate kiss.

I shuddered against him, pent-up excitement and nervousness mingling into one. He kissed me deeply, plunging his tongue into my mouth as he threaded his fingers through my hair from temple to crown.

I felt a slight tremble from him too, beneath my own fingertips. And it stunned me. Was he trembling from excitement? Definitely not nervousness. What on earth did he have to be nervous about? He'd done this...

Well, more times than I wanted to even think about, I was sure.

For such a seasoned pro, though, he was going slow, taking his time, running his hands all over my body—my belly, my hips, my thighs. Until his hand rested at the juncture of my legs, the very place his mouth had stirred such ecstasy not long before. His fingers slipped down the crease of my sex, gently separating me there, working themselves inside.

He kissed and kissed me, making me dizzy once again with desire as his fingers slipped against my clit, sometimes rubbing me there, sometimes entering me—but always slowly, methodically.

His head dipped then to fasten around my nipple, and in conjunction with the movements of his hands, he was stirring me to greater heights like before. "You like that, baby girl." It wasn't a question but a statement. He said it as if he was very proud of himself for making me feel so good. I caught my breath as his fingers slipped deeper, and he lifted his mouth to turn attention to the other nipple. "Don't hold back. Let me know everything you're feeling. What you like. What you don't."

My voice was so breathy, I doubted I made myself understood very well, but I tried. "I like everything you're doing right now."

"Mmm. Good. Because I love the way you taste. The way you feel. You are one damn sexy woman, Gray, and don't you ever fucking tell me otherwise again." Then his mouth resumed its soft sucking, and I wasn't thinking words again for the next few minutes.

I was only thinking in sensation as my spine curled in on itself again, and I was calling his name as I hit that second orgasm.

Holy macaroni.

"God, I love it when you say my name. Especially when you say it like that, all breathy and satisfied."

"Mmm," I grunted as I rolled my head to press against his rippling shoulder to plant a kiss there. "You're spoiling me."

He tucked my hair behind my ear. "Oh, I enjoy spoiling you. A lot."

I smiled and put my hand on his cheek, turning to meet his burning gaze. "But I want to use that condom."

He smiled. "So do I." And without another word, he turned to the nightstand and scooped up the foil package, tore it open, and slipped it on, all while I stroked his back and neck with the back of my hand. Once it was on, he straightened, tossing the foil wrapper onto the floor next to his shorts, then he rolled close to me, so that part of his body was overlapping mine.

His mouth sought out my neck, and I closed my eyes. How could I feel even more hunger after he'd made me come—twice?

But I did. And he was. And when his mouth found mine again, our tongues tangling, he moved on top of me, gently settling himself between my open legs.

His rock-hard erection pressed against my sex, and he seemed to hesitate before I lifted my hips toward him, clamping my hands around his huge shoulders. "I want to feel you inside me, Ryan."

With a wordless growl, he pressed forward—perhaps more forcibly than he was planning because he drew back slightly the moment I flinched. I had been willing myself not to flinch. As this was my first time, I knew it would likely hurt. I'd been preparing myself for it.

But, disappointingly, I still flinched. I lifted my hips to him again and said, "Go ahead. I'm fine."

He pushed deeper and my breath hitched, but other than that, I didn't move. It was strange—how it hurt and felt good at once. Alien and natural at once. Everything and nothing that I'd imagined it to be at once.

Ryan continued after another minute's pause. With another smooth ease of his hips, I realized there was still more of him.

When he stopped moving, he let out a shaky breath and met my gaze. I smiled, and with only the briefest of hesitations, he smiled back, then leaned in for a kiss.

He moved again and everything changed.

Chapter Nineteen
Ryan

T HIS WHOLE NIGHT HAD A SURREAL QUALITY—IN THE best of ways. Never in a thousand years would I have thought it would end up like this, with this beautiful, amazing woman's body pressed to mine, open to me.

I closed my eyes, relishing every moment of this, pressed my mouth to hers though I was reluctant to stifle those melodious sighs, each one striking a new chord of desire deep inside of me. My hands ran along the length of her body, that soft, creamy skin.

Moving my hips again, one step closer to my own climax, I was mindful in every moment that I had to go slow, be gentle, give her time. Part of me didn't want to.

And part of me was consumed by this alien feeling that I shouldn't be here. That I didn't deserve this, didn't deserve *her*. That I was an unworthy traveler on pristine, hallowed territory.

It was true. I did not deserve this. I knew it as I met that jewel-like green gaze, as wide open to me as her body was and as unguarded as her heart. *Gray Barrett, what are you doing to me? And how are you doing it so quickly?*

Once more I sank into her heat, reminded of her inexperience by the daunting tightness of her body. My mouth landed on her temple. Her hands clung to my shoulders, her eyes now closed, and we moved against each other, consumed in each other, feeling only the connection of our bodies, each other's breath on our faces, the places where our hands held us fused together.

Control was quickly slipping away from me as she started to move her hips in conjunction with mine, like a well-practiced, intimate dance we'd known all along without realizing it. This dance was only ours—Gray's and mine.

I buried my face in her sweet-smelling neck and quickened my pace, listening carefully for any change in her breathing, the tension in her body. Instead, I heard encouragement. "*Yes—that feels good.*"

Fuck, this woman was blowing my mind. She wasn't the proverbial iceberg floating on the water, mostly hidden. She was the glacier to my mountain, carving new patterns in my soul, leaving her indelible mark.

Careful, I warned myself. *This one could hurt. A lot.*

Then again, I had the immense power to hurt her as well. Just as right now my body was hurting hers. She was being very brave about it, I knew, but I could tell that when I moved certain ways, it caused her pain. It was temporary, yes. But I *was* hurting her.

And I had the potential to hurt her a lot more than this.

I vowed right then and there with everything in me that I wouldn't.

My eyes squeezed closed, feeling the familiar cues of my body and where they were leading. Her hands were on my back now, cupped around my shoulder blades, her harsh breathing in my ear as I sped up, racing toward climax, my body tensing in that pleasurable trek toward the summit.

She arched her back beneath me, gasping my name, and that was it for me. I was lost in her. Every muscle in my body tense, my breath stilling as the throes of climax swept over me, submerging awareness of everything else, contracting over and over again. Like a waterfall into the most pristine, clear forest pool, I emptied myself into her.

Sweaty and out of breath, I all but collapsed on her before quickly rolling to the side, though it had taken every inch of my willpower to pull myself away from her. Too much. Too powerful, these sensations, these feelings.

Quick as I could, I ducked into the bathroom to get rid of the condom, then came back into the bed. She'd crawled under the covers, so I joined her there.

A poignant high washed over me. Before she could say anything or even move, I reached over and pulled her to me, so that she lay across my chest. Because the thought of being even inches away from her right now was intolerable.

I needed her body against mine, her skin on my skin, her breath mixing with mine, her sweat and mine—all night. I wouldn't have it any other way.

She pressed her soft cheek to my chest, and my eyelids slowly closed. I could lie like this for days and have everything I wanted in my arms. The most comforting contentment enveloped me at that moment. My fingers found the soft nape of her neck, the silky strands of her short hair. *She was precious.* And maybe, just maybe, I *could* deserve her. Eventually.

"Well, that certainly wasn't how I was expecting things to go tonight," she said quietly after a long while of us simply caressing each other. My hand stroked the soft skin of her back, hers smoothing over my chest and abdomen.

"Can't say I'm unhappy in the least," I said through a grin.

Her head popped up, and she returned my smile. "Me either." I kissed her soundly along her jaw, her neck, the salty taste of her driving me to distraction. And those urges, so recently satisfied, were now reawakening.

"Hmm," she said, arching her neck toward me. "Better take care, there, Commander Tyler. Or there's going to be an encore performance."

I grinned wickedly against her neck. "Oh, you can bet on it. There is definitely going to be a round two."

I was ready now, but that would be too fast for her. I stopped stroking her back and held her close instead. I didn't kiss her again, and I tried to think about something else besides rolling over and starting this all over again. But damn, I sure wanted to.

Surprisingly, I liked doing this almost as much.

"Mmm, this is nice," she drawled lazily, tracing some kind of idle pattern across my stomach. "You aren't ticklish though."

"Nope. I'm an insensitive bastard, even in that way."

Her hand stopped, and she turned to look into my face. "Who said you were insensitive?"

I shrugged. "I've lost count."

Her dark brows rose. "Bed partners?"

I hesitated, not wanting to talk about other bed partners. For some reason it felt like that would trivialize what this was. This was so different—in ways I didn't even want to examine. The tangle of feelings vying for dominance inside my chest, for one. "I don't cuddle after sex, ever."

"You mean, like you're doing right now?"

"This is an anomaly." And I swallowed a pang of emotion.

"So you've had lovers—"

"—sex partners—" I corrected.

"—accuse you of being insensitive because you won't cuddle afterward?"

"Or call them later, yeah."

She grinned. "This mean you aren't going to call me?"

I pushed her hair back from her face, not so much because it was in her eyes as because I loved to touch her hair. "Given the fact that we are cuddling right at this very moment—and that you've been living here—I doubt it."

"Is your body rebelling right now? Screaming out in protest of the cuddling?"

I brushed my thumb across her cheek, down those irresistible ridges above her lip. She put her lips together and kissed the tip of my thumb. My body was rather enjoying this, in all honesty. As much as I wanted to fuck her again—and ASAP—I also wanted this. *What was this?*

"Nope." I gave the simplest answer. The one that wouldn't give her ways to dig deeper, like she usually did.

"Oh God. This isn't some...pity cuddle, is it?" Her head came up, her eyes wide. "You're not doing this because it was my first time and so you think I need comforting or something?"

I smiled at her honest fear. "I am not feeling one ounce of pity right now. Pity is the furthest thing from my mind."

"Good," she said, still running her fingers across my skin. I closed my eyes, relishing her touch. It was like that touch of rain and fresh air against my face the moment they'd open the Soyuz capsule on the Kazakh Steppe after landing from the ISS. It was my first assignment of nearly half a year on station. Nothing had been sweeter than that first breath of fresh air after six months shut inside a can of recycled air, no matter how much it had hurt to return to full gravity.

And she was that same sweet breath of air in human form. Her cool, soft skin pressed to mine. The smell of strawberries and the salty tang of her sweat. I could feel myself drifting away. I was almost in lucid dreamland when she shifted slightly beside me and my eyes opened again. "So I guess, in the end, it was a good thing I turned off that lamp." She let the statement drift off.

I knew her well enough by now to know that wasn't an offhand statement. Nevertheless, even the slightest hint she might turn off the light and bring in the darkness again was enough to make me tense involuntarily.

She felt it, lifting her head to look into my face. Whatever she saw concerned her enough to frown. "What is it that terrifies you? What do you see in the dark?"

I stared up at the ceiling, ignoring her scrutiny. I wanted to blow off the question. But something pulled at me to respond— maybe it was the almost tangible feel of her eyes on my face? My barriers softened, and I let out a long sigh. Weary, down to my bones. I could no longer fight to keep that all up. My lids closed, eyes squeezing shut.

"On the far side of the planet, when it's nighttime, it's very dark. During the day, Earth is this brilliant blue-and-white glowing ball that outshines everything, so that you can't even see a star in the sky when you look out into space. But during the night, you can see spots of light outlining the cities, but the blackness of space, the dark station above. It..." I shuddered involuntarily.

She pressed a long kiss to my chest, her arms tightening around me, reassuring me of her presence. I started to stroke her hair but still did not look at her.

"It's the last thing he saw...Xander—he even said. He said that he couldn't think of a more spectacular view to be his last one."

She was silent for a minute, perhaps wishing for me to continue. But I had no desire to.

"But what do *you* see...in the dark?"

I shook my head, trying to blank out the image that rose in my mind—a corpse, suffocated in his own suit, drifting on orbit, a man-sized, man-shaped satellite. Waiting, just waiting until orbital decay and inevitable immolation in the atmosphere. Instantaneous cremation.

Xander's sightless eyes. Xander's voiceless, perhaps open mouth. Silence and blackness. His spacesuit turned into a coffin. I shuddered again.

She smoothed her hand on my chest. "You could tell me if you wanted to. It might make you feel better."

I blinked. Tell her? Unburden myself of the truth that only I knew? I swallowed a monstrous lump in my throat.

She reared up on one elbow, propping herself there, and leaned in to kiss my face, then caressed my cheek softly with her hand. "There's no judgment here. At all."

I blew out a breath, feeling pressure mount in my chest, beneath my skin. That same anger—anger at Xander, yes, but more fury at myself. I shook my head. "I told him not to. Damn it all. He was so fucking stubborn."

The rhythmic stroking of her fingers slowed only a little before resuming. When I said nothing else, she asked, "What did you tell him not to do?"

Was I holding my breath? Why did my chest feel so tight? I forced myself to let it go. *Let it go.* Every breath was painful, tight, suffocating. I'd never revealed this to any living being and yet—it wanted to come out.

I could hide the truth from everyone else. But from her?

"Do you know about how things went down during the accident?" I asked.

"I read the public transcripts. Watched the documentary and read some other articles. You guys were out there to repair an unexpected minor ammonia leak."

I nodded. "But when a blast of pressurized ammonia blew us back against the truss, my suit was breached. Xander panicked, but he couldn't get to me because his tether was tangled." My last bit of breath escaped my lungs with that admission, and my heart sped up like I was in the middle of a workout.

I hadn't told her anything that wasn't on every official record of the accident. I sucked in a big gulp of air, thankful for her silence while I got this out.

"He asked for permission to untether himself. I said no way. CAPCOM told him no, too. The leak in my suit was slow, and I had time to get the job done. So I made my way up to the valve to shut off the ammonia."

Here it came. The room whirled for an instant as my blood pressure shot up at the mere thought of verbalizing this. Where was the relief I was supposed to be feeling? Pain racked my body instead. Like a festering wound that needed to be dug out, drained.

"He could see the leak in my suit, the gas escaping. And closing the valve was a two-man job." *Air, more air.*

She noticed my quickened respiration, her head coming up off my chest as if that would help me catch my breath. No chance of that.

"Without warning, he was at my side, even though I knew he couldn't have untangled his tether that quickly." Was this my voice that sounded so strangled? "Houston kept wanting to know what happened, and I couldn't say anything. Couldn't reprimand Xander over the comms, or they'd know. As far as they knew, he'd untangled his tether. But I had visual confirmation otherwise." I gulped air like it was my last breath. Beside me, she pressed her sweet body against mine. My grip around her tightened, but all I knew, all I saw...

"I'm making my way to you now, Ty," comes Xander's voice over the comm.

"Oh, you've untangled yourself? Excellent. Come join the party. We'll have this done in no time."

He doesn't reply, and I don't think anything of it until he's within eyeshot. His helmeted head pops up from below as he clings to the truss segment opposite me. I can confirm visually that he's okay. And it's clear that he's no longer tethered to the station.

And of course, if I make a comment on it over the comms, he'll be in massive amounts of trouble. Our eyes meet, mine widened, and I shake my head vigorously. He doesn't respond.

My eyes squeezed shut. *God forgive me.* And yet, I didn't believe in God. And I knew it was useless to call out to some higher power. I should have said something the minute I'd noticed his tether undone. I should have told them. Xander might still be here had I spoken up.

Why the fuck did you do it, Xander?

"He had everything to live for." It was spilling out of me now, as if out of my control. As if this little sorceress in my arms had cast some spell on me to draw out the truth so that a curse would no longer harm my soul. But I knew that was impossible. This sin was mine to own. Mine *forever*. "He threw his life away to save me."

She murmured softly against my skin. It comforted me, like a prayer. "I will bet any money he didn't think of it like that."

My eyes stung and I blinked, staring unseeing at the ceiling. "He had no fucking right to make that decision. He had no right. He had a wife. A kid. I had no one. Jesus," I croaked, tears threatened to spring from my eyes. "You had to be a fucking hero," I rasped in a dead voice.

I reached up, rubbing my eyes through closed lids, praying she wouldn't notice the tear that leaked out the corner before I managed to get myself under control. She said nothing for a long time, just held me, pressed her cheek to my shoulder.

My strained heartbeat calmed. When my breathing matched it, she spoke again. "It's okay to be angry at him."

I swallowed nails. They impaled my esophagus, my stomach. It made me feel like shit to be angry at him. I ground my teeth together.

"You can't understand," I finally said.

"You're absolutely right. I can't."

"I can't look at them—Karen and AJ. I can't talk to them. I— Knowing what I know. That he traded his life for mine."

"Did he, though? Did he know he was doing that? He saw your suit leaking. He saw that you needed help. He untethered himself to get to you faster because you were in distress, because he was worried about you. You would have done the same for him."

"I had less to lose." That hung in the air between us. She had nothing to say to that because it was the truth.

"What happened next? I mean...I know what happened in theory. But somewhere along the line, things went wrong again. I know when you got to the valve it was frozen."

I ran a palm over my forehead. "It hadn't been touched in a decade. We were trying to work it loose, and it wouldn't budge. I braced myself for leverage and—when it gave, it *really* gave. The torque sent us off-balance. I got yanked back because of my tether. But Xander fell against the array. The live current was what fried his suit."

Exhaustion settled over me and I was weak from the aftermath of having let that secret go but I was still angry. "I told CAPCOM I was going after him, but they wouldn't let me. They cut off our communication with each other, and I couldn't see where he'd bounced off to."

"But your suit was leaking. You couldn't have gotten to him in time to get back to the airlock. And then you both would have died."

She was right, of course. All this, I knew. But it didn't change how that made me feel and how I still couldn't look Karen and AJ in the eyes knowing I kept that secret.

After another long pause, she cleared her throat. "So this is the real reason NASA fired you? Because you wouldn't come clean about Xander untethering himself?"

I blinked in surprise, impressed at how quickly she'd leaped to that conclusion. "They have their suspicions, and they tried like hell to get me to admit what happened. I wouldn't. They shitcanned me and blamed it on the fight with the flat-earther. Obviously, it's a secret that can't get out."

She nodded and looked into my face. "And you won't tell NASA what really happened because then they'll pin the blame for the accident solely on Xander."

"I don't want any of that to discredit his memory. Xander posthumously received the Congressional Space Medal of Honor. That's the highest award an astronaut can get."

She nodded. "You received it too."

I shrugged but didn't say anything. Naturally, she called me on it.

"Yours doesn't mean any less, Ryan. That award is for important feats, but also for bravery during a space emergency— and preventing a major space disaster. *You* did that. Even if things didn't end up the way you wanted. Xander saved you. You saved four other astronauts and the entire station. And accepting the accolades for that does not mean you are forgetting Xander's sacrifice in any way. You sacrificed too. Xander is a hero. But so are you. You aren't lesser because you lived. It just happened. And you can't control what happened. But you can stop tormenting yourself about how it turned out."

My hand brushed down her delicate spine as she talked. I absorbed every word, took it in like it was water and I was desperate to drink. My arm tightened, and I hitched her body against me.

Did I believe what she was telling me? Not necessarily. But I appreciated where the thoughts were coming from. And though this baring of my soul had been downright painful, it also felt good. So good to let someone in this close. Every muscle relaxed, and I closed my eyes—I was exposed, vulnerable. Yet with her, I felt safe.

She smoothed her hand across my cheek once again, and I turned to look her in the eye. "Tell me what you are thinking," she finally said.

I rolled to my side to face her, my hand resting on her hip, pulling her against me. "I'm thinking about how sweet your lips taste." I leaned down and kissed her soundly, aware that the surface temperature of our skin was quickly heating up. Her lips opened to mine immediately as if it were the most natural thing in the world. "And how much I want to keep tasting them—and every inch of you."

She leaned back when I would have gone in for a second approach, and our eyes met. "You're using sex to avoid this subject, aren't you?"

A brow raised, and that soreness still niggled at me beneath the surface. I wanted to forget. I wanted to lose myself in her again.

"Perhaps I am. Do you have any objections?" My mouth sank to wrap around one of her perky pink nipples. She gasped, arching toward me. I sucked harder and her hips jolted. She let out a long, slow moan that ignited my blood. "I take it you are on board with this evasion tactic."

Heavy breathing met me in answer. I nudged her shoulder, so that she lay flat beneath me. Our gazes locked and she swallowed. "I need you," I ground out between my teeth, watching her through narrowed eyes.

She licked her lips and stared up at me with those beautiful green eyes.

My mouth sank to devour her neck, and she squirmed beneath me. *Heaven.* Slowly, so slowly that pain, that rawness of opening up was fading, cooling as I immersed myself in her. Like a healing salve. I rolled her onto her side, facing away from me, and lay behind her in a spoon position. She murmured unintelligibly as I pressed my erection to her firm, round bottom. My mouth enveloped her earlobe. "I want inside you again, Gray. *Now.*"

She whimpered against me in response, but she was nodding, and eventually, she supplied a breathy, "*Yes.*" This sent me digging for another condom, sheathing myself effortlessly before pressing against her from behind, my arm wrapped around her waist, holding her to me as I entered her again.

As before, it was a tight fit. And I went slow. Thankfully, she didn't flinch this time. In fact, she kept absolutely still, leaning her thin shoulders back against my chest. Once again, her heat swallowed me, and I squeezed my eyes shut, letting loose an involuntary curse.

Fuck. It felt so good. I moved my hand to her clit. "I want you to come when I'm inside you. I want to feel it when you're wrapped around me." She moaned loudly as my hand moved over her, stroking her heat, her wetness, I moved inside her while my hand strokes quickened in pace. Her lithe body undulated against mine, responding to my movement.

Good God, this was blowing my mind, pulling me into an inescapable gravity well—our own event horizon. Time slowed, and all I became aware of were her movements against my body, her vocal responses to my touch. The smell of her arousal, her sweat-soaked skin sticking to mine. *Jesus.* She was destroying me.

I became acutely aware of the mounting tension in her body. She'd gone stiff against me, her eyes squeezed shut, her head thrown back against my shoulder, every stroke met by a strong vocal response. Like a long, intimate conversation. My hand moved, my cock gently thrust inside her, and she moaned and writhed against me, pressing the globes of her pert little ass into my groin, making me lose my mind.

I stilled when she hit her climax, her muscles clenching, gripping me ferociously. It squeezed the air from my lungs, and I couldn't move—couldn't breathe until her crisis had faded and she was limp against me once more. I brought my mouth down to suck her neck, and I resumed my movement, more insistent, more urgent than before.

The tension in my pelvis, my legs, my chest, everything tightened, and I couldn't think again until I was coming— mindless pressure spasming in pleasure waves as I stilled, thrusting inside as deep as I could. Fuck. Fuck. *Fuck.*

It felt so good.

Long minutes after that, riding that wave of heady afterglow, the bed moved as she left it, and I rolled onto my back, dazed, knowing I should probably follow her. I did manage to pull off the condom and dispose of it. Somewhere in there, I cleaned up before stumbling back to bed, pulling her to me and falling into a restful, dreamless slumber. A type of sleep I hadn't experienced in months. Maybe even a year.

Chapter Twenty
Gray

I'M NOT SURE WHERE THE DAYS WENT. THEY FLOATED BY IN a delightful but delirious haze. I know I got my work done. I know I was accomplishing things—working on my side jobs for the Mars Analog team and compiling studies for other colleagues. I know I maintained my fairly modest social life when I could.

But damn if it wasn't all done through a Ryan-colored filter cast over my life. I saw everything as if looking through him. If it were a color, it would definitely be one of the warmer, more pleasant ones, maybe a golden-yellow hue. It made the world more pleasant, colors more vibrant, bright things even brighter. Experiences more vivid. Tastes more intense.

And it was stunning how much I thought about him every day. And not only when I was in bed with him making all kinds of new wrinkles in his sheets. Not only when I saw him at work and we had to fight not to grin at each other like idiots and gloat over our stunning little secret.

I thought about him most of all when he wasn't around me. When I was trying to focus on my work or write up reports. When I was in meetings with the psychology team, trying to work out new training schedules and protocols for the astronaut team.

I even thought about him when I managed a rare moment to slip away on a Saturday to have a long-delayed lunch with Pari at the outdoor patio of a vegan restaurant—her choice—near where we worked in Seal Beach.

She had a bowl of lentil stew with a big chunk of dark bread. I munched on a vegan burrito with a side salad.

"It's about time you come hang out with me." She pouted in between spooning bites of the fragrant brown mixture into her mouth. "I was beginning to think maybe my deodorant wasn't working anymore."

I rolled my eyes. "I'm sorry. I've been really busy."

"With your babysitting job...yes, I know. How is the astro-hottie, anyway?"

I smiled, *astro-bae,* indeed. Quickly, I shoved the burrito into my mouth to cover for the blush that was now bathing my skin. She didn't miss it.

"What was that?"

I flicked an innocent glance up at her, eyes wide. Any moment now, I was going to start busting up. I wouldn't be able to maintain this for long. But I hadn't decided yet on how much I could or should tell her. I mean, I trusted Pari implicitly, but I wasn't sure who I could confide in about this.

And yet, if I didn't tell *someone,* I risked spontaneously combusting. The Ryan-colored filter was even seeing that as something ridiculously positive. Jeez. In some ways, he was better than what I'd imagine a psychotropic drug to be.

"Fess up. Now. Are you crushing on him? Or is there more?" She scrutinized my face as I slowly chewed my bite. I was usually so good at masking my emotions. With my parents, I'd had to become an expert at it at a very young age, but damn, this was hard. *Hard.*

I'd never ever felt like this before—like I had a thousand champagne bubbles inside my chest, fizzing and burbling all the time—and it was damn hard to conceal.

Her eyes widened, and she slapped the table beside her plate, rattling all the silverware and startling the couple sitting nearby. She turned to them, sheepishly muttering her apologies.

Then she was back at me, making frantic "gimme" gestures with her fingers. "Spill it. Now."

I faux-scowled at her. "Why do I have to talk about my stuff when you are the one walking around with all the secrets?"

She threw me an exasperated look. "What secrets? I have no secrets."

"Victoria?" I raised my brows at her expectantly.

She ripped off a chunk of bread and sat back in her chair, thoughtfully gnawing on it as she considered me. "Touché."

I forked a bite of my salad into my mouth, satisfied that I had shut her up. Yes, it was weird that an almost-psychologist was happy to shut her friend up instead of getting her to talk about something that was obviously bugging her.

A myriad of emotions crossed through her dark eyes, indecision, curiosity, doubt, and even a little fear before she set the remaining chunk of bread aside on the table next to her plate and leaned forward.

"Fine, I'll tell you what's going on if you tell me about you and Ty."

"A tell-all?" Should I call her bluff? I put my hand to my chin and tilted my head. "An interesting idea."

"Are you in?"

"You first." I said slowly, throwing her a look under my lashes. I knew better than to trust Pari. She'd milk all my details and then throw me a bone or two in return, an unequal exchange.

Her mouth quirked. "No fair. You have all your psychologist skills you can use on me to pull everything else."

I arched a brow. "Untrue. Besides, you love to brag about how you're immune to my 'psychological voodoo.'"

She narrowed her eyes suspiciously. "Fine. About four months ago, I had a one-night stand."

I frowned, waiting for her to continue, staring straight into her dark eyes. Our gazes locked and I made the connection she was hoping I'd make, likely so she wouldn't have to speak it. "Holy crap. You...and Victoria?"

She blinked and looked away, a pained look crossing her features before it was gone.

I let out a long breath and rubbed the bridge of my nose. I had no idea what I was expecting her to admit, but it wasn't that. It felt weird because while Pari was freely sharing with me about her personal sex life, Victoria had not. I bit my bottom lip, knowing that, ethically, I had to proceed carefully.

"So one or the other of you was hoping for more, I take it? Not just a hookup?" And if I knew Pari, I already knew which one that was.

She shrugged and shook her head vehemently. "I didn't mean to hurt her. I thought she was down for some fun. I—" She let out a breath and sucked in a new one.

I held up a hand. "Okay, no details. I don't need details."

Her brows rose. "Are you sure? Because I sure as hell am going to ask you deets about yours."

I raised my brows at Pari. "You should talk to her."

She rolled her shoulders, covered by her military-inspired khaki windbreaker. "What on earth would I say? 'Thanks for the stellar lay. Sorry, you got your feelings hurt expecting more?'"

With my arms folded against my chest, I tilted my head at her. "Why can't there be more?"

She blinked, staring at me like a deer caught in the headlights. Clearly, my question had caught her off guard. "Well, we, uh… We work together, for one."

"Not together. You probably go days or weeks without seeing each other. So, she doesn't do it for you?"

She drew back, looking almost offended. "Uh, no. Have you *seen* her? She's fucking gorgeous. Everything about her is…" She shook her head almost wistfully.

"Too good for you?"

She stared into midspace between us, then blinked, as if pulling herself out of a trance. "Yeah." She cleared her throat. "Like what the hell do I have to offer her?"

"I bet she'd have some very valid and thoughtful answers for that, if you asked her."

She swallowed visibly as if terrified by the thought. But she didn't say a word. The silence hung between us, filled only by the sounds of the diners around us.

"Maybe you should just work on the idea of doing it. Imagine yourself having the conversation. Get the courage up. Because you know what? You *do* deserve her. You're smart and beautiful yourself. Even if a little too over the top in the snark department."

Suddenly, she laughed. "There ya go. Psychologizing me again."

I snickered, grabbing my water glass and raising it to my lips. "That's not a verb, Pari."

"It is for you." I sighed, and she hardly even let a beat go by before she started in. "Okay, your turn. Spill about you and Ty."

I clenched my jaw and then relaxed it, knowing it was only fair that I "spill my beans" in turn. But I had to be careful. Pari also worked with Ryan. And many of these "deets" were not mine to spill. I glanced around to see if anyone was listening to us. "First off, let's not use his name out here, okay?" Pari's eyes widened, and she nodded. Since I'd lowered my voice considerably, she leaned forward, resting her chin in her hands.

"Okay, well. We are...involved."

"What does that mean? You can't exactly date."

I nodded. We couldn't go out much in public. He got recognized pretty much wherever he went.

Her brows went up. "Are the two of you...?" She made a gesture with her hands.

I wiped my mouth with my napkin. "Cone of silence, Pari?"

She looked at me as if I was an idiot. "*Of course.*"

"Then...yes," I finally croaked.

Her eyes were as huge as if they'd been drawn for anime.

I rolled my eyes. "Don't look at me like that."

She blinked, then spoke in a harsh whisper. "Oh, I'm gonna look at you like that. You lost your virginity to an American icon. That's brilliant. How was it?"

I blushed beet red. "Pari—"

"Well, I imagine with as much ass as he gets, he's really good—" Then she stopped herself. "Oh shit, sorry. I didn't mean to make it sound like—"

"Like I'm just another piece of ass?"

She bit her lip and looked at me.

I made a gesture with my hand and picked at my salad. "It's okay. I get it."

"Well, well, well. Our little Gray is all grown-up. Magnificent." Her lips curved in a tight smile. "But you aren't...you're not getting feelings for him, are you?"

I flicked a look up at her. "What, you mean because he's the first guy, so I have to be madly in love? No." I had no clue about what being "in love" truly meant and had already recognized that many of my symptoms—including the Ryan-colored filter—would be attributed by most in my field to infatuation.

I was happily infatuated with him, and I wasn't afraid to admit it—if only to myself.

Pari bit her lip and reached across the table in an uncharacteristic gesture, to touch my wrist. "Just be careful, okay? Please. Guard your heart."

I smiled and pointed to myself. "It's me. Guarding my heart is my specialty."

I was good at playing it safe, as Ryan was fond of calling me on.

Playing it safe was admitting that this was infatuation, nothing more. Nothing more than an enjoyable fling while we worked toward a common goal.

Playing it safe was keeping my head on my shoulders and remembering that, even if I had to chant it every day like a mantra.

And as for the man himself, I didn't see him until that night. He'd gone to the gym to work out and then out with the guys. I hoped he'd choose not to drink. He'd been doing so well lately. The day before, I'd had a chance to casually glance at the measured levels on the bottles in his wet bar. According to them, he hadn't touched a drop since returning from Houston.

Here's to good things continuing.

When he got home after dinnertime, he found me at his kitchen table, my laptop open as I finished an email to my team members.

Without a word, he came up behind me and put his mouth on *that* spot. The one he knew made my heart race instantly. Right at the base of my neck where it joined my shoulder.

I moved my head to the side, stretching my neck for him, and he obliged, kissing his way all the way up.

"Did you have a good day?" I asked.

His hands came around and cupped my breasts, kneading them to desperate, aching points. I blew out a breath. We'd had sex this morning, but he was acting like he hadn't touched me in weeks.

I turned my head and inhaled deeply, feeling that pleasant zing I always got from his smell. But more importantly, I didn't smell alcohol.

"I will tell you all about my day," he said gruffly with my earlobe in his mouth. "*Afterward.*"

And with that, he scooped me out of the chair and carried me into his room like a caveman.

Now, I don't normally go in for the Neanderthal type, but that did turn me on. A lot.

He lowered us both to the bed, slowly, as if returning to full gravity after a bout of weightlessness. When we hit the bed, our mouths fastened together.

Our bodies soon joined in that same, gorgeous dance. And, as always, he left me sweaty and breathless and oh-so-full of afterglow.

Afterward, we took a shower together, and out of the blue, I thought about Karen. I hadn't sent her an update on him this week.

"You know what might be awesome?" I asked as I soaped up his back.

"More sex after we get out of the shower?" he shot back immediately.

I laughed. "Aside from that."

"There's nothing even close to that."

"I was thinking. Maybe you could send Karen a text. Maybe a picture for AJ or something."

Silence.

Well, at least he didn't stiffen and tense under my hands when I brought it up. "I just thought, you know, something simple. She asks about you."

He turned around to rinse his back and looked at me for a long time without answering.

I shrugged. "I'm not going to push it. Think about it, okay? Maybe start with something easy."

His look told me that there was nothing easy about it for him. I leaned forward, threw my arms around his neck and kissed him. "You decide what you're up to doing. I was just putting that out there."

He kissed me back, then grabbed my butt and pulled me flush against him, deepening the kiss. We at least made it out of the shower without having sex, but it was touch-and-go there for a few minutes.

As we were drying off, he stared into space, thinking. Then he looked up and said, "I'll text him a picture I took of the guys at work the other day." I nodded. No picture of himself, but of the other astronauts that AJ undoubtedly knew very well.

Small steps. Good. I smiled but decided not to make a big deal out of it. "Great idea."

We fell asleep soon after, and I couldn't help but think how much I enjoyed looking at life through my Ryan-filter. Infatuation or no, I could enjoy this for a while.

Maybe even a long while.

CHAPTER TWENTY-ONE
RYAN

W E SPENT THE NEXT FEW WEEKS IN A THRILLING, exhaustive haze of work, hours of sex, and long talks in between. At work, we were complete professionals, hardly even crossing paths. I was too busy gearing up for the first round of full flight simulations, and she was finishing up some projects that she described to me in detail in bed between bouts of hot sex.

We were like teenagers discovering orgasms for the very first time. And it was addictive.

"I'm going to have to start doing monthly questionnaires with the astronauts," she told me one afternoon. We'd barely made it in the door after work before proceeding to rip each other's clothes off in the living room and fucking right there. Now I was contemplating how famished I was, and she was lying across me on the couch, idly twirling my chest hair in her fingers. "Will that be weird for you? Should I get someone else to do you?"

"You're the only one I want to do me," I laughed.

Her hand stilled, and I wondered what I'd said when I replayed how that sounded. My gut tightened instinctively. Normally, I was careful about the language I used with the women I slept with—on the few occasions that we had involved conversations. I always tried very hard and meticulously to keep it casual. Not to give a woman a reason to think it might be anything more than that.

But it was hard with Gray. Our lives overlapped a great deal and—well—for some reason, I kept slipping up here and there like that. Making it sound like this was something that could last.

Maybe it could?

***

Days later, our astronaut group of four emerged from the flight simulator for the first full simulation. We went through an entire debriefing afterward attended by the astronauts, Tolan Reeves, our CEO, and Adam Drake. Adam had worked on a great deal of the simulation programming design via a virtual reality company he had recently acquired.

We spent hours going over the simulation, examining how it had gone, how it could be improved, discussing possible variations, and imagined catastrophes to test and prepare any astronaut who would be going up in a Phoenix capsule.

"Things are looking great with your 'romance,' Ty. I don't normally follow gossip, but I've been paying attention to the coverage. Well done," Adam said after the meeting as the other astronauts filed out. I'd held back to have a few words with him. Upon hearing this, Kirill's head jerked around, and he shot me an accusing stare. I puzzled at that and sent him a "What's up?" look as he jerked his head away and disappeared.

I frowned, wondering if he thought there was actually something going on between Keely and me. Maybe he'd lost his usual cool with this girl and had gotten more attached?

But Kirill played things so close to the vest, who knew what he was thinking? Sometimes I doubted even he knew.

I finished up my chat with Adam and Tolan and left to hit the gym for a workout before the day came to a close. Gray had a meeting with her advising professor at UCLA this evening and wouldn't be back for hours, so I had some time—and excess energy—to blow off.

The gym was spacious and occupied the majority of the multipurpose rooms in the west wing of the XVenture facility. It was for all employee use, but at this time of day, it was usually deserted. I'd made that delightful discovery almost by accident when I'd come here around this time weeks ago. It had been an excellent way to work off the sexual frustration I'd been building up by hanging around Gray without being able to touch her, despite desperately wanting to.

Thank God those days were over.

All the guys were in the gym when I got there. Apparently, they'd headed straight here after the meeting.

"Well, look who it is. The man of the hour," Noah called out when I walked in. He was spotting Hammer on the bench press. Kirill was doing pull-ups on the chin-up bar, pumping his arms up fast as if his gym shorts were on fire. He stared fiercely straight ahead and didn't acknowledge me when I came in. What was up with him? He seemed pissed off and was playing it off with typical cool Russian attitude. But I knew him well enough to know something was bothering him.

I blew it off and went through my own workout, figuring it would come out eventually.

And I was right. It didn't even take that long.

Afterward, in the showers, the guys had decided to tease Kirill for all the scratch marks down his back. The man seriously looked like he'd gotten in a fight with a wet alley cat. Wolf whistles abounded, and he grinned sheepishly.

"Kirill getting lucky with my fake girlfriend." I laughed, grinning ruefully. "Way to go. Apparently, she's a hellcat in bed?"

Kirill's face clouded. "I'm not only one getting lucky, though. Am I?" His ice-blue eyes clashed with mine, and I frowned, looking away. He knew, clearly, about Gray and me. Either he'd seen something or Keely had or—who knew—girls talked. Maybe Gray had told her.

Apparently, Kirill wasn't happy. Well, at least he wasn't hiding it anymore.

I snatched up a towel and wiped my face, hoping he'd keep his mouth shut in front of the guys. But no, apparently that hope was in vain. Noah straight up asked him what he meant.

Kirill jutted his chin at me and said. "Ask him."

I shook my head and headed out of the showers and into the locker room. Fuck this shit. I was not ready to talk about it. And I sure as hell wasn't going to trade literal locker room stories about Gray. No fucking way.

Because she meant more to me than that. The thought of it even made me sick to my stomach.

"Is Kirill right?" Noah asked. "Are you getting pussy on the side? Aren't you afraid the press will discover it and out you as 'cheating' on Keely?"

I dropped the towel and proceeded to dress as quickly as I could. I was not doing this.

"It's worse than that," Kirill said softly, and I turned, only partially dressed, to stare him down.

"Don't start this," I said to him in Russian.

"Worse? What do you mean, worse?" Noah asked.

Kirill shook his head but didn't take his eyes off mine. I took a deep breath and let it go. Then held the next one. But I didn't speak as every muscle in my body tensed.

"If you are jeopardizing entire program, don't you think Noah and Hammer have the right to know before they break ties with NASA or anywhere else?" Kirill's thick brows rose over his pale blue eyes.

I folded my arms and leaned back against my locker. As I had no shirt on, the cold metal settled against my shoulder blades.

"What's he talking about, Ty?" Hammer asked from where he sat on the bench in front of his locker.

"Exactly how is my relationship with Gray going to jeopardize the entire program?" I said to Kirill, ignoring Hammer's question.

"Wait, what?" Noah shut his locker and turned to me. "Relationship? With Gray Barrett? As in, daughter of Conrad Barrett?"

There was a resounding silence between the four of us as his question sank in. Their accusatory stares pinned me down as unspoken allegations bounced off the polished cement floor beneath our feet.

"Are you screwing the billionaire's daughter?" Hammer asked, clear disbelief on his face. "Have you lost your mind?"

Kirill shook his head. Ripping his eyes from me, he muttered expletives in Russian—things I'd learned from my grandpa when I was five. Bad shit he didn't normally say out loud.

"I'm not just screwing her. Not that it's any of your fucking business."

"But you *are* screwing her. And it is our fucking business." Hammer groused. "If her dad finds out, what do you think is going to happen? Our money vanishes."

"Jesus, Ty." Noah huffed, turning beet red. "You need to keep it in your goddamn pants for once instead of fucking everything that moves. You're risking trashing the program for a piece of ass?"

Rage set my skin on fire, tensing every muscle, and I turned to him, staring him down. How fucking dare he? My fists clenched at my sides in clear warning.

And then he took his shitty diatribe and pushed it over the edge. "Really cashing in on that American Hero persona no matter what the cost to the rest of us, huh?"

I leaped off that locker and over the bench to slam Noah against his own locker, my face inches from his. "I *said* it wasn't like that. Did I stutter, asshole?"

"Fuck you, Ty," he gasped as he fought against me pinning him to the cold metal.

I grabbed his T-shirt, twisting it in my hand. Shaking my head at him, I hissed between my teeth, "You've been wanting at me for the past year, Noah. Let's do this now. I'm sick of all the shitty side-eye and the muttered comments. Let's settle it like men."

Both Hammer and Kirill were at my shoulders, pulling me off of him. Noah stared at me like I'd lost my mind.

"Come on," I shouted as they dragged me back. "We all know you fucking blame me for the accident, so let's go, goddamnit!"

I shoved against Kirill's hold, but Hammer yanked me back. I might have been a match for one of them, but not both. Not without bloodying myself up pretty badly.

And Noah wasn't taking the bait, the fucker. My jaw clenched. I wanted at him. And I wanted it *bad.* I was sick of all the pussyfooting around.

Once upon a time, he was one of my closest friends.

But since the mission...since I'd gone up in his place, everything had changed. Noah should have been the senior astronaut on that spacewalk. But not long before the launch, he'd developed an abscess in his jaw that had prevented him from going up.

And I'd thought myself a lucky bastard as his backup. I'd have my second mission in less than two years—almost unheard of under normal circumstances. *Lucky me.*

I always knew that Noah firmly believed that if he had been on that spacewalk with Xander instead of me, things wouldn't have gone down the way they did. And I would have been sitting in Mission Control in Houston as the CAPCOM instead of him.

Now, his words confirmed that—but for that wretched twist of fate, he'd have saved the day.

I backed off from him, my heart banging in my chest, adrenaline pumping. Noah watched me, wide-eyed.

"We should calm down now," Kirill said, tightening his grip on my arm as Hammer went to Noah in case he decided to come at me. Apparently, they'd determined that the best solution was to physically separate us as far from each other as possible.

Fine. It wasn't like I was going to sit down and talk this out with the bastard.

"You're the one who fucking started this shit," I growled at Kirill.

I yanked my arm away from his grip and went to my locker, cramming shit in there as quickly as I could.

"We are worried." Kirill replied. "About this program. About you. This destructive—"

I tensed, but my fury had muted me. I yanked the zipper closed on my gym bag and grabbed my other shit, getting ready to bolt, determined to finished dressing in the bathroom.

"Now that the intervention is over, you all can go fuck yourselves," I ground out as I left.

I seethed the entire way home. Their mere suggestion that I was sleeping with Gray to get my rocks off was offensive beyond belief—and I tried not to question too closely why that was. The logical side of my mind knew where they were coming from.

But this wasn't logical. She wasn't just a lay. She was more. *So much more.*

I wanted some vodka badly when I got home. And I'd been good. I hadn't even wanted it. But damn, I almost poured myself a shot. The only thing that stopped me was the thought of her reaction when she got home and smelled it on my breath. Instead, I went for a run in the canyon. By the time she came through the door, I was well and truly exhausted.

***

Needless to say, I did not socialize much with the guys in the days after that. We were cool and cordial to each other at work. Did what we had to do together, and that was it.

Days later, I had a local gig with Keely—a charity dinner at a fancy hotel in Beverley Hills. I showed up in the tux for the red carpet, the pictures, and the meal, then filed out a side door and went home to where I honestly wanted to be—in Gray's arms.

Daily, we continued with the flight simulations. I aced every one of them. We processed, discussed, tweaked, and they threw variations at me. Everything was smooth sailing.

And with Gray, my nights sizzled. Smoldered. I couldn't get enough of her.

Every time I saw her again after being apart, it was thrilling. My heart sped up, my breathing hitched. I hadn't felt like this since...

I blinked, thinking about it.

I had never felt like this.

I sat on her couch, watching her as she tucked some clothes and personal items into a suitcase for me to take to my house so she wouldn't have to come here as often to get her stuff. Later, her dad was going to pick her up for their weekly meal together.

"You know," she said as she dumped yet another pair of jeans and a small stack of T-shirts into the suitcase. "One could argue that you are doing so well now that you don't need as much 'babysitting' anymore. Isn't that what you were arguing for in May? Maybe we could meet daily at work?"

"Nope. Vetoed. I definitely need closer constant supervision."

Especially in my bedroom.

My eyes had riveted to her fine little ass as she bent. Any other woman and I would have suspected she'd purposely given me that angle for seduction purposes. But not this girl. She didn't operate like that.

Everything about her said straight shooter. Maybe that was why I'd grown to trust her so quickly. Because frankly, it was shocking even to myself how fast it had happened.

She turned and shot me a wry smile and then went to grab her tablet and a few books to tuck into her luggage.

"Yes, you definitely need to keep coming to my house—I mean, *at* my house," I said, my mouth in that cocky grin she had told me drove her nuts.

"I thought I had a rule about that? No sex while I'm under the same roof?"

I laughed, resting my head against the back of the couch and looking at the ceiling. "Ooh boy, we blew that one right up, didn't we?"

She grinned, walked to the couch, and bent over me to land a kiss on my mouth. "Multiple times."

"More like exponential times. Or at least, on our way to it." I winked at her and copped a feel. Her boobs were *right there.* I never missed an opportunity.

She smiled and straightened, politely removing my hand from her chest. "We are wasting time."

I smiled. Not a waste of time in my opinion. I half felt like packing up the rest of the apartment and moving it in if it meant she'd stay with me. We hadn't talked about that yet—that our arrangement had an expiration date to it. The test flight was still a couple months off, and we were deep in the middle of summer. But when fall came, what then?

I still didn't know. The only thing I did know was that I wasn't ready for this to end. And I didn't think I'd be ready in two months either. Of course, we had yet to pin down and declare exactly what this was.

I swore I'd do anything I could to avoid breaking her heart.

And with the tightness that blossomed in my chest, I wondered if it was her heart I needed to be the most worried about. As she settled on the couch beside me and leaned in, her strawberry and mint smell enveloping me, I blinked, wondering.

Because inadvertently, I'd been relying on her. So where would I be when she was no longer there?

If, Ryan. If she was no longer there.

I blew out a breath. *Fuck.*

Of course, she sensed the change in my mood immediately. "What's wrong? You want to come along for dinner that badly?" she joked. "I know you're Conrad Barrett's number one fan."

I laughed. "More like the other way around. I wasn't the one roasting him over the coals in that investment meeting."

She reached up and sifted her fingers through my hair. "Oh, you can take some good ol' boy prodding from my dad any day of the week. He's all bark and no bite."

I hooked my arm around her waist and pulled her into my lap, facing me, so that she straddled my lap.

"So I guess he wouldn't be much of a fan of this, would he?"

She paused, and her eyes roamed my face as she shifted, getting comfortable on my lap. Her weight added pleasant pressure through my jeans as she settled against the budding bulge of my erection. In response, I grew harder and half of her mouth quirked up in a knowing smile.

"I haven't said anything to him, if that's what you're asking. And the main reason is that, well, we don't know what this is."

I nodded but didn't otherwise respond.

"Do we?" she asked quietly, and I lifted my head to meet her gaze.

My mouth twitched as I watched her, all pretty and innocent. She'd never done this before and neither had I, and we were stumbling around what should be an important conversation. An inelegant dance where we approached, then shied away.

Like we were constantly falling. Like gravity.

The force that not only drew us nearer and nearer to each other but kept us in each other's orbit, constantly circling without getting closer.

And an object in orbit around a larger body was in a constant state of free fall. And this...this felt like free fall too.

My arms tightened around her hips. Dare I tell her that? That this felt like the beginning of something more? That it was so different from anything that had come before.

And dare I voice that now? And dare I think she'd want to be in my orbit?

My head was still a little too fucked up to think about starting something like this now. It was too precious, too new, too bright for me. I was still looking out at it from the darkness.

I swallowed.

"We're having fun, right?" I deflected.

An unsure smile crept onto her mouth, causing a dimple to show above her chin. "Yeah," she breathed.

"Come here," I said. With a hand pressing her on the back, I brought her to me, our mouths connecting in a steamy kiss. Her mouth opened, and her tongue slipped confidently into mine. If I wasn't fully aroused before, then I certainly was now, especially when her arms came around my neck and her chest pressed against me. Her nipples tightened under her tank top, driving me insane as they rubbed me through my shirt. A second later, my hand was under the thin material, toying with the tight bud as she sighed against my mouth.

All blood rushed south, and her hands were on my shirt, pulling the buttons open as quickly as she could. I resisted the almost overpowering urge to push her down on the couch and bury myself inside her. Instead, I figured that while she was on top, I'd let her pilot the ship. And while she still might be a novice at sex, she had caught on rather nicely.

And boy had I had a lot of fun showing her the ropes. As often as I possibly could.

So I sat back and kept my hands on her hips as she kissed her way down my body from my neck, over my bare chest, spending time lavishing as much attention on my chest and nipples as I tended to do on her in my turn.

And while it felt very good, I was anxious to cut to the chase. "Dammit," I hissed. "Now you're just torturing me." She was moaning and grinding on the bulge in my jeans as she dragged her hot mouth across my chest. *Fuck.* It was torture. Sweet torture.

When I went to take off her top, she pushed my hands away, letting me know she clearly had this. And, with no warning at all, she slipped off my lap. Maybe she wanted to lead us into the bedroom instead of doing this here. I glanced at the clock. Her father wasn't getting here for a couple hours yet. We had time.

Delicious, achingly sweet time. Time just for us. When I went to get up from the couch, however, she put a hand on my shoulder and sank to her knees in front of me. We locked gazes and my chest tightened. I swallowed, my breathing doing triple time. Merely seeing the hunger in her eyes, her hunger for me, made my pulse leap with excitement.

For the last year or so, sex had only been something to get done, a quick and numbing escape. I mean, I'd been highly motivated to get it done—and often. But the act itself hadn't been anything special.

Until lately. Until Gray.

She ran a hand over the bulge in my jeans, groping me through the thick denim. "I've been thinking about how much I need the D."

I laughed. "I'm more than happy to give it to you. Whenever you want."

She grinned, holding my eyes with hers. "I know you are." She reached forward and unbuttoned my fly. I released a long breath and put my hand over hers, helping her navigate the zipper around the tight fit. She grasped the waistband, tugging it down, freeing my hips from the jeans.

She was now kneeling, leaning forward over my lap, between my open knees. Her intentions were clear, and I, well, I was right on board with this plan. I couldn't tear my eyes away from her mouth, anticipating the feel of being enveloped by her heat, feeling her tongue and lips slide around my cock. My hips jolted when she fished my erection out of my boxers, exposing it to her inspection as she smiled at me, licking her lips.

Fuck.

Slowly, she leaned forward. Her hot breath bathed my sensitive skin, and I closed my eyes, savoring the anticipation. Her tongue lashed out, tasting the head of my cock. My breath stilled as pleasure zinged through my body. Then, her lips touched me there. The lightest stroke started at the very tip before opening to take it in, sliding down my length, devouring me.

My eyes shot open as I watched more of me disappear into her mouth, that hungry gleam in her green eyes sharpening. *Beautiful.* So very beautiful. She was a lioness. And I was her happy prey. For now.

Thrilled to be hunted down and swallowed by her.

I reached out, threading my fingers through her soft hair, encouraging her to continue, letting her know it felt good. In some cases, gently guiding her movement when it was appropriate. She didn't seem to mind, the way the thirst in her eyes intensified, and she'd let out a throaty moan.

She was so damned delicious that I was about to lose it embarrassingly fast. One small hand gripped me at the base of my cock, the other ran her fingers through the fine hair near my navel. Pure pleasure clamped itself around me, grasping control and taking me along for the ride.

I let it. Let her take me there.

My hand cupped her breast, fingers quickly finding her nipple and working it to a peak. And I wasn't sure what was turning me on more—the feel of her hot mouth on my aching cock or the small whimpers she made deep in her throat.

Whatever it was, it got me to where I was going, quickly and without delay. Soon I was feeling the familiar build to climax. For her part, she kept going even if sometimes she needed to slow down and readjust her angle.

Her mouth sucked, my pleasure spiked, and I knew it was inevitable. "Gray," I rasped. "I'm coming."

I started to pull out of her mouth, but she shook her head and thrust forward, taking me deeper as I squeezed my eyes closed and tensed, stilling as pure pleasure washed over me and I shuddered.

I fell back against the cushions, happily depleted as she got up and went into the bathroom, returning a few minutes later with a washcloth for me. I took my own turn in the bathroom and cleaned up.

When I came out, I saw we still had at least an hour. So, as she zipped up her bag, I instead scooped her up, throwing her over my shoulder as she shrieked in surprise. Carrying her to her bedroom, I pulled off her leggings, buried my head between her legs and returned the favor.

Making her scream was quickly becoming my new favorite thing to do.

She barely had time to dress for dinner and usher me out the door. Even though I knew I'd be seeing her in a few hours, I made out with her a little in the stairwell before I hopped down to the parking lot, loaded with her suitcase.

We had months together, yet. And there would be no more talk of sleep studies or working through my issues. There was only some good clean—and sometimes dirty—sex followed by well-deservedly restful sleep.

I waved to her from the parking lot as she smiled down at me, watching me make my way to the car.

I drove home with a smile on my face the entire way.

CHAPTER TWENTY-TWO
GRAY

D INNER THIS EVENING WAS DAD'S CHOICE SO, naturally, it was at his favorite haunt, Applebee's. He was famously fond of the inexpensive chain of restaurants, and the media thought it almost an adorable quirk that he used coupons when he ate there.

But tonight, he was unusually quiet, studying the menu for long minutes without looking up. Which was ridiculous because he always ordered the same dish.

When the server arrived, I ordered a chicken Caesar salad, which of course my dad scoffed at. He hated salads and eschewed most cooked vegetables too. I often joked that he had the palate of a toddler.

"How are you feeling tonight? You look a little peaked," I said when he'd rearranged his silverware and polished every piece with his napkin multiple times.

He shrugged. "I'm fine."

"Are you not feeling well?"

"I'm fine, Gray. Stop nagging. Just had a long day."

My brow went up at the waspish snap, so unlike him, normally. Maybe he'd had a bad meeting earlier. "You're still checking your blood pressure every day, right? With that automatic monitor I got you for Christmas?"

Now, he looked exasperated. So, I held out a palm face up. Resting my chin against my other fist, I gazed around the restaurant, noting the couples, the small families. I understood why Dad liked coming here. When stuck in offices and in the world of finance and sycophants, someplace that brought him back to his middle-class roots would be a welcome break.

"How about you?" he finally asked after our meals had arrived.

I chewed my bite of salad and looked up at him. "How about me, what?"

"You seem busy. My assistant told me it took her days to get hold of you to make this appointment."

I smiled. "Sorry. The day job and all the side jobs—the reports and studies I've been working on."

"And this whole babysitting thing. How's that going?"

I nodded. "Just fine. He's doing so well. I keep sending you links to the media mentions. I hope you've been looking at them. The public's been eating up that romance."

He snorted and dug into his fettuccine.

"I'm concerned about your schooling," he said a while later after he'd stayed uncharacteristically silent for long minutes while enjoying his meal.

"Nothing to be concerned about. I've got a plan to start getting clinical hours this fall—"

He shook his head. "You should be working on all that now. Get the whole thing wrapped up."

I stopped mid-chew to throw him an exasperated look. "Well, you're the whole reason I've been doing this work with Commander Tyler in the first place. Or did you forget that?"

I frowned. What was up with him? Now he was backpedaling? This was so unlike him.

"That's all been a waste of time," he snapped irritably.

I dropped my fork so that it clanged against my plate—loudly. "Excuse me?"

He stopped eating and stared at me, and my face flushed. Now, he was pissing me off. But would I ever in a million years tell him that?

No. Hell no. I clenched my jaw and quickly picked up my fork again and stabbed at my salad, taking a breath and mentally counting to ten before I spoke again.

"Dad, why didn't you fully fund the XPAC, then?" There, my voice was smooth as silk. I was proud of myself.

He didn't answer for a long time. "I want you to succeed, and I want you to love what you do. I'm afraid you're not going to finish what you started."

I shook my head. "The only way that will happen is if the XPAC isn't funded. Then I won't have the job." Might as well shove a little additional pressure for him to keep from backing out whenever I could.

Some strange mixture of emotions crossed his face, and he looked weary. He must have had a bad night's sleep. That happened to him sometimes. But I refrained from mentioning it because it only seemed to make him more ticked off with the mood he was in.

We didn't linger over our plates tonight, nor did he order dessert, which cut things short and confirmed to me that what he was lacking was some good rest. We drove back to my place in silence. In the parking lot of my building, I gave him a big hug and landed a kiss on his cheek.

"Get some sleep, Dad."

"Love you, Gracie," he said in an odd sort of monotone.

I had a forty-five-minute drive back to Ryan's house that night, and so I cued my oldies playlist and listened to Diana Ross and the Supremes sing about how you can't hurry love.

It made me wonder, again, what love was and where the line was between what I was feeling and love or infatuation.

In my field, some had published on the subject, saying that love was definable by certain behaviors and characteristics. A focus on the positive—like my Ryan-colored filter. An emotional instability heavily dependent upon the object of one's desire. Given the way my moods were swinging these days, that would definitely qualify. That central dopamine rush like the flow of a drug—as I'd often compared that feeling to. An intensifying attraction—and yes, he was much more handsome to me now than even when I'd first noticed him. I still appreciated those flawless physical characteristics, but now that I knew more about his heart—his good heart underneath the cocky asshole façade, I couldn't tear myself away.

The list went on. Intrusive thoughts, emotional dependency, daydreaming about the future, possessive feelings, craving emotional union. I had them *all*.

Goddamn.

I was in love.

As I gripped the steering wheel and exited the freeway, headed for the hills in the north, I swallowed the oncoming tidal wave of exhilaration, happiness and cold fear.

I was deeply in love with Ryan Tyler.

I caught my breath again, trying to calm my respiration. I could hear the clicking, even over the music. Should I tell him? And how should I tell him? And if not tonight, then when?

Ordering myself to calm down, I turned into his neighborhood, flipping my headlights on to high beam so I could see better. I blinked and forced myself to think it through calmly.

I was never ever known for getting carried away with my emotions. No. I was Gray, the girl who played it safe. And I'd be as calm and rational about this as I was about everything else. I wasn't going to let being in love for the very first time make me lose my head.

No, I'd let things play out naturally knowing that my intuition would lead me to divulge that wonderful secret at exactly the right time.

And hopefully, God, I hoped, he'd feel the same way too.

CHAPTER TWENTY-THREE
RYAN

THE NEXT MORNING IN THE ASTRONAUT OFFICE, WE were prepping for our next full real-time simulation. Noah, as my backup on this mission, was helping me go over the timing and checklists for each step from pre-flight to touchdown. Fortunately, we'd managed to keep it professional since the blowup in the locker room the week before last.

As a group, we were preparing to go out to Cape Canaveral, Florida the following month for launchpad tests, and we had to have the timing down to within fractions of seconds in order to be ready for them.

"Stack thirty-five," Hammer was saying. "Go at T minus twenty—"

The door opened, and Tolan's assistant poked his head in.

"Sorry to interrupt. Mr. Reeves wanted to know if Ty could meet him across the street at the restaurant at three for an informal meeting with some of the investors."

My brow shot up. That seemed sudden and weird. "Did he say who?"

The assistant shrugged. "Just said to make sure you got the message and that you'd be there."

"Okay." I shrugged. "Got it."

Weird or not, I'd go.

The guys said nothing, and we went back to work.

Not long before three, I left the building and crossed the street to hit the old haunt. When I got there, I saw that Cheryl was on shift today. She perked up when she saw me coming. "Here to meet Tolan," I said when she greeted me with a menu.

Her eyes widened. "Right, he's in the back room. With some famous guy. Or at least that's what the guys in the back are saying. I have no idea who he is."

My brow went up. "Famous guy?"

She nodded. "Of course, you're famous too, so it's not a big deal who that old man is."

I frowned. Famous? Old man? With Tolan? His assistant had said it was to meet with some investors. Maybe it was someone new who wanted in? I speculated over that as she led me to the semiprivate room in the back—meant for corporate parties or people who requested more privacy.

Still, this bar and grill wasn't all that fancy and an odd place to meet someone important. Tolan should have brought whoever it was over to the plant, given him a tour, introduced him to all the guys, not just me.

When we stepped into the room, I immediately understood why Tolan had chosen not to bring him to XVenture.

My stomach bottomed out as Conrad Barrett looked up from his conversation with Tolan when I walked in. Not the famous guy I was expecting—though I had no idea who I'd been expecting. But it sure as hell hadn't been him.

I clenched my jaw before forcing myself to relax. I held out a hand to shake Barrett's. He looked at it, and instead of taking it, waved me off toward a chair. "Sit down, Tyler. Join us. Shall I order some appetizers? Are you hungry?"

I blinked, hesitating, and then pulled my hand back, oddly reminded of that first day when I'd put my hand out to Gray. She'd stuffed her hands into her pockets rather than shake my hand. I never did ask her why she'd refused that handshake. But the irony was not lost on me.

"I'm fine, thanks. Had a big lunch a little while ago." His eyes took me in from head to toe. I sank into an empty seat across from him and Tolan. And I waited for one or the other of them to clarify for me why the hell I was here.

"How about a beer, then?"

I looked up at Cheryl. "Mineral water with lime, please."

Barrett ordered himself a Diet Coke and a bowl of chips and salsa. Tolan, instead of ordering, stood up. "I'm going to let you two chat. I've got to get going."

I frowned at that. Clearly, this had been the plan. That did not bode well for whatever Barrett's agenda was. I frowned at Tolan, then turned my gaze to Barrett, a question evident in my glance.

"Tolan's indulging me. I had some questions about how things are going with the program, wanted to hear it straight from you." He nodded at Tolan. "Thank you."

Tolan acknowledged Barrett's comment and then nodded to me and left the table. Cheryl appeared with our drinks and the chips and salsa. Barrett proceeded to load his plate with a handful of chips before pointing to the bowl. "Help yourself."

"I'm good." I sipped at my beverage, bracing myself. This was not some generic meeting to follow up with concerns. I knew that much. Conrad Fucking Barrett did not deign to bother himself with such banalities. If I hadn't figured that out from his down-home public persona, then hearing Gray talk about him for the past month and a half had helped me figure that much out, at least.

I leaned back in my chair and watched him attack his chips and salsa with gusto. I blinked, waiting. He didn't seem all that in a hurry to get started. And that added to the sinking feeling in my gut.

Classic blow-off tactics—summoning me to a meeting, then putting me off by making me wait. The magnanimous offer of food and drink—alcoholic, if possible. Yes, Barrett had an agenda, and if I was a betting man, that agenda involved his daughter. "What can I do for you, Mr. Barrett? You had questions?"

"Mmm." He held up a hand to hold me off while he finished chewing his mouthful and washed it down with a sip of Diet Coke. "My daughter would kill me if she knew about the soda. Not supposed to have caffeine."

I swallowed but didn't say anything. We held a long, meaningful gaze.

He knew about Gray and me. I was certain of it.

But would he have the balls to be the first to bring it up, or would he wait until I cracked and confessed? He was toying with me, that much was certain.

I put a hand on the table and leaned back in my chair. "You didn't have questions about the program, did you?"

His dark brows twitched up. I scanned his face. I saw nothing of his daughter there. She clearly must resemble her mother. No wait—his eyes. They were that same shade of green. Shrewd. Clever. They saw everything. Just like hers.

Except, where I got the feeling she was noting, cataloging, and empathizing, he was looking for weaknesses for an entirely different reason. No empathy in the older Barrett. No. He acquired knowledge for exploitation. I knew his type well.

You are the type. I heard Gray's comment in my head then. She'd said that once when we'd been discussing her father. Perhaps I did know his type so well for that reason. *Perhaps.*

But like him, I wasn't one to give up, especially when it was something I wanted. Something I wanted a lot.

And at that moment, I made a decision. I wanted Gray. And I needed her. And as far as I was concerned, she wasn't going anywhere, no matter how much her father was going to try to scare me off.

Resolve solidified inside me, and I stared the man down. Let him crack. Let him be the one to bring up the subject. Let him approach me from a position of weakness.

Let him come. I wasn't afraid.

Barrett abandoned his pile of chips after another sip of soda. "I do have a question about the program, Commander Tyler." He held up a finger. "Just one. How much do you really want to fly?"

I held his gaze and refused the bait. "I'm very excited to fly again."

His tongue rolled under his cheek as if he were cleaning out his mouth. "That so? Because it doesn't seem like it. You don't seem very *focused* on that goal."

I blew out a breath. "In what way? I've stuck with the plan. The PR stunt has gone exactly as it was laid out. My training—"

"And Gray? How does she fit into all of that?"

"She's been a very integral part of the whole—"

"That's not what I'm talking about, and you know it." His eyes narrowed. "I can take a lot, Commander Tyler, but one thing I cannot take is BS."

I shifted in my chair and held his gaze. "Then how about you come out and say what this is really about."

His lips thinned. "Last night, I picked my daughter up to take her to dinner. As I'm sure you're aware."

He paused. I stared, neither confirming nor denying his suspicions.

"I do all my own driving, as I prefer. I get motion sickness otherwise. But I had to take a call from China before picking her up. Hence, I got to her place ahead of time and sat in the car to take the call. I parked in full view of her front door. You follow me?"

I blinked. Well, that pretty much laid it all out, didn't it? Was there any point in denying it now? He'd seen her walk me to the stairwell—also in full view of the parking lot—give me a long kiss goodbye with her arms wrapped around my neck and while I grabbed her ass. Then me leaving with her full suitcase. Yeah, he'd seen enough to incriminate.

"What do you want, Mr. Barrett?"

He pursed his lips. "For you to stay away from my daughter, in case it wasn't already obvious."

"Your daughter is a consenting adult with her own decisions to make."

"As are you—a man capable of making his own decisions about his life. So, I ask again, Tyler. How much do you want to fly?"

I laced my fingers together in front of me and stared at them for a long moment. "You have the wrong idea of what this is. It's not just—"

"Not like all the other women you've had in your life—" he turned his hand in a circular motion "—one after the other—for the past year, at least? Each and every one of them featured in the tabloids? Not like that? You tell me what man in this universe would want his daughter involved with the likes of you?"

"Gray is capable of—"

"I know full well what she's capable of. I've known her for her entire life. She's a fighter. I'm not here to coddle her. I know she's strong. But she's never dated. And I don't want her to fall prey to—"

I shook my head. "She's not my *prey*. Not anyone's. Gray can—"

He held up a hand, stopping me with a look on his face that made it clear he'd brook no bullshit—from me or anyone else. "She's young. She's inexperienced in this area. You've been through women like underwear. I don't want her anywhere near you. And, because I'm sick of beating around the bush, I'm going to lay this out how it is. Should you choose to continue this unwise course of action with my daughter, then I will have no choice but to pull the plug on my investment."

My hands, where they were laced together, clamped tightly. I'd known it was coming. Why the hell was I so surprised? "And by pulling out of this, you risk alienating yourself from Tolan, and even your own daughter. By yanking your support of the program, you effectively stifle their dreams too. This program is not all about me."

Conrad Barrett's eyes narrowed shrewdly even as his face flushed with obvious anger. He took another long, lingering sip of his Diet Coke and nodded. "Exactly, Commander Tyler. Exactly. This program is not all about you. Something you should definitely remember when you make your decision. Do we understand each other?"

"How about asking me what my intentions are, or—"

He shook his head and laughed. "I don't care what your intentions are."

I blinked. "So just like that, you want me to...And risk alienating her from you anyway."

"I think it goes without saying that she doesn't need to find out about this little meeting. Am I right? We all suffer disappointments in life. Better it happens for her now than later."

I shook my head in denial, but before I could speak, he continued.

"What on earth gives you the arrogance to assume you even deserve her? All that shit they put in your head about being a *hero*? You're no hero, Tyler. Your friend died. You left a man behind. Your best friend. To die and decay in orbit. You let down NASA, and they fired you in disgrace. You'll let her down too, inevitably. I'm the one who picks up the pieces when you shatter the precious gem that is her heart. So, don't. Pull out now."

I sat back, as stunned as if he'd landed a kick right to my diaphragm. And, noting my reaction, he stood and straightened the jacket of his ill-fitting suit. "I've given this matter all the time it deserves. Don't get up." He exited the room, leaving me sitting, watching him go. Gap-jawed at the abruptness.

Well.

Fuck.

I buried my forehead in my palms, fingers threading into my hairline as a server I didn't know came to clear the plates. The asshole had thrown down a twenty to cover the check, and the server quietly took it without attempting to engage me.

I had to think. I had to...

But, fuck. Who? How? Where?

I got back to work as most everyone was packing up for the day. Fortunately, the guys had no idea that the "investor" who had been waiting for me across the street was Barrett or they would have all been giving me *I told you so* looks.

I put on a brave face—I was used to that. It was one of the things I did best. And met Gray at my car. Our schedules had coincided, so we'd ridden in together since most knew she'd been staying at my house for the purpose of her assignment.

Still, we'd been sure to be discreet about it, arriving early, parking at the farthest part of the lot, and not heading out to the car together.

We were halfway home when she finally turned from looking out the window. "You're quiet. How was your day?"

My fellow astronauts are barely speaking to me because they found out about us, and your bastard father just gave me the ultimatum to end all ultimatums.

I kept my eyes on the road. "Good. Yours?"

She nodded. "It was good. I spoke with Marjorie about the conference with my advisor. She's going to give me more duties so I can get my clinical hours. I'll be Dr. Barrett before I know it."

I forced myself to smile. "Awesome."

"Pari wanted me to catch a movie with her tonight."

"Sounds great. I could use a good long walk in the canyon."

She looked at me. "You don't mind?"

I frowned. "Why would I mind? We aren't attached at the hip."

She snorted. "Not right now. But hopefully, we will be later."

My insides clenched. Aching. My jaw squeezed shut.

I wanted nothing more. But everything was so up in the air.

I needed some breathing space.

"Text Pari. I'm going to go hang out with the guys, I think," I lied.

My voice was quiet, my face placid. I would have fooled about ninety-nine-point-nine percent of the population. But not Gray.

She looked up from her phone. "Just did." She watched me for a long moment. "You sure you're okay?"

"Headache." Another lie.

Once she left to go to dinner with Pari, I went for a long walk in the canyon, making sure to find my way back to the well-lit streets of the neighborhood well before sundown. Then I walked those streets for hours more.

I was gone for a chunk of the evening, thinking, running that conversation with Barrett over and over in my head. Thinking about Gray. What it felt like to be with her. Her smell. The sound of her voice. The way I couldn't hide anything from her. Even when I tried, she knew something was up.

And thinking about how much I didn't want to hide anything else from her.

I'd bared my deepest secrets to her.

Why keep this one?

Because. *Because...*

I had no right to damage her relationship with her father, despite how much of a bastard he was.

She'd told me they were close. That he was her support, her foundation. I couldn't rob her of that, no matter how undeserving he was. I hadn't had my father for more than half my life. I'd give anything to have him back. I couldn't rob her of hers.

Because I was even more undeserving.

In truth, I had no idea where this was going and had had no answer for her when she'd asked. I had nothing to offer her. I was broken. We both knew that.

The old man was right. I didn't deserve her.

When I got back to the house, it was almost midnight.

I turned on my phone to find a few texts from her asking where I was. Then telling me she couldn't wait up any longer. Exhausted, she was going to bed.

I showered in a guest bathroom and crept into my bedroom, knowing she was in that bed.

She'd left all the lights on for me. And she was curled up on her side, facing my side of the bed. A lump collected in my throat. I could hardly breathe around it.

Yeah, it made logical sense to end this, but—

But.

These *feelings.* What did they mean? Was this...

What was it? I shook my head.

I couldn't stop this now. Not before I found out.

With a long sigh, I slipped under the covers. A second later, I had her wrapped in my arms. She stirred, murmured something absolutely unintelligible, and rolled her head onto my shoulder.

I turned my face toward her and breathed her in.

That warm scent that was *her.* I had gooseflesh. Everywhere. My eyes closed.

Oh no, I fucking wasn't giving this up.

It wasn't happening.

That old man could go fuck himself.

Gray and Ryan's story concludes in the next book in their duet, High Reward (Point of No Return, book 2).